PRAISE

FORTUNE'S CHILD:

MW00851504

GRAND PRIZE 2019 Best Book, Chanticleer International Book Awards

KIRKUS REVIEWS: A historical novel set in sixth-century Constantinople charts the extraordinary ascent of a woman from poverty to royal power.

Theodora is born into inauspicious beginnings: Her Greek father, Acacius, is a bear trainer in a circus, and her Syrian mother, Asima, is a dancer. Their fortunes only grow worse when Acacius dies in an accident. Theodora is only 5 years old when the tragedy happens and is forced to work by the time she is 10. Her life is brutally hard—she is raped with impunity at 12—but she is also dauntlessly ambitious and refuses to resign herself to a lowly station. Theodora learns to read and write and works as a prostitute and an actress, but she pines to escape the "fringes of the theater circuit." She eventually becomes the mistress of Justinian, the nephew of the emperor, destined to take the throne. Martin weaves into the tale a crucial subplot—a poor Syrian boy, born Sufian but renamed Stephen after he's sold to an unscrupulous magus, discovers that he's "singularly adept at languages" and lands a high-ranking position in Justinian's court. He befriends Theodora, but she betrays him. Later, as empress, she demands that Stephen—wasting away in jail—become her biographer, giving him an opportunity for both freedom and revenge. In this ambitious novel, the author vividly brings to life the cinematic story of Theodora's life, chronicling her rise, more halting than meteoric, to spectacular power ("Theodora set about to prove wrong her sister's assertions regarding the roles of women. She wanted to affirm that her own role in life was not preordained—and that she had some talent, some gift"). Martin's command of the historical period—not just the chief political events, but also the nuances of its cultural mores—is masterful. Furthermore, he conjoins that scholarly rigor with novelistic excitement—the entire tale is intelligently conveyed with great emotional poignancy.

A meticulously researched historical account presented in the form of a thrilling political drama.

Chanticleer
2019 BEST BOOK
GRAND PRIZE

Fortune's Child
James Conroyd Martin

CIBA
Chanticleer International Book Awards

PRAISE FOR
TOO SOON THE NIGHT

"*Too Soon the Night* is a gorgeous tapestry of impeccable research and intricate worldbuilding. Martin brings Byzantine Constantinople to vivid life through the eyes of Stephen, a resourceful court eunuch tasked with recording the memoirs of the enigmatic Theodora, one-time actress turned Empress of the civilized world. A must-have for any fan of ancient-world historical fiction!"

~Kate Quinn, bestselling author of
The Empress of Rome Saga and *The Rose Code*

"Readers will become enchanted with the inimitable Theodora found in this elegant novel."

~Eileen Stephenson, bestselling author of
Tales of Byzantium and *Imperial Passions*

 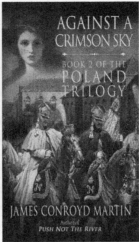 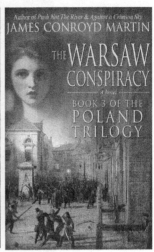

Check out The Poland Trilogy: https://goo.gl/93rzag

Based on the diary of a Polish countess who lived through the rise and fall of the Third of May Constitution years, 1791-94, **Push Not the River** paints a vivid picture of a tumultuous and unforgettable metamorphosis of a nation— and of Anna, a proud and resilient woman. *Against a Crimson Sky* continues Anna's saga as Napoléon comes calling, implying independence would follow if only Polish lancers would accompany him on his fateful 1812 march into Russia. Anna's family fights valiantly to hold on-to a tenuous happiness, their country, and their very lives. Set against the November Rising (1830-31), *The Warsaw Conspiracy* depicts partitioned Poland's daring challenge to the Russian Empire. Brilliantly illustrating the psyche of a people determined to reclaim independence in the face of monumental odds, the story features Anna's sons and their fates in love and war.

Winner of a 2018 Gold Medal from the Independent Publishers Book Awards
Best Regional E-Book, Fiction

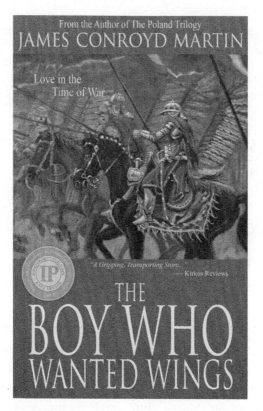

Aleksy, a Tatar raised by a Polish peasant family, wishes to become a Polish winged hussar, a Christian lancer who carries into battle a device attached to his back that holds dozens of eagle feathers. As a Tatar and as a peasant, this is an unlikely quest. When he meets Krystyna, the daughter of the noble who owns the land that his parents work, he falls hopelessly in love. But even though she returns his love, race and class differences make this quest as impossible as that of becoming a hussar. Under the most harrowing and unlikely circumstances, one day Aleksy must choose between his dreams.

Winner of a 2017 Gold Medal from the Independent Publishers Book Awards
Military/Wartime Fiction

Too Soon the Night

A Novel of Empress Theodora
The Theodora Duology Book Two

James Conroyd Martin

HUSSAR
QUILL PRESS

CHICAGO

Too Soon the Night: A Novel of Empress Theodora
Copyright 2021 by James Conroyd Martin Trust All rights reserved
First Print edition: June 2021
http://www.JamesCMartin.com

Edited by Mary Rita Perkins Mitchell
Cover and Formatting: Streetlight Graphics
www.steetlightgraphics.com

Hardcover ISBN: 978-1-7340043-1-1
Paperback ISBN: 978-1-7340043-2-8

Art:
Front cover: ***Teodora,*** circa 1887
By Giuseppe de Sanctis
Public domain

Back cover and title page: ***Empress Theodora and Her Attendants detail***
Mosaic, Basilica di San Vitale, Ravenna, Italy, Public domain

Opposite Chapter 10: ***Empress Theodora at the Coliseum, 1889***
By Jean-Joseph Benjamin-Constant
Public Domain

Also: ***The Hippodrome of Constantinople,*** print
Public Domain

No part of this book may be reproduced, scanned, or distributed in any printed or electronic form without permission. Please do not participate in or encourage piracy of copyrighted materials in violation of the author's rights. Thank you for respecting the hard work of this author.

While some characters are based on historical personages, this is a work of fiction.

ALSO BY JAMES CONROYD MARTIN

The Poland Trilogy:
Push Not the River
Against a Crimson Sky
The Warsaw Conspiracy

and

The Boy Who Wanted Wings
Hologram: A Haunting
Fortune's Child

AUTHOR'S NOTE

Long ago and far away in Los Angeles, I took an adult Art Appreciation course. When we studied the Byzantine mosaics located in Ravenna, Italy, the professor pointed to the figure of Theodora and said, "I'm not a writer, but if I were, that is the woman I would be writing about."

Click!

I immediately went to the Hollywood Library and took out a dozen books on the period and the empress. I had already started my first novel, *Push Not the River*, so I planned for Theodora's story to be my second. As the first novel was going to press, I started work on Theodora. Ah, but St. Martin's Press had a different idea: they wanted a sequel to *Push Not the River*, so that led to other books and the passage of years. At some point during those years, the eunuch Stephen came to life and shared the stage with Theodora as her biographer, thus making a duology necessary, hopefully a necessary pleasure.

Enjoy…

For John Rdzak and
Kathryn Killackey Mitchell

Thank you for reading *Too Soon the Night.* I think you will enjoy it, and I'm hoping you'll reward me with a brief review afterwards on Amazon, B&N, Google Books, KOBO, Smashwords, Apple Books, or Goodreads. Thanking you in advance!

PLEASE subscribe to my **Newsletter** for rather infrequent announcements about freebies, bonuses, booksignings, contests, news, and recommendations: **http://jamescmartin.com/announcements/**

LIKE me on **Facebook**: https://www.facebook.com/AuthorMan/

Follow me on **Twitter** @JConMartin

Follow/add me on **Goodreads**:
https://www.goodreads.com/author/show/92822.James_Conroyd_Martin

JConMartin on **Instagram**

Ravenna

Rome

Carthage

W E

S

The Byzantine Empire
550 A D

Thessalonica

Constantinople

Antioch

The Pentapolis

Jerusalem

Alexandria

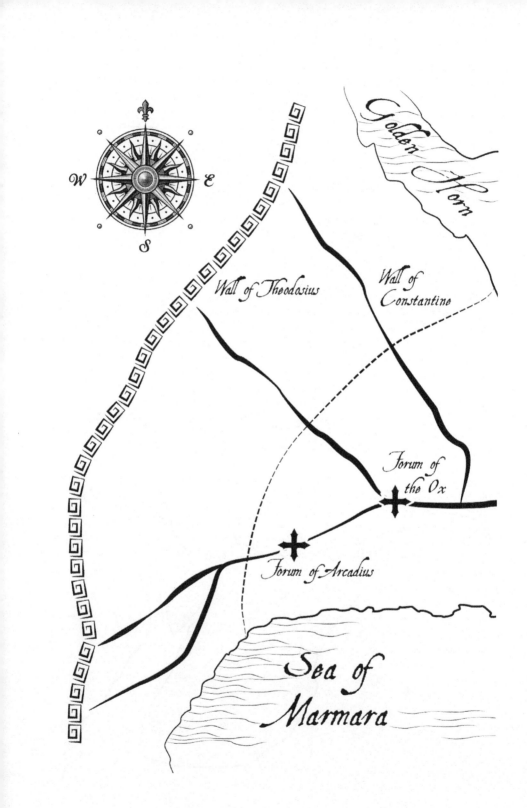

Bosporos

1. Hippodrome
2. Palace of Hormisdus
3. Milion
4. Church of Holy Wisdom
5. Augustaion
6. Baths of Zeuxippos
7. Chalke
8. Kathisma
9. Prosphorion Harbor

Forum of
Constantine

Forum of
Theodosius

Great
Palace

Constantinople

PART ONE

1

28 June 548 CE
Constantinople, The Great Palace

HER SACRED RESPLENDENCY THE EMPRESS is dead. Theodora—daughter of a bearkeeper, actress in living pictures, lover to many, concubine to Hecebolus, supporter of Monophysitism, advocate of women's rights, wife and equal partner in power to Emperor Justinian—is no more.

On the day of her death, a Sunday, I am called to the women's quarters of the Imperial Apartment at Emperor Justinian's request. What could he want with me, I worry, as I leave my suite and make my way up to the floor above.

I find the emperor overtaken with grief. His face is red, his eyes wet and little more than slits, as if he is trying to shut out the world. I bow and he moves toward me with such a look of familiarity that I think for a moment he means to embrace me. He stops a pace away. Emperors do not embrace eunuchs.

"Ah, Stephen," he says, "you must do your lady one last favor. It is for me, too, this favor."

I have no words—and not a clue as to the meaning of *his*.

He is flushing. "Her women are dressing her now." He pauses, pivoting slightly and averting his gaze. After a long moment, he turns back, half-hidden gray eyes holding mine. "You loved her, too. Do not imagine I've missed that. Not from the start when you brought us together, a bit reluctantly." His eyes are pooling. "Now, hold out your hand."

I obey.

He places in my hand a needle already threaded with translucent thread.

"I am so ashamed, Stephen—but I cannot will myself to do it." With his head so low that his chin touches the top of his rumpled purple tunic, he hurries from the room, tears giving way.

And so, I am left to perform the task only a loved one is allowed to do. I am holding my own hot tears at bay and shaking like a sapling in storm when I screw up enough courage to go into Theodora's bedchamber to bind her mouth closed so that her soul would not escape into the night.

In my room I sit at the desk in my study. My old suite located on the floor beneath the Imperial Apartment of the Daphne Wing had been returned to me. In place of my former servant Piers, I am waited upon by a stout, middle-aged eunuch, Basil. A tangy breeze from the Sea of Marmara stirs the curtains of sheer silk at the balcony door and sets the flames of my lamps dancing. Two days have passed since Theodora's magnificent funeral, the ceremony so regal and elaborate that the Augusta herself would have approved—were it not celebrated in the Orthodox rite, rather than in her chosen Monophysitic sacrament.

I look down at my empty pages and an undertow of bile and bitterness tugs at me. At her orders, I spent five years in the dungeon beneath the Daphne Palace, a wing of the Great Palace complex. Also at her orders, I was released so that I could once again be of service. For years prior to my incarceration, Theodora held me enchanted in a spell as strong as Circe's. And even upon being reprieved from below, I found myself promising Theodora I would write her life story and tell it true. "Others will tell it slant," she said. Despite the wrong done to me, she trusted me not to embellish the facts.

The finished pages laid out to my left detail her early life, pages created before her death at forty-eight. Cancer, the physicians said. I am indeed tempted to emblaze her life with wicked fiction in requital for my lost years, but something restrains me, something about this proud and complicated woman in whose veins compassion and cruelty comingled.

Am I to continue with this quest to set down the truth? Why should I spend the days, months, and perhaps years that it would take to satisfy the wish of a dead woman? Merely because I promised her that I would? I recall the many hours of interviews wherein she related her life, describing in detail every important event, every attendant thought and emotion, often employing her early talents on the boards to act out scenes. I wrote it all down so that her story could be told. The many diamond-shaped shelves of neat manuscripts in my study bear witness to her life and wait now for me to blend them into one codex, one life's story. The pull of her personality remains strong and the promise weighs heavily, yet I consider renouncing it and living my life for myself.

Suddenly, the breeze from the sea escalates into a strong gust, and several stone oil lamps sputter and go out, except for a metal lamp stationed on a stand nearby. Lazy shadows play in the darkened room. My friend Tariq would call me superstitious, but I feel her presence. She and I—both of Syrian blood—would trade gambols about which of us might possess the sight credited to Syrian sorcerers. Sometimes, however, I think we did afford the notion some credibility.

The wind rises again, the current this time extinguishing the lamp next to me, chilling me. My arms turn to gooseflesh.

I recall now her reasoning, passionate as it was, for leaving behind an accurate chronicle of her life. Her spies had informed her that Procopius, palace lawyer and historian—no friend of mine and Theodora's nemesis—was writing his own account of her life, one that is false and base.

It is enough to set me in motion.

The hour is late and the hall, lighted at intervals by sconces, eerily quiet. As I come to the stairwell, I hear the clatter of boots. The nighttime contingent of palace guards passes my floor and continues to the Imperial Apartment on the floor above, where they will relieve the daytime detail. Justinian has not shown himself since the funeral, so great is his grief. The two—emperor and empress—had become as one and, for now, he is lost.

Taking the stairs, I go to ground level and exit the Daphne Wing. The summer night is still warm. I make my way down the white marble stairs set into the escarpment bordering the Sea of Marmara, descending from one artfully landscaped terrace to the next until I reach the Palace of Hormisdas at the water's edge. Here the salty scent of the sea tempers the perfume of the jasmine vines that grow near the shore. I come and go at all hours within the Great Palace complex, and so I am admitted by the excubitor on duty without question. I move noiselessly. This was Justinian's palace when he was a prince, and it was also where I lived and worked upon my arrival in Constantinople. I have with me a torch, and lighting it now from a sconce, I use my key on the latch and pull open the high double doors of the one-time magnificent dining hall Justinian had fashioned into his massive library and scriptorium.

I move up the middle aisle of the high desks of copyists. It is here I worked in the early years. I excelled at languages and my linguistic skill made possible a rise in stature that I, a slave and eunuch, could not have foreseen. In time, even my handwriting became—well, adequate. Others will say it was my relationship with the empress that pushed me up the palace ladder. Well, there is truth in that, too.

Fronting the rows of copyists' desks is a bank of bays lined with honeycombed shelves of manuscripts. I come to the last bay, the one appropriated to Procopius for his own workspace and manuscripts. I take a deep breath and enter, knowing he would have me flayed alive if he knew I had trespassed on his sacrosanct domain. As long as a guard on his rounds does not interfere, I feel comfortable in my stealth, for Procopius has accompanied General Belisarius and the army on the Italian campaign to win back Italy from the Ostrogoths.

I place the torch in the holder on the wall and begin my search. I know what I'm looking for, what the dead empress has commissioned me to find, find and destroy, but I don't know for certain if it even exists. Her spies were insistent that Procopius was recording her life in the most unflattering way imaginable, and so I am determined to find out whether he has left behind any clue as to such a project.

The shelving is arranged in a u-shaped fashion around his desk. Thinking he would want it out of reach, I rifle through the codices and scrolls on the upper shelves first. I find nothing other than tedious accounts of the military campaigns on which he had accompanied General Belisarius as legal advisor, secretary, and historian—roles he carries out with a swagger of self-entitlement. I go on to search the middle shelves, wondering if he would be so confident of his privacy as to place it in plain sight. Half of an hour of searching reveals only manuscripts detailing the architecture Justinian has initiated in the capital, and the smoke from the flame is irritating my lungs. Now come the lower shelves. I go to my knees and crawl from one niche to the next, pulling out dusty scrolls and replacing them after quick inspections. A number of them pertain to the governance of a large bureaucracy and are of little interest. I come to the last shelf, find it empty, and sit back against the bookshelves, defeated.

Wouldn't it make more sense for him to keep such a work secreted in his apartment in the Daphne Wing? I had feared so from the first. But how am

I to enter his locked, private residence when he has an ever vigilant staff? Or perhaps he has it on tour with him, anticipating a moment when his dark imagination would ignite and spew out calumny. The empress's spies could have been wrong. Perhaps he did boast of such a lurid venture—but might it be no more than that, an empty boast? Would he really pursue it?

Like my own energy, the torch sputters. From my sitting position on the floor, I glance up and gauge that it will go out in a matter of minutes. So what, I think, I'm finished here. As I bring my gaze down, I notice something strange. Attached to the underside of Procopius's desk is a large square object. It is visible only from where I sit. The desk I had worked at in the early years had no such thing. Neither did, as far as I knew, any of the others belonging to copyists.

Crawling under the desk, I examine my find: a hidden drawer that slides along metal rails and comes free in my hands. I set it on the floor and remove a manuscript. I unroll it and observe Theodora's name. Scanning the scroll, I see that it occurs again and yet again. I don't have enough light to read it here, so I roll it up and plant it in my voluminous sleeve. I replace the drawer on its rails and stand, feeling victorious just as the bay goes completely black.

It is of no concern because I know my way about the library in the dark. I take the dead torch and leave the bay, moving into the main chamber of the scriptorium.

A noise.

I halt in the middle of the large hall and look to its source, the exit. Through the seams of the double doors the flare of flame appears. Someone is out there. I hold my breath, praying he will pass, but the light does not move away. The sound of a key in the latch breaks the silence. My heart races. I am about drop behind a desk when I think again, conjecturing it is a guard to whom I would owe no excuse. I steady myself and wait.

Both doors open now, abruptly, as if to admit someone of importance, not a guard. A man enters.

When my eyes adjust to the light of his torch flickering on his face, I note that it is someone of—*self-importance*. I halt, my mind spins in frenzy. *How is it possible?*

The man looks up with startled eyes to find someone in the darkened room at this late hour.

Procopius.

I freeze. Fear runs like a poison through my veins. He could have only just arrived in Constantinople. I would have heard otherwise. Some malignant force has contrived to bring him here first thing. I curse myself for not having hidden.

My thoughts race, blurring with old, negative emotions. I attempt a smile. Our relationship has always been adversarial.

His surprise dissipates at once, and he arranges his face into one of annoyance. "What in Satan's name are you doing here?" he demands.

My fear accelerates. I realize that my right hand has gone to the sleeve that secures my treasure. I am without words, heart pounding like a drum.

Procopius marches up to me. "I asked you a question!" He thrusts the torch out, toward me, as if to burn me at the stake.

I am trying to formulate some story when he says, "That's your old desk, isn't it?" He moves the torch as a way of pointing. "The one you worked at before *she* brought you up in the world." He sneers. "The dead one. I am broken of heart to have missed her funeral."

My first master, the magus Gaspar, had a designation for one such as Procopius: "cold-blooded as a fish."

I look down. I hadn't noticed but he's correct. It is my old work station. I take his observation as evidence that I must have been an annoyance of some significance to him then. "I couldn't sleep," I say, ignoring his comment. "I often walk about the palace grounds."

"Indeed?" His eyebrows move up in a show of skepticism. "And you come here out of—what, nostalgia?"

I thank the gods in whom I hold no faith. Procopius has supplied me with the excuse—however weak and unlikely—I had been searching for. "Exactly," I say.

"I don't believe you."

"It's true," I insist, my stomach knotting as his gaze flits over my shoulder, toward the library bay I had just left, *his* library bay.

His eyes come back to me. "You've been here a while if your torch has spent itself."

I lift my torch for his inspection. "Ah, I heedlessly picked up one that was nearly depleted already." Without allowing him time to respond, I wish him a good evening and dash past him.

I come to the doors, lift the latch and pass through, but in taking care to close them behind me, the stolen scroll slips from my sleeve and falls to the floor. I reach down in the darkness, recover it, and hurry toward the exit.

Having no religion, I am at a loss to whom I should pray Procopius does not discover the theft tonight. I stop on the third landing of my climb up the escarpment stairway, turn, and fling the dead torch out into the Sea of Marmara.

The yellow-orange of dawn breaks shyly through in the east, taking only minutes to boldly fire scarlet-red before drifting through purples into the blue of day. My new custom is to savor the drama from my balcony in an attempt to consign to oblivion my many days spent without natural light. The effort usually works, but it proves fugacious today once the blue dominates and day fully breaks.

Still calming myself from my encounter with Procopius, I retreat to my study and sit at my desk with his manuscript before me.

I begin to read, marveling at the neat flourishes of his pen.

Theodora's spies were not mistaken.

Procopius has done more than exaggerate. The manuscript has a sprinkling of truth, but it is little more than a compilation of falsehoods touching on palace scandals and excoriating Emperor Justinian and his minions. More attention, by far, goes to the empress. He writes of Theodora's "cunning and misdeeds" as she conspired to seduce Justinian, not with charm, but with charms. Oh, I've heard such malicious gossip before, so such an argument as this seems a waste of time. Still, the masses can be gullible, as well as have a taste for the sensational.

I am well aware of Theodora's imperfections. As I read on, however, coldness takes hold of me at my core, paralyzing me like hardening ice in winter. I have born witness to many shocking things in my forty-three years, but I find his libel concerning Theodora's supposed sexual history so disturbing and disgusting that, even sitting alone, hot blood rises into my face and sets my temples throbbing.

I am thunderstruck. The account, descriptive in places and yet little more than an outline, strikes me as unimaginable, repellent, scurrilous.

Half of an hour brings me to its end.

The empress was well informed by her spies. Given his dark venture, Procopius would see to it that Theodora's place in history will be vilified in unspeakable specifics. The lies are monstrous.

If ever I was hesitant in writing an accurate account of Theodora's life, I am no more. Procopius's philippic eclipses any bitterness I still harbor for my five years of incarceration at her whim and brings to the fore the loyalty—and love—I still hold for her.

My hands involuntarily tighten on the manuscript. I am struck by the intensity of my own feelings, staring at the document, wanting to tear it to pieces and set it ablaze. But there's no destroying it now because he would know. With Procopius's proximity to Belisarius and Emperor Justinian himself, his steps to have me punished would be extreme. He would see me banished—or worse.

I take a breath, think. My head begins to clear. One thought breaks through the fuzziness: this is nothing but a fragment. I must return it to that hidden drawer. The whole manuscript must be found—if indeed it is finished. Only then can I take my own steps. No joy accompanies the notion that I am now a sleuth.

Neither do I feel any sense of guilt in my venture when I consider the caliber of Procopius's character. I once asked my friend Tariq for his estimation of the man. He replied: "An ass thinks an ass is a pretty fellow."

I return the manuscript to the hidden drawer the next day, blessedly without incident. Just one day later, I learn Procopius has left for the Italian front after having parleyed with Emperor Justinian about the war effort. General Belisarius had sent him as an emissary to beg for reinforcements. Word has it that sickness has significantly culled the army, and yet Justinian made no commitment to send troops.

No doubt Procopius made a show of more sincere condolences to a grief-stricken Justinian than he made to me.

I return to his library niche and the hidden drawer. The manuscript is missing. Had Procopius destroyed it? Instinct—or is it the sight?—tells me he did no such thing. I become certain that he is forging ahead with his project to undo an empress.

A double burden has fallen on my head now: to bring an end to Procopius's story—and to continue with Theodora's account, beginning with the early years on the throne.

Lacking a means to act on the first task, I partake in a solitary meal of bread, cheese, and dates before settling in at my desk and beginning the latter.

PART TWO

2

I N THE HIGHLY-VAULTED GOLDEN AUDIENCE Chamber, Theodora sat still, silent, her gaze fixed on the two men prostrating themselves before her and Justinian.

"Enough, enough!" Justinian cried, joy in his voice. "Rise—rise up!" He jumped up from the throne as if he were twenty and not forty-six. With a wave that dismissed the new protocol that they were to kiss a red shoes of both emperor and empress, he stepped down from the dais and embraced one, then the other. Theodora would have words with him later about such impulsive behavior.

Once seated again, her husband went on to receive them as if they were long-lost friends, rather than soldiers. He had told her about them a number of times. They had been palace excubitors to former Emperor Justin, who personally singled them out for their leadership abilities, advancing them in rank and reward.

The two had just returned from Persarmenia, where their mission was to stave off aggression by Persia, the empire's inveterate enemy. To hear them give their account—one supported by an earlier report from Procopius, who had accompanied them—they had succeeded in winning a significant victory over Persia, bringing back treasure and slaves. Their faces alight with pride and confidence, they detailed their experiences to the emperor.

After awhile, the exchange between her husband and his officers fell into relief as Theodora studied the two in their clean tunics and bronze cuirasses polished to a high sheen. Stephen had told her how, in just a few days after their return, they had ruffled the plumage of jealous senators and turned the heads of women.

On the right stood the lean Sittas. Like so many Armenians she had known, he was striking with his long, curved nose, wide forehead, and dark hair, brows, and beard. He was handsome enough, but his appeal was eclipsed by the man at his side.

Belisarius was as tall as any Thracian she had encountered and as wide-shouldered. His black hair had a wiry curl to it, his beard camouflaged a face otherwise a bit too long, and the appeal of the bright brown eyes and high, eastern cheekbones no doubt fetched countless admirers. As he spoke here in the audience chamber, white teeth flashing, his demeanor bespoke his confidence, as did a genuine, clear laugh.

On occasion, his dark eyes stole away from the emperor and commanded the empress's attention. Theodora felt a faint flush coming into her cheeks. In a past time and place he might have proven a temptation.

Today, however, her thoughts were elsewhere. She had two sisters and a dear friend to whom she had promised husbands when she took the throne. Here were two men of distinction who might fulfill two of the three promises. The day before, when Justinian could not attest to their marital status, Theodora's palace spies assured her that neither was married.

Later, at their evening meal, Justinian spoke of his two favorites. "They are marked for greatness, Thea, I am certain. Belisarius especially—why, he's brought a new day to the army."

"How?" It was a question Theodora felt compelled to ask.

"He's put together his own private regiment of cavalry. He calls them his *bucellarii* and they are a mix of nations, recruited for the most part from prisoners he's taken—Persians, Huns, Goths and maybe a dozen more nationalities. He respects them, pays them well, and provides them with the best armor and weapons. In return, they are fiercely loyal."

"Is that so good, Justinian? Shouldn't they be loyal to *you*?"

Justinian shrugged. "As long as *he* is loyal to me, they will be loyal, as well. And, Thea, he has been schooled at Adrianople in accountancy, rhetoric, and law—all attributes necessary in a fine military leader."

"Law?" Theodora asked, feigning surprise. "If that is the case, why is it that he needs Procopius as legal counsel to accompany him?"

"Besides providing legal advice, Procopius is to record the history of his military exploits from an objective point of view."

"And," Theodora replied, "you think Procopius is capable of writing an accurate history? Of being objective?"

Justinian turned to Theodora, his eyes narrowing at her challenge. "Thea, why do you persist in your aversion to Procopius?"

Theodora allowed his remark to pass. Any past attempts to undermine his closeness to Procopius had always failed. She could not bring herself to tell him of the defamatory things Stephen had heard Procopius say about her prior to the royal wedding. And why should she bother? After all, it was good fortune that Procopius should be away from the capital for long periods of time while on campaign with Belisarius.

Theodora found Antonina and Comito waiting in the reception room of the women's quarters, as requested, but she did not expect to find them locked in a high-pitched argument. She found her younger sister Anastasia there, too, an observer to the scene.

"Well!" Theodora exclaimed. "What is this all about?"

The three, standing in a semi-circle, turned toward her. Antonina and Comito fell silent, shamefaced.

"They're arguing over a man," Anastasia said, a lilt in her tone.

"If we were backstage at the Old Royal Palace," Theodora said with the air of a schoolmaster, "I would laugh at your antics. However, we are in a genuine palace now, and I will not have my servants talking about the behavior of my sisters and closest friend."

Comito's and Antonina's serious faces reflected proper admonishment, but anger seethed near the surface.

"Comito says she's in love!" Anastasia said, her tone at once timid and smug.

"Indeed? Well, that is something." Theodora looked to her elder sister, who was blushing to the roots of her dark hair. "And who is the object of your affection?"

"It's Belisarius," Anastasia blurted. "That's who!"

"Really?" Theodora asked, sucking in breath, stunned that the subject of the earlier audience was their topic of discussion. "Just why would your infatuation cause the argument I overheard?"

"It's not a mere infatuation! You said you would find us husbands, Thea!" Comito cast what seemed the evil eye at Antonina, whose back visibly stiffened.

"Antonina's in love with him, too!" Anastasia said, asserting herself as more than an onlooker.

Theodora's head spun. Belisarius was, in fact, the subject of this altercation, but things were running off into strange directions. "I suggest we sit down."

Theodora sat on the couch opposite that of Antonina and Comito. Anastasia remained standing immediately to the right of Theodora.

"Nina, is this true?" Theodora could not read her expression.

Bending low, Anastasia whispered, "She says she has already seduced him."

Theodora looked up at her sister. "So, Tasia, are you to play Pheme, goddess of gossip?" she asked, holding back a smile.

Anastasia wiggled her eyebrows. "Pheme has her good side. She did well by me when I was on stage."

"Did she?" Theodora put away her smile and patted the cushion on her left. "Come, sit next to me and try to be quiet."

Anastasia obeyed.

Theodora fixed her gaze on Antonina, who stared back. They had been friends too long and come through such adventures that Theodora had no doubt that she had indeed ensnared Belisarius. She was beautiful and resourceful, as ever. Theodora had often envied her for her golden hair and blue eyes, which drew men to her like flies to honeyed dates.

Theodora let out a long sigh. "They say one cherry tree will not hold two jays. Or has every woman in the palace fallen for this Thracian brute from the Balkans?" She turned to her younger sister. "You, too, Anastasia?"

Anastasia's eyes went wide. "No, Theodora."

"Good!"

"But—with your help I should be happy with Sittas," Anastasia replied, black eyes sparkling.

Theodora's mouth fell slack. She had much to do if she were to properly stage-manage this little family drama.

An extended, convoluted, and sometimes heated exchange played out through the afternoon. Of the three marriage-minded young women, only one went away happy. Citing Antonina's seduction of Belisarius, an accomplished fact, Theodora pledged to pursue her friend's interest, rather than her sister's. In reality, she wanted the strong-willed Antonina to accompany Belisarius as his wife in order to keep an eye on both Procopius and a commander who might become so proud and ambitious as to think the throne would one day welcome him. Generals like Belisarius and Sittas could not always be trusted. Justinian, she knew, could be too unsuspecting of both men.

Theodora's further promise to play go-between for Comito and Sittas—rather than for Anastasia and Sittas—invited scorn and recriminations from both sisters.

Still, Theodora was confident things would play out the way she had planned before entering the room. She was confident that Belisarius and Sittas would not resist the partners she chose for them. Antonina and Comito were attractive women, each with connections to the throne. Besides, Theodora had long ago become aware that her wishes carried more weight now than in the days when she trod the boards. Her wishes today were the demands of an empress.

Now, she had only to find someone suitable for Anastasia.

Despite demands on her life as an empress, Theodora and I still played an occasional round of *Shatranj*, an Indian board game I had taught her during my visits to her humble home on the alley above the Hippodrome. The Persian Gaspar had taught it to me. Here in the Daphne Wing, we were hovering over the light brown checkered board when she insisted—not for the first time—that I move into permanent quarters in the Daphne. I had not yet learned what so many others were learning at the start of the new reign—that one says *yes* to Empress Theodora. My tiny subterranean room in the Palace of Hormisdas had been comfortable enough. I was close to my place of work as a copyist in Justinian's large scriptorium there. Theodora was a shrewd woman and forced from me the real reason for attempting to decline her invitation. My face flamed hot with embarrassment as I told her of my attachment to a mural on the wall of that windowless cell. The exquisite mosaic features a dark-haired boy seated on a parapet around a pond.

"I named him Jati, 'honest one'," I told Theodora. "I commune with Jati almost nightly. You'll think me foolish or unhinged, but I open my heart to him and sometimes I sense a response." She looked at me, the lids of those dark, lustrous eyes lowering. Certain that she was going to laugh at such superstition, I prepared myself for humiliation.

"What kinds of things do you confide in Jati?"

My face must have burned scarlet, for I could not tell her how often I relayed to Jati my love—the unrequited love of a slave and eunuch—for a free woman, a free and beautiful woman. A woman now an empress.

"You think me silly, don't you?" My question was meant to divert from having to answer her question.

Her response came as a surprise. "I have Syrian blood on my mother's side. They say Syrian blood is more inclined to gain insight into a world outside of ourselves. I sometimes believe I have contact with some power, some invisible force. Spirits, perhaps. Call it the sight, or what you will, it is there to support me or perhaps warn me. They are feelings I have learned not to ignore. Who's to say how they communicate, such spirits? So this mosaic boy by the fountain—this Jati of yours—he may be your guardian spirit. My father was Greek, but both of your parents were Syrian, so you might be doubly blessed."

I sat thunderstruck by her words, by her thoughts.

"Confer with Jati tonight," she continued. "Consider my offer as you do so. If you accept, I will have the mosaic disassembled and placed in one of your rooms here in the Daphne Wing." With that, she smiled neatly, leaned over the game board and captured my *shah*, winning the game in a move I had not seen coming.

As I took my leave, head spinning, she called out: "By the way, Stephen, I have just the suite in mind for you."

I took her advice regarding Jati. Or was it a command?

That night, I sat staring at the mosaic boy, revealing my heart to him not in words but in thoughts. My lamplight flickered, catching the water, the fish, the black crown of hair. But the eyes remained dark. I felt nothing.

Nevertheless, in the morning I made the decision. I lay there, eyes on the wall. "We will be moving soon," I told Jati, "although you were no help in my coming to a decision."

How could I have considered rejecting the offer? In the morning, when the corners of Theodora's mouth lifted a bit at the news, a little thrill ran through me.

"The rooms are large and lovely, Stephen. You will have a personal servant, too, more if you wish. They are as plentiful as the blades of grass. You will, however, have to wait just a little while."

Of course, I wondered at the reason for the delay, but I dared not voice it.

Her eyes locked onto mine and she deciphered my thoughts. "The current tenant will be moved out when Belisarius goes on campaign."

Suddenly, I knew that someone who didn't like me was going to like me even less.

Theodora saw that I understood and nodded. "You will be taking Procopius's suite." One of her eyelids flickered. "Won't he be surprised?"

The surprise of the moment, I must admit, was the fact that an empress had winked at me.

In no time at all, I—and almost everyone at court—became aware that Antonina had indeed succeeded in bewitching Belisarius. It took no prompting by Theodora, merely an official introduction to the golden-haired beauty, one that granted legitimacy to the seduction. The general fell hard so that by the time he and Sittas left to resume their campaign at Persarmenia, marriage plans were being made. Sittas, too, fell prey to Theodora's propensity to move people around as if they were pieces on her *Shatranj* game board. Comito's response to his entreaties was not as enthusiastic as Antonina's to Belisarius's overtures, but acceptance came in the end, nonetheless.

When Procopius left with Belisarius, I became the lucky new tenant of his luxurious rooms in the Daphne, directly below the Imperial Apartment. Theodora arranged for my pitifully few belongings to be moved, but I personally directed the removal of my mosaic boy by palace artisans, who numbered each piece and saw to their careful application to the wall of my new study.

A week later, I sat luxuriating at my highly polished oak desk. Across the room, dark-haired Jati once again sat on the retaining wall above a pond, the flickering light cast from a single oil lamp on the tesserae providing the illusion that the gentle waters were undulating, the golden fish wriggling. But the boy was not watching the fish. His head was up, face forward, the overly large, black eyes glistening and staring out, as if watching me, as if assessing me.

"Like me," I said to my muse, "you have come up in the world." His eyes drew me in, but in a blurry moment they were not his eyes, but the tearful eyes of my mother on the last day I saw her. How I longed to see her again. What would she think of me today? What would my father think to see me here in the New Rome and at the very source of power? Had he thought to give a ten-year-old a better life—or to gain the gold coins a Persian magus placed on the kitchen table? And what would he think to know that the wizard would, in turn, sell him to slavers who would have him cut?

Over the years I learned the bootlessness of spending time on that tear-worn subject, so I turned my thoughts to Procopius, who had once promised me rooms in the Daphne Wing of the Great Palace if I would work with him to thwart the romance between Prince Justinian and Theodora. I refused, of course, only to find myself installed in his very suite. I looked up at Jati, wiped at my eyes, and smiled.

With my new post came a servant whose job it was to keep the rooms clean and orderly, prepare meals, and oversee the care of my wardrobe, one that was increasing in size and quality of garments. In his mid-fifties, Piers was bald, plain of looks, stocky but not excessively fat. He was a nervous fellow, a trait I attributed to his having been in the employ of the volatile Procopius. Considering his prior loyalty, I at first planned to replace him, but his genuine desire to please and what I took to be relief in his change of employer made me think again.

Piers was one of a stream of cut ones sent to Constantinople from the east, Paphlagonia, on the southern coast of the Black Sea, to be exact. On our first meeting, I told him of my interest in languages and asked him what language was spoken in Paphlagonia.

He blinked and tilted his head at the question. "A language I've nearly forgotten," he said, his tone dry as sand, "Paphlagonian."

"Of course!" I exclaimed, laughing and swatting my forehead.

My laughter gave him warrant enough to join in. The ice was broken. In very little time we came to trust each other.

I assumed that my duties as Personal Secretary to the Empress in the Daphne would be light and that I could continue my copying duties for Brother Leo in the scriptorium of the Palace of Hormisdas. After all, how many letters would Theodora wish me to write for her? The fault in my assumption was soon clarified.

I was putting things in order at my desk when Piers, his face a stage mask of surprise, announced Theodora's arrival mere seconds before she hurried into my study. His demeanor had been shaken, he assured me later, because she had never visited Procopius.

"How are you finding your rooms, Stephen?"

"More magnificent than I imagined, Theodora." I stood. "What will Procopius say when he finds out?"

My question tickled her—but the light laugh died quickly. "Who cares—Leave him to me."

"Will you sit?"

"No. I've come to tell you I must have a command of Latin. I need your help, Stephen."

"My own knowledge of Latin is rudimentary, Thea."

"Then we shall learn together, yes? You see, I'm well acquainted with the Greek dialect spoken in the streets and high Greek in the palace, which is not to say I couldn't use some improvement in the latter. But Latin is the language in which palace business is done, and I don't intend to be left out."

"I can make a list of Greek terms in one column and Latin in another next to it. I could group the terms by subject, say, for instance, food items or aspects of law."

"Excellent!" she said. "You are a quick thinker. I like that. And your list making is to be done in your study here in the Daphne Wing."

I must have displayed a quizzical expression.

"I have a small but growing pile of Greek codices I wish you to copy."

"From Greek to—?"

"Greek!—Oh, don't look so perplexed. I must have the lettering made larger."

Ah! I understood. Her vision at close range was poor. I nodded.

"Oh, there will be many Latin-to-Greek codices having to do with law that will need translation, you'll see. At least until my Latin is fluent." Theodora paused, the nearly wedded dark eyebrows rising to presage something of gravity. "Now, everything you do for me is to be kept between us, do you understand, Stephen? I do not want anyone, not even my husband, to know what texts I am having you copy."

"I do understand." I suspected also that she didn't want word of the imperfection of her sight to be known.

She gave me a long, hard look as if to determine my sincerity, granted the briefest of nods, and hurried from the room.

So—my position in the Daphne was to be full time. There would be no return to the scriptorium at the Palace of Hormisdas. I drew in breath. I would miss my friends there.

It occurred to me that I was just another game piece to be moved around on her royal game board at her wishes or whim. The truth was, I did not mind.

3

A T THE HEAD OF THE long, polished cherry wood table, Theodora sat next to Justinian in the Hall of the Consistory, where a series of round-arched windows ran the length of one wall and a painted map of the Roman Empire's massive territories took up much of the other. The meetings of the emperor's councilors—numbering a dozen—were called Silences because, once they concluded, the participants were forbidden to speak of what went on within the chamber.

Theodora was the only woman ever to sit in on a Silence. This was Theodora's eighth such occasion. The councilors had all been surprised at such an intrusion by a woman, but some seemed especially horrified, and two or three had dared give her the evil eye. She would remember them. One of these was John the Cappadocian, an accountant of the War Office. Justinian told her he was priming him for the high post of Praetorian Prefect of the East, replacing the elderly Julianus. The prefect would be empowered to collect and raise taxes, powers that invited cruelty and corruption from a person of questionable character.

She had not delivered up her own opinions in those meetings; instead, she bided her time, watching these men in their political habitat as a hunter might take care to study the game, waiting for the time when she would speak.

Today, Justinian announced an edict creating a commission meant to establish an inclusive codex of Roman law, an enterprise he had told her about long ago. Theodora looked down the table at Tribonian, a lawyer and official of the praetorian prefect who was to head the commission that would edit and codify the many thousands of verdicts rendered by earlier Roman jurists. He sat erect, the expression on his simple face one of self-congratulation. Noting his thickening body and receding hairline, Theodora guessed him to be in his late thirties. In previous meetings he had expounded on matters of law. Her spies told her he was not liked in all quarters and that he had his eye on the post of Quaestor of the Great Palace, the senior legal authority responsible for drafting laws. She determined from his demeanor that he was vain, but her spies told her he was greedy, as well, a trait at odds with running a forthright revenue office. Further, they told her of evidence he still adhered to paganism.

While Justinian delved into the details of simplifying centuries of Roman law, Theodora's mind wandered back to that morning when Belisarius and Sittas presented and prostrated themselves in the Golden Audience Chamber, having returned from Persarmenia. This time the news they brought laid waste to the memory of their recent victories. The New Rome forces had been routed in an appalling defeat. The two generals brought home no slaves, no plunder, no ground gained.

Justinian fell silent as the two bowed before him, shamefaced. Long moments ticked by. At last, the emperor sighed, drew breath, and spoke: "It was Pyrrhus who said, 'Another victory like that, and we are lost'." He stood now, stiff as a stork, and allowed another minute to pass, holding nearly everyone in the room suspended over an abyss.

Belisarius lost color in his face, and Sittas visibly flinched. While they no doubt feared for their military futures, Theodora—mind racing—could think only of how their loss and possible demotions would impact the impending marriages she had arranged for each of them.

"However," Justinian said, "I am blaming only myself for not having sent enough reinforcements." He went on to elucidate how palace decisions—his decisions—might have contributed to the outcome.

Theodora knew her husband spoke the truth, and she reveled in the fact that he accepted responsibility. She knew someone like her one-time lover Hecebolus would have found someone else to blame. She released a silent sigh of relief, and yet she still worried over the future of her planned marriages.

A heated argument broke out at the table now, snapping Theodora from her thoughts. The subject concerned the earthquake Antioch experienced at the end of November. The city had been leveled two years before and a wealth of government funds were spent then to aid the survivors in rebuilding.

"I beseech you, master," Tribonian was saying, "We have spent enough on Antioch. Let it remain a pile of rubble. Our treasury is gushing money faster than any tax revenues can replenish it. What of all that has been spent on that city since 526? It's come to nothing. And now we are to do it again?"

As he rattled on, Theodora thought of the friends she had made there a few years before the devastating earthquake and resulting fire Tribonian cited. Her friend and mentor while she was there, Macedonia, had survived that cataclysm—but had she been so lucky this time?

Tribonian now called into the room two witnesses in support of cutting off funding: Urban Prefect Eudaemon and Peter Barsymes, a banker who had risen to an office within the staff of praetorian prefect. Each man argued quite convincingly that Constantinople itself had pressing needs and that enough Antioch relief monies had already dropped into a void as deep as the chasm at the Oracle at Delphi.

John the Cappadocian himself spoke up now, addressing Justinian. "Master," he said, standing with eyes averted from Theodora, "may I add that to rebuild the city is a foolish and expensive task? However, the Consistory may be disposed to send food and limited funds to the stricken city."

When Justinian didn't respond, John sat down, a satisfied smile on his lips, nonetheless. Theodora's dislike for the man deepened. Did he think he already had the title of Praetorian Prefect of the East?

As the discussion went on, Theodora could see Tribonian and his witnesses were having their effect on a good number of the Imperial Consistory. Perhaps the councilors were of one mind.

Heart pounding, Theodora drew in breath and rose to her feet. "My lords," she called out, a slight quaver in the voice, "Are we not all good citizens of the New Rome?"

The hall hushed at once. The councilors sat back in their chairs, eyes lifted in her direction. Theodora felt Justinian stiffen slightly at her side.

"Do we not want to see all the cities that pay tribute treated fairly? What example will we set if we are to abandon one at the time of its greatest hardship? Unlike the chariot track in the Hippodrome, the road of loyalty runs both ways. In the previous Antioch earthquake, two hundred and fifty thousand people perished. Only God knows how many have died this time."

Theodora's gaze had been leveled just above the councilors' heads, but now she dared to lower her eyes and stare them in the face, moving up one side of the table and down the other until she settled her gaze on John of Cappadocia. "What good are limited funds and food if there are no roads, no buildings, no forums in which to gather and trade and be governed?" When she took note of John's eyelids lowered in retreat, she turned her attention to Tribonian, who was drawing in breath and squaring his shoulders in preparation to continue his argument for withdrawal of aid.

"Lord Tribonian," she said, bringing him up short, "isn't it true that when the emperor came to the throne, the empire had in its treasury twenty-nine million gold solidi?"

Tribonian stood to answer. He paused glancing from Theodora to Justinian and back again, then mumbled something unintelligible to her.

"I'm sorry, Lord Tribonian, I did not understand that."

Tribonian cleared his throat. His face ran red. "I said, Mistress Theodora, that His Clemency the Emperor inherited some twenty-eight million, eight hundred thousand solidi."

Theodora heard two or three muted gasps from the others.

She felt the heat of blood flooding into her face. "A small enough difference, but you are right to correct me."

"Oh, mistress, I did not intend—"

A dismissive wave from Theodora silenced him. "Never mind, Lord Tribonian. What is important is how much is in the treasury *now*. Can you answer that?"

"No, mistress." Tribonian bowed and sat down.

"What with the increase in trade these past months, are we not better off?" she continued. "Are we not to help fellow citizens of the empire?"

She noticed now that the only person to meet her gaze was the banker, Peter Barsymes, and his slight, sympathetic smile made an impression on her. No one else responded or even lifted his eyes to her.

When Theodora sat down, her perspiring palms resting on the carved arms of the chair, Justinian momentarily placed his hand over hers before standing.

"It is my decision to grant the Governor of Antioch the funds in full that he has requested. Now, If there is no further business, my Lord Councilors, I pronounce our Silence at an end."

The councilors remained seated as Justinian took her hand to lead her from the hall. She held her face averted in the event the smile she was holding back would break through. Elation fired up her heartbeat, drumming warmth through her body.

It was a double victory. Besides winning on the matter of funds for Antioch, she had proven herself capable of winning the emperor's support in the face of his councilors' opposition.

It was more than she had been able to do years before at the Pentapolis.

Later, in the women's quarters, Justinian told her that not only would Belisarius and Sittas escape rebuke, but he had promotions in mind for them.

Theodora closed her eyes and quietly released a long breath. The marriages would go forward, according to her plans.

Without missing a beat, Theodora whispered to her husband, "Is Peter Barsymes married?"

"He is not, Thea."

"Ah, is he Greek?"

"Syrian."

Even better.

Theodora personally orchestrated the wedding between Belisarius and Antonina. I did not attend the ceremony in the Church of the Holy Wisdom nor witness any of the festivities. Within the palace complex, I did hear gossips wonder whether Antonina could truly put her colorful past behind her, observing also that her two children by previous attachments were nowhere to be seen.

Comito did not attend the wedding, either.

"She is still smarting from her failed infatuation," Theodora told me, having summoned me to her study in the women's quarters of the Imperial Apartment. "She is my sister and has been loyal to me since our childhood. I must convince her, Stephen, that I do not place my friend Antonina above her. You can help me do that."

And so it was that the next day I stood in front of a palatial residence two streets above the Hippodrome, heart pounding at the prospect of my mission. Most of the buildings accessible to the Mese, the main thoroughfare, were made of lumber and had only facades of marble, but this magnificent private home was fully clad in the costly gray-white marble from an island in the Sea of Marmara. Was it possible that it was, as Theodora said, owned by a eunuch, one who, in earlier years, had loyally served Emperor Anastasius?

"I am to see Lord Antiochos," I told the stern-faced and beardless servant.

"Do you have an appointment?" he asked.

"The empress sent word that I was coming."

The servant's eyelids lifted slightly. "This way."

A long passageway brought us to a few steps leading down into a sumptuous office of polished dark woods, strong with the scent of bees wax. The servant announced me and, at a slight hand movement of his master, disappeared.

Antiochos, richly robed in a wine-colored mantle over a white silk tunic, rose from behind his wide ebony desk. It was my guess that he was into his sixth decade. "Welcome," he said, smiling. "I'm at the empress's command—and yours. Be seated, my friend." His intonation of the word "friend" clearly referenced our like status as eunuchs, if not in wealth. We differed in another way, too, in that I had been cut after puberty, whereas his voice had the high timbre and his waist the wide girth of one who had been cut before puberty.

I sat on a cushionless chair placed in front of his desk. My mouth had gone dry with the thought of my visit's purpose. I drew in breath. "You may know that Comito, the empress's sister, is to be married."

"Yes, indeed. The talk has reached us here. I may no longer serve at court, but I have my ears."

I nod.

"Word has it that she would like to use my humble dwelling for the festivities after the services. Is that not correct?"

Another nod.

"So—she has sent you to do the asking. Scarcely a year on the throne, and she has learned to be so diplomatic. I am impressed beyond measure." Antiochos released a cheery laugh. "Very well—I'll spare you the asking. "Yes, of course, she may make use of the house! I'd be delighted."

"The empress will thank you."

"Indeed—but between the two of us, I hope she doesn't have too many unmarried sisters." He laughed again.

I avoided an answer. If he was as well connected as he implied, he knew that she had another sister—Anastasia, whose fortune in marriage was still an unknown.

"What is the date?" Antiochos asked. "You see, I shall have to remove a few things."

"You have another residence?" I asked, although I knew the answer.

"Oh, yes." Antiochos leaned forward, his elbows on the desk. "Why, I have two! On the day that Anastasius's throne was placed in peril, I gave him much-needed advice and was well rewarded. It was fortuitous for both of us. Perhaps you will be able to supply the empress with similar advice one day. Shall I call for some wine?"

I shook my head. "Lord Antiochos," I said, "there is more to the empress's request."

"Is there?" He blinked. "Well, then, she shall have it, whatever it is. What, besides the house, does she wish? The house is hers."

Here was my opening. Despite a thickening in my throat, my words spilled out: "And that *is* her wish."

It took a moment for him to take in my meaning—the faded gray eyes dilating—and when he did, he went as white as the shock of hair on his head. "My house?"

I nodded.

He stood. "She wishes to buy it?"

I cleared my throat. "There was no mention of money, my lord."

Antiochos did not seem surprised at this twist. He knew as well as anyone what power the throne wielded. As for me, I was learning.

"So, I am to make a gift of it to Comito and General Sittas?" He took his seat and his tone took on an edge. "Well, then, she is no Empress Euphemia, is she, content to see to the running of the Daphne while the emperor attends to matters of state? I hear that Her Sacred Resplendency the Empress attends the Imperial Consistory meetings and questions his councilors. They say she sides with the Monophysites and seeks to put the whoremongers out of business."

I could neither contest his observations nor condemn him for his faintly disguised barbs, so I said nothing. I did not appreciate this task Theodora had given me. One minute expanded into two, and then three. I grew uncomfortable in my chair.

His face as still as stone, he was facing me but his eyes appeared unfocused.

At last, I stood to take my leave. "What shall I tell the empress?"

The eyes came alive as if he had just awakened, as if he had just realized he had spoken ill of the empress to one of her servants. Antiochos summoned up the energy to stand and present me with a smile. "Why, tell her the house is hers—or rather, her sister's. I'll make all the arrangements." He rang for his servant to show me out. "She has learned the game, my friend. She is empress. Give her my best."

I gave him a note from the empress that contained only the date of the wedding. It was, in essence, his eviction notice.

I turned to go, bewildered by his compliant surrender. As I reached the three stairs that would return me to the passageway, I heard him mutter, "God help us all."

Not long after the wedding, Justinian announced the new commissions for Belisarius and Sittas. They would be parting ways, for Belisarius was named Master of Soldiers in the East while Sittas was promoted to Master of Soldiers in Armenia.

On his first visit to my new rooms, my friend and fellow scribe Tariq remarked that the new commissions seemed to have been done quietly.

"You're right. They came back from a defeat with their tails between their legs, so I doubt the emperor wanted to appear to be rewarding them for what was an embarrassment to the throne."

"Just the same," Tariq said, his dark eyes above an Egyptian nose locking onto mine, "there's the matter of Hypatius, the man Belisarius is replacing."

"From what I hear Hypatius has not had a victory to his name and that his military career has been lackluster at best."

"That may be the case, Stephen, but he is the nephew of Emperor Anastasius."

"That bit of history is before my time here. Why would it matter?"

"I'll tell you why. People thought his bloodline gave him a clearer right to the throne than that of Justinian's uncle, who had merely been Commander of the Imperial Guard. A soldier, you see, without a drop of royal blood."

"Ah! So you think his coming back to the capital might create some discontent?"

Tariq shook his head. "The man is said to have little enough ambition for himself, but *should* there be discontent, his presence might add fuel to the flames."

"I feel a bit removed since moving into the Daphne. You no doubt have your finger in the air more than I do. *Is* there cause in the streets for discontent?"

"Always, Stephen. The Blues and the Greens are always going at it. Justinian is smart enough to hold down dissent by playing one faction against the other. You need to get out from under the empress more. You're missed in the scriptorium."

"Oh, someone will take my desk, sooner or later."

"Let's take some walks now and again."

"I'd like that, Tariq."

"Good! You'll have to dress warmly, though. January is coming and with all these waterways around us, the cold can cut right through you."

4

J ANUARY BROUGHT A THIRD WEDDING. Theodora had been impressed by a banker who had appeared before the Imperial Consistory—not for the wordless bit of support he had relayed to her regarding her plea for the funds to rebuild Antioch, but for his wealth and status, or so I suspected. Her infatuation with Sittas apparently forgotten, Anastasia seemed happy enough to accept Peter Barsymes.

I was happy, too, because the banker owned his own house, freeing me from having to requisition another one for a sister of Theodora.

With hurried steps, Theodora entered her husband's study. "Justinian ... do you have a moment?"

The emperor looked up from his desk. "So formal, Thea?"

"Did you think I would call you *Tino,* as your aunt did?"

"I was referring to your tone. It's rather serious."

"I have been reading a section of the codex that Tribonian and the commission have been working on."

"Oh, it's been put in effect."

"Nonetheless, I have a concern." Theodora approached the desk.

"Why haven't you raised it before this?"

"It's an enormous amount to read, Justinian." She would not reveal even to him that she'd had to wait for Stephen to recreate the codex in a larger script, as well as coach her in some of the Latin.

Justinian cocked his head. "And your concern, my love?"

Theodora leaned forward, placing her palms on the desk. "My concern is the edict which closes the Academy of Plato in Athens. Why would you do that?"

"I'm not closing it. I'm ending the funding. Oh, I don't intend to take action against the teachers. The last thing I would want is to make heroes out of Plato's latest generation of students."

"I don't see the difference. Without funds, the school will close."

"Indeed! Thea, it's a school of pagans, devoted to paganism."

"Why should that pose a problem?"

"Because, dearest, I intend, as you well know, to remake the Empire of the New Rome into what Western Rome once was. I will do it in all matters—legally, militarily, and—"

"In religion?"

"Of course. To unify this New Rome we must be of one true apostolic religion."

"And so, am I to conclude the edict condemns not only pagans, but Samaritans and heretics of every variety?"

Justinian nodded. "It does." He looked up at Theodora, his eyes widening. "Ah, I see—your concern is for your Monophysitic friends in Alexandria, for Patriarch Timothy and the rest."

Theodora drew herself up. "And for myself."

"So—there it is. You consider yourself a Monophysite."

Theodora paused for a moment before taking up a different thread. "You well know your uncle persecuted Monophysites just a few years ago." She avoided mention of the fact that Justinian himself had played some role in the mistreatment, to what extent she didn't know.

Justinian stood and came around the desk to stand in front of Theodora. "Just as you and I have compromised on some things, I hope to repair the breach between Dyophysites and Monophysites."

A part of her longed to play the actress, as she had done on occasion with Hecebolus and a dozen others. Theodora knew that a smile, a veiling of her eyelids, a certain tilt of the head could work wonders on any man—but as yet, her interactions with Justinian had been natural and sincere. She would not change that now. She looked up into his earnest face and spoke her heart. "How is that possible if this edict is so unforgiving? Would you alienate Syria and Egypt, where you know Monophysitism is strong? What with our threats from Persia, Syria is a valuable friend strategically and militarily. And without Egypt, where would we buy our wheat?"

"You've been to both and all along the Levant. I'm envious of your travels."

"And I found good Christians along the way, Justinian. The Monophysites are separated from Orthodox Catholics by just a few words regarding the nature of Christ. Was Christ incarnated *in* two natures, as Dyophysites profess, or *from* two natures, as Monophysites believe?"

Justinian placed his hand over Theodora's. "You make the chasm between the faiths seem tiny. But you are correct: we cannot turn Syria or Egypt against us. We will take our good time to think and to mediate."

"And if any of my friends come from across the Middle Sea—?"

"I am giving you the Palace of Hormisdas." Justinian leaned over and kissed the top of Theodora's head. "I ask that the library and scriptorium be maintained as before and the copyists and scribes be allowed their subterranean rooms. Otherwise, use it as you wish, dearest. Entertain whom you will."

I took respites from my copying duties for Theodora to take walks through the city streets with Tariq. Our white tunics with gold trim and purple emblems on the upper sleeves identified us as palace eunuchs of some station, garnering for us nods of respect from some and hard stares from others, some quite hostile. On one such occasion we had finished our walk and were standing just within the Chalké Gate saying our goodbyes when a little parade of more than a dozen colorfully clad women and girls entered the complex, preceded and followed by excubitors, as if they were under arrest.

"What's all this, now?" Tariq questioned.

"I don't know." The words were no sooner out of my mouth than a woman's discordant voice cut through the air: "Stephen! Stephen!"

I looked up to see that a rotund woman in an orange tunic had broken ranks and was barreling her way toward me.

"My God, Stephen!" she cried. She halted right in front of me, her painted face, marred by tears, staring up at me. "Oh, you do remember me? I could not forget you. I had never seen such a handsome eunuch."

"Yes, my lady," I said. Of course, I remembered her. I had been dispatched by Justinian to rescue Antonina from her indenture at this woman's house of bad repute. He had paid her handsomely.

"You are friends with the emperor. I know that. You can help me, I know you can!"

"Have you been arrested?"

"No! But it's just as bad—or worse!" She took my hand and held it in both of hers. I looked down to see that every one of her short, chubby fingers bore a jeweled ring. "I'm to be brought before the praetorian prefect. I'm to lose my business!"

"It's the edict about the houses?"

"Yes, yes, the edict! Oh, Stephen, you can intercede for me! Please! I will be out on the street unless I find a way." Her hands tightened on mine, rings cutting into my skin.

By now, one of the guards had taken notice of his wayward charge and was hurrying over. "Come forward with the rest!" he ordered. "We don't have all day, woman!"

"I have no influence," I said. The guard pulled her away, freeing my hand. "I'm sorry."

"I did what he asked—the emperor!" She was no match for the guard who quickly hustled her toward the others. She twisted her head in my direction. Her voice loud and shrill, she cried, "I released Antonina with the golden hair so that she could live here in luxury and find a handsome husband as she has done. Now, what's to become of me?"

And then they were gone from sight.

"Mother-of-pearl!" Tariq cried. "If she talks like that before the prefect, she might not see daylight again. Good God, Stephen, who is she?"

"That, my friend, is Madame Flavia, colorful owner of one of the stylish brothels in The City. Justinian had me rescue Antonina from her clutches because she is Theodora's oldest friend."

"And now the brothels are being closed?"

"Indeed they are. The prefect is asking the brothel keepers under oath how much they paid the parents of the girls. Then, when they go before the empress, she will give them up to five gold pieces for each girl's release."

"Theodora herself?" Tariq asked.

I nodded.

"What of the harlots?"

"The youngest girls will be given a fresh tunic and a gold coin—and sent home. The empress is working at finding a kind of group home for the older ones. The brothel keepers are forbidden to resume their trade."

Tariq whistled. "She's making her mark, isn't she?"

"You don't know the half of it. She is seeing to it that daughters will have equal rights with sons to inherit and that a wife's dowry is returned to her upon the death of her husband. Now—I have a codex to copy, so I must say goodbye, Tariq."

I returned to my suite and dropped onto my desk chair only to stare rather stupidly at the codex I had been copying. I felt sadness for the eccentric Madame Flavia, whose life—albeit a ridiculous one—had taken a downward path, but a bit of hope ignited in my heart for the girls and women who might have better futures because of Theodora's dissatisfaction with the status quo.

5

A T PRECISELY NOON, THE *CARPENTUM* drew to a stop in front of the marble-clad mansion. The carriage, with its four thoroughbreds standing abreast like bearers of a chariot, blocked much of the narrow avenue and drew stares from a gathering crowd. Theodora was handed down from the purple cushioned and draped interior. She looked up, impressed by the edifice she had expropriated for her sister Comito. Antiochos had given it up without a whimper. Should they cross paths one day, she would remember to be nice to him. She moved quickly up the several steps, leaving the dozen excubitors to wait for her. She had brought no handmaiden for accompaniment out of fear that the business and banter of three sisters would set tongues wagging in and out of the court.

A croaky voice from the street called out now: "Glory of the purple, joy of the world!" Theodora paused, turning to see an old woman, her veiled head bowed. She knew any empress in purple might enkindle the same greeting, but her arms went to gooseflesh, nonetheless. She was determined that one day she would merit such praise, not just from an old woman, but from throngs of her citizens, the powerful and dispossessed alike.

One of the palace eunuchs afforded to Comito and Sittas admitted her into the grand vestibule and led her into the atrium where he announced her. Comito and Anastasia sat on a couch at the far end, on the other side of the pool where four marble water nymphs stood beneath a square of open roof, their hands cupped and held up as if to catch the rain.

Anastasia stopped her chatter and hurried over to embrace Theodora. Lagging behind, Comito avoided an embrace, instead taking Theodora's hand and kissing the ring with the rare purple sapphire that Empress Euphemia had once worn.

"You look like you are about to cry," Theodora said.

"Oh, she's just emotional today," Anastasia chimed, her manner more irritating than illuminating.

"*Is* she?"

Motioning toward the smaller rooms off to the side of the atrium, Theodora said, "Perhaps one of those rooms will be more private. Out here it's like we're onstage."

Anastasia giggled. "And we three have been on the boards more than once!"

"Hush!" Comito commanded, her eyes scanning the bank of rooms on one side, then the other, before nodding toward her choice. "Let's sit in that one."

The room was small but richly appointed. Two red couches sat perpendicular to each other on the one side and a large table with a chair behind it was placed on the other side.

Comito ordered refreshments before sitting down next to Anastasia on the couch across from Theodora's. "This serves as Sittas's office although he scarcely used it before he was off to battle."

"There's news," Theodora said.

"Yes, indeed!" Anastasia declared.

Theodora's gaze went directly to Anastasia. Before she could ask what her sister meant, Comito spoke up.

"What news, Thea?"

"Your husband has scored a significant victory in the borderlands."

"Oh, you gave me a fright for a moment—I thought—"

"No, no, I should have said that it's good news."

Comito brightened for the first time. "Thank the gods, pardon the expression, one of Mother's. It's just that talk of the Persians at the borderlands is all one hears these days. It's distressing when one's husband is in the thick of it."

Anastasia released what seemed a stage sigh. "You're right, Comissa. It's all people talk about. It's mind-numbing, don't you think?" Her gaze moved from Comito to Theodora. "Why can't the Persians stay within their borders, where they belong?"

Theodora laughed. "And what of us Romans—we who have claimed most of the earth around the Middle Sea?"

Anastasia tilted her head as she took this in but had no riposte.

"Tasia," Theodora said, "did you mean to say a moment ago that *you* also have news?"

The corners of Anastasia's mouth drew up into a sly smile and her jaw fell slack as if to speak but no words came. She turned her head to Comito. "Perhaps Comissa should tell you."

Before Comito could speak, a servant appeared in the doorway. At her nod, the corpulent, gray-clad eunuch entered, carrying a small table that he placed close to where the two couches met. He was followed by two female servants who deposited cups as well as plates of olives, cheese, and honey cakes on the table. A second, younger, eunuch entered with a large bowl of mountain tea that he ladled into the cups. The four wordlessly left the room.

As Anastasia's attention was drawn to taking up a honey cake, Theodora trained her questioning eyes on her older sister.

"I am going to have a child," Comito said, her eyes luminous.

Theodora blinked and sat back against the bolster. Her two sisters had been married some months now so that such an announcement should not have come as a surprise—and yet it did. Theodora had been so intent on affairs of state, not the least of which was providing an heir for the empire, that thoughts of her sisters' new marriages were on the far peripheral of her thoughts.

"This is good news," she said, fumbling a bit as she tried to appear more delighted than she felt. She knew she should rise and make a fuss over Comito, but could not gather the initiative.

"She's to have a little Sittas," Anastasia cried, crumbs falling from her mouth, "a little warrior. He's likely to enter the world waving a sword."

"Anastasia!" Comito exclaimed. "That's most irreverent."

"A tiny sword, I meant."

The silly joke somehow fit the moment and the three laughed together.

"So," Comito began, turning serious, eyes on Theodora, "was this a significant victory? Will people praise him and talk about him the way they are talking about Belisarius's victory at Daras? I'm sick of hearing about him."

"Comito, are you thinking of your husband now and the respect he's due—or are you unsettled with the ... the—"

"Marriage you arranged for me?"

Anastasia let out a little gasp and returned a piece of cheese to the plate.

Theodora drew in breath. "Well—are you?"

"No, I'm not, Theodora. Belisarius was not meant for me, but I have not forgotten that you wouldn't let me go on campaign with Sittas, while you *insisted* Antonina go with Belisarius."

Anastasia laughed. "That's because Antonina has the coin purse of a man, isn't that so, Thea?"

Theodora tried not to look at her younger sister but could not hold back a smile at the bawdy joke. Comito, however, was not amused, so Theodora rearranged her expression to one more serious. "Comissa," she said, "considering your present condition, it was a good decision. Now, listen, Sittas has much to be proud of. He actually had *two* very significant victories, one that completely repelled an invasion by the Sassanid Empire. It's regrettable that Belisarius gets all the acclaim. I put that on Procopius, who travels with him and sends back long, glowing reports of Belisarius's glorious victories. Despite his talents, Procopius is such a bootlicker that he has Justinian in the palm of his hand, and I am powerless to do anything about it. But I shall see to it that Sittas is given a royal supper when he returns. That will help set things right, don't you think?"

"Perhaps," Comito said, not without the hint of a grudge.

Theodora turned her attention to Anastasia. "And you? When are you to have a child, Tasia?"

Anastasia's back went rigid. "I'm not—not if I can help it."

"And sometimes you can't," Comito quipped.

Theodora wondered whether she was speaking generally, or if it was a snide allusion to the child she herself had given up before leaving The City with Hecebolus.

"I'm not the motherly type," Anastasia said.

"Tasia, your husband will expect children," Theodora said.

"And so does the law, it appears." Anastasia brushed some crumbs off her tunic. "The new edict that your friend Tribonian dreamed up states that nature created women for the express purpose of bringing children into the world, *and* that this is woman's greatest desire. Did you not see that, Thea?"

"I did, but I don't always see things in time. I must wait for Stephen to copy out the edicts because … Oh, never mind. So, in parroting Roman law, Tribonian got away with a bit of posturing. Meanwhile, I was seeing to other initiatives that mattered more. One must pick one's battles."

"Initiatives?"

"Yes, Tasia, like running the brothel-keepers out of The City, returning young girls to their homes and freeing the older ones, supplying them with a home if they need one. Divorce and inheritance laws are to be revamped and a dozen more changes need to be made."

"Thea," Anastasia said, her voice but a whisper, "you've had a child. Were you frightened to give birth? It terrifies me."

"It's a hard thing, but you survive it."

"Does Justinian know you have a daughter?" Anastasia asked.

"He does."

"When will you tell Hyacinth you are her mother," Comito asked.

"I don't know," Theodora answered, noting that her interest appeared sincere. "When the time is right."

"Why, she'll be of marriageable age herself soon, Thea."

Comito was right, and the idea struck Theodora like the crash of a cold wave. Plans for her daughter must be made, and soon, she thought—before the adoptive parents marry her off to some farmer. Theodora could not think about Hyacinth, the girl child she left with Comito in Constantinople when she set off for the Pentapolis, without unwelcome thoughts of the baby John she had left behind in Alexandria. "Enough questions!" she declared.

"Just one more," Comito pressed. "Doesn't Justinian want to have children?"

Theodora felt the rush of blood to her face. "Yes, of course. And the empire needs an heir.—I should take my leave now. I have an appointment this afternoon." She stood, as if to go, paused, and sat again. "Comito, as your time gets closer, I want you to take up residence at the palace."

"I will be fine here, Thea."

"No, I insist. You are to give birth to my nephew or niece in the royal lying-in chamber."

Anastasia gasped. "In that little red building?"

"More purple than red, Tasia. It's porphyry from Egypt."

Comito paled. "But it's for—"

"Future emperors, yes," Theodora snapped, "but it's been decades since it's served that purpose. Justinian was not born there and neither was Justin."

"They weren't royal," Anastasia interjected. "Isn't that right, Thea?"

Theodora shot her sister a sharp look, to little effect. "That's correct," she said, immediately pivoting to Comito. "Please, Comissa you are to plan on it." She stood abruptly. "Now I really must go."

Later, inside the purple luxury of the *carpentum* as it moved toward the Mese and back to the palace, Theodora wondered what her sisters thought about the way she unceremoniously bolted from their presence. She had done so out of fear of revealing secrets. Blurting out things one regretted sometimes happens with sisters. Why, she had almost disclosed to them that Stephen had to copy out documents and codices in larger handwriting that she could read. But that secret paled in relation to the other two. She had kept from her sisters the knowledge that she had given birth to a son in Alexandria. Although she trusted Comito completely, Anastasia had a way of speaking out of turn.

And then there was the other matter—that of providing a royal heir. Theodora and Justinian had high hopes of having children, but as time went on she felt less and less confident. Her courses ran on schedule, she knew that much. Was it possible that Justinian had been made sterile by the bout of orchitis he had suffered seven years before? When the physician Philoxenos had been tight-lipped—to her and even to Justinian—about possible complications from the abnormal inflammation of his testes, she had Stephen scour medical texts for the truth. No matter what, *if* the disease had rendered Justinian sterile, she did not want him to know that he was likely the cause of their childless relationship. She would rather have him think she was barren. *No one must find out. No one must know, ever.* The physician had died a year or two later. Only she knew now—and Stephen.

Still, she did not abandon hope that she would bear another child, a child for the empire.

Theodora drew back the curtains as the *carpentum* came into the crowded Augustaion. A number of voices rose up, not quite in unison: "Glory of the purple, joy of the world!" Her gaze went to the center of the square and the column that supported a silver statue of the city's founder Constantine astride a horse. At ground level stood statues of two of his sons. Even as a child chasing pigeons in the square, she had recognized the significance of royal lineage.

Her generosity in her invitation—or insistence—that Comito give birth on the palace grounds and in the purple opulence of the royal lying-in chamber had been impulsive. But it was not done without foresight. Dropping the curtains into place, she sat back, praying that one day she, too, would follow suit.

As it turned out, it was Antonina, on campaign with husband Belisarius in the East, who won the first birthing boast. Just a week later, news arrived that Antonina had given birth to Belisarius's child, a girl, Joannina.

Theodora sat seething, having just summarily dismissed Stephen, who had read her the letter. It seemed as if marriages all around her were bearing fruit.

"Comito and now Antonina!" she cried aloud and threw her wine goblet toward the firebox, but it missed its mark, shattering on the white marble hearth. Staring at the spattered red wine, she cried out, "Why not me?"

6

A PALACE EUNUCH CAME TO MY suite one afternoon to tell me that the empress was on her way down to see me. I found this odd. While we always had two games of *Shatranj* in play—one here and one in her rooms—this was neither the day nor time when we sat across from each other eyeing the black and white pieces on the game board. "What now, Jati?" I said aloud to my mosaic boy on the wall. I left my study, which was less than tidy, and received her in my small reception room.

Theodora arrived unattended, as was her custom when she came to my rooms. She placed a brown garment on a chair and seated herself on the couch. I took a cushioned chair opposite.

"Stephen," she began, clearing her throat, "no doubt you have heard much of the Samaritan revolts in our Diocese of the East.

"I have." Here I stepped lightly because I knew from Brother Leo and my former fellow scribes and copyists in the Palace of Hormisdas that the rebellions staged in Samaria were caused by certain of Justinian's pro-Christian edicts which leaders aligned with Constantinople carried out, not without bad feelings and widespread bloodshed. When the rebels gained some leverage, they demanded an independent state. Instead, the full force of the East Roman military, along with Arabs from that area of the Levant, brought pressure to bear all the more, crushing the revolt and killing tens of thousands.

Theodora gave a tight smile. "This morning Justinian met with Abbot Sabbas, who asked for a private audience with him. I watched the meeting from a recess in the audience chamber. He is here to requisition support for the Dyophysite Patriarch of Palestine, which lies right between Syria and Egypt with their Monophysitic bishops. Oh, he's a saint, to be sure with his wiry form and white, white ring of hair and long beard. He's founded a hundred monasteries throughout the Levant." She paused, tilting her head in a pose of skepticism, or perhaps annoyance. "Justinian not only dispensed with having a holy man of ninety prostrate himself, but the emperor stood, stepped down from the dais and welcomed him with a kiss on the dusty forehead."

"But—*you* don't hold him in such esteem." It was more a statement than a question.

"Ha!" Theodora snarled. "I can tell you he's most intolerant of what he calls the 'filthy Monophysitic heresy'."

"Does he seek soldiers or money?"

"In essence, both, if we give the patriarch what he requests—a lowering of taxes, protection from raiders, and a pilgrim hostel. Justinian is inclined to grant him his three wishes. And he was so much in awe of the holy man that he offered to fund his monasteries. Sabbas refused the offer."

Theodora's eyes came up and she read the question on my face: How would she—a fierce friend of Monophysites like Patriarchs Severus of Antioch and Timothy of Alexandria welcome a full-throated Dyophysite? I knew for a fact that she was sheltering Monophysites in the Palace of Hormisdas.

"Yes, the monk and I are at odds with our core beliefs, but I shall surprise you, Stephen. I will—like my husband—humble myself. And in doing so, I need your help."

"Mine? What can I do, Thea?"

She nodded toward the garment she had brought. "Tomorrow morning you will bring him that clean new tunic. Why, you should see the filthy rag he wore for his audience! Narses said it smelled of camel dung. You are to tell him it's a gift from me and that I beg his presence. Give him time to bathe and change. You are to accompany him—here to this room so that there are no witnesses."

Theodora stood, turning to leave. She knew the question I held back because she halted at the door, and without even a glance back, said, "You'll know why soon enough, Stephen. Just be certain that he is here at noon."

It happened that way sometimes. Either we knew each other extremely well, or the Syrian blood we shared did carry a trace of the sight we often talked about.

I sat there thinking about Narses' camel dung comment and chuckled to myself. He did have a dry wit on occasion, but he was a hard man to get to know. His advancement within the government had come quickly. When he purchased me in Antioch for service in the Great Palace, he was a steward to Prince Justinian. In little time, he became Commander of the Imperial Guard, and then Grand Chamberlain. Both the emperor and empress trusted and valued him.

Allowing time for the holy monk Sabbas to wash and dress, I hurried down the stairs to the floor beneath mine, where he had been given rooms. I could see at once that he had yet to bathe. And Narses had not exaggerated about the odor, which caused my throat to tighten. I took my breath through my mouth. It was not the lord chamberlain's dry wit; it was stark truth.

The monk accepted the garment but laid it aside, saying that his grooming would come later in the day. He was wearing the tunic Theodora had disparaged. Despite the intolerable odor in the closed apartment, I forced a smile, telling him that I would have the empress wait until then—or until the next day if that suited him.

"No, no," he said, "I will see her on her schedule."

It was a bad plan, made worse by the fact that I had to remain in his company attempting small talk until it was nearly noon. We dared not be early.

As we made ready to leave some twenty minutes later, I noticed his dirt encrusted sandals near the door and realized he meant to meet the Empress of the New Rome in bare and begrimed feet. "We have but one floor to climb, yes?" he asked when I suggested he wear the sandals. At my slow nod, he waved his hand dismissively and moved out into the hall. The subject was closed.

It was as we were taking the stairs that he struck me dumb with a question meant to appear offhand. "Is it true, Stephen, that Theodora is hiding Monophysites in the Hormisdas Palace?"

My heart quickened as we reached the landing, passing the silent excubitor on duty there. I pretended not to hear him. No doubt the guard had heard him, and it crossed my mind that he could easily be one of Theodora's many spies.

Thankfully, we arrived at the door to my suite, and he had no time to repeat his question. We entered just as the water clock cymbal chimed noon.

That Theodora was already present was not the biggest surprise.

Theodora awaited the holy monk dressed in her purple and gold. I blinked. She was kneeling! "Good father," she said, "I welcome you to Constantinople."

Now she stretched out and lay prostrate on the floor, arms extended as if on a cross. I saw that she had removed my carpet so that she was on the cold, dark marble.

I was so shocked by the sight that I found myself stepping back against the wall, forgetting to announce the visitant.

The holy monk advanced, nonetheless, feet slapping lightly on the marble. "Rise, mistress, rise."

Theodora spoke with her eyes on the floor. "I beg your blessing, most Holy Father. I beg you to intercede with the Lord God for me."

"The Lord will provide glory and victory for your empire, mistress. Now, rise."

By now I had come up to the side of the tonsured monk. Theodora looked up at him, then me, and back to him. If his ragged appearance and stink shocked her, she did not show it. She was an actress, after all.

Theodora lifted herself to her knees. "Holy Father, I beg for prayers that I might conceive a child, a son, for Justinian."

The monk's head, its crown still caked with dust from the road, tilted slightly. "The Lord will provide glory and victory for your empire, mistress."

Theodora stood. Though not particularly tall, he was still a head and shoulders taller than she.

"You have passed through the Levant on your travels, I understand, mistress."

Theodora swallowed and appeared to collect herself, holding reins on what emotion I could only guess.

"Am I to understand, mistress, that in North Africa you came under the tutelage of Patriarch Timothy and Patriarch Severus?"

Theodora's black eyes widened. I think she and I both knew at this point the difficulty of the situation. "They were saviors in my time of need, Abbot Sabbas, desperate need. They were not merely teachers; they were saviors and friends."

"Indeed, indeed. I see."

"Abbot Sabbas, if you care anything for our emperor and for the empire, this Christian New Rome, you will intercede for me, praying that I can deliver a healthy son, a proper heir to the empire, one who can hold Christendom together for another generation."

The old man nodded obsequiously, as if he agreed. And yet he repeated,

"The Lord will provide glory and victory for your empire, mistress." Squaring his shoulders, he said, "I beg your leave now, mistress."

Theodora stared up at him many moments, her porcelain complexion turning paler still. She drew in breath and turned to me, her face hard. "See him to his rooms, Stephen."

We bowed and backed our way to the door. It was a ritual Theodora required of me only when in the company of others.

In the hall the old man moved remarkably fast, his bare feet slapping on the marble, muttering as we descended the two flights. When we came to his doorway, he turned to me, wheezing with breath hot and fetid, "You know," he said, "it matters not a particle of sand to me what life of depravity she led before coming to the throne. But does she think I would pray for the empire to fall into the clutches of heretical vipers? Monophysites!" His eyes held mine. "Better it is she is barren!" He pivoted now and stepped into his rooms and shut the door.

I returned to my suite, wondering whether he had spoken out of emotion or because he expected me to repeat his words to Theodora. I was no fool to bring such a message to her. Besides, I knew her well enough to know that she already had a grasp of the man. No child would be born out of his prayers.

Not at all certain of the scene I was stepping into, I entered my reception room to find Theodora had not waited for my return. The tension left me like a bow suddenly unstrung. I moved to cross the room when a flash of sunlight on glass drew my gaze down to the black marble floor. Amidst shards of glass, bronze mechanical pieces, and water lapping at my sandals lay the remains of my water clock.

Abbot Sabbas stayed four months as Justinian's guest. Theodora never spoke to him again.

17 April 531

Theodora found it hard not to fidget in her chair, harder not to speak up. For the most part, she merely observed the Consistory at work at the Monday Silences. Justinian's councilors had become used to her presence, but the resentment of a few still simmered so that she found it more efficacious to watch and dictate notes to Stephen afterward. If she wished to make her opinion known, it was usually to Justinian, later and in private. The meetings could be a trial, often tedious and uninteresting, but not so today. Today it was disturbing.

Despite reservations she had raised to Justinian about his naming John of Cappadocia Praetorian Prefect of the East, he had done so just the same. "Oh, he is not schooled or cultivated like Demosthenes, who held the office under my uncle," Justinian had told her the night before, "but he has considerable expertise at cutting costs. Why, even our rich patricians and senators are holding tight to their purses having heard of the reforms he has in mind."

Although Theodora could read hesitancy on the faces of those men at the deliberation table, no one voiced an objection to the promotion. At the far end sat the Cappadocian's predecessor, old Julianus, a tired mule put to pasture. She would miss him. He offered no arguments when she requisitioned funds for Patriarchs Timothy and Severus, as well as for dozens of other Monophysites seeking her help. Saving money for the empire was all to the good, but she did not want to be made to defer to the Cappadocian in her spending.

The mood at the table this Monday was far from celebratory. The topic turned now to the war against Persia. They had found out only that morning that on Easter Saturday Belisarius had been dealt a humiliating defeat by the Persians at Callinicum, in Syria. The military messenger had told of a battlefield with even forces of twenty thousand. Belisarius merely wanted to prevent the Persians from invading Syria, but his men were inebriated with their past successes and demanded they attack, threatening mutiny if Belisarius demurred. The general bent to their will. Heavy losses were taken on both sides, but it was Belisarius who was forced into retreat. Still, the rout brought with it one satisfying result: because the Persians had lost so many men, their aim of taking Syria was blunted. In his absence, Belisarius had both supporters and detractors at the table, but the calls for his replacement won the day.

Justinian rose, his arm raised high to bring the discussion to a close. "General Belisarius is my friend," he announced, "nonetheless, I find myself in agreement that it is time to bring him home. I will need to hear from him—and from Procopius who has been scrupulously recording the events."

Theodora sat stunned. Would Belisarius—husband of her greatest friend—survive what seemed a crippling blow to what had been a promising future? Oh, she would be happy to see Antonina. But not Procopius. He was no friend of hers.

"Master Justinian," Tribonian said. "That is all very well, but who is to take his place at the Persian border?"

A quiet murmuring went the rounds of the table.

"It is an important post," Justinian answered. "We all agree on that, yes? I am sending someone already familiar with the Persian frontier. Familiar and successful, I might add. I am assigning that post to Sittas."

Now came a second stinging. Not because of the change in post for Comito's husband, a post that offered an opportunity to excel, but because Justinian had not discussed with her the future of their brother-in-law before this announcement.

With nods and affirmative words, the men around the table were at one with Justinian.

"I am sorry that I did not take you into my confidence, dearest," Justinian said at their evening meal, "but I decided only this morning, minutes before the Silence."

Theodora nodded, choosing not to belabor the point. The hurt would pass.

"As for Belisarius," he continued, "I have no intention of disciplining him, you can rest your mind on that. Why, it was more of a Pyrrhic victory for the Persians, after all. But I felt the councilors needed some show of action."

"Oh?" Using fingers to tear a piece from her grilled pike, Theodora lifted her eyes to her husband, who sat on the couch next to her. "You must know, my love," she said, "that the whole dozen of them taken together do not measure up to you." Her gaze stayed steady even as she lifted the nugget of fish to her mouth.

Justinian gave her a half-smile. He understood her purpose. Now and then she would remind him that he was no longer a peasant from Romanized Illyricum, just as she thought less and less about her days acting in the theater or wandering the deserts of the Levant.

He came to her in the women's quarters that night, as he did several nights a week. Their passion for each other had not dimmed. It had grown. Theodora felt a sense of freedom in their coupling here in the Imperial Apartment that she had not experienced when they lived down near the sea, in the Palace of Hormisdas. There, a cloud of uncertainty hung over her. Even after the death of Empress Euphemia, who hated her and worked to scuttle her relationship with Justinian, other detractors were at work, not the least of whom was Procopius.

Justinian seldom stayed the entire night because he slept so little. He seemed to require just a few hours of sleep, instead spending nighttime hours in his study going over the laws prepared by Tribonian or other issues of importance.

This night, naked, lying on her side with her left hand propping up her head, she watched him as he dressed.

"Justinian, what if … what if—"

"Shush," he said at once. His tunic in place, he came to her barefoot and found space to sit beside her on the sleeping couch, his warm hand on her hip. "Do not despair, dearest. God will hear our prayers."

"And if He doesn't? What then?"

Theodora felt his hand move to her midsection. "Unripe grapes get sweet as honey," he whispered, "but at a slow pace."

It was a favorite proverb of his, but for her it had worn thin. She gave him a smile, hoping that in the amber light of the beeswax candles he wouldn't recognize it for what it was—a stage smile.

Justinian leaned over and kissed her. I'll see you in the morning."

Theodora knew there was no amending his poor sleep schedule. He had even more extensive and vigorous changes in mind than his quest to compress and codify thousands of old Roman laws into one digest, the *Codex Justinianus*; thus, he spent his nights planning in his War Room beneath the Daphne Wing. She had seen the room once. Secret documents were locked away there and maps of the world were laid out on a massive table. He had told her how he longed to regain the Roman world that had once completely encircled the Middle Sea before the rise of barbarian tribes, how it was his destiny. At the City Arsenal, he showed her a laboratory where chemists were trying to perfect a flammable compound that could be used in naval warfare. He had begun the building of a fleet of dromons, warships meant to sail the Middle Sea, retaking Hippo and Carthage on the African coast before setting sail for the River Tiber and the reclamation of Rome itself. By replacing square sails with triangular ones, Justinian's shipwrights created navy ships no longer dependent on square sails that relied on wind from behind, but galleys with Lateen triangular sails that could be employed to take the wind fore-and-aft.

At first, Justinian's quest had appeared untenable to Theodora, just as it had to certain councilors at the Silences. But as he voiced his determination and enthusiasm within the Silences and within their Imperial Apartment—

and as the two of them seemed to transform into one ruling power—he began to win her over.

After he had gone, Theodora rose from the couch and moved toward the window. The fire in the grate still gave off enough heat so that she did not draw on her robe. Outside, the full moon shone nearly as bright as day. Coming to the window, she looked down through the wavy glass, her sight trained on the round roof of the little palace of purple porphyry where young empresses had their lying-in.

Only the week before, beneath the gold-leafed roof, Comito had delivered a girl that Sittas named Sophia. Theodora's insisting her sister give birth there had been done on impulse, but not without thought. No matter what she told Justinian or herself, she knew in her heart she had not done it to merely please Comito. That their niece be born there could one day have resounding consequences. *I am preparing myself for a childless nursery.* The thought, like the impulse, had come unbidden, and for a moment, just a moment, she believed she had been visited by the Syrian sight. This notion brought with it the sensation that the skin on her arms and at the back of her neck was tightening. She shivered as if taken by a cold wind and quickly shook it off, along with the notion.

While the birth of a royal niece should have pleased her, an unbearable sadness descended. For her, there was time; she would be just thirty-one in June, and she had already brought two children into the world, but she was dogged by dark thoughts of the prognosis the physician Philoxenos had so carefully avoided a few years before. If it came to pass that Justinian himself was the reason for their lack of a child, an heir, she would take that knowledge to the grave. No one on earth shared that secret—except for Stephen.

Theodora's eyes moved down to the double brass doors on the red building. She drew in a long breath, her hand moving down over her flat stomach. She recalled the warmth of Justinian's caressing hand. Her husband's hand.

A wave of jealousy swept over her as she imagined Comito holding her new daughter.

Will I ever sit in the jewel-encrusted birthing chair?

7

MY BEFUDDLED MANSERVANT PIERS ENTERED my study a step or two behind the empress. "The Mistress Theodora," he choked out. I stood for another of her unannounced visits. I had gotten used to them. Piers had not. His lips and chin trembled.

Theodora gave him a slight nod, and he knew to disappear.

I invited her into my reception room where we settled ourselves on facing couches, our standing *Shatranj* game board on a table between us. "Thea, I am behind by two or three codices." Even though she carried nothing with her, I was fearful she had yet another codex of Tribonian's laws for me to copy in large script.

"It's nothing like that, Stephen."

"Good!" I said, pulling a face.

She laughed. "It's an errand."

"I see."

"You're to find someone."

"Yes, of course."

"My daughter, Hyacinth."

I tried not to show surprise. "Where am I to find her, Thea?"

"She and her parents sell chickens in the square at the Forum of the Ox. I've not seen them since that day there was an attempt on my life, but Comito tells me they still go there on market day. They are allowed a space in front of a spice shop."

"I see. What am I to say to her—or to them?"

"You are to deliver up a truth that they will not believe at first."

"Hyacinth—she doesn't know—"

"No, nor do her adoptive parents. She was given over to them when her mother was a nobody, a nothing, getting ready to sail to the Pentapolis. No one could have guessed … this." Theodora made a sweeping motion of her arm as if to take in our surroundings. "So, this is a delicate mission I have chosen you for."

I swallowed hard. "I am to tell them that Hyacinth's mother is the empress?"

Theodora nodded.

"What if they don't believe me? Who would?"

"You are to give them this," she said, opening her hand to reveal a gold earring. It resembled a tiny gold shield from which dangled three gold pendants that terminated in green stones. I could see the gold was merely paint because bits of it had worn away.

Theodora read my expression. "It's nothing but stage jewelry, of course, but Comito attached its mate to the baby blanket she wrapped Hyacinth in all those years ago. The mother will recognize it. She'll believe you."

"And—"

"You are to ask Hyacinth to visit. I say *ask*, but you are not to accept a refusal. She'll be nearly fourteen now. Tell them we'll send a coach for her the next day—Sunday."

"Her parents?"

"If they wish to come, yes, they may do so."

"When should I—"

"Tomorrow, early."

"Shall I bring excubitors?"

"No, absolutely not. This is to be done in secret."

"What about my friend Tariq?"

"Is he trustworthy?"

I nodded.

"Yes, then take him with you."

Saturday, 10 January 532

Wearing wool cloaks against the cold, Tariq and I started out at eight in the morning. We got no farther than the Chalké Gate before having to stand aside to allow a group of some forty or fifty soldiers to pass into the complex.

We recognized the leader as General Belisarius, who had been recalled to the capital.

"The general has an impressive bodyguard," I remarked.

"Those are but a few of his household army. They're quite a brew according to Leo. He holds tight to longtime Greek friends for his lieutenants but for soldiers he culls the best from those he defeats. Rugged and ruthless, they are—but loyal as hell to him. He calls them his *bucellarii*."

"His *biscuit-eaters*?

"Your Latin is sharpening, Stephen. Yes, the army often has to sustain themselves on the twice-baked biscuit."

"Thus the name, ha!"

"I wonder if he is here for his demotion," Tariq said.

"Not according to Theodora. She says Justinian has other plans for him."

"Who's left to hold Persia at bay?"

"The old Persian king is near death," I said, "so Justinian has replaced him with General Sittas. He's also sending Hermogenes with a pot of gold to barter for a lasting peace."

"I'll believe that when I see it," Tariq replied. "You know Mundus is here, too, come from the Danube with his thousands of Heruli, who are Christians on the face of it but still wild and no more than a generation past human sacrifice."

"It makes one wonder, doesn't it? All these mercenaries converging."

"Oh, don't play coy, Stephen. You know plenty. Why, when Justinian reopened the naval arsenal for the building of the ingenious dromons, the people caught on at once that they were war galleys. The emperor wants a new war. The people don't. Now, what's gotten into his head?"

I had no cause to prevaricate. "Let's walk," I said. We passed through the bronze gates into the Augustaion. "Justinian wants war with the west," I said as we moved toward the Mese. "He wants to regain Old Rome's lost holdings all along the North African shore of the Middle Sea, move on to Sicily, and finally to sail right into Rome itself."

Tariq whistled. "A nice feat that would be."

"Indeed. He says that in the years before the barbarian invasions the Middle Sea was completely encompassed by land under Roman rule and that it was known as *Mare Nostrum*."

"*Our Sea*?" Tariq clucked his tongue. "Well, I guess it was, when I think about it. It belonged to Rome, every drop of it."

"And could be again?"

"With Justinian and Theodora? Perhaps."

"Ha! Indeed, Tariq."

Following the Mese, I soon noted something odd about the city this day. The main avenue seemed sparsely populated, the usual loud mingling of languages diminished. Even the brisk breeze following us from the Sea of Marmara was surprisingly unsullied with the usual bouquets of bakeries, perfumeries, spice shops, and grills with frying fish. Shops were shuttered, makeshift stands missing, beggars gone. As we climbed the second hill, we came upon the massive Praetorium on our left, headquarters of Urban Prefect Eudaemon, as well as those of Praetorian Prefect John of Cappadocia. An unusually large number of urban police were stationed in front, lances to the sky, eyes alert. Citizens of a threatening mien gathered there while others streamed from the side of the columned structure where the latest schedule of fees and taxes was posted. No doubt intimidated by the police, they spoke in low, grumbling tones.

We stopped to take in the sight. "Not a joyous group, is it?" I asked. "It's the tax increase, I take it."

"New taxes and new orders. You have not gone walking in a while. The city is in a tumult. Justinian has been pushing things a bit far. If you had brought stylus and parchment, I could dictate a list of grievances the people nurse." He gave a little hiccup of a laugh and continued, "At the Harbor of Prosphorion Justinian came upon foreign sailors squatting at dice with crew members of his barges. He went to Eudaemon and had him issue an ordinance against all public gaming. And then, last fall at the harvest festival at Hebdomon Park, the usual free wine had been forbidden. More recently, on the eve of the Nativity no one from the Great Palace showed up at the steps of the Church of the Holy Wisdom to hand out the silver coins. The tradition was ignored and no mention made of it."

I was about to respond when Tariq raised a hand that served to both muzzle me and point at the group of discontents. "You see there the people's reaction to the latest taxes," he said. "The most recent one has been levied on the Street of the Bakers, so that every man, woman, and child pays a tax on the bread they lift to their mouths."

"So—they blame Eudaemon?"

"Oh, they know the money squeeze comes from the new praetorian prefect, so they hate John the Cappadocian all the more, not to mention Tribonian.

"Oh, but—"

"You're going to tell me Tribonian has a first-rate legal mind and is integral to Justinian's new code. That may be true. But since he was given the office of Quaestor of the Great Palace, just two years ago, he's built a reputation as a corrupt Minister of Justice most concerned with filling his own treasure chest."

I nodded, for I had heard exactly that myself. "As for the Cappadocian," I added, "last year Theodora attempted to dissuade Justinian from naming him Praetorian Prefect of the East, but you see how far that went. It seems Justinian finds them both invaluable to his plan for the distillation of Roman law."

We pushed on. As we made our way through the throng, I realized that there appeared to be an equal number of Greens and Blues and that they seemed not to be at odds with one another; rather, some were openly commiserating, quite out of character.

The Forum of Constantine was nearly deserted, as was the Forum of Theodosius. It was a longer distance to our destination, the Forum of the Ox, and I was a bit tired by the time we arrived.

Even though it was market day, very few stands had been set up. "What goes, Tariq? It is bitter cold and blustery today, but since when would that keep a merchant from turning even a brass coin? And there's not a whiff of fish—grilled or fresh."

"It's not the weather, Stephen. Look, there. It's because most of the permanent shops along the colonnade are closed."

We took just a few more steps into the square before Tariq grabbed my arm and pointed to the right. A gallows had been erected in the far corner. Two bodies twisted slowly in the wind.

"My God!" I whispered, staring stupidly. I had never witnessed such an event. It came home to me now how palace eunuchs lived lives largely away from the public—like monks. "Here? And on market day?" I turned away.

Tariq was unconsciously stroking his throat. His face had paled. When I began to think he had not taken in my comment, he sighed and said, "No doubt the urban prefect wanted to make a statement to the largest number of citizens."

"And made them vanish in the process," I said. "One thing's for certain—there's no farmer selling chickens here today."

Tariq gave a low whistle. "Your friend in the Daphne Wing will not be pleased."

"You're right. She won't be pleased at all. Ha! Thanks for pointing that out, good friend." I started for the colonnade on the south end.

"Wait up, Stephen! Where are you going?"

I took long strides and stepped up onto the covered walkway and stopped before a shop. "This must be the spice shop Theodora spoke of."

Tariq caught up to me. "It looks dark inside."

I took hold of the handle on the wide door and my heart leaped a little when the door opened, spilling a profusion of scents, sweet and sharp.

"Ah," Tariq intoned, "a festival for the nose!"

I entered, Tariq on my heels.

An ancient Indian man came shuffling forward.

"Not much business today," I offered.

"No, not once the urban prefect and his henchmen arrived, pushing people around with the tips of their spears. My customers scattered like bugs."

I motioned toward the exterior. "What was their offense?"

The proprietor's face went blank. "No idea. Dicing perhaps.—What can I help you with today? A nice mountain tea? We have several varieties. Or perhaps a minty salvia? I am Saatvik, here to serve."

"No, Saatvik, no tea today. I am Stephen and this is Tariq. We're looking for a farmer who comes here each week with chickens to sell. I was told they always set up in front of your shop."

He nodded. "The farmer himself died a while ago, but his woman and their daughter carry on although their business falters. Fewer and skinnier birds they have now. They were here today, but like I said, everyone scattered like bugs."

"Like bugs, yes. Tell me, Saatvik, is the daughter's name Hyacinth?"

"Why, yes, it is—and she's pretty as the flower, I can tell you. What business do you have with them?"

"Do you know where their farm is?" I asked.

A shadow of suspicion passed over his face. "I think you are seeking more than a chicken, yes?"

"Perhaps we are," Tariq interjected.

The man's eyes narrowed, moving over us like the beam of a lantern. "Ah!—Those are the palace whites underneath your cloaks, yes? I didn't think you look like the buyers for the royal kitchen."

I had to laugh. He recognized the garb of palace eunuchs. "No we're not here to buy chickens, but we are on a mission."

"Not from the urban prefect, are you?"

I thought that an odd question but didn't pursue its logic. "Listen, Saatvik, it's private business, and believe me, we intend no harm to the family."

The shopkeeper went silent for several long seconds.

"We're on the empress's business," Tariq said, a sharpness in his tone not lost on the Indian. "We would not wish to disappoint her.—No one does."

The man turned to me, his expression questioning, fear floating in his dark eyes.

I merely nodded my agreement, inwardly impressed by my friend's mettle.

"They have a little farm," the shopkeeper said. "It's off the road to the right just outside the walls."

"The Walls of Constantine?" I asked.

"No, no, the Walls of Theodosius."

"Christ!" Tariq blurted.

"You're sure?" I asked the man.

"I am. Follow the Mese to the Second Military Gate. Then look for a ramshackle stone house with several wooden outbuildings behind it."

"Thank you." I tried to give him a silver coin for his trouble, but he backed away, his hands waving me off.

Outside, Tariq said, "I didn't know a person of Indian descent could turn so pale."

"Evidently," I said with a laugh. "The empress has made an impression on The City, it seems. Now—are you ready for a good walk?"

"Do I have a choice?"

"You do," I said, "but I don't."

"Let's go."

After a while we passed through the Forum of Arcadius, which had no more activity going on than did the Forum of the Ox. We continued on, discussing the hangings, the mood of the people, the animosity against the administration that very clearly was on the rise. From there, we talked— speculated, really—on the reasons for Theodora's wish to contact her daughter at this particular moment in the lives of each. No one speculation seemed to hold more water than another. While I had confided the nature of my mission to Tariq, I was careful not to allude to the second child Theodora bore in Alexandria.

When we came to the Military Gate, we did, in fact, use Theodora's travel passes I had thought unneeded. The sentry's eyes widened at the empress's seal and signature.

It was no distance from there to the farmhouse the shopkeeper had told us about. The building was modest enough, with thick stone walls and a clay-tile roof. We had to bang hard on the door. At last, a woman, early-fifties, plain-faced with gray-streaked dark hair, answered our knock. She wore an undyed, well-worn, but clean tunic.

"Yes?" she asked, squinting at me, then at Tariq. She held to the latch as if she might slam the door in our faces.

"We've come from the palace," I said.

Although the muscles in her face sagged and her complexion lost color, she didn't seem surprised.

"I thought the urban prefect would send someone." She pulled back the door. "Come in out of the chill, will you?"

The typical farmhouse storeroom was placed at the front. This one had been turned into a henhouse. We followed the woman into the living quarters, shuffling past two dozen or more scrawny, squawking chickens.

"It's cold today," the woman said. "I brought them in early. Can't leave them in the henhouses no more these days."

"Foxes?" Tariq asked.

She turned to face us. "Two-legged foxes," she snapped. "Thieves. People are hungry these days. Times are hard, people are hungry. They steal."

Like the storeroom, the main room had a dirt floor. A low fire burned in the grate that served to heat their food, as well as the house. "We're not from the urban prefect," I said.

"No?"

"Why would you think that?" Tariq asked.

"We owe on our taxes." Tears pooled in her brown eyes. "They've increased beyond measure, and since my husband died last September, we've had a hard going of it."

"I'm very sorry," I said. "How … how did he die?"

"He got into a scuffle with one of the Greens who meant to take some-thing by force."

"One of your chickens?" Tariq asked.

The woman's eyes went to Tariq, then to me. "My daughter," she said, a catch in her voice.

My mission was becoming more complicated by the moment. "I'm very sorry," I repeated and awkwardly introduced Tariq and myself.

"I am Hestia," she said with a little bow of the head. "I expect one day the urban prefect will send someone to question me about the Green who killed my husband."

"What could you tell them?" Tariq asked.

Hestia stiffened as she took in a large breath. "That I'm glad the Green is dead—and—" The woman suddenly stopped speaking.

Somehow, I knew at once that it was she who had killed the Green. It might have been her aborted comment, tone, manner, or pale coloring, but I was never so certain of something.

A long, awkward moment ensued.

I sensed that Tariq was about to speak, and anticipating he might pursue the subject or say something indelicate, I said at once: "Indeed, who could blame you? Hestia, do not be alarmed, but we have come about your daughter."

She took a step back, her head at an angle, shoulders lifting.

"Hyacinth, isn't that her name?" I smiled, hoping to put her at ease.

A little whimper-like gasp came from behind the blanket hanging in the doorway that led to what I supposed was their sleeping room. The girl was listening.

Hestia fastened her dark eyes on me. "You have no business with my daughter. Others have come here the last few years wanting to spirit her away, to what bad end, I can only guess." She drew herself up. "You should leave now."

"It's the empress who wishes to know of her health, Hestia."

The woman's eyes went wide and her lower lip curled. "The empress! You're lying!"

Moving close to her, I took the pass Theodora had given me and showed it to her. "We've come from the palace, Hestia."

She could not read the words, but her eyes dilated a bit at the royal seal before darting up to me. "What could the empress—"

I leaned into her and whispered, "Does Hyacinth know you adopted her?"

"Yes, she does." Hestia blurted, making no attempt to lower her voice. "My foolish husband told her one day when she tried his patience. Children do that. But—how do *you* know this?"

"Do you recall that it was a young woman named Comito who gave the baby over to you?"

"I do," she said. "The woman said the baby was her sister's and that she couldn't care for it."

I nodded. "Hestia," I said, my mouth going dry, the words a whisper. "Comito is the sister of the empress."

The woman's eyes went wide and she laughed. "That's a lie! This woman was a—a—"

"Actress?"

"Yes," she replied at once, setting her jaw.

I reached into my inner pocket, withdrew the earring Theodora had given me, and held it out in my open hand.

Hestia's face drained to the grayish white of linen, and I thought she would faint dead away. I took hold of her upper arm to steady her and placed the earring in her hand. "You do recognize it, yes? Comito attached its mate to the baby blanket."

Hestia stared at the earring, turning it over with hands well accustomed to work.

"Will you call her now?"

Hestia looked up at me, then to Tariq, and back again. "Hyacinth," she called, a tremble in her voice.

Tariq gave a gentle tap at my elbow and nodded toward the blanket at the entrance to the back room. The heavy cloth was almost imperceptibly stirring.

"Hyacinth," Hestia called again.

A hand came from behind and pushed aside the blanket. A girl stooped a bit and stepped through the opening.

"Come here, child," Hestia said.

I saw at once that she was tall, at least a full head taller than Theodora. When she stood in front of us, Tariq gave out with a gasp. As for me, my arms went to gooseflesh.

Hyacinth's face was shaped a bit differently from Theodora's—more round-faced than heart-shaped—and her complexion was colored by the sun rather than porcelain white, but she had the same penetrating black eyes under heavy dark brows that nearly met above her perfect nose. "What is it, Mother?" she asked. Her voice had the same musicality and—even at her age—sultriness of her mother's.

It was dark and cold by the time we returned to the palace. Tariq went to his quarters in the Palace of Hormisdas. I knew not to delay my news, so in no time a silentiary was ushering me into a small reception room in the women's quarters of the Imperial Apartment.

I had scarcely sat down when a breathless Theodora rushed in, a purple blur, her royal demeanor forgotten. "Well?" she demanded, coming to stand in front of me. "Tell me!"

I started to get to my feet.

"No, stay where you are Stephen. Just tell me."

"She will come tomorrow. I told her we would send a carriage for them."

"Them? Her parents, too?"

"Just her mother—"

"She's *not* her mother!" Theodora snapped.

"Oh, yes—stepmother. Her stepfather died recently."

Theodora blinked. "Oh. That is too bad. But it does make things smoother, I should think. I want them to live here on the grounds. I'll have a little house prepared. Very well, thank you, Stephen."

I nodded even though her plans took me by surprise. "They don't know that."

"Of course not. I needed to know their situation first. Listen to me, Stephen. This *must* be kept quiet, so I want you to be the one to go tomorrow and collect Hyacinth and the woman and what few things they absolutely wish to bring. They will be provided for here. You're certain that Tariq warrants your trust?"

"Yes, Thea—and yours."

"Good. I ask because I've been fooled before."

"I should say that we witnessed, Tariq and I, a good deal of discontent as we walked. People were gathering at the Praetorium and complaining loudly enough. And at the Forum of the Ox, two men had been hanged. Very little trading was going on."

"That fool Eudaemon. Surely we had a better choice for urban prefect. That forum is not the proper place for executions. Oh, my spies have been warning me of the unrest. That's why I want Hyacinth out of harm's way at once. Take two excubitors with you tomorrow just in case. Be certain to swear them to secrecy."

I forced a smile. The responsibility made me anxious.

Before I reached the door, Theodora said, "Make certain that you and Tariq are armed, as well."

8

"ARMED, YOU SAY?" TARIQ MUMBLED when I routed him from sleep. "Well now, the empress appears to have her finger on the pulse of the city."

"I agree," I said, "and that answers our question as to why she has chosen now to reclaim her daughter. Oh, and no palace whites today."

"We have one problem as I see it," Tariq said as he dressed, making short work of pulling on a plain tunic and attaching his sheath and dagger to his belt before pulling on a woolen cloak. "If there is unrest today, we will be easy game sitting in a coach from the palace, even with two excubitors. Good god, when did a palace guard in his pristine and polished livery actually face an enemy?"

Tariq had touched the crux of the matter with a needle. "You're right," I said, my hand reflexively going to the belted dagger beneath my cloak.

A lengthy discussion followed, and at the risk of raising the ire of the empress—not an inconsiderable one—we decided to forego the coach and excubitors.

"You've driven a mule before?" I asked, as the stable master fastened one to a four-wheeled cart that had benches in front and at the rear.

"How hard can it be?" Tariq quipped.

At least, I hoped it a quip.

The City was relatively quiet, the Mese clear, so we made good time along the thoroughfare. The Forum of the Ox appeared normal, with people shopping in the colonnade and merchants selling their wares from stands and wagons in the square. At the far end, the gallows stood empty.

We arrived at the chicken farm at midmorning. Both Hestia and Hyacinth looked as if they had not slept.

"I should explain something," I said, once we were all sitting at their little table.

"I'm going to bring four of our fatter chickens," Hestia said, as if she had not heard me. "Do you think she will be pleased?"

"I—I am sure she will be delighted," I lied, thinking how little the simple gift would matter at this time. Fearing Tariq would say something rude or make a joke, I shot him a cautionary look before pivoting back to the worried mother. "Hestia, do you have someone to look after your farm?"

She drew back in her chair. "Why?" she whispered.

"The empress wishes for you to stay on the palace grounds."

Her hand went to her mouth, the fingers pulling at her lower lip. "For how long?"

"I couldn't say. She wants to see Hyacinth—and you—safe."

"I see." Hestia said. She sat quietly for a long minute, her hand moving to her heart, as if she could control the measure of its beats. Suddenly, she turned to a pale Hyacinth and directed her to locate a cousin who could manage the farm and its dwindling supply of chickens.

"I don't think she should leave here on her own," I said.

"It's fine," Hestia said. "He lives out here beyond the walls on my brother's farm. There won't be any trouble. She's made the trip a hundred times. Hurry, now, Hyacinth. And come back directly."

I made no further objection because the girl was already at the door. "Yes, Mother," she shot back—and then was gone.

Two long hours passed while we waited for her return. Like a bird, Hestia moved quickly around the house tending to small tasks and pulling together things she meant to bring.

"She's fearful of losing her daughter," I whispered to Tariq.

"I would be, too," he said. "But, you know, with her husband gone and this little business failing, I think she feels a sense of relief at the same time. It's as if the gods have stepped in and drawn her back from the abyss."

"Like the *Deus ex machina* device in the old tragedies? Why, Tariq, sometimes you surprise me. And you might be right."

Hyacinth arrived at noon with her seventeen-year-old cousin trailing. Nestor was an awkward youth, thin as a reed and wide-eyed at the fortune of suddenly having a farm, albeit small, to manage. Whether his dazed look reflected good fortune or bad, I could not decipher.

In no time Tariq was directing the old but sturdy mule back along the Mese, the way we had come. Hestia and Hyacinth sat on the back bench, their cloth bags of belongings and a wooden cage of four chickens on the floor in front of them.

The two hours we had lost waiting for Nestor undid my plan to return to the Great Palace while The City was still calm, and this became painfully apparent as we neared the Forum of the Ox and heard the clamor and cries of an angry, riotous crowd.

Our cart plodded slowly into throngs of people, some women but mostly men wearing their blue or green dalmatics. "Something's happened," Tariq said. "Look!" he cried, pointing to the far side, where the gallows had been built. The horizontal beam meant to hold the ropes with nooses at the end had fractured in two. "What do you suppose—"

"Who knows," I snapped, "but if the two factions are going to go at it, you need to hurry us along. We have the two in back to consider."

Tariq nodded. "Not to mention the empress," he muttered. He reached for the whip, but at this point, the crush of people became so excessive we came to a dead stop. Tariq and I began to shout at the people in front of us to move aside, but for our efforts we received only hard looks and an occasional harsh word or gesture.

"Saatvik!" The high, excited voice came from nearby. When I turned around, I realized Hyacinth was its source. "Saatvik!" she called again. The voice, almost musical, could have been Theodora's.

I followed her line of vision and saw that she had gained the attention of the shopkeeper who had given us directions the day before. We had stalled very near his spice shop. He waved at us and stepped down from the colonnade.

"What a day! What a day!" he said as he approached us. When he came up to the side of the cart, his eyes swept over occupants, bags, and chickens. Any sense of surprise at the oddness of our menagerie passed without a question. He gave a little bow to Tariq and me, then turned and bowed to Hestia and Hyacinth. "Greetings!"

"What's happened?" Tariq blurted.

"Ah! You have missed the excitement although there might be more to come, who knows? Come into the shop and I will tell you."

"We don't have time," I said.

Saatvik looked from me to Tariq and back again. "Not wearing your palace whites today, I see. A smart choice should things get desperate."

"Oh, Saatvik," Hestia called, "tell us!"

"Yes, Saatvik," Hyacinth echoed, "tell us."

I wanted to push on, but the crowd in front of us wasn't moving, and before I could object, Saatvik launched into his tale in a voice loud and expressive, his accent most noticeable when he rushed his words.

"We had three more hangings not an hour ago. Faction members, of course. Who else gets into trouble these days? Two Green and one Blue. Instead of scaring the shoppers away like yesterday, the event today drew a swarm of people. The square was even more crowded than what you see now. You know the type who comes to see executions? Many are not very pleasant, if you know what I mean. They're the ones who like to see dark things, horrible things."

"So you stayed in your shop?" Tariq asked, his tone teasing.

"Oh no," Saatvik said. "I locked up the shop." He paused now, his face coloring, ensnared as he was in his own words.

"You saw it up close, then," I said. "Tell us."

He shrugged off his embarrassment and continued. "The three were lined up side by side. But the middle convict—by Zeus, he was the fattest fellow I've ever seen! Well, when the floor dropped out, his weight broke the beam when he went down."

"Did he die?" Hyacinth demanded.

"That he did. Must've broken his neck. But the ropes of the other two fellows slid across the beam to where it was broken—and they fell free. Landed, they did, atop the mountain of a man. It was the strangest thing to happen."

"And to see!" Tariq put in. "So they took the two lucky ones away? Saved for another day, at least?"

"The story gets stranger, my friends." Saatvik rubbed his hands together as his dark eyes swept over his little audience. "You see, just a little while earlier three of the monks from the Monastery of St. Conon were here to buy tea and spices. I know them, good customers they are. It seems that when they left the shop they joined the crowd, perhaps to offer a prayer, who knows?"

"And?" Tariq pressed.

"The two lucky ones were wiggling atop that pile of flesh. Their hands were tied behind their backs, you see, and the ropes were still around their necks. In no time, a handful of urban police were about to descend on them. Well, the crowd wasn't having it. They surged forward, crying out things like,

"God's wonder! Let them live! Let them go free!" Before you knew it, with the crowd holding off the urban prefect's men, the monks lifted the two off the dead man, untied them, and spirited them clean away, easy as you please."

"Where did they go?"

The shopkeeper pointed to the north. "Toward the Golden Horn. To what destination, I don't know. I will say that I would not want to be near the urban prefect when he hears about this."

"The emperor might not take the news so well, either," Tariq said.

I looked back at Hestia and Hyacinth. The story had clearly enthralled them, Hyacinth especially. Her beautiful dark eyes were wide as an owl's.

The crowd was now streaming out of the forum, most of them going in our direction, toward the Sea of Marmara. "We had better continue," I said.

Tariq prodded the mule and with quick goodbyes to Saatvik, we began to trundle forward.

Dusk was falling when we finally passed through the Chalké Gate into the palace complex with Theodora's daughter in tow.

Theodora sat at a little table in her reception room, attempting to focus on one of Tribonian's legal codices that Stephen had copied for her. A dozen lamps had been lighted to offset the setting sun. Suddenly, she heard footsteps and a small commotion in the anteroom to her suite. Fearing that Narses had misunderstood her message to watch for Stephen and direct them to the little house that would be her daughter's, she felt her pulse run fast. Her eyes went to the closed doors, her hand to the dimpled area in the collar bone beneath her throat, an old nervous habit. She had no wish to meet her daughter this night. She felt ill-prepared, and—allowing for truth—frightened.

At the sound of the light knock, Theodora took a deep breath and gave permission for the silentiary to enter. She stood, already practicing in her mind a smile and lightened tone of voice. But—what to say? She had yet to create a mother-daughter script.

The double doors opened and the silentiary entered and stood to the side, allowing for a woman in red to follow him. "The Lady Antonina!" he announced.

A surge of relief and genuine delight coursed through Theodora's veins. "Antonina!" she cried, nodding at the servant. Only when he had left, closing the doors behind him, did she rush to embrace her lifelong friend. "Oh, Nina, it's been too long!"

"Long for you, Thea, here in the seat of luxury and culture. Much longer for me trekking from one campsite to another. You have no idea."

"Ah, but you are here now, dearest, and you look radiant! I should be hurt, Nina. You and Belisarius have been in your suite two days and you are only now coming to see me—"

"Ha! I slept for those two days so that I could look radiant, as you say."

"The child—how is the child?"

"Joannina." Antonina shrugged. "She is fine."

"And Belisarius?"

"Anxious, considering the circumstances."

"What circumstances?"

"Why, Justinian replaced my husband with Sittas. You know Belisarius did all he could do in Persia. And now—to be recalled!"

"Oh, that's just the way government works sometimes. Justinian has not lost faith in Belisarius, believe me."

"No?"

"No, not in the least!"

"He'll be given another position?"

"Of course. Come, let's sit." Theodora took Antonina by the hand and led her to a couch. They sat side by side. "So—you have missed The City. I can understand that. I missed it terribly all the many months and years I was on the other side of the Middle Sea. But barring that, you have been happy—yes?"

"Sometimes, yes."

Antonina averted her eyes and Theodora noticed that her friend's hands were in her lap atop the red tunic, one hand gripping the other's wrist. "Sometimes?"

Antonina nodded.

"Look at me, Nina."

Long seconds elapsed before Antonina brought her gaze back to Theodora. The blue eyes were half shaded, and a blush suffused her cheeks.

Theodora drew in breath. "With Belisarius?"

"You know, Thea, sometimes I wish you *had* matched him to Comito instead."

"What's wrong, Nina?"

"Oh, he's a handsome man, you know that. And he's good—perhaps too good."

"Too good?"

"He adores me. In his eyes I can do no wrong. And yet …"

"But you have—done wrong. Is that it, Nina?"

Antonina looked away.

"Nina! Is Joannina—"

"Oh, Thea, she is his, rest assured."

"But—"

"Now, don't be shocked, Theodora. You know my history. Why, it's *our* history isn't it? However, you have a throne to sit upon and a man you love as much as he loves you. That's what people say."

Theodora released a long sigh. "You've been discreet?"

Antonina chuckled. "You could send out criers down the lines of his men bellowing out my—*misdeeds*, shall we say, and, by Hera, he would remain oblivious."

"That's little enough assurance, Nina. You know he has someone close to him who is all ears and mouth."

"You mean Procopius, of course. You were right about him. He is a snake and a bootlicker with an agenda. The way he struts about, some stranger might take *him* for the general instead of Belisarius. Lucky for me, he's always hidden away writing his histories of the battles."

"Going forward, Nina, you'll be good? I mean, with Belisarius."

"I don't set out to be otherwise, Thea. It just happens." Antonina thought for a moment. "Is it for me you appeal to my better angel—or is it my value to you as a spy you're thinking of?"

"Both! But you first, Nina. You first!"

"So, Theodora," Antonina said, employing a light tone as she picked up a new thread of conversation, "Comito has birthed a little girl."

The words stung. "She has. As have you."

"Yes, despite my taking the old precautions. I had planned to wait. It's not easy moving from battlefield to battlefield. But, what of you? The weight of an empire doesn't rest on our shoulders—as it does yours and Justinian's."

"Nina, it hasn't happened."

"You still have hope, Thea? You're—that is, *we're* still young." Antonina's eyes locked onto Theodora's.

Theodora swallowed hard, holding down the despair she had come to feel.

Did her friend know the depth of the cuts she was delivering? She avoided mentioning the secret arrival of her daughter Hyacinth, turning the conversation now to the unrest in The City.

"How bad is it?" Antonina asked.

"It's more of a perceived danger, they tell Justinian. At least I hope it is." Theodora did not add that her own spies were less optimistic.

A half hour of lighter conversation and reminiscing brought the evening to a close. Antonina embraced Theodora and said her goodbye. In walking toward the doors, she detoured to the window and stared out into the gloom. "That little round house down there is the one made of red porphyry from Egypt, isn't it?"

"It's the royal lying-in chamber, Antonina.—And it's *purple* porphyry."

"Ah, indeed. Well, goodnight, Thea."

Theodora sensed at once that her friend knew Comito's baby had been birthed there. She watched Antonina glide out the door, seemingly unaware she left in her wake another cut, one that ran deep.

Several minutes later, Theodora found herself at the same window, staring down at the gold-leafed roof of the little building, heart racing. She recalled her mother's voice: "You're overly excited, Theodora. Take deep breaths."

Her gaze moved further down the gravel walkway now, passing over several small buildings to the Blue House she had provided for Hyacinth and her mother. Lights flickered in the windows. Few things made her nervous these days, but the prospect of trying to form a relationship with Hyacinth seemed laden with obstacles and pitfalls. *Is it a mistake to even make the attempt? Maybe the girl was better off living the only life—simple as it was—she has known.* But it was too late to change direction now. How long could she put off meeting her nearly grown daughter?

Her eyes traveled back to the round birthing house. "I'm not thirty-two yet," she said aloud. "I still have time."

9

Monday, 12 January 532

I AWOKE EARLY, NOT HAVING SLEPT well because of noises and angry cries that came, not from within the palace complex, but from the adjacent streets and alleys. Dressing quickly, I hurried out and down the terrace steps leading to the Palace of Hormisdas, my first home in Constantinople.

I was about to enter the library when the door nearly struck me in the face as a figure hurried from the room, his shoulder grazing mine in the shadowy hallway. He passed me in a blur, but before I could enter, he stopped and pivoted toward me. I recognized the perfectly pressed brown robe, thin form, and narrow face. "Stephen," he said, the stentorian voice lending confirmation.

"Lord Procopius," I said, watching him retrace his steps until he stood inches away.

"I noticed your old desk was occupied by a newcomer."

I nodded, waiting for what choleric comment would follow.

"In short order," he said, "you have risen from copyist to Private Secretary to the Empress."

I held my tongue.

"Tell me, are your new rooms comfortable enough?"

"They are," I said, attempting to mask a smile, as well as avoiding the wicked temptation to turn the question on him. I had already heard that he threw a holy tantrum when he heard that no sooner had he left The City with Belisarius than Theodora commandeered his suite for my use as her secretary. His belongings were transferred to a smaller apartment in the bowels of the Daphne Wing.

Procopius appeared as if he were about to explode with curses, but he suddenly drew in breath and took hold of himself. He turned now and hurried away.

I entered the library, found Tariq and convinced him to take a break. Knowing how news quickly circulated in the library, I was certain he would have heard something of yesterday's events at the Forum of the Ox.

Bundling ourselves in our wool cloaks against the cold gusts of the Sea of Marmara, we found a stone bench close by where we could talk in privacy.

"The City is a tinderbox, Stephen," Tariq said. "We found the empress's daughter not a moment too soon. I would not trust taking to the streets today. We got some details from a friend of Brother Leo, but oddly enough, most of what we learned came out of Procopius's mouth. You just missed him."

"No, I didn't," I said, snickering. "He bumped into me as he made his stage exit."

"Really? He was delighted to see an old friend, no doubt." Tariq tossed off his mischievous smile. "Did you rub it in about his rooms?"

I laughed. "I didn't have to. My expression when he brought up the subject did the job. Now—back to the matter at hand. What has transpired since the two convicts were plucked off the fat man by the monks?"

"Well, the two monks Saatvik told us about took the two prisoners to the Church of St. Laurentius, up near the Golden Horn. He was right—one was a Blue, one a Green. They were given food and cots. Sanctuary, in other words."

"And?"

"Word got to the urban prefect, of course, and Eudaemon sent a dozen of his men to the church. By the time the urban police arrived, separate honor guards of the Blues and the Greens stood in solidarity. They meant to protect the condemned men. The police dared not break sanctuary, but they staked out the doors to keep people from entering or leaving. What's interesting is that according to Procopius, the two Colors talked and commiserated among themselves."

"So, each has a deadlier enemy now?"

Tariq shrugged. "All I can say is that The City is ripe for something."

"That's everything we know so far?"

"It is—except …"

"Except for what?"

"Procopius's demeanor as he spilled out his details to Leo and the rest of us."

"Go on."

"Well, here he is well favored by Justinian to write the history of Belisarius's war with Persia, and to hear him tell it, he is to write the *entire* history of Justinian's reign. However—as he spoke of the botched hangings and ensuing events, you would have thought he was sword and cudgel *against* Justinian's government. Now, maybe he's merely stirred up because he will be able to write what could be an exciting chapter in The City's history. But ..."

"But?"

"Well, Stephen, he had such vigor about him, even a sparkle you might say, and in his voice a silvery quality that made me think he is delighting in this crisis."

"Maybe he is, Tariq. Maybe he is." I staved off a shiver, one in no way the result of the January wind.

Sitting with Justinian at the end of the long deliberation table, Theodora drew in the beeswax scent of the newly polished cherry wood, but it was the breath of fear permeating the Hall of the Consistory that captured and held her. It happened to be Monday, so the Imperial Consistory was already scheduled, eliminating the need to call an emergency meeting to confront the current crisis in the capital.

Her eyes took in the men on the right side of the table and moved down along the faces on the left side. How many of these twelve or fourteen councilors—officials, senators, and generals—were true friends, loyal to the throne above all things? How many in the Great Palace complex would remain true in times such as these? Her spies kept her apprised of the many in the Senate House and elsewhere who still grumbled about the new regime.

The urban prefect stood far down at the opposite end of the table, relaying the events of yesterday. Eudaemon was stout but so short one would think he was giving his testimony from one of the leather cushioned chairs. She listened. Her spies had previously informed her of the mismanaged hangings and tense standoff at the Church of Saint Laurentius between the urban police and the Blue and Green factions, each there in support of their man. Eudaemon failed to mention some Blues and Greens had dashed back to the city center to inform their respective leaders. Was the urban prefect downplaying the crisis, she wondered, or were her own sources better informed than his?

Justinian fidgeted in the chair next to hers. "The situation is clear, Eudaemon," he said. "We're at an impasse. I understand that. Now—what's to be done about it?"

"Master, we must at all cost show firmness. We should not do anything that would make the rabble think they have the upper hand."

"They're asking for the two criminals to be freed, is that it?"

Eudaemon nodded. "It is, master."

"It seems little enough.—You don't recommend granting mercy?"

Eudaemon drew his head back slightly. "Master, it would be a grave mistake to show weakness. There is no telling what they would next demand."

Theodora understood the need to show strength. Yet the fact that one of those claiming sanctuary was a Blue and one a Green gave her pause. While both she and Justinian favored the Blues, Justinian often feigned sympathy with the Greens to keep a sense of equilibrium within The City. In doing so, they allowed no faction to become too powerful. But—what if the longtime enemy factions were to combine their muscle?

In the privacy of the bedchamber, she had posited that possibility the night before. Justinian entertained her opinion, in fact confessing similar concerns himself. He withheld making a decision as to policy, however, instead looking forward to conferring with his councilors.

As an actress, she had learned to read faces, whether of fellow actors or audience members. What she observed now up and down the table was complete agreement with Urban Prefect Eudaemon. The government should not back down. The prisoners should be kept in sanctuary until such a time when they might be forced to leave and face the noose once again. Soon her observation was borne out as one after the other gave verbal assent to holding a hard line, including Generals Belisarius and Mundus, who had been asked to sit in on the Silence.

Justinian was not convinced. "And how," he asked, "are we to apprehend the miscreants without breaking sanctuary?"

All eyes went to the urban prefect.

Eudaemon drew himself up. He had an extraordinarily large head, Theodora noted, one that appeared to rest on his shoulders without benefit of a neck. "My intention is to keep the overly helpful monks at bay and to starve the criminals out."

The hall went quiet. Theodora stifled an urge to question the plan. She had not spoken since that day she voiced her support for sending aid to the earthquake devastated Antioch. One must pick one's battles, she knew. Besides, Justinian picked up her line of thought and peppered Eudaemon with questions about how long such a course of action would take, going on to question the efficacy of the prefect's approach. "You do realize, Eudaemon," Justinian said, "I have some knowledge of church architecture, and I can tell you that beneath the monastery and church there is a labyrinth of tunnels and tombs running from one to the other that provides access. Let me add, too, that a tomb can serve as a handy larder."

The prefect stood silent as a stone.

No one came to his defense.

"Setting aside this little conundrum," Justinian said, "we must face the fact that tomorrow, Tuesday, is a racing day. The Hippodrome is always full. Shall I allow racing, as usual?"

It took no more than a glance at the faces around the table for Theodora to augur the answer.

"I have another mission for you," Theodora said. "Sit down."

I had thought that perhaps I had been called upstairs to the Imperial Apartment to be thanked for safely delivering the daughter of the empress to the haven of the palace complex. Then again, Theodora often surprises me. I sat.

"The races are to be run tomorrow," she said.

I nodded. I knew as much, for the criers had already run the streets with the news.

Theodora did not take the seat across from me. Instead, she paced back and forth, her mouth drawn down, brow furrowed. "I'm not at all sure it's the right thing to do, but there it is, good as done." She halted and pivoted in my direction. "What is the mood of the people, Stephen?"

I shrugged. "I'm not sure I'm a good one to ask."

"Oh, I know Brother Leo and his tribe of copyists, scribes, and illuminators have their ears to the ground. Do you not still visit with them?"

"I do, but Thea, you have a whole covey of—"

"Spies?" she snapped. "Oh, I have that, but … Well, I don't want them to see me as you see me now. The concern I have." She began to pace again. "I can't trust them, any of them. If they sense Justinian and I are the least bit concerned about this matter with the two criminals, it will get out, don't you see, and it will add to the discord in the air."

"What can I do?"

"Leave that for the moment. First, tell me what the word is in the library."

I knew to tread lightly. Theodora was known to sometimes blame the messenger. "There is discord, as you say, Thea. The people up and down the Mese are grumbling louder than ever. Word has it—"

"Word! From whom? Someone must bring it. Who?"

Swallowing hard, I drew in breath and blurted: "Procopius seems to have his sources throughout The City."

"Procopius!" she snarled, turning on me. She paused a moment, as if to catch her breath and calm herself. "And … he brings his observations to Brother Leo and anyone who will listen, I suppose."

I nod, refraining from telling her that Tariq characterized Procopius's attitude about the mounting antipathy toward the government as nothing short of exultant. After all, I had not borne witness to his chronicle. What if Tariq was wrong?

"Procopius—why should I be surprised?" Theodora approached me and sat on the opposite couch, leaning forward and lowering her voice. "Stephen, I want you to be my eyes and ears tomorrow."

"As you wish, Thea. Just how am I to do so?"

"I want you present in the Hippodrome for the races."

I no doubt looked stunned.

"You've attended them before, yes?"

"A few, times, Thea, but never for a full day."

"Well, you're likely to get bored if you stay for the usual twenty-five races, unless you wager on them."

I smiled. Oh, I had come up in the world, living in the Daphne Wing of the Great Palace now, but I had little disposable income. I was still a slave.

"I must admit," Theodora continued, "I was held mesmerized the one time I sat through them. I was five and my mother, my sisters, and I were granted a dispensation from the rule that excludes women. I've told you about that day."

"I'll go early so I can find a good seat."

"No need. I'll have Narses take care of finding you a place. Just be certain to find him in the morning. He'll be looking for you."

"But if the lord chamberlain is there—"

"Why do I need you? You see, Stephen, while he may be as observant of little things, as you are, he is hesitant sometimes to offer information that might displease us and so will sugar it over. I trust you will not. You and I have always spoken as equals." Theodora stood now.

Our interview was over. *Well, not quite equals*, I thought, promptly getting to my feet. I changed the subject. "I trust Narses saw that Hyacinth has settled in, along with her … stepmother?" I said, narrowly avoiding my previous blunder regarding her title. I couldn't help but ask, so curious I was to know how the mother-daughter meeting had gone.

"What?" Theodora shot me a pinched expression. "Yes, I think so. I've not seen them yet."

I left thinking how the woman was a mystery to me. She went to great pains to reunite with the daughter she gave up years ago and yet appeared to have put off the actual meeting. Was it the tumult in The City that unnerved her—or was she afraid to face the judgment of a young woman she had abandoned?

The Hippodrome of Constantinople, print

Empress Theodora at the Coliseum, 1889

10

I SAT GAZING DIRECTLY ACROSS AND down at an immense bronze obelisk situated on the long spina that divided the length of the race course. To the right, three bronze entwined serpents climbed a column that had been looted from the sanctuary of Apollo at Delphi. Next to it sat another obelisk; this one, formed of pink granite some two millennia before, had been plundered from Egypt.

I could only imagine that the haphazard winds of fate that had brought monuments of other times and places to the low wall below must be of the same variety that swept up a shepherd boy from the hills of Syria only to drop him in the kathisma, the imperial sky-box of Constantinople's Hippodrome.

Then again, perhaps such things were less the whimsy of fate, and more the machinations of man.

There I sat in a gilt chair on a plush red cushion—eyes wide, pulse racing—looking out at the vast amphitheater, now filling with men of every social stratum, for admittance was free. My chair was placed next to a support column in the front row at the very right of the box so that, once seated, I enjoyed excellent sight lines below the railing and between the metal balusters. I was unperturbed by the heavy purple curtains, the folds of which grazed me and collected at my elbow once drawn open. Narses had done well by me. He was seated three seats over, at the middle aisle. Between us were two senators who made no effort to speak to me. No matter—the moment was rife with a mix of tension, excitement, and anticipation.

The amphitheater was a little more than half filled when the music struck up from some recessed area, and dancers—men and women with impossibly long legs—began sprinting and scudding up the raceway, those dressed in green ribbons on the other side, those in blue on this, the traditional side of the Blues. Few of those audience members already seated paid attention. The several entrances kept spilling out spectators like drains gushing storm water. The people entering via the entrance just below the imperial box spoke at full volume as they pushed toward their benches of wood planking and brick supports. Most wore heavy cloaks against the January cold, and many carried cushions. Every so often, the men's heads would pivot back and up to the kathisma, eyes lifting in the direction of the throne, which sat in the middle aisle on a dais a few rows back, empty. The men turned back to one another, heads down, words exchanged. Their faces were hard to read. Were they disappointed that Justinian was not there to jeer at? Did they feel vindicated because they had laid down bets that he wouldn't show? Even though Narses had assured me Justinian would make his entrance at the start of the first race, I was not totally convinced he would. I knew by now that Justinian could often be indecisive. The two senators on my left were wagering between themselves whether he would attend.

Two troupes of acrobats replaced the dancers now, one troupe dressed in bright green, the other sky blue, parading up the parallel lengths of the racecourse, jumping, tumbling, balancing on balls, barrels, and one another's shoulders, each team trying to outdo the other. Attention paid was minimal and the hubbub of the thousands only increased. These were old tricks and stunts, and not even the added Blue-Green rivalry seemed to catch fire.

The crowd did settle once the bear tamers, one in blue and one green, came on the scene. I marveled to myself at the thought that the Greek father of Theodora, Empress of the Roman World, had been a bear tamer here in the Hippodrome. I wondered anew about fate. Is it directed by some deity, like the Greek Goddess Tyche, as some still believed, or is it our own decisions that determine our destiny?

I blinked the thought away and focused now on the bear tamer of the Blues as he herded a family of brown bears—parents and three cubs—down the track, stopping right in front of the kathisma, where they danced in circles. The two grown bears stood on their hind legs, allowing for the cubs to somersault beneath them. This had gone on for some time when one of the citizens seated in the front row—on a cushioned marble bench reserved for the wealthy elite—waved a red scarf back and forth at the bears. Evidently well into his cups, he shouted something at them, threw down the scarf and began hurtling small candies of some kind at them. This did take the full attention of the large male bear, who turned, snarling, went to all fours, shoved aside one of the cubs, and raced toward the patron.

A shrill cry went up at once from the crowd and those on the fashionable marble seating in the bear's path began to flee.

Suddenly, the bear halted, realizing, just as did the audience, that he was teetering on the edge of a well-filled moat, a device usually meant to keep overly enthusiastic spectators from running out onto the concourse. A collective gasp of relief went up now as the trainer went to retrieve his charge.

The excitement ebbed as the bears were led away and workers arrived on the scene with wheel barrows to prepare for the races by laying down sand on the hard earthen surface. This took some time, during which faces kept turning toward us in the kathisma, impatient for the emperor to show. Talking fell to a low male hum and throb. Expectation and apprehension, palpable as smoke, rolled through the amphitheater.

My attention was drawn to some movements out of the corner of my eye. I turned toward the row of starting gates situated at the north end, where they were shaded by an extensive roof that supported sculptures of four copper gilt horses, elegantly prancing abreast and drawing a bronze charioteer in a chariot. Proud and majestic, the sight of the *quadriga* never failed to take my breath from me. At the midpoint of the boxes, a worker stood on the roof putting in place a pennant to indicate that the races were about to begin. He unfurled it now, revealing its color as purple. Wasn't this all the evidence the crowd needed to accept that the emperor would indeed attend the day's racing?

Soon, all eyes in the stadium—at full capacity now—were gawking at the royal loge. The throne remained vacant. What if the emperor had decided to stay away? While the crowd certainly had no interest in a palace eunuch, I felt a multitude of eyes upon me now, and I felt myself slumping in my seat, wishing I could hide myself in the folds of the curtain at my right.

Then came the sound of a dozen trumpets that were placed along the uppermost levels of the amphitheater—and when next I looked, Emperor Justinian stood in front of his throne, prepared to receive the adulation of his people. Even without Theodora, I thought, the man does know to make an entrance. Oh, it was a very confounding stir he created because it wasn't all adulation, by any means. People stood facing him making a variety of bows. I took note of the number who did not bow, as well as the number whose body movements seemed to indicate they were doing so out of habit or fear.

Oh, there were enough unhappy celebrants on this, the Blues' side, the faction often favored by the throne, that in my head I doubled the likely number for the hot-tempered citizens on the Greens' side.

As the emperor sat back on his raised throne, chariots were pulled into position at four of the twelve boxes. Narses told me that once all twelve gates had been utilized in a single race, but that it made for a cluttered concourse and a good deal of splintered chariots, ripped limbs, and broken bodies. He exaggerated, saying that often it was the case that fewer combatants were leaving the concourse by the Great Gate near the kathisma than those quickly transported to the exit they call the "Dead Gate," where bodies were claimed by loved ones. Over time, the number of competing chariots dwindled to eight, and now, most often four. At first these represented the four factions, before the red and white ones weakened and were incorporated into the stronger green and blue factions, respectively. Most recently, it appeared that the standard was for two four-horse chariots of the green faction to race two of the blue. The drivers drew their gate numbers by lot.

When the trumpets blew again, the crowd quieted, and a herald—located somewhere above us, atop the kathisma, announced the first race. In a deep and full-throated voice, he further stated that the games today would consist of twenty-five races and that the first three were limited to drivers under the age of seventeen, while drivers of the next five would be between seventeen and twenty-three. The remaining races would be open to drivers over twenty-three, "veteran drivers of skills worth your wagering," he joked, before going on to name the young drivers of the first race.

In short order a single trumpet blast signaled the opening of the chariot boxes—and the race was on. The *quadrigae* moved to their left to take the length of the field so that they passed the kathisma first on the initial lap. The chariots were tightly clustered as they moved past, the fierce-faced child-drivers in their short tunics of green and of blue, all looking pitifully small and young but for one of the greens, who was singularly tall.

As the four teams rounded the far end of the concourse, the first of seven metal cast sculptures of dolphins was removed from the base of the spina, indicating to the audience that the chariots would have to pass by six more times, then as they thundered on to and around the starting curve, the first of seven metal cast ostrich eggs was removed from the spina there, signifying that a full circuit had been completed.

And so it went for six laps, whips flying, the crowd cheering, calling for victory. "Nika, Blue!" came the call from the near side. "Nika, Green!" the other side chanted. As they came around the turn to begin the seventh lap, a baby-faced Blue and the tall Green were in the lead, neck and neck, with the Green holding to the wall of the spina. The others were falling farther behind and jockeying with one another not to come in last. A worker removed the final dolphin and the chariots rounded the curve and moved up the other side, the judges at the finish line vigilant. By the time the front pair crossed the line, the tall Green was in the lead, winning by no more than a foot or two. All four drivers acquitted themselves respectfully, but that did not quell the cheers from the Greens nor the taunting from the Blues. There on the concourse, beneath the sculptured *quadriga*, the Green accepted a gold emblem, a silver helmet, and a small purse that contained gold coins, purportedly newly minted, with Justinian's image on one side, Theodora's on the other.

In the short time it took for the track to be raked and for the next four chariots to be put into their boxes, something most unusual occurred. Two men stepped out onto the concourse directly in front of the kathisma, men of middle age, one in a green tunic, one in blue. These were the demarchs, the leaders of the two Colors—and longtime foes. They bowed in the direction of Emperor Justinian.

The Green, a tall, ruddy-faced man, took a step forward. "Master," he said, without lifting his eyes to the imperial loge, "we do you reverence, for you are thrice August. Wishing you long life, we come to beseech your imperial pardon."

The Blue stepped up beside him. This rather small man also kept his eyes cast down in obeisance. He projected a surprisingly powerful voice. "God has seen fit to ordain two men free of the sentencing imposed by the urban prefect. Twice they have been rescued from death, on the gallows and through the intervention of good monks. You, oh, most victorious one, you are God's vicegerent on earth. Thus, we implore you to recognize the will of the Divine and rescind the sentences against the two men now in sanctuary at the Church of St. Laurentius."

The two demarchs lifted their eyes to the emperor, as did everyone within hearing distance. Even those who could not possibly have heard the double plea seemed to sense the drama of the peaceful—even polite—interaction between these two inveterate enemies and fell quiet but for scattered whispering. I turned to my left, as did the senators in my row, and looked to the emperor. My first thought, strangely enough, was that Theodora maintained that when he played *Shatranj* with her, she could not possibly guess his next move, for his plain face wore an expression indiscernible, absent of any emotion or reaction. Her observation rang true now.

The moment lengthened.

I looked out to the masses. People stirred in their seats, stretching to gawk at their emperor. Word of the request was quickly circulating, it seemed, for whispering mounted, burgeoning into loud muttering, even catcalls coming from unknown individuals at enough distance that guards could not seek them out.

I turned again to the emperor, whose mask of indifference had not cracked. A man sitting behind the emperor leaned forward, whispering something in his ear. Justinian's mouth moved only slightly, and the man immediately sat back in his chair, his face flushing. This was the emperor's personal herald, the spokesman who relayed the words and wishes of Justinian to his citizens.

The emperor stood now and the crowd quieted in momentary suspense.

Is he going to answer the request? Or is he going to leave?

Justinian's gaze moved down and to the right, toward the starting boxes. He raised his right hand now, palm upward, giving the usual signal for the next race to commence.

He took his seat once again, eyes forward, as if he had not heard a syllable of the demarchs' pleas.

As the herald began announcing the names of the next drivers, reclaiming the attention of much of the crowd, I could not imagine how this little drama would play out. I had no doubt Justinian had been warned by Urban Prefect Eudaemon and others to ignore any request for leniency for the two men in sanctuary. But here he sat—and I with him—in a massive amphitheater with many minds that I feared were capable of turning against him.

The second race began and it went much like the first. "Nika, Green!" came the cry. "Nika, Blue!" was the response. This time it was a victory for a Blue driver, who accepted the gold emblem, silver helmet, and purse of coins.

I was absently watching the raking of the concourse when the two demarchs once again stepped out onto the raceway in front of the kathisma, heads lifted in the direction of the emperor, eyes cast down. This time the Blue spoke first: "Master Justinian, servant and arm of God here on earth, we implore your mercy." The Green Demarch stepped forward to deliver the crux of the request for the release of the two in sanctuary, doing so in nearly the same words as the Blue had done after the first race. That the two inveterate rivals were working together so harmoniously bewildered the crowd and made for a hum of male mumbling and murmurings.

I turned to check the emperor's reaction. The herald was sitting a bit forward in his seat as if anticipating that the emperor might have him respond to the demarchs.

However, Justinian made no such move. He sat stoic as a rock, facing forward, seemingly staring at—and as immobile as—the bronze obelisk in his line of sight. After a tense minute, he stood and raised his hand for the third race to begin.

The third race got underway and with it the dueling clamor of "Nika, Green!" and "Nika Blue!" On the final circuit, one of the young Greens brought his chariot too close to the wall on the second-to-last turn, and in an eye's blink he was jettisoned from his carriage. His head struck the wall of the spina as his body dropped to the ground. I could see the sand darkening. While handlers took charge of the wrecked chariot and team of horses, others speedily transported the slack body toward the Dead Gate exit. The other Green won the race, so little attention was paid to the boy whose career and life had been snuffed out in an instant. My throat tightened with dryness, and my eyes kept going back to the stained patch of sand. I wondered if his father was here to receive the body and how much hope his family had placed in his becoming a well-known and wealthy charioteer.

Theodora had suggested I might become bored with the repetition of twenty-five races, and when the Blue and Green Demarchs stepped forward yet again with their rehearsed request only to be ignored as before by Emperor Justinian, one might think her guess an apt one.

Such was not the situation. With each race came neither boredom nor excitement, but the escalation of tension and anger all across the wide amphitheater. By now even those well out of earshot of the demarchs had been told of their request for leniency so that each time the emperor failed to respond, jeering and taunting flamed anew on the part of both the Blues and the Greens.

No, I was not bored.

The fourth race followed.

And the fifth.

By the sixth, I was caught up with the dark mood of the crowd and uncaring as to which color team had won. It was disturbing.

Two drivers—ages between seventeen and twenty-three—were injured in the seventh and yet the drama between the two demarchs and the emperor played out again, along with the mounting agitation and distemper of the crowd, Blues and Greens alike.

By the tenth race, during which a veteran driver was killed and hustled toward the Dead Gate, I had stopped taking mental notes of what I was witnessing. The impressions of the day's events were being scored deeply enough in my memory that I anticipated no problem providing an accurate account to Theodora.

How long can this go on? Fifteen more races? I realized I was perspiring profusely under my tunic and that I held my arms clasped together across my middle, as if I were hugging myself.

While the two demarchs were reciting their lines after the fifteenth race, I turned to see Procopius leaning over the emperor, who spoke to him with his hand cupped over his mouth. Whereas Justinian's face had previously been set in hard, stubborn lines, now I saw uncertainty. He appeared to be asking for Procopius's advice. Where had Procopius come from? Perhaps he had been sitting in the back of the kathisma all along. Would the emperor rely on him for advice? Who knew where Procopius's true allegiance lay? Not I. What advice would he provide?

At first, Procopius was nodding as he listened to Justinian. Now, however, he shook his head vigorously as he provided his caution at a volume he chose not to moderate. "No, master," he said, "to accede to their demands would only encourage them to ask for more. The prefect was right. Stand firm."

The emperor gave a subtle nod, waved Procopius away, and went on pretending he could not hear the demarchs.

The races continued. By the twenty-first, I was counting down the last five, anxious to see the final one even as hope dimmed that the Syrian blood thrumming at my temples—each throb a warning of imminent danger on the wing—was merely imagined. As for the tenor of the massive crowd, it had grown uglier. The crashes and injuries were eliciting more cheers than were the victorious charioteers. Justinian rallied at each victory with a painted smile and staged applause, but each time the demarchs retraced their steps in the track's sand to the front of the kathisma, his face went dark, his line of vision sharply focused on the darkening winter sky-high above the stands across the way.

It was after the twenty-second race that a door to hell was unbolted.

The Blue and Green demarchs took up their position once again, both with backs straight as swords, crabbed faces, and set jaws. The racing day was nearly at an end, yet they had not swayed their emperor. This time there was no wishing the emperor long life. The Blue stepped forward and proclaimed in a steady, low-pitched manner, "Long live the merciful Greens!" The five words resounded with menace. The Green stepped out a pace now so that they stood together. "Long live the merciful Blues!" he called out, his tone louder and more truculent.

The senator next to me gasped. I knew the cause. Justinian had managed to achieve something with his intransigence that no one had accomplished in living memory. He had quite literally united the two groups who had always been at knife point with each other. Now they shared a common enemy: the Justinian and Theodora regime.

I knew at once that no priest, magus, or emperor would be able to contain what had been loosed. Out of thin air, my father's old interjection formed in my mouth: "Holy mysteries of Mithra!" There would be no final three races. No assuaging the rage in the stands. My stomach tightened and the urge to flee rose up inside me.

As if to christen the dark compounding of the two factions, a chorus arose from the nearby stands that no doubt had been planned by the factions beforehand. "Long live the merciful Blues and Greens! Long live the merciful Greens and Blues!"

The chant spread quickly around the U-shaped stands of the amphitheater, each repetition taking on volume and aggression. Some younger faction members—young toughs, really, eager for a fight—began jumping up and down on their wooden benches.

I looked to the throne. Justinian no longer appeared as an imperturbable, unblinking stone statue, ready to wait out a storm. He was rising, his face ashen. At the back of the imperial box, the emperor's personal excubitors were rushing down the stairs, hobnailed boots frantically clicking on the stone steps.

Narses, the two senators, and I—prime targets here in the front row—stood at once. Before we could put our feet into motion, our attention was drawn to a huge uproar occurring on the other side of the amphitheater. No longer an audience now, this was a mob, and they were tearing the wooden planks from the brick bench supports and heaving them like missiles out onto the concourse. Others were making for the exits with purpose, their intention set on—what?

I looked again to the throne. It was empty. The personal guard detail had hustled Justinian away. My heart contracted. Two dozen well-armed excubitors could not protect him—or us—from a maddened swarm of sixty thousand or more. I gave thanks to the architect who had fashioned the kathisma so that it was at the highest level and that it jutted out over the eastern tiers. It was, in effect, unapproachable to those in the stands.

"Hurry!" Narses called to me. He was standing aside, allowing the two senators to make their escape before taking me by the arm and leading me to the rear of the kathisma. We passed through the suite of rooms where a mere five years before Justinian and Theodora had waited to be hailed by a capacity crowd as *Justinian Augustus* and *Theodora Augusta*. A spiral staircase took us down into the safe confines of the Daphne Palace.

But even there, following us was a new chant, staccato and angry: "Nika! Nika! Nika!"

"It's the thrice-repeated victory cry used for the factions' charioteers," Narses told me. I knew as much, of course, but what he said next left me speechless. "Only now, Stephen, I fear it has taken an alternate meaning. The word means 'victory,' but it also means 'conquer'."

His meaning was clear. "Nika" was now being used as a rallying cry for the populace to overthrow one regime and supplant it with another.

11

I WENT DIRECTLY TO THEODORA'S RECEPTION room in the women's quarters. She received me at once.

Even in ill temper her dark beauty radiated. "Well? What should I know before I go into the Silence that my husband will be holding this evening? Sit down, Stephen. Is it as bad as what I hear coming from the streets?"

My first inclination was to say *Worse, Theodora. Much worse.* Although I resisted such a lead-in, I did not mince words and told her exactly what I had seen and heard at the Hippodrome.

Theodora stiffened in her chair when I mentioned Procopius. "You say you heard him tell Justinian to stand firm?"

"I did. I believe he was citing Urban Prefect Eudaemon's advice."

"I see. Tell me, did he sound sincere—or was there a stage quality to his little speech?"

"I took him at his word. What are you driving at, Thea?"

"What I'm driving at, Stephen, is that had Procopius been attempting to invite disaster into the palace, he might have given my husband just the advice he did."

"Ah," I said, sighing, "thus achieving the very result that is happening out in the streets."

"Exactly! Although my husband would never believe him capable of treason."

Procopius was a mystery. And I felt a naive fool for not having considered that he might be giving false advice. It came home to me now that I would make a most deplorable spy.

"You know, Stephen, there are times when one must choose one's battles and times when one runs a diversionary tactic—or even retreats. My husband may have missed his moment—and at the prompting of his favored historian."

I knew not to deliver up an opinion on what could become a combustible matter between the royal couple.

Theodora's gaze and thoughts seemed to drift away.

I gave a little cough. "If that will be all, Theodora—"

"What?" The empress snapped to attention. "No, Stephen, that will *not* be all! I have two tasks for you to perform. The first is to visit the little Blue House below where my daughter and her—her stepmother are staying. See that they are comfortable and assure them they will be kept safe."

I nodded. I knew the house she spoke of. "Have they settled in, Thea?"

A dark look accompanied her sharp reply: "That's for you to tell me!"

So—she had yet to meet her daughter! She had put it off. Even for an empress as strong as Theodora, there came moments of fear and uncertainty. Human moments.

She fell silent and the pause lengthened.

Finally, I asked, "And the other matter?"

"Ah, yes." She drew in breath. "In the house next to my daughter's are Pompeius and Hypatius." Theodora took note of my reaction. "Oh, don't look so surprised. We brought them here to the palace for everyone's good. Theirs and ours."

"I see."

"You know Emperor Anastasius had three nephews who also had links to the throne."

I did. By saying "also," Theodora meant to imply that Justinian's uncle, Emperor Justin, had a link to the throne. However, this was not the case. Pompeius and Hypatius were brothers and of the noble Anicii clan with strong Roman roots. This, in contrast to Justin, a peasant who rose through the ranks of the army to become commander; merely by chance had a peasant been chosen over the three nephews, a significant event that would serve only to undermine the Justinian-Theodora reign and one I ignored, speaking the obvious: "You're concerned that one of them might use the chaos in the city to reestablish the Anastasius royal line."

Theodora's wide collar of cascading pearls lifted slightly in a shrug, and her right hand went to the hollow of her neck. Something serious concerned her. Was she thinking about her own unlikely rise from the shadow of the Hippodrome, one even more spectacular than that of her husband's uncle? Finally, she said, "I got to know their mother well during my stay in Alexandria. As I confided in you years ago, she did me invaluable service, and yet—" Theodora drew herself up and changed the thread of conversation. "I want you to check in on them, Stephen. Strike up a conversation. Try to gauge where their true alliances stand."

"But they'll surely know my purpose."

"No doubt, but nonetheless, you're a good judge of character and human behavior. See what you can ferret out. You will need to carry my seal to gain access."

"Oh—they're under guard?"

Her eyes went wide, and she gave a smile of the sort she might give to a half-wit on the street. "Of course."

As I left the Daphne Wing and came out into the evening air, an acrid stream of smoke caught in my nostrils, but I was too lost in thought to realize garbage was never burned on Mondays. Arson was the cause, I would realize in short order.

My thoughts, however, were on the delicate precipice upon which the two brothers—Pompeius and Hypatius—no doubt found themselves perched. They had become like two game pieces on the board of *Shatranj*, Theodora's game board.

I moved toward the little house that Hyacinth and her mother had been allotted. Two silentiaries stood, each at one of the modest twin marble columns of the portico. Like Pompeius and Hypatius, the women, were under guard. I could not hold at bay my feeling that Theodora's plans for her daughter ran deeper than merely keeping her safe. Hyacinth was yet another game piece for Theodora to move about. And, typically, Theodora's sharp mind hovered several moves ahead.

I kept my visit short, fending off their anxious questions as to what was expected of them, when they would be presented to the empress, and whether the trouble in the streets was a true threat. I assured them with as much persuasion as I could muster that the Empress Theodora would see to their well-being.

In making my exit, I passed the house where Pompeius and Hypatius were being held. It was known as the Yellow House. I deferred seeing them at the moment because I wanted a bit of time to figure out how to approach them if I was to glean their true motivation and intentions. Hurrying toward the stack of terraces leading down to the Palace of Hormisdas where Tariq had his room, I realized the smoke was thickening.

In no time at all I could scarcely see a few feet in front of me. Men were running in all directions calling out garbled alarms. Had the bronze gates been stormed? My mind was in ferment when from the rear a hand came down on my shoulder.

"Stephen!" came the voice at my ear.

I turned to find Tariq at my side, his face pinched and streaked with smoke. "What is it?" I asked, trying to filter any fear from my voice.

"The Chalké Gate—they've set it afire!" he shouted, even as he handed me a leather bucket and pulled me toward a large fountain.

"But—but the gate is bronze. It won't burn!"

"Oh, no? Well, the wooden structure around it and the timbers of the roof are burning nicely and the frame is bent from the heat." We fell into a line of excubitors and an odd mix of slaves, silentiaries, and eunuchs waiting to fill the buckets.

"And the people?" I asked.

"The *mob*, you mean?" He turned to face me, his eyes merely slits. "They've set fire to the Senate House and the Great Church, Stephen. Cranked up, they are. Keen as mustard to get at us and cut our throats!"

The news struck me dumb. The Senate House sat on the eastern side of the Augustaion, and while I had not had occasion to see its interior, I was awed by the columned white marble façade that stood like a bold and elegant fortress against the deep blue of the Sea of Marmara. It was the loss of the Church of the Holy Wisdom, however, that cut me to the quick. I'm not Christian, of course, but that sacred building, with its architecture, mosaics, and statues, had held me mesmerized on the occasions of Justinian and Theodora's wedding and coronation.

I said no more while we filled our buckets and ran toward the gates, water sloshing on us as we went. The square-like structure of the Chalké Gate that served as a kind of vestibule for those entering and leaving the Great Palace complex lit up the darkening night like an orange torch as we moved toward it. Even as I realized there was no saving it, its timbered roof unloosed a daunting cracking sound and collapsed. The heavy statuary it held—including that of the gold-encrusted Christ—came crashing down with it.

"The gate is lost! Put those buckets to better use!" An excubitor stood in front of our line, diverting us toward the nearby stables that had caught fire. Grooms were leading snorting and squealing horses from the interior, several so frightened they were attempting to rise up against their handlers. The fifty or so of us in the makeshift bucket corps would be unable to save the structure—that much was clear. Nonetheless, we kept at it, dousing and refilling for hours, it seemed.

On one return trip to the fountain, I collided with a woman wearing a hooded cloak of velvet red, startling both of us. Her lovely face was slashed with terror, eyes wide, lips and chin trembling. I'm not sure she recognized me. She looked from me to the sight of the fallen Chalké Gate behind me. "Holy Hera," she said, turning toward the burning stables, her terror deepening. She backed away from me in clumsy, jerky steps, pivoted, and ran, retreating in the direction from which she had come.

Tariq pulled me along. "Who was that?"

"You didn't see?"

"No, her hood blocked my view."

"Antonina," I said. "Antonina."

"I might have guessed by her red cloak," Tariq said, "had I my wits about me."

The stables burned to the ground despite our night-long efforts. All the horses survived. The excubitors made use of their time by building an unholy and mountainous shrine of rubble, melted bronze, and broken statues. These remnants of what had been the welcoming vestibule of the Chalké Gate now stood as a forbidding barrier to the mob milling outside.

Theodora left the women's rooms and moved toward the Golden Audience Chamber in search of her husband. As the two silentiaries opened the doors for her, she realized he had another visitor: Urban Prefect Eudaemon. Even viewing him from behind, she recognized his short, stout form and exceptionally large head.

She startled him as she stepped up and took her place on the throne. "Mistress," he muttered, proceeding to prostrate himself and kiss the toe of her shoe.

"Eudaemon has only just arrived," Justinian said.

"In some haste, it appears," Theodora said, noting his quick breathing and perspiration all about the face and neck.

"He says the Praetorium has been overrun by the rioters," Justinian offered.

"And yet you are here, Endaemon." Theodora's gaze settled on the prefect. "Are you not in charge of keeping order?" She saw his Adam's apple move as he gulped before responding.

"There were too many of them, mistress."

"What did they want?" Theodora demanded.

Eudaemon swallowed hard. "Me," he said. "Several of my urban police were killed outright. Others deserted, mistress. The rioters released a good number of prisoners and set fire to the building. I escaped through a secret egress that opens into a back alley." He turned to Justinian. "I beg you allow me to stay, master."

Theodora responded before Justinian could do so. "Is it the two convicts that prompted this?"

"At first, mistress, but I heard chants before they broke in calling out my name—and others."

"So," Justinian said, "your decision to use a heavy hand dealing with the two even though the winds of fate appeared to be at their back when they survived the hanging—"

"Was a mistake, master, especially since Fortune placed those monks in the square when the hanging went sour."

Theodora scoffed. "Ah, Tyche is always the first to take blame, yes?" She turned and could see in her husband's paling face that he was acknowledging his own missteps in not acceding to the requests of the demarchs in the Hippodrome. "What's done cannot be undone," she said, directing her words at the prefect. "You said the mob chanted your name and 'others'—what others?"

Eudaemon looked to Justinian and then to Theodora, his face blanching. "Tribonian's, mistress."

Theodora sensed her husband shrink back at the mention of one of his inner circle. "And?" she asked, her eyes on the prefect.

Wiping perspiration from his brow, the prefect paused, looking from her to Justinian and back again.

"And?" Theodora demanded.

"John of Cappadocia's, mistress."

"Indeed?—Who else?"

The prefect's eyes went wide. "No others, mistress."

"Just the three of you?" Justinian asked.

"That's all I heard, master."

"I understand their ill temper with you," Justinian said. "But what is there about Tribonian and John that has provoked what we hear even now coming from the streets?"

"I—I hesitate to say, master. It was just a chanting that I heard. Anything I say would be nothing more than conjecture."

When her husband had no immediate reply, Theodora spoke. "Then make your conjectures, prefect."

"I don't wish to sully anyone's reputation, mistress—"

"We'll take that into account, prefect. Now, what might Tribonian have done to stir up the blood of the people?"

Eudaemon saw no way out of the predicament he had made for himself. "They—they believe he has perverted justice, mistress. That he sells his verdicts to the highest bidder and has made himself wealthy preying on others."

Theodora sensed an unnatural stillness in Justinian's posture. He didn't like what he heard. She focused on Eudaemon, asking, "And John of Cappadocia?"

Eudaemon took in a long breath. "He has brought about new taxes daily, it appears, all on the heads of those who can least afford it. But he deals mercilessly with the wealthy, too, impoverishing them, not only to bring money into the treasury, but also into his own personal coffers."

Theodora held back on expressing the secret pleasure that ran through her upon hearing about John of Cappadocia's failings. She hated the man.

Evidently, Justinian had heard enough from one of his principal ministers about two others. "You're dismissed," he said. "Leave us,"

"Master, may it please you for me to remain here under your protection at the palace?"

"Yes, yes—go find Lord Chamberlain Narses and have him find you rooms."

Justinian sat in silence a good while after the prefect left. Theodora felt certain he was chastising himself for having mishandled the situation at the Hippodrome. Procopius's advice to ignore the pleas of the factions' demarchs in such a public setting had proved a monumental mistake. She reached over and placed her hand on his, wondering how she would have reacted to the same situation, Procopius or no Procopius.

Lord Chamberlain Narses entered now, his haggard face smeared with smoke. In his high-timbred voice, he gave an accounting of what had gone on in the Augustaion, detailing how the Senate House, Church of the Holy Wisdom, and Chalké Gate were lost to fire. The loss of the Praetorium paled in her thoughts now as she listened to Narses tell of the destruction.

Justinian sat to her right in his seat of the double throne, morosely silent, his body slumped. "They torched the Great Church?" he asked. "It's not possible!"

"It was the North wind, master, that carried the flames from the Chalké Gate to the church and the Senate House."

"That matters little!" Theodora snapped. Heat flared up into her face as she clenched and released her fists on the arms of the throne. "They are still responsible. And now, you're telling us the rioters are at the very gates of the Great Palace."

"They cannot breach the Chalké Gate, mistress. It's badly damaged but it's piled high with rubble and broken masonry—and it is well guarded."

It was only too clear to Theodora that Eudaemon had known about the mob's actions following their attack on the building housing his urban police force, but he was afraid to be the bearer of such news. She drew herself up, her back hard against the ivory marble. "The urban prefect was just here," she said.

"I saw him, mistress, and told him where he could find lodging."

"We're giving him comfort when it was he who prompted this uprising with his failed executions?" It was not a question for which she expected an answer. But she had another: "If the gates have been blockaded, as you've told us, Narses, just how did Eudaemon gain entry?"

"He came in through the hidden door to the baths, mistress."

"So, the Baths of Zeuxippus were spared plunder?"

"They were, mistress."

"And now?" Justinian asked, stirring himself. "Are the urban police impotent?"

Narses drew in a long breath. "They are scattered, master, and without orders."

"Have some sympathized with the rioters?" Justinian pressed. "Have some gone over to them?"

As if afraid to verbalize his answer, Narses shrugged.

The chamber went silent and Theodora closed her eyes for a moment. We are living in a nightmare, she thought, dizzy as events and their world seemed to be spinning out of control.

Opening her eyes now, she gulped down breaths to hold her anger in check. She looked deep into Narses' dark eyes. It was her way of divining truth in a person. In a tone sharper than she intended, she asked, "Do you, Narses, have any *good* news for the emperor?"

The chamberlain's delay was short. "The fires are dying out and the people are tiring, mistress. Most appear to be drifting back to their homes."

"Perhaps their homes should be torched," she muttered, glancing at Justinian. She saw that her husband's face had gone flaxen as a ship's sail. Her gaze went back to Narses, silently pleading another morsel of hope.

"I've seen this before, master," he said, taking her cue. "The crowd has done their damage. Tomorrow will be a new day, I'm certain."

Theodora found his certitude wanting and noted that it had little effect on Justinian, as well.

Narses took his leave. The royal couple was standing in preparation to return to their private rooms when a woman in a red cloak rushed in, breathless and in a panic. She violated imperial protocol by neither bowing nor prostrating herself.

"Antonina!" Theodora cried. "What is it? Have the cries of those drunkards from the street so scared you?"

Antonina drew herself up, took a deep breath. "They may very well be within the palace walls by now, Theodora!" Her gaze moved to Justinian, and she afforded him a contrite bow of her head. Her hood fell back, loosing her blond curls.

"Indeed not," Theodora said, summoning up some of Narses' optimism. "We've just heard from the lord chamberlain."

"Narses? A lot of good he is! The excubitors did not moisten a single blade with the blood of that lot! At his orders, they stayed within the palace walls the entire time."

"Antonina," Justinian said, employing the patience of a parent, "did you expect them to go out into the crowd and take them on?"

"Yes, of course!"

"Ah, well, they did not do so for several reasons. They would have been outnumbered many times over and the rioters might very well have gained entrance. Antonina, had we drawn blood, we would have had the whole city down upon us by dawn."

Antonina blinked and appeared to weigh the logic.

Theodora could tell that her friend remained unconvinced. "Not to mention, Nina," she added, "our excubitors do not see battle, ever. Why there's not a scratch to be found on their bright cuirasses, I can tell you, unless it's from wrestling with some drunk out in the Augustaion. Narses himself would admit as much."

"Then you must call in men who bravely bear the scratches on their cuirasses and their bodies!" Her blue eyes shifted from Theodora to Justinian. "Why, master, it is your good luck that you have recalled my husband. As you well know, Belisarius has his true and loyal men, his *bucellarii.*"

"I do know that, Antonina."

"Mundus is here, as well, with his sizable force. Together they would not have allowed such a thing as is happening today at your very gates without lopping off a few heads."

Justinian's body tensed. "Thank you, Antonina." He nodded.

That this was a dismissal was not lost on her. She turned to Theodora, her expression pleading support.

Theodora drew in breath as if to speak, caught herself, and gave her friend a tight smile.

Doubly dismissed now, Antonina offered a perfunctory bow and backed out of the room as court etiquette prescribed, her face red with silent rage.

Once she was gone, Theodora turned to Justinian. "You know, husband, there is meat in my friend's suggestion. Perhaps Tyche has provided us with a blessing."

Theodora had not just now thought of using Belisarius and Mundus, but Antonina had given the idea fuel. She reached out and lay hold of Justinian's arm. "Perhaps there is something in what Antonina is suggesting."

Justinian's head retracted slightly in surprise. "Violence? That is what giving Belisarius and his foreign mercenaries free rein would warrant, Thea. Who's to say where it stops? Perhaps with our own downfall. No, I won't hear of it."

"Well, you must call off the races, at least. No sense in affording the mob a meeting place."

"No, The City will go on as before. The races will allow the crowd to vent its spleen, as they say. Time to take a breath.—Oh, do not fear. I'm not without plans. I'll send Narses out early in the morning with purses full of gold for the Blue and Green demarchs. They'll soon quiet their factions. And, earlier Eudaemon suggested sending out a parade of priests to tamp down the spirits."

"What?" Theodora scoffed. "Do you think that a religious procession would work magick?"

"It's worth a try."

Theodora tightened her grasp on her husband's arm. "We might not have time to experiment."

Justinian's gray eyes peered down at her for a long moment before he forced a smile and patted her hand as if she were a child. When Theodora released her hold, Justinian stood and began to move out of the room. "You're right, my dear," he called back. "Tomorrow I'll have the herald announce that Eudaemon, Tribonian, and John the Cappadocian have been dismissed."

"What?"

"Coming?"

Theodora stood as if fastened to the floor. The three were no friends to her, quite the opposite in John's case, and yet thoughts of the concession Justinian was making brought on lightheadedness; and that her opinions of them might have goaded him into it made it all the worse.

Something about her husband suddenly reminded her of Hecebolus, the man she had followed to another continent. Even on the voyage to Africa amidst a squall at sea, Hecebolus had shown fear, and at the Pentapolis he had yielded too easily to small-minded men who felt threatened by a woman who dared speak her mind.

She watched Justinian pass through the double doors, the silentiaries in the anteroom coming to attention. Within her husband were threaded thick veins of goodness, like gold in a rich mine. Could she trust that veins of iron also bound within him the strength of will required of an emperor?

Or, did he—like Hecebolus—possess weakness in the face of crisis?

A chill in the room took her now, and she shivered.

12

Wednesday, 14 January 532

I SLEPT BUT A FEW HOURS and awoke coughing at mid-morning. Smoke had penetrated the Great Palace complex, seeping even into closed rooms. I found a reasonably clean dalmatic and dressed quickly, all the while fighting off a sense of dread.

Piers usually kept out of my way in the morning, but he surfaced in the doorway now to announce—between his own coughs—that Tariq was waiting in my study.

"Am I to assume the mob has returned, as well?" I asked.

"You don't know a piece of it," he replied. "Do you want something to eat?"

"Later, Piers."

"Very well, Stephen. On your desk you'll find a sealed note that only just came."

"From?"

The servant pursed his lips, and using the forefinger of his right hand, pointed to the ceiling.

The Imperial Apartment.

Tariq had moved out onto my balcony by the time I read the message and secured the sheathed dagger to the belt I wore beneath my dalmatic. I had new instructions from Theodora.

"So they have not cooled off?" I asked, as I joined Tariq.

"Indeed not."

"What's the damage?"

Tariq pointed in a northwesterly direction to the nearby Baths of Zeuxippus, where scattered plumes of dark smoke were thinning but still rising.

"The baths?" I asked.

Tariq nodded. "Just this morning. You must have slept through the pandemonium."

"Let's go down to the gates," I said, giving him no time to respond.

The Chalké Gate was as we had left it in the early hours of the morning: piled high with stone, iron, and ash, allowing neither entry nor exit. Employing the wide sleeves of our dalmatics as masks against the smoke, we moved toward the unobtrusive door in the palace wall that led directly into the baths. Two excubitors who stood guard stiffened as we approached. "No entry," one announced.

"Is it still burning?" I asked.

"No, it's well burnt out. Quite a party they had, toppling and desecrating the sculptures."

"What's become of the crowd?"

"Filthy mob, you mean. They've gone into the Hippodrome, all of them. The races are to go on despite everything, if you can imagine that."

"We'd like to go in," I said, discerning Tariq flinch slightly at my side.

"To the baths?" The excubitor shook his head. "Narses' orders," he said, his haggard expression an indication he had not slept since the riot began the night before.

"I'm on the business of the empress," I said removing the pass with the royal seal I had used in searching out Theodora's daughter. Tariq was almost as surprised as the excubitor.

The guard in charge gave out with a great breath. "You're quick to put your life on the line, you are. Your white robes will give you away as palace servants, you know. If you run into any of that swarm of wasps, you won't live to see another emperor."

I blinked at his words. "You're right," I said. I turned and tugged at Tariq's arm. "We'll be back!" I called as we hastened away.

The stable master's shanty survived the fire, and it was there we found grooms' robes, albeit dirty ones, that we put on over our whites.

"Stephen, what do you think this is going to accomplish?"

I shrugged at his lack of enthusiasm and pushed the voluminous sleeves of my whites up into the shorter and tighter sleeves of the undyed tunic.

"Ha! It's your cursed curiosity more than anything. Admit it, Stephen!"

"You know me too well, my friend. What's most curious, Tariq, was the excubitor's warning."

"Hades take it," Tariq swore as he wiped a cinder from his eye. "You mean we might be throwing ourselves to our deaths?"

"Yes, he said that, but he went further. Didn't you hear? He said we might not live to see another emperor."

"I did hear that." Tariq shot me a knowing look.

There was no need to say more. Things had become deadly serious. We both knew some excubitors had little love in their hearts for the royal couple. I was certain a good many of them were waiting to see from which direction the wind might blow. I suspected that was at least part of the reason Narses had not sent excubitors out into the Augustaion the day before when the very gates of the palace were under attack. He was fearful the mob would turn them.

"Let's go," I said.

The excubitors at the door to the baths gave no argument when we returned. We were admitted and the doors closed behind us, the sound of a bar falling heavily into place.

One of my last tasks in Justinian's scriptorium before moving into the Daphne Wing had been to translate from Greek to Latin a codex of epigrams by the poet Christodorus, each epigram devoted to one of the eighty statues lining the baths. I had meandered through the beautifully landscaped paths on a number of occasions, matching up the poems to the statues of the mythological and historic figures they represented. As an immigrant, I felt the thrill of walking through the history of this New Rome, as well as the old one.

The Baths of Zeuxippus had been built on the grounds of the Temple of Zeus more than three hundred years before. For only a follis or two, any citizen could gain access to the baths, luxuriate in its waters, and appreciate its ancient beauty. Now, Tariq and I picked our way through broken mosaics, desecrated sculptures, and the smoking remains of timber roof trusses. Here lay marble torsos, limbs, and heads of Julius Caesar, Aristotle, Plato; there lay those in bronze of Homer, Virgil, and Zeus himself.

By the time we came to the entrance at the Augustaion, hot tears were beading in my eyes. I dared not look at Tariq for fear they would spill. An old man in a soot-smeared dalmatic sat with his head in his hands on a marble block that had been the base of a statue of Hermes, one winged foot still attached.

"Timon," I said, my voice no more than a whisper. He was the head ticket taker at the baths, had been for years and years. From time to time, we had chatted about the statues I had come there to study, and I would recite the corresponding epigrams for him. On one occasion, Justinian was with me and his obsession with the artistry of the Roman aqueduct system led him to detain the man from his occupation, chattering on about the Aqueduct of Valens and how the waters came almost two hundred miles from the hill country of Thrace to feed the baths. Justinian nearly put the man to sleep.

Timon was looking up at us now, his gaze moving from me to Tariq and back again. My groom's robe seemed to confuse him at first, but he soon recognized me. "Lord Stephen," he said, his voice breaking, "oh, look what they've done."

At a loss for words, I nodded.

"How could they?" he pressed. "This was their place, the people's place. It cost almost nothing and when one had forgotten his purse or was too poor, I looked the other way. Some of these broken statues came from Rome, from the East, even from Egypt. Oh, there is no replacing them, no rebuilding this place."

I put my hand on his shoulder. "Justinian will do his best."

"The emperor will rebuild," Tariq offered.

"If he doesn't, you can be certain the empress will see to it," I said.

"This was the palace of the people," Timon choked out. "Their house! They did this to their own dwelling."

I knelt, my knees pressing into jagged tesserae. I looked into his hooded and tearful eyes. "You stay strong, Timon. Stay strong and one day you will take tickets again. You will be needed more than ever."

He looked up, his face brightening a little. Did he believe me? Or was he merely allowing me to take refuge in my own hope?

Tariq and I left him there and moved into the Augustaion, where we were appalled and saddened by the fire ravaged Senate House and the Church of the Holy Wisdom.

"*How* is all this to be rebuilt?" Tariq asked, sighing.

"That's for the emperor to consider. Come, let's go," I said, allowing him no opportunity to demur. I had a mission.

Just as we passed Timon again in doubling back, a searing cry came from the nearby Hippodrome, stopping us in our tracks. "That didn't sound like a cheer," Tariq said.

"Oh," Timon replied, "you don't think the usual races will humor that bunch, do you?" He looked up from his seat on the statue's base, his lined face screwed up in painful bitterness. "They've had their taste of power. Drunk on it, they are. Who's to say what will satisfy them?"

My arms went to gooseflesh as I left my old friend there.

"The old man sounded like a soothsayer," Tariq said, shadowing me.

"Let's hope he's as inaccurate as most of them," I answered, moving toward the Mese.

"Hey!" Tariq called, running to catch up to me. "Where are you going?"

"We haven't much time, Tariq. Pick up your feet."

"For what? You *are* acting on *her* orders, aren't you? Holy Mithra! Stephen, just what business has Theodora engaged you in that takes you—us, I should say—out into the jaws of … of who knows what?"

As we hurried along the strangely deserted thoroughfare, I explained that we were to take Probus from his home and lead him through the back alleys to the palace. Tariq fell silent. He understood the situation and Theodora's fear. Since Hypatius and Pompeius were secured on the palace grounds, the rioters—if they were bold enough to seek to replace Justinian—would turn to Anastasius's third nephew.

How would this all end? I asked myself, my eyes scanning ahead. The streets and alleys were tinderboxes of frame buildings that could flame up like torches. And, while the façades of imposing buildings we passed along the Mese were made of marble impervious to fire, the city code allowed for the other walls to be constructed of wood, every bit as flammable as their wooden trusses and roofs. All of Constantinople could end in a shambles more severe than the earthquakes that had twice leveled Antioch.

Once past the Forum of Theodosius, we took the northwest branch of the Mese and found our destination close to the top of The City's fourth hill. Probus's house was just as Theodora described it: the only significant mansion with a façade of gray-white marble situated directly across from the Church of the Twelve Apostles. Before I could rap at the door, Tariq pulled at my sleeve. "See there!" he hissed.

Turning, I could see movement farther down on the Mese. Countless people were moving up the hill as if the entire Hippodrome had emptied out, as if they were on a hunt—and we were the hunted. But no, they were not coming for us. They were coming for Probus. Still, the chances of our getting caught up in a maelstrom of violence were great. Heart pounding, I turned away from the sight, tightness taking hold of my shoulders. I pounded on the door.

No answer.

I pounded again. "Open at once!" I shouted.

I pivoted to check the progress of the crowd. The incline of the hill slowed them, but they pressed on and would arrive soon. I turned back to knock again, but found the door open, a young man in an undyed tunic standing there, his face like white marble.

"Your master—Probus—tell him to come out at once!"

"Pr. . . Probus?" he stuttered.

"Yes, Probus! Where is he?"

He stared dumbly. I was about to push my way past him when he muttered, "G … gone off, he has."

"Gone off?" I demanded. "Gone off where?" My first thought was that he was lying, that he was told to lie, that Probus was hidden within.

"To his pistachio farm."

"What?"

When the servant stupidly repeated himself, I judged him to be telling the truth.

"Where?"

The boy shrugged. "West of The City."

Of course it was west. I was about to admonish him for saying the obvious when he looked over my shoulder, toward the incline of the road, his eyes dilating.

By now the clamor of the rioters could be heard. They were closing in.

"Who else is here?" I demanded.

"I am alone," he said. His frightened eyes came back to me.

"You won't be for long. You'd best take yourself away at once, do you hear?"

"They're coming here?" he asked, trembling. "Here … here?"

"Never mind that!" Tariq shouted. "You don't have time. Run away now or you'll be torn to shreds!"

"Come with us!" I ordered, certain he would not be able to save himself.

The three of us turned and made for the wide portico of the massive church. Thankfully, the doors were unlocked. We entered the narthex and desperately looked for ways to bolt the three sets of doors. We found none. Before we could think out our next step, a black-robed figure appeared, standing atop the several steps leading into the nave, his arms crossed, a large ring of keys dangling from one hand. The sharp scent of Frankincense from an earlier service followed him into the vestibule.

The old priest's curious gaze moved from me to Tariq, falling last upon the boy. "Spiro!" the priest exclaimed. "What is this about?"

The boy looked from him to me, his brow wrinkled.

I called up my deepest voice. "I'll explain, good father, but first, if you came to lock the doors, you best get on with it."

"Yes, of course."

The priest stood inert. "What's that noise?" he demanded, alerted to the raucous sound of the mob's front line as they began to arrive at the house of Probus.

"It's the sound of death approaching," Tariq interjected, "unless you lock the cursed doors!"

I don't think it was so much Tariq's high-pitched order, but rather the shouts of angry men out in the street and the implied violence that made the gray-haired priest jump to, searching out the right key even as he scurried down the marble steps.

No sooner had the priest's key driven home the bolts in the wooden block locks than we heard the sounds of sandals on the front stone steps and the desperate tugging on the doors.

We froze in silence.

After some minutes, I whispered to the befuddled priest what I knew of the rioters' intent.

Across the way, not finding Probus at home—just as we had done—and knowing nothing of his whereabouts, the crowd grew agitated, angry, hostile. We soon heard the sounds of things being broken as they gave vent to their frustration by looting and tearing apart the villa.

"Will you lead us to another exit?" I asked the priest.

He thought for a moment, nodded. "The crypt below runs from the church to my rectory. There will be a safe exit for you there."

"Thank you, Father."

"And the boy?" Tariq asked.

"I'll see he is reunited with Probus," the priest said. "You may count on it."

Before we could leave the narthex, an acrid smell overpowered the scent of incense. I think we all turned to look at the doors at once. Dark smoke was seeping into the church through every sliver of space all around the six doors.

Across the way a raucous cheer went up, one sounding oddly joyous and angry in equal measure.

Theodora watched the slight but spry Narses advance toward the double throne. His slightly bent posture and downcast eyes spoke volumes. Something hardened at the pit of her stomach.

"I already know that no races were run today," Justinian said, waving his hand dismissively in a motion that freed Narses from the usual prostration.

The audience chamber had been emptied except for the three of them. Even the silentiaries were placed outside the doors. No one within the palace walls was to be trusted.

Justinian leaned forward. "The piles of gold you left with this afternoon did no good?"

Narses shook his head. "Oh, the Blue and Green demarchs took their purses, but neither would guarantee they could control their factions."

"Not even the Blues?" Theodora inquired. "We've always found mutual ground." She knew, however, that often enough the two factions had occasionally been treated alike to avoid the appearance of favoritism.

"No, mistress."

"But you proceeded with the next steps of our plan?" Justinian pressed. "You told them the two Green and Blue convicts are being released?"

"I did. And that you are replacing the three officials they hated most." Narses paused, sighing. "It did little good. 'Too late, too late,' the demarchs said. They said neither they nor their men could be pacified by a purse."

"And yet they took the gold," Theodora snarled. "What *would* pacify them?"

Theodora had never witnessed Narses without his imperturbable self-confidence, but as he paused and straightened his back, she detected a quivering on his beardless chin.

"The news of the replacements merely darkened their mood, mistress."

Justinian cocked his head. "Why is that?"

"I'm afraid, master, they took it to mean you are in a weakened position."

"I knew it!" Theodora cried. "And so now they want *our* heads! Isn't that so?"

Narses stood silent.

Justinian looked to Theodora and then back to Narses. "Is that so, Narses?"

Narses bowed his head in response.

Justinian wet his lips. "What was the chant we heard come over the wall from the Hippodrome?"

Narses tilted his head and closed his eyes, no doubt wishing for some way to avoid answering. With his eyes still shuttered, he said, *'Allon Basileia tei polei.'*

Justinian let out a little gasp. "'Another emperor for The City.'" He fell back in his throne as if struck by an arrow.

"Your hesitancy to speak the facts will do us no good, Narses," Theodora said. "The rabble are aware Hypatius and Pompeius are here on the palace grounds, are they not?"

"They are, mistress. Word has gotten out."

"Since I don't hear them at the Hippodrome any longer, I wonder why we don't hear them at our gates, which are being reset. I went down to see them for myself, not an hour ago. They are bent and misshapen."

"They are, mistress." Narses drew himself up. "As for the people, they would not storm the palace while Generals Belisarius and Mundus are present with their foreign troops."

"So, we have been blessed in that," Theodora said. "I surmise they have something else in mind, then. Is it Probus?"

Theodora's deduction didn't warrant even a blink from Narses. "It is. They went to his house but found him not. My sources told me he left the city. Out of anger and frustration, they torched his house."

"They burned his house?" Justinian asked, his back stiffening against the back of his throne.

"Only after destroying or carrying off anything of value in it," Narses answered.

"You're certain he wasn't found?" Theodora asked.

"No, mistress. I had spies within the crowd."

Theodora wondered if he had willfully disappeared or whether Stephen had found him in time.

Justinian stood. "If unrest continues tomorrow, see that Belisarius has some forty or fifty of his men at the ready."

"Yes, master. What of the plan for the patriarch to lead a delegation of prelates out into the streets carrying icons and calling for calm?"

"Do *not* give him the consent. The time for such peaceful measures has passed." Justinian raised his hand to give Narses leave and then stepped down from the dais.

Theodora watched Narses back out of the room, the weight of the world on his shoulders. She stood now, turning to her husband. "Forty or fifty?" she asked.

He pivoted to her, the gray eyes dark and penetrating. "It's to make a statement, Thea, not to encourage a full-scale revolution, but, hopefully, a bloodless one. After all, with Belisarius's *bucellarii* and Mundus's Heruli recruits, the number doesn't exceed two thousand. Not enough to wage against a revolution."

"If only they had brought their entire forces.—Just where are these men?"

"Belisarius's *bucellarii* are here within the palace walls. Mundus has camped his Heruli on the lands extending from the Church of Saint Euphemia and the Palace of Antiochos down to the Harbor of Julian."

"Close enough, then," Theodora said, amused that Comito's palace was still known as belonging to the eunuch Antiochos. As she stepped down, Justinian took her hand, and they started toward their private rooms. It gave her some ease of mind that the household army of Belisarius and the Heruli of Mundus were not Greek and held no sympathy for the citizens of Constantinople. These were mercenary soldiers, many of them pagans, who were fiercely loyal to Belisarius and Mundus. On the other hand, no one, not even Narses, could vouch for the loyalty of the Imperial Guard—nor for the scores of senators who had recently taken sanctuary within the complex.

Her thoughts turned to Hypatius and Pompeius now.

Tariq and I stood near the Yellow House occupied by Pompeius and Hypatius, just out of earshot of the Imperial Guards at their door. Tariq was supplying bits of the brothers' background Theodora had omitted. While I felt guilty I had waited to attempt the interview she had ordered, knowing their cousin Probus had fled The City colored the situation and gave me something to work with in trying to ferret out their intentions.

"Are you certain I'm needed on this little venture?" Tariq asked.

"Oh, I know you're tired, Tariq, but yes, I'd like you to observe. Theodora herself taught me that when one *expects* to see specific reactions in a person, one might easily *imagine* seeing exactly that and draw the wrong conclusion."

"So you need another pair of eyes?"

"Ears, too, my friend," I said, turning and moving toward the steps.

The guards scarcely looked at the empress's seal before opening the door. We entered and rapped on the open door and in short order Pompeius appeared, shooting a puzzled glance at me, then Tariq, and back again. He was of average height, with a broad chest and a middle fat as a pigeon. He was balding, but his well-trimmed beard offset a face lined in suspicion—and perhaps fear. "Two beardless ones," he said loudly, closing the door. "To what do we owe this pleasure?"

"This is Tariq," I said, ignoring the insult. "And I am Stephen."

"Secretary to the Empress, I know."

I nodded.

"On Theodora's business, I presume." He tilted his head, as if weighing the situation. He was no fool.

This task was already proving difficult. "You might say so. She asked me to check in on you to see that your accommodations are adequate."

"Oh, really?" His lips flattened into something of a smile that could not obfuscate the sarcasm in his tone. "Come in. My brother's in here."

We followed him into the dining chamber. Hypatius sat upright on his couch at a square table, pouring wine from an amphora into his goblet. That part of his angular face not hidden by an unkempt, grizzled beard was florid, his eyes clouded. Upon being introduced, he exhibited none of his brother's wariness, possibly because he was in his cups.

"You play *Shatranj*," I said, noting the board game in front of him.

Hypatius did not respond.

"We were just about to play," Pompeius said, "but my brother has a hard time focusing on games."

Hypatius looked up at me with reddened eyes. "Are they still running the streets and setting fires?"

"We trust the night will be quiet," I said.

Hypatius took a gulp of his wine. "Are we safe in here?"

"I told you, Hypatius," his brother shot back, "we are in the safest place in all of Constantinople!"

Hypatius grunted and topped off his goblet.

"Perhaps our guests would like to quaff *their* thirst?" Pompeius looked from me to Tariq.

Knowing liquor loosened tongues, I nodded and Tariq followed suit.

Motioning for us to sit, Pompeius went to a sideboard and gathered up goblets and an amphora. I took the couch across from Pompeius's, and Tariq faced Hypatius. Pompeius poured the wine and we drank. No toast was offered.

Pompeius noticed that I was looking at the finely carved *Shatranj* pieces laid out on the tan squares of the game board. "Do you play?" he asked.

"I do." I avoided mentioning that I taught the subtleties of the game to the empress herself.

"Then we shall have a game!" He turned the board so that the white pieces moved away from Hypatius and arrived in front of me, the black in front of him.

After we played through several turns with Hypatius drinking and Tariq watching, Pompeius said, "Now, just what is it the empress wishes to know?"

I laughed to myself, realizing Pompeius and I had the same intent concerning liquor and the loosening of tongues. "Only that you are comfortable and at ease."

Hypatius stirred on his couch. "Comfortable! I want to know if we're safe. I want to know that … that Justinian is not going to put us out."

"He won't," Pompeius replied. "Now, hush."

"Hush? We should have gone with Cousin Probus. He knew to leave The City in time! I should not have listened to you, Pompeius."

So—they knew Probus had fled. Interesting.

Pompeius moved one of his pieces and looked up, locking eyes with me. "Stephen, you haven't answered me fully. Why would the empress care about our comfort?"

"She knew your mother," I said, thankful Theodora had told me of the relationship.

Both brothers registered surprise. "How could she?" Hypatius demanded. "Why, before she married Justinian, Theodora was nothing but—"

"Never mind that!" Pompeius interrupted his brother before he could give voice to slander—or truth. He turned to me. "*How* did she know our mother, Stephen?"

"Well, while she was in Alexandria and under the care of Patriarch Timothy, Lady Caesaria—your mother—took her under her wing at what was a critically low moment in her life. She was a great comfort to Theodora."

I read the astonishment in both brothers' faces. They would have been doubly surprised had I not been sworn to secrecy about the son Theodora had delivered with the help of Caesaria. "She didn't say what brought your mother to Alexandria," I lied, intending to draw them out.

"Our mother was a Monophysite," Hypatius said. "She had sought out Patriarch Timothy when Justin took the reins and started persecuting Monophysites. She would not convert to the Dyophysitic belief."

"So it caused a family divide? You and Hypatius ascribed to the Chalcedonian Creed?"

Pompeius stiffened on his bench. "Yes. We maintained that we are Orthodox believers."

"Rather than go against Emperor Justin and lose your standing here?"

"Yes, rather than lose everything." He blanched. I had touched a nerve. He quickly redirected the conversation. "What you say about Theodora's owing a debt of gratitude to our mother may be true, Stephen, but Justinian and I have a bit of history that should warrant some loyalty on his part, as well. He need have no suspicion about us. You see, I rode on two military excursions with Justinian before Tyche smiled and dropped him onto the throne—"

"Smiled?" Hypatius blurted, a tiny rivulet of red running from the corner of his mouth. "Ha! The Goddess of Fortune no doubt gave forth with a good and hearty *laugh* as to what she was perpetrating!"

Pompeius shot his brother a cautionary look.

Seeing an opening here, I said, "You mentioned suspicion, Lord Pompeius. Has there ever been reason for the emperor to be suspicious?"

Wine splashed from his goblet as Hypatius set it down and managed another interruption. "He was not suspicious enough when the siren came calling."

"Enough, brother! Enough—unless you are trying to have us thrown to the mob. Or, more likely, the dungeon below the Daphne." Pompeius turned to me. "Please excuse Hypatius and know that the wine is talking." His eyes widened as he dropped his chin to his chest. "What he says, Stephen, need not be repeated."

"Of course not," I said, "but the truth is, there might be cause for suspicion, yes?"

"What do you mean?"

"Well, I was not here, so you may correct my history lesson. In the year when your uncle, Emperor Anastasius, died, his three nephews—you two and your cousin Probus—were carrying out duties far from The City. The people were insistent about proclaiming an emperor *at once*. Justin was in the right place. Otherwise, the diadem might have gone to any one of you."

Pompeius winced. He did not correct me.

"And," I said, eyes on the board as I pushed a game piece forward, "after Justin was installed, at an advanced age, it should be noted, people said you were conspiring with the Persians to subvert the chances of his nephew Justinian being named successor."

"Rumors! Lies! No Greek worth his salt would conspire with the enemy in order to advance himself—no matter the slight."

No matter the slight, I thought. Giveaway words. Resentment dies hard. What I said was, "Of course not. Such conspiracies occupy only the Roman Caesars. "

"None of the three of us has ever shown that kind of ambition," Pompeius insisted.

"So, not one of you imagined yourself deserving of the diadem when your Uncle Anastasius was on his death bed?" My gaze moved from one brother to the other. "You three were the closest to him."

"That was fourteen years ago, Stephen," Pompeius said. "I can speak only for myself. I enjoy living too much and would no doubt buckle under the many pressures of being emperor. However, if you were to consider which of us might be *deserving*, he is here at my right hand."

Hypatius winced and waved one hand dismissively while raising his goblet to his mouth with the other.

"While the three of us have served as consuls and as generals in the Emperor's Army," Pompeius went on, "only Hypatius, as Commander in the East, held the title of *magister militum*, a position second only to the emperor."

"I see," I said, avoiding a riposte even though I was well aware Hypatius' army career was notably lacking in success.

Pompeius wasn't finished. "Of course, my brother did marry into the noble Roman Anicii clan."

I nodded. The implication here was that both Justin and Justinian descended from peasant stock.

I cleared my throat and changed the subject. I meant to be direct. "Have any of the senators—or anyone—contacted you here in this house?"

"About what?" Pompeius asked.

"About the rioting."

Pompeius caught on at once. "So—some senators are suspected of treason, yes? Do you think they might wish to draw us into overthrowing Justinian?"

My response was a shrug.

"Never!" Pompeius shot a look at his brother, one I could not decipher. "My brother and I are loyal to Justinian. We came to him hoping for sanctuary from the mob."

Hypatius moved from a semi-reclining position to one fully erect, as if the white game pieces still sat at hand instead of in front of me. "Stephen," he said, "you've set my mind to thinking."

"Oh?"

Hypatius leaned forward, elbows on the table. "Are the guards at the doors placed there for our safety—or are they to hold us in house arrest?"

"I—I'm not sure," I lied. "Perhaps it's a little of both."

Hypatius bristled at my answer and his gaze went to his brother.

"Now, Hypatius," Pompeius said, his tone placating, "the important thing is we are safe, is it not?"

At this point, suspecting I would learn little more, I deliberately made a couple of foolish moves on the board. I was willing to give Pompeius the win so that Tariq and I could make our escape.

Outside, I turned to Tariq. "Your thoughts?"

"I don't see much of a threat in either of them, Stephen. However, if the offer of the diadem were to present itself, I'd lean toward Pompeius as the one most likely to grab at it."

"I see."

"What is your thinking?"

"I'm thinking the two brothers are a team, each reliant on the other, and if such a situation does arise, one might persuade the other. One would be emperor; one, chief councilor."

"Who would persuade?"

"Pompeius, of course."

"Which one for the diadem, do you suppose? Pompeius, as well?"

I shook my head. "I would not wager on it. I'm not sure."

"Is that what you will tell the empress?"

I thought for a moment. "It is. Not very definitive, though, is it?"

13

THEODORA LAY AWAKE, WATCHING THE gray winter light brighten as it filtered through the partially opened shutters. She had slept little, waiting for the noise of the rioters in the streets to cease. The sound of the discontented had ebbed somewhat, but it had not ended. While Stephen's report appeared to indicate Pompeius and Hypatius were of little threat to the throne, it provided little reassurance that a hostile takeover would not occur. The brothers might be weak and afraid, but as long as they remained in the city, they were a double menace.

She rose from the sleeping couch, shooed away Phaedra, her handmaiden, dressed herself, and went in search of her husband. She found him alone, pacing around the long, rectangular deliberation table in the Hall of the Consistory.

Justinian smiled weakly, turned away from her, and moved to the window. "Something had to be done," he said, as a way of greeting. "This is intolerable."

"What is it?" Theodora asked. "What?"

"Two hospitals and three churches have gone up in smoke."

"What's been done?"

"I've given Belisarius orders to restore order to the streets nearby. To do so, he has just taken fifty fully armed soldiers out."

Theodora approached him. "Good. I'm glad."

He turned toward her but shrank back slightly. "You mean to say I've waited too long. Is that it?"

"No. You've been patient, that's all."

"Too patient, I'm afraid." Justinian averted his eyes.

Theodora reached out and grasped his forearm. "There's something else, isn't there?—What is it, Justinian?"

"There's a ship docked below."

"A ship? In the royal harbor?" A sudden coldness ran through her. She looked down but could not bring anything into focus. "For us, you mean?"

"It's being well stocked. You must set your women in motion to see that anything you wish—"

"You mean the situation is such that we will have to escape by ship?"

"It's a precaution at this point, only that, Thea."

"But once word gets out we intend to flee, the situation will worsen. The rioters will assume they've beaten us."

"Narses is seeing to it that it's done quietly. Once the ship is loaded, it will be anchored far out—but at the ready should we need it."

Theodora took several moments to digest this information. "Where would we go, Justinian? Where?"

"To somewhere on the southern coast of the Black Sea, where people are still loyal to us. We'll be able to collect ourselves, put forces together and re-take The City."

This brought new concerns to the fore. She wondered how many monarchs driven from their thrones had ever succeeded in once again wearing the crown. She was about to give voice to her doubts when a sustained tumult exploded outside on a nearby street. The window did not afford a view of the clash of toughened soldiers with the populace of the city, but she and Justinian turned to peer out just the same.

At an hour past noon, Stephen and Tariq stood near the burned-out stables and watched General Belisarius and his men return through the Chalké Gate. Members of the Imperial Guard stood by idly watching. The general rode with his back straight in his saddle, his head held high like a returning hero; however, his glazed eyes found no place to settle.

His face, limbs, and polished bronze cuirass were spattered with blood. He had a gash on his forehead. Most of the white-faced men following him were in worse shape with wounds visible and invisible. Some tear-streaked riders held onto the reins of riderless horses.

In the evening, Stephen and Tariq heard the full story from one of the soldiers who had been involved. Belisarius's assault on the rioters initially met with success. He and his men forced the mob back from the environs of the Augustaion and the Hippodrome and into the narrow lanes and alleys. Many of the law breakers appeared to be scattering, perhaps heading for their homes.

Then—at the most inopportune moment—a procession of priests and monks descended from a street upon which a once magnificent church sat smoldering. This surprisingly thick collection of churchmen carrying crosses and holding up icons painted on boards moved right into the thick of the street battle, praying aloud and chanting for both sides to lay down their weapons and welcome peace back into The City.

The patriarch had engineered this little stunt without fully taking into account that Belisarius's loyal men were neither Greek nor Christian. These were men of a private army, beholden only to their leader, and they were killers when the occasion arose. They had no regard for the city, its citizens, or its faith. Thus, the priests and monks found themselves caught up in the melee and trampled, their crosses thrown to the ground, the icon boards crushed beneath the hooves of horses. Two monks were killed outright.

Thus, just when the mob appeared to be dispersing, its members were fired up with new resolve. They were not about to allow esteemed members of their faith to be so sacrilegiously attacked. They turned back upon the mounted soldiers with renewed energy and any kind of weapon at hand, be it a rock or old man's cane. The soldiers found themselves in tight alleys and lanes with attackers on all sides and little space to maneuver their horses. Lances were useless. Catcalling women turned out at windows and upon roofs, showering the soldiers with any weighty household item—including pots of night soil—that could be sent like missiles to their targets.

Frustrated with the tactics of the rioters and livid at his own men for the injuries done to churchmen, General Belisarius called for retreat.

14

Friday, 16 January 532
Noon

THEODORA CLOSELY WATCHED PROCOPIUS AS he approached the dais. Relief was evident in his face when, with a little wave of his hand, Justinian exempted him from having to prostrate himself. It was a dispensation she would not have allowed.

Procopius bowed toward her, then toward Justinian.

"Where is Belisarius?" Justinian asked, an edge in his tone. "We expected *him*."

"The general suffered a head wound yesterday, as you have most likely heard, master. Today he was sleeping soundly, so Lady Antonina insisted I be the one to report."

"I've heard quite enough about the debacle yesterday, Procopius. I wanted to hear from Belisarius what plans we might make going forward. Did he speak of our prospects?"

"He did not, I'm afraid."

"Well, then," Justinian said with a sigh, "while we are dependent on the disposition of the general's wife, perhaps you will tell us about the state of things, as *you* see them. You are, after all, keeping the history of the empire, my empire."

"Yes, master, of course." Procopius pivoted slightly, casting a quick, wary look at Theodora before returning his attention to the emperor. "The unrest continues, master. It seems the people have developed an appetite for arson. Nearly every public building has been set ablaze. And the strong north winds today have led to the destruction of The Church of the Holy Peace, and those of Saint Theodore and Saint Aquilina, as well as the Eubulus Hospital and the Sampson Infirmary. Private homes have gone up, too, along with the Baths of Alexander."

"This is intolerable," Justinian muttered, "intolerable."

"So much for outside the palace," Theodora said, "what are your observations concerning conditions *within*?"

"Within, mistress?" Procopius turned his gaze to Theodora. An attempt at a smile twisted into a grimace.

"Yes, inside!" Justinian bellowed. "Answer the empress's question. Are my people within loyal to me?"

Procopius shifted his body a bit to the left, toward Justinian's throne, but his eyes were cast downward. "The Imperial Guard," he began, "are, that is to say, they say they are loyal to the emperor as long as, as—"

"Yes, yes, as long as he is the emperor. Narses has given me his all-too accurate assessment of his, that is, my guards. I'm well aware their loyalty is dependent on the wind. What I want to know, Procopius, has to do with all the many senators who have been given sanctuary here behind palace walls. Are my senators loyal? You've made it your business to know them. You have always had one ear to the ground, yes? If not to a keyhole. Now, tell!"

The color drained from Procopius's face as he cleared his throat. "I will say, master, you have pleased many of them of late."

"You mean," Theodora said, "the firing of John of Cappadocia has pleased them."

"And that of Tribonian, too, mistress. Those two preyed as much upon the wealthy and privileged as on the ordinary citizens in the streets."

"I see," Theodora said, "but did the firings come too late?"

Procopius gave a little shrug. "It's hard to say, mistress."

"Don't play us for fools, Procopius," Justinian uttered, his voice low and threatening. "You know more than you let on. They've had unreported meetings, I've been told. So do this, my friend, right now, without too much thought, place in your mind any ten of our good senators."

"But, master—"

"Silence! Just close your eyes and do it!"

Procopius obeyed, his closed lids fluttering.

"Now," Justinian went on, his patience ebbing, "just how many of those ten will remain loyal to us, no matter what the rabble does."

Procopius's discomfiture was palpable. Theodora doubted that Procopius had ever witnessed the emperor in such an agitated state. After less than a minute, he opened his eyes. "Master—"

"How many?"

"Perhaps … perhaps, one."

Justinian's lower jaw dropped a bit. If he released a gasp, Theodora did not hear it. "One?"

Theodora said nothing, biting at her lower lip. She was less shocked than her husband, but her heart tore for him. She wished she could shield him from such truths. And her disgust for Procopius aside, she felt he was indeed delivering a truth. When Justinian and she should have been nurturing the good will of their people, patrician and peasant alike, they had turned an admiring eye to the wealth those two officials brought to the government and a decidedly blind one to the wrongs they were inflicting and the people who were being wronged.

"Names, Procopius," Justinian pressed. "I want the names of those you suspect of disloyalty."

As her husband pursued more information from a reticent Procopius, Theodora considered this committed enemy of hers. How loyal was he to her husband? Was he playing both sides? Why wouldn't he consider his own future should Justinian be overthrown? She was certain he would do just that.

Justinian dismissed him without having gotten the name of a single senator. He turned to Theodora, his face white as milk. "He didn't have to name names, Thea. They are all against us. All! How can that be?"

"It may not be the case," she said, attempting to hold down his doubts, as well as her own.

Justinian wasn't listening. He jumped up and raced to the door, opened it, and ordered one of the silentiaries to go for Narses at once.

Somehow, as Theodora watched him return to his throne, she instinctively knew what he was planning, and it sent a shiver down her back. She wondered if she could stop him, but by the time Narses hurried in, she had thought of no alternative.

She said little as the plans for the morrow were discussed and agreed upon.

15

THEODORA AWOKE WITH A START, her body drenched in perspiration, her heart racing in fear. The nightmare had been so very real. She had relived her last day in the Governor's Palace at the Pentapolis, the day of the seventeen-year desert locusts. At a distance, the sky had darkened with them, as if it had been a massive storm approaching, but it was something much more terrible. Amidst a harrowing drone, the creatures came, field by field, devouring the crops that had yet to be harvested. When they reached the immediate grounds, the governor—her lover Hecebolus—and everyone else retreated from the balcony into the palace. All but she; racing down into the garden, she took a shovel to them and struck at them, over and over, until her body was covered with them, until she lay in a heap expecting death, accepting death. Somehow she had survived, but her days as the governor's concubine had come to an end.

Theodora shook the cobwebs from her brain. Had she gotten any sleep? She was alone now in the women's quarters. Justinian had not come to her bed. Pushing herself into a sitting position at the side of the sleeping couch, she used the corner of a blanket to wipe at the wetness on her face and about her neck, and as she did so, the horror of recent days came back to her. The dream suddenly took on dark meaning as it came to her that the locusts of today were the many thousands who had become a murderous mob angry enough to destroy a city. Pushing the gory images of the then and the now from her mind, she rose from the sleeping couch.

Theodora could hear a din of activity outside on the palace grounds. She looked to the water clock. It was morning and the word, Justinian's order, had gone out. The senators—all of them—were being ousted from the palace. In his interview with Narses the night before, Justinian had become overwrought with the sense that treason was all about him, that from the beginning, the riots had been planned by men of some power as a way to depose him. She did not know if eviction was the right decision, and so had not spoken against it. She had left them arguing over the fate of Anastasius's nephews. Justinian insisted on removing Hypatius and Pompeius while Narses argued against it, positing that should some force attempt to put one of them on the throne, they were best observed under guard here in the palace. She wondered now at the outcome.

Theodora dressed quickly and went in search of her husband. He was neither in his rooms, nor in the Hall of the Consistory. She found him in the Golden Audience Chamber, pacing, gray panic flashing in his eyes.

"Well, you've missed the excitement, Thea," he said.

"I can hear it going on outside," she replied, approaching him.

"It was here inside not long ago with every senator and his wife or mistress trying to gain entrance to this chamber. Chaos it was. Enough to overpower the silentiaries. Narses had to have the doors bolted and excubitors called to banish them from the palace."

"All with requests?"

"Yes, mostly to stay behind the palace walls, but when they were told the order was emphatic, then they wanted gold, money. I suppose to leave the city or to ransom themselves should the mob take hold of them. They were met with the bolted door."

"Do we have enough in the treasury, that is—"

Justinian took her hand and drew her to the window that looked out at the Sea of Marmara. The acrid stink and smoke of fires, old and new, hung in the air.

"Out there to the north, Thea, though it's just a dot on the horizon."

"The ship?" she asked, although she knew he meant exactly that.

He stood behind her, his mouth at her ear. He whispered, "The treasury is on board."

Theodora took in a deep breath, one that held. The blue of the sea blurred as if shrouded in a fog only she could see. Feeling a tremor start at her middle and run through her body, she crossed her arms and held them close to her chest. *This is real*, she thought. *This is happening.* Before, it had seemed so foreign to her, so impossible. But now, for the first time, she was being forced to accept the fact that Justinian might very well have to give up his claim to the Empire of the New Rome, that The City and the empire might fall to the rule of a mob, and that she and Justinian might, indeed, have to flee for their lives.

Justinian's hand came down on her shoulder in what was meant as a caress, but it was one that caused her to shudder.

"There, there," he said in response.

Theodora turned to him and his hand fell away. "It's just that your hand is cold," she said.

Justinian nodded. "It's chilly here by the window. Let's go sit."

"No—tell me first—about Hyacinth."

"Don't worry, she and her stepmother are safe in the Blue House. I've had Narses double the guard. They'll not get caught up in the leave-taking."

"And they will—" Allowing a flick of her eyes to finish the question, Theodora turned her head to the sea.

"Of course, Thea, they will go on board with us, as will your sisters."

His assurance, compassionate as it was, brought little comfort.

He took her hand now and began to lead her toward the double throne at the far end of the chamber. Even as they walked the many steps, her mind's eye pictured them sitting there in this closed and barred room, talking between themselves, their words echoing in the emptiness, with no senators, no ambassadors, no servants, no followers.

Theodora fended off dizziness and despite an odd ache at the back of her throat, she stopped and turned to her husband. "What—what did you decide about Hypatius and Pompeius?"

"They're gone by now, I suspect."

"Gone?"

Justinian nodded. "When they were told I was not holding court for anyone at all and accepting no pleas, Narses brought a letter authored by Pompeius begging me to reconsider and allow them to stay."

"Did Narses think you should—reconsider, that is?"

"He might have, but by then he knew my mind. Why, the letter made me even more suspicious of them. Narses would be the first to admit that the loyalty of the Imperial Guard wavers, so I did not want them to have an alternative right here under their noses."

"I see."

"You seem troubled, Thea. I did send them with a few of Belisarius's soldiers, and I gave the brothers enough money to get them to their country estate."

"How do you know that's what they'll do."

Justinian shrugged. "I don't, but Narses informed them it was for their own good."

When Justinian again tried to set her in motion toward the throne, she held her ground. "So," she said, "with the palace emptying out, Justinian, who—who is left?"

Justinian's lips thinned into a smile that wasn't a smile. "Belisarius and his *bucellarii* along with Mundus and his Heruli. We have protection."

Only behind these walls, she thought. The combined armies of two thousand would not succeed against the citizen mob of three hundred thousand, who fought with a cat-and-mouse strategy, sallying forth, striking, and retreating into narrow alleyways and passages, while others took aim from windows and roofs. She looked hard into Justinian's eyes. "And who else?"

"Narses, of course, and most of the Imperial Guard. Oh, and Eudaemon."

"Eudaemon? You've allowed him to stay? So we have given sanctuary to the former urban prefect? The man whose botched hangings started this revolt?"

"I did, Thea," he said, all innocence. "My spies have assured me the revolt was a conspiracy supported by some of our own senators. The botched hangings were merely the catalyst."

"And what of Tribonian and John of Cappadocia?"

Justinian averted his gaze. "They are here, as well," he said, his voice dropping, eyes toward the sea. "I've granted them safety."

Theodora blinked, staving off a weakness at the knees. The three men whose dismissal the Blue and the Green factions had demanded—in the rarest example of unity—have been given refuge and preferential treatment. She wondered if they would also be afforded cabins in the waiting ship out on the horizon. Her throat closed just as she was about to speak. She could not find the words to ask. The likely answer frightened her.

In the early evening, Justinian held a Silence in the Hall of the Consistory. Theodora sat at his side, looking down the length of the table at the many empty chairs. Those present were Belisarius, Mundus, Narses, Tribonian, Eudaemon, Peter Barsymes, and John the Cappadocian.

"I've come to a decision," Justinian said. "I'll not be dissuaded, but I would welcome any embellishments."

Theodora noticed the posture of his councilors tensing, eyes hardening. Her husband's future was their future.

Justinian sighed deeply. "As I speak, the criers are running the streets announcing that games will be held in the Hippodrome tomorrow and that I will be in attendance in order to address the citizens of Constantinople."

Theodora's gaze moved quickly over the faces of Eudaemon, Tribonian, and John. She read tenuous relief in their expressions. Because they didn't wish to sail to some unknown foreign destination, they were quick to grasp at Justinian's plan, especially since it did not place them in jeopardy.

Justinian went on to detail his intention to carry with him the gospels and to humbly offer to put off the diadem. "The mob of criminals has yet to become organized into something resembling a government. We dare not wait until a leader knits them all together into one fabric of revolution. I plan to accede to some of their demands."

Theodora witnessed Eudaemon turn pale. Was he fearful he would be given over to the bloodthirsty rioters? Of course, everyone in the room knew Justinian was hoping to successfully imitate Anastasius who, twenty-one years before, had saved his throne by appearing contrite and humbled in the Hippodrome, where, having put aside the diadem and the purple, he voluntarily offered his resignation to the stunned crowd. Amidst the following shock and confusion, planted voices placed in various positions in the amphitheater began calling for Anastasius to pick up the diadem and take back the purple. Unprepared for an alternative, the befuddled multitude followed suit, and the emperor saved his throne.

Earlier, in their private rooms, when Justinian had revealed his plan—courageous as it was on the surface—Theodora thought it one of weakness and humiliation and, worse, one likely to fail. It went against the very core of her being, and when she started to object, he raised a finger of caution to her. He had made his decision and would not so much as entertain hearing her reservations.

Late into the night, she sat in her own chamber, feverishly brushing her hair, as if she could bring back the comfort doing so had inspired in happier times.

Abruptly, she stood and went into her study, where she sat and penned a quick note.

16

Sunday, 18 January 532

I N THE EARLY MORNING, A note arrived attached to a purse heavy with coin. I read the missive several times, attempting to grasp the empress's directions. She had written it in a state of agitation or panic. The convoluted wording was so unlike her usual explicit demands. I was to accompany Justinian to the kathisma and observe the goings-on, as I had done once before. And yet, I was to locate Hypatius and Pompeius—if they were still in the city—give them the money, and see that they were quickly escorted to the Golden Gate at the far end of the Mese.

I sat lost in this quandary when Piers announced the arrival of Tariq, who was more amused by the note than I. "Well, Stephen," he said, chuckling, "it seems she thinks you have the power to appear in two places at once."

"Yes, but I'm not the Holy Spirit."

"As if you believed in one," Tariq quipped. "My suggestion, my friend, is that we join Justinian's entourage. I saw them gathering below at the Ivory Gate to the spiral staircase. He had yet to join them."

Tariq was right. Time was dictating which task to follow first. "Let's hurry, then."

Below, we found Narses, a few senators and councilors, and a contingent of Imperial Guards awaiting the emperor. Narses did see us join the group, but he looked less than approachable, so I said nothing to him about my instructions.

In a matter of minutes, Justinian arrived, followed by his personal herald, who would address the audience. As Theodora had hinted in her note, the emperor was dressed in the undyed tunic of a commoner. He wore no diadem to cover his grizzled hair. I found him an odd sight.

Tariq and I fell in behind the silent and somber group and began the climb. At one point, I glanced up the rounded stone steps and caught a flash of red. *Holy Mithra!* Despite wearing the costume of a commoner, Justinian had not put off the red shoes of an emperor.

Once in the imperial loge, Narses motioned for us to sit in seats at the back. I was only too glad not to occupy the front row again. Not today. This crowd was out for blood.

The gold-tasseled purple curtains had yet to open, but the maddened voices of those in the stands were enough to raise the hairs on the back of my neck. Tariq shot a look at me that said, *What have you gotten me into, Stephen?*

Justinian took his place on the raised throne, his face dark, his lips all but invisible. The herald sat behind and a little to the side of him. Time—a good hour—passed slowly as the two quietly discussed their approach. This was no ordinary racing day. The level of noise on the other side of the curtains increased, running the gamut from raucous to shrill to angry. The sounds reverberated with latent violence. Every so often, Narses, hands trembling slightly, pulled at a side curtain and spied down upon the crowd.

Finally, Narses nodded at Justinian, who stood and waved his hand. As if by magick, the curtains began to pull back. It was a sunny Sunday, yet it was cold and the air in the loge turned icy.

"Look! Look!" Impassioned shouts went up from the crowd and the clamor fell away for two or three minutes as everyone caught sight of the emperor. The crowd stood in dumb, collective surprise, not only because Justinian had shown the nerve to present himself, but because he came before them—shoes well hidden—in such a show of humility. They saw a man simple of face beneath a shock of graying, windblown hair and dressed in an undyed tunic devoid of decoration, not even a plain fibula visible. He could have been a baker or fishmonger.

Like a good actor, Justinian waited until he had the full attention of the stadium. That accomplished, he carried a codex down to the balustrade situated at the front of the royal box, where he was in good view of nearly everyone. He stood there, stiff and formal as a priest at the altar rail. The quiet deepened further.

I held my breath. Even though the kathisma jutted out and was positioned well above the benches and out of immediate reach, the emperor appeared a tempting target for this enraged throng.

The herald followed him down with hesitant steps and skittish head movements, coming to stand at his left side. Justinian began to speak at normal volume, pausing to allow the deep-throated herald to relay the message with surprising clarity and firmness.

"My fellow Romans!" the herald announced. "Good citizens of this, the New Rome, I beg your attention. Allow me to stand before you. Allow me to offer a heartfelt apology. I come to you bareheaded—without the diadem and without the purple."

A low murmur rippled through the stands.

With both hands, Justinian held up the oversized codex. The herald continued relating Justinian's words: "What I do bring are the gospels! I hereby swear upon them my oath to redress the wrongs of my administration."

The crowd slowly settled, waiting, as if for the prologue to a play.

"On Wednesday, the demarchs told you the Blue and the Green who were held in sanctuary by the monks of St. Conon have been freed. You were also advised that I dismissed the Urban Prefect Eudaemon and other men of my administration. Today, I can tell you that Tryphon is the new urban prefect and that John of Cappadocia has been replaced by Phokas for praetorian prefect. Phokas is known for his reserve and sound judgment. Last, Tribonian's post of quaestor has gone to Basileides, a man whose fairness cannot be questioned!"

Just hearing the names of the offenders seemed to initiate a swelling of curse words.

"Together, Romans, we will seek and find the answer. Together, we will bring peace and calm back to this great city and empire." While the herald trumpeted his words, Justinian handed off the codex to Narses.

Someone on the other side of the Hippodrome's spina called out, "Too late for you!" A few other voices picked up the cry, but it fell away as the herald began again.

"I will ensure that the churches, baths, and homes that have been destroyed will be rebuilt better than before. I guarantee you a new Church of the Holy Wisdom that will be unparalleled in its size and architecture. These things I promise!"

Someone close to the starting gates called out, "Justinian, take back your diadem!" Another call came from the far turn of the track: "Emperor, take back the purple!" A low male murmuring ran through the crowd as two or three other similarly spaced and worded cries rang out.

I was certain Narses had engineered the pleas. This very stratagem, applied to a similar audience calling for Anastasius's head some twenty years before, had worked. But would the gambit work now? How many here were there that day? How many could discern the royal trickery?

The voices calling for the emperor to hold onto the royal trappings fell silent, and things quieted as the herald bellowed. "If you forgive your emperor, so too, will I forgive you, and we will move into the future together. I am granting amnesty to everyone in the here and now!"

"Amnesty be damned!" someone screamed and others took it up. "Amnesty be damned!"

"Go to your homes now! If they have been destroyed, they will be rebuilt. This I swear!"

"Donkey ears!" someone screamed. "Donkey ears!" It was an insult against Justinian heard occasionally on the street. While it might have started as a gibe about his appearance, it had come to disparage Justinian's stubbornness or his readiness to accede to the whims of Theodora, just as a donkey accedes to the whip. No one had dared toss off the epithet in front of the emperor. Until now. Hundreds picked up the taunt: "Donkey ears! Donkey ears!"

Color was draining from the emperor's face, and his hands reached for and held onto the loge railing with the grip of a charioteer at full speed.

A strong voice from the other side carried across the Hippodrome with surprising force: "Demon!" The mob—for it was a mob now—took it up and the combined voices of many thousands rose to a thundering roar: "Demon! Demon!"

"Go to your homes!" the herald pleaded. "Go now and in peace."

The emperor's words were drowned out as the curse of "Demon" mutated into the victory cry so familiar in this amphitheater to the Blue and Green factions who wagered on their favorite charioteers: "Nika! Nika! Nika!" The cries rang out with deafening, murderous intent.

The mob raised angry fists toward the kathisma. Some moved closer, climbing over others as if they could reach the emperor and pull him down into their midst.

Justinian, his face white with fear, turned to Narses, who motioned for him to leave.

I stood and leaned over to Tariq. "You go to the empress. Tell her what we've witnessed. *Exactly* what we've seen."

"Me? What about you?" He rose to his feet and grasped my arm, pulling me close, panic in his dark eyes. "Justinian himself will tell her. Why should I—"

"Because she wants a more neutral judgment of the situation." I pulled away from his hold. "You'll do fine, Tariq. She won't take your head off. I need to follow up on her other order, if it's even possible." Without waiting for his response, I made for the entrance to the hidden and little-used staircase winding down into the stands. The excubitor on duty allowed me to pass. I heard the heavy bar drop into place behind me as I rushed down the stairwell and soon found myself caught up in the crush of the exiting crowd.

I did not look back and up into the kathisma. I had no wish to see an emperor forced to flee for his life from his own people.

Theodora had been accurate in her directions. The brothers lived in typical Roman villas, side by side on the fourth hill some distance past the burnt-out structure of their cousin Probus's more ostentatious mansion. Looking to the right of it as I passed, I was surprised to find the Church of the Twelve Apostles still intact.

I knocked at Pompeius's home. Receiving no response, I hurried next door to Hypatius's villa.

Pompeius answered the door. "Yes, we're still here," he said taking in my disappointment. I had hoped they had taken the empress's advice to leave The City and that my errand would end with two empty homes. "We've been arguing over what to do next."

I removed the purse of gold from my inner pocket and held it up. "The empress sent something that might smooth the way."

"So she thinks money will take us out of The City, yes? Out of her domain?" Even as he said this, his hand reached for the purse. "Come in. But I warn you my brother is in quite a state."

His lips reddened with wine, Hypatius looked up at me from his chair in the reception room, and what seemed a glint of hope appeared in his eyes. "Ah, Stephen! You must tell Pompeius that we should leave at once."

"You must!" cried a woman as she rushed into the room.

I was introduced to Hypatius's wife, Maria.

"Please talk some sense into Pompeius," she said. "They will come for one of these two, they will—just as they came for Probus. My husband doesn't want the diadem, but he doesn't want to flee without his brother."

I turned to Pompeius, who gave a little shrug. The purse was nowhere to be seen. "And you?" I asked.

"Me? No, I told you that I would not want the responsibility that goes with the purple and that my brother is more deserving."

"What about the *danger*, then—for your brother?"

Pompeius stood silent. That he didn't contradict me was telling.

"Listen," I said, "We have no time to lose. You are standing in the way of danger as we speak. Justinian pleaded for forgiveness to the racing crowd today. The factions did not accept, and he was routed from the stadium. This could be the end of his reign. The crowd has probably heard by now that Justinian evicted you from the palace complex. So, Maria is right—they *will* come for one of you."

Pompeius squared his shoulders. "We will be firm in our refusal, then."

I looked into his eyes and judged him less than sincere. He was waiting to consider his options. "Do you think a mob will take no for the answer?"

"We've made a provision in that case," Hypatius piped. "Maria, go get the letter."

Maria grimaced and shot her husband a questioning expression. When Hypatius nodded, she bustled to the rear of the house.

"A letter?" I asked.

"Yes," Hypatius said, "if one of us is hauled off to the Hippodrome for some mock ceremony, the letter will go to Justinian. It states our loyalty to Justinian and Theodora, and if Fortune is with us, then all his enemies are in one place and the time to overcome them is at hand. His generals should take action."

Pompeius stiffened a bit and wet his lips as if to say something, but then kept his silence. I inferred that this was the first he had heard of this scheme.

I digested the plan even as Maria hurried in with the scroll. It sounded foolish and extremely risky.

"It's well sealed," she said to me. "I'm sorry."

Pompeius reached out his hand, motioning for Maria to pass him the letter. Maria's eyes went wide with caution. She paused, glancing at her husband, trust in her brother-in-law lacking.

"I'll hold onto it for safety's sake, Maria," Pompeius said. "If it's needed,

I'll know who to give it to so that it gets to the palace. Stephen here might even provide the means to assure its delivery."

Hypatius looked from his wife to Pompeius and back again. He took two or three beats and then he nodded. Maria seemed unconvinced, but nonetheless handed it over to Pompeius. I noticed it had been sealed in red wax and that it bore the seal of the Royal House of Anastasius.

Pompeius's face yielded no emotion. He tucked it into an inner pocket of his dalmatic.

The subject closed now because events were hurtling toward us with some speed. We could hear the approaching mob in the street.

"Is the door barred?" Hypatius asked.

"It is not," his brother replied.

Maria's face darkened. "I'll see to it," she said.

She took just a few steps when Pompeius caught her by the arm. "That's not a good idea," he said.

"Let me go," Maria pleaded, struggling against his hold.

"If you lock the door, they'll set fire to your house just as they did to Probus's. Is that what you wish?"

"No," she spat, pulling free. But his argument had worked. She stood still, rigid and somberly waiting.

As did we all.

Theodora sat at her makeup table in the women's quarters, staring into the box mirror of polished metal, something she did only when alone because some believed that a woman too attached to her reflection possessed a weak character. She recalled the myriad times in her stage days when she had sat applying her makeup. Today she wished she could prepare an appropriate face to meet her husband, who had been sent from the Hippodrome in humiliation.

What am I to tell him?

She already knew what he would tell her. Tariq had just left after providing a halting narrative of what had transpired. It was a sparser telling than one Stephen would have provided, for speaking before the throne so inhibited Tariq. Still, he had told her enough of an outline that she could fill in the many gaps.

Theodora staved off a trembling at her core. Today she was certain she experienced the sight passed down from her Syrian mother. Before Tariq delivered the details of how the mob had received her husband, and even before Justinian had left to make his humble plea to the Hippodrome audience, she had known how the scenario would play out, as surely as if she had seen it on stage a hundred times. It would end in self-abasement and ignominy. And it had.

She stood, ready to leave the women's rooms. Justinian would most likely repair to his study.

A knock came at the door. Theodora looked up to see Antonina push past a silentiary and enter, her face drawn and dark.

"Theodora—" she started.

"I've already had a report, Antonina," she said in a sharper voice than she intended.

"Oh. And you're not surprised?"

"No, I'm not.—Did I think the uneducated rabble would have forgotten the ploy Anastasius had successfully used all those years ago? Perhaps. But there are enough of the educated among them—senators, in fact—who would recall and see through my husband's restaging, no matter the sincerity he brought to it." Theodora was tempted to bolt from the room, but the stunned seriousness in her childhood friend's face caused her to think again. "Come sit, Nina. I can spare but a minute or two."

The two moved to an alcove beneath a high window and sat in facing chairs.

"What are your thoughts, Thea?"

"Ah, my thoughts? I thought I would ask *yours*—and your husband's."

"Both Belisarius and Mundus are ready to do the emperor's bidding, whatever may come of it."

"Are they?"

"They are. And as for my thoughts, I am confused."

"Aren't we all, Nina? What is the nature of your confusion?"

"It's the ship."

"Ah, the ship of desperation. Our ship to some netherworld. What about it?"

"I'm concerned that it's no longer anchored far out and that it sits in the Harbor of Hormisdas. This is a bad situation, Thea, unless we are to leave at once. It shows to the rioting devils that they have us—the emperor—on the run. It shows them that they've already won."

"I know that. I fully agree. It's still not clear who ordered it to shore or why, but I reversed the instructions, not more than an hour ago. The harbor should be empty."

Antonina's hand went to her heart. "Thank Almighty God! But should we need it after all?"

"A code using a mirror will be sent to the ship's captain if we need it."

"What are the chances of that? Tell me honestly, Thea."

Theodora stood, anger rising at being forced to think of the worst outcome. "Do I look like Tyche, Nina? I have played her onstage a time or two, but I don't know our future." She took a breath, fending off misdirected rage, and attempted a smile. "I do have a favor to ask of you, Nina."

"Yes, of course."

"I'd like you to look in on my daughter Hyacinth and her stepmother."

"Certainly. They're in the little Blue House."

"How did—"

"Oh, it's gotten around that she's here. Secrets are hard to keep at court, Thea. I caught sight of her, too. You do know, she is the striking image of you."

Theodora swallowed hard. "Yes, well, I want you to assure them that they will be safe."

"I will do that for you, Thea. But, tell me, have you not been to see the girl?"

"No, I have not," Theodora snapped, lowering her gaze. "Now, you must excuse me. If I know my husband, he will be calling his councilors to a Silence at once. I must find him." Theodora abruptly brushed past Antonina.

Three senators whom I recognized led the noisy delegation to Hypatius's home. They and a group of some thirty Greens crowded into the villa's atrium. A larger crowd waited outside, chanting for a new emperor, namely Hypatius.

The only one of the rogue senators I knew by name, Origenes, realized at the start that Hypatius was in his cups, and so in a quiet conversation to which I was privy, he spent some time trying to convince Pompeius to address the crowd and accept the diadem instead.

Pompeius was adamant. "I won't have it. My brother is the one."

No amount of pleading had an effect. I had doubted his preference for his brother, but now I was convinced he was sincere. It was also my conclusion that if Justinian were overthrown, Pompeius meant himself to be the de facto leader, the power behind his brother's throne. I had already witnessed him manipulate Hypatius.

Origenes relented at last. "Very well. We need to bring him before the people at the Forum of Constantine. Prepare yourselves."

"Must it be now?" I blurted. I still held out a bit of hope that I could spirit the brothers away, as I had been asked to do.

Origenes turned, taking close notice of me for the first time. "And who are you?"

"That's the empress's secretary!" one of the other senators said.

My leg muscles tightened. The thought came at once: *Run!* But I was enclosed by men who took notice now. Origenes' eyes narrowed. "Ah, yes."

"Stephen," I said, scanning the crowd and attempting to keep calm, aware that danger—like a wolf pack—was closing in.

Origenes gave a skeptical tilt of his head. "Your purpose here?"

"I'm a friend."

"Are you?"

"Yes, and you can see for yourself that Hypatius is in no condition to—to stand before the populace."

Origenes snarled. "He'll sober up soon enough."

I shook my head. "Allow him a day with his family and—"

"Out of the question!"

"Two hours, then."

"No. The white dalmatics that you eunuchs wear have such voluminous sleeves," Origenes said, pulling at one of mine. "One never knows what one may find in them." He smiled, cheered by his own joke, but in moments his face tightened. "Your loyalty is now to be tested, Stephen. Will you be faithful to your friends here—or to the empress?"

"I would like to be loyal to both."

"Not possible! Is it merely coincidental that you are here at this moment?"

"Actually, I was only just now taking my leave."

One of the other senators motioned Origenes over, and they went into a parle.

I weighed this as my only opportunity to escape, so I pivoted and slowly made my way through the crowd, eyes on the door.

Those in the atrium had gone silent in an attempt to listen in on the senators' whispered conference, so that when Origenes shouted, it pierced the air. "Halt!" he cried. "Stop him!"

A heavy hand clamped onto my shoulder. I was roughly spun about and pushed back by multiple arms toward Origenes.

"Off to tell the actress that two of her players have been kidnapped, are you? And that one is to succeed the demon emperor?" The speaker was an old, thin senator standing next to Origenes. He hardly struck one as the type to be fomenting a rebellion.

"No, I—"

"Never mind your lie!" a rotund senator spat. As he swiveled away from me to address Origenes, I could not help but notice how small his perfectly round head appeared atop his body of great girth. "We can't," he announced, "allow this eunuch secretary to go running back to the palace!"

"Indeed, you're right, Leonidas," Origenes said, his eyes not leaving me. "You will come with us, Stephen." He then appointed four of the young Greens to guard me. These young toughs—with their Gothic hair styles and muscled arms—had no doubt played their parts in the destruction and violence of the last week. The wolves had me.

"Hypatius," Origenes ordered, "stand erect and face your destiny. It's your time."

As Hypatius rose unsteadily from his chair, his wife, who had been standing in the doorway, her hand on her heart, raced to his side. "You must not go, Hypatius! You cannot!" She grasped his arm.

"He has been chosen," Origenes told her.

"Chosen to die, you mean!" Maria screamed, her face flaming red. "Hypatius, these men are leading you to your execution!"

Pompeius stepped up to his sister-in-law. "There, there, Maria," he said, "I won't allow my brother to come to harm." Once he had her attention, a knowing lift of his brow and a light touch to his heart brought to mind the letter he had placed inside his dalmatic, the one created that, hopefully, would keep them in good stead with Justinian. She read his nonverbal message and lightened her hold on her husband.

Origenes seized the opportunity and moved in now, fully separating the couple. In a matter of minutes, the wolf pack had closed around me and the brothers.

"No, no, no!" Maria cried. "Don't go!" She was pushed to the side as we were forced from the villa and out into the street.

Halfway down the hill, I could still hear her shrill scream: "Hypatius, no! It will come to a bad end, it will!"

If I slowed a bit, one of the Greens gave me a push. I was now one with the brothers, prisoner of the mob, my future as doubtful as theirs.

Theodora found Justinian alone in the dressing area of his bedchamber, hunched over on a white couch, head in his hands. He was still dressed in the undyed tunic of a peasant.

They could read each other well these days, so that when he glanced up, his face as white as the couch damask, she could see that he knew she had been fully informed of the debacle in the Hippodrome. Tears gathered at the corners of his eyes.

His appearance jolted Theodora and caused a strange fluttering at her middle. She took quick, long strides toward him and dropped to her knees in front of him, the folds of her dalmatic puffing up around her like the petals of a purple flower.

Her hands closed over his.

"It's a loss," he said, the tears threatening. "All the dreams lost … everything we planned for this New Rome gone, like water through a sluice gate."

Theodora squeezed his fisted hands. "Don't be so quick to give it up, Justinian."

"It's being *taken*," he said, shaking his head, unable to meet her eyes. "Who can we blame but ourselves?"

"There has to be a way out of this. It's like a labyrinth, I give you that, but even labyrinths have an exit."

"They do, dearest, but in our case the way out is like the Dead Gate in the Hippodrome."

"Unless we board the ship, you mean."

"The ship! Yes, the ship! I ordered it to harbor, Thea. And it's not there! I expected to see it by the time I returned from the kathisma. We're truly lost without it."

"I ordered it away."

Justinian sucked in a long breath. "You did what?"

Theodora nodded. "I did. Don't you see, having it near at hand sends the wrong message?"

"What message?"

"It tells the mongrels out there in the streets—*our* streets—that we have lost, that we are prepared to flee like rabbits."

"But, we are—"

Theodora shushed him by lifting a forefinger to his lips. Suddenly a fear flooded her that the prediction she made to Antonina was wrong. She looked into the gray eyes of despair and lowered her voice, asking, "You're going to call for a Silence, aren't you?"

"I don't know how much good it can do." His lips widened into an unwitting smile, holding her suspended several seconds.

"You must call for a Silence!" Her heart continued to race. "Justinian! Tell me!"

"Yes, yes, I already called for one!"

"Good!" Theodora stood, drawing her husband up with her.

"It may do *little* good," he said, his head tilted down toward her, as if he were speaking to a child.

"You'll not put aside your dream for finishing the *Codex Justinianus*. And if the Roman world is ever to be united again, *you* must do it!"

His eyes softened, questioning hers, as though she were Tyche herself with the key to the future.

Theodora stood, drawing Justinian from the couch.

"It's time to put aside that despicable tunic, Justinian. You must go into the Silence properly dressed in the purple."

When we came into the Forum of Constantine and found an even larger group of treasonous senators applauding, it dawned on me that this revolt might have begun spontaneously, but now it went to the heart of the government and its forward motion was anything but random. The ceremony was to take place beneath the pillar holding the statue of Constantine, an implicit statement that Hypatius—with his bloodline—deserved the royal throne, whereas Justinian, a soldier and nephew of a soldier, did not.

The forum still swelled with men coming from the Hippodrome and from every intersecting street. The chant "Hypatius August, May you conquer!" began. It was repeated over and over again, its volume building, "Hypatius August, May you conquer!"

Hypatius, still uncertain on his feet, was dropped onto a shield, as was the custom of Roman emperors acceding to a vacant throne. Four muscular Greens lifted it from the ground. Senator Origenes stepped forward and placed into Hypatius's visibly trembling hand a scepter with the Roman eagle atop it.

No diadem had been procured for the crowning, however. Instead, Origenes carried a torque featuring a gold medallion of the royal eagle. With both hands he held it high to the chanting mob, and in a stentorian voice announced that Emperor Theodosius had once worn it, whereupon he placed it—not around Hypatius's neck, as was the purpose of a collar—but upon his head so that the eagle rested on the furrowed forehead, the oddest of diadems.

The chorus shifted now to "Long live Hypatius!" It went on a long while.

Hypatius motioned for Pompeius to come near. I was close enough to hear him demand in a slightly slurred voice that his brother give me the letter declaring his allegiance to Justinian and see to my release so that I could bring it to the palace. Pompeius nodded, moved away, and passed by me without saying a word.

Origenes called out in a voice as strong as a herald's, directing the throng back to the Hippodrome. Hypatius, still cross-legged on the shield, was lifted higher into the air and swept along the Mese with the swarm of men toward the Hippodrome. His hands locked to the sides of the shield to steady himself, he cast a fear-infused look back at Pompeius and me, but he was soon lost to sight. Pompeius turned around, ordered the four Greens to keep close watch on me, and then hurried to catch up with the unwilling usurper, having said nothing to me about the letter. Clearly, Pompeius's interests were not the same as his brother's. I found myself being prodded and shoved toward the Hippodrome in a crush of bodies that offered no opportunity for escape. We entered the amphitheater through the main entrance, whereupon the shield bearers tipped the shield forward, allowing Hypatius to alight, his face white with wonder—and no little fear, I thought—gaping at the amassing crowd. Origenes led the way behind the stands, toward the hidden stairwell leading up to the kathisma. It was much narrower a passage than the spiral staircase leading from the Daphne Wing. Hypatius moved slowly, supported by Pompeius, who held onto him beneath the shoulder.

We reached the top floor. A complicit silentiary or excubitor within the Daphne Wing must have unbarred the door. The imperial loge that not many hours before housed the emperor and his entourage now filled with faithless senators and an unwilling usurper, his brother, along with a number of young toughs, mostly Greens. Origenes saw to it that the heavy iron door leading to the Daphne Wing was barred, thus prohibiting the arrival of Justinian's excubitors. I had to wonder if his imperial soldiers would dare confront a crowd of such a magnitude as now filled the Hippodrome—even if they remained loyal.

The gold-tasseled curtains were open so that the stands below presented a chaotic canvas of color as the citizen-mob searched out places to stand or sit. I was made to sit in the back of the box—ironically in the same seat I had occupied earlier. Hypatius was ushered down to the raised throne, but before sitting, he turned around, his reddened eyes locking onto me and growing larger as he no doubt came to realize that I had not been sent to the emperor with his letter. Grasping Pompeius's arm, he made demands I could not hear above the cacophony within the stadium, but they were demands I could easily imagine. He viewed me and the letter as his insurance that Justinian would not hold him responsible. For now, it was undeliverable. He was asking his brother why I had not been sent to the emperor.

Pompeius spoke with visible fervor, one arm making a sweep toward the throngs in the stands, many of whom were just now noticing Hypatius standing in front of the throne. "Long live Emperor Hypatius!" someone cried and the crowd took up the chant. Pompeius's other arm rested on his brother's shoulder, pressing down, guiding him into his seat.

Origenes approached the two brothers now and delivered some news. Pompeius smiled but there was a more significant change in his brother's visage and attitude. Hypatius's eyes widened with the knowledge, and a smile formed as he leaned back against the throne, as if he deserved their praise, as if he was accepting his role in the rebellion.

It was news, indeed, initiating the change, and in no time it swept through the stadium, inciting a rolling wave of cheers.

The senators in the kathisma were all smiles. It appeared I was the last to learn what had happened. My Green guards were speaking with great animation among themselves in a low dialect I could scarcely follow.

I placed my hand on the arm of one of the Greens. "What is it?" I asked. "What news?"

The Green sneered and pulled away as if I were a leper. "Your new job with Emperor Hypatius is now secure, eunuch."

"What do you mean?"

"The ship with the demon-emperor and wicked empress has sailed. It was in the harbor all morning. Now it's gone. Poof! *They* are gone!"

"That's not true," I said. "It's a rumor. It must be!"

The Green laughed and shook his forefinger at me. "They are gone and will not be back, eunuch!"

Over the next hour, word that the new emperor now occupied the kathisma spread through the city faster than the fires of the previous week, filling the amphitheater to capacity. Although Hypatius still occasionally looked back at me with nervous, darting eyes, little by little, he began to soak in the enthusiasm of the ever-increasing crowd. Meanwhile, Pompeius, Origenes, and some six or seven senators held a war council at the rear of the kathisma very close to where I was being guarded.

"With Justinian gone," the fat Senator Leonidas said, "we should take the palace now."

Origenes' face clouded. "You're forgetting that he's left behind a number of the Imperial Guard, and two foreign armies, and while the Imperial Guard likely can be swung to the people's side, the forces of Belisarius and Mundus could stand and fight. So, I say we should wait them out. They'll run out of supplies soon enough."

"What if they don't?" a senator responded. "Look out there, into the stands. Even trained soldiers of their armies could not stand against this multitude when we lay siege to the palace. They are fired up with zeal *now*."

"Senator Hector is right," another said. "We can't lose this moment. If we allow these men to go back to their homes, their passion will fade. And Belisarius and Mundus will be emboldened to leave the drill grounds of the strategium in order to find and arrest the ring leaders."

This speech was not lost on a number of the senators, men whose wealth and power had been compromised by the Justinian-Theodora reign, and who had still more to lose if there was no change of regime. On the other hand, should the coup fail, they would lose everything. The talk droned on.

As for me, I would not believe that the royal couple would flee. Would they leave the trappings of the richest and most powerful empire to live in ignominy? Not Justinian with all his plans to revamp the laws and glory of Rome. Not Theodora, who had weathered so much in her short life and come so far.

17

F ROM THE WINDOWS CAME THE cheering of the crowd within the
Hippodrome.

"Does no one have a suggestion?" Justinian bellowed. "No one?"

Theodora looked down the length of the deliberation table from one grim
face to the next, from her brother-in-law Peter Barsymes to Narses to the tri-
umvirate who had just lost their positions: Tribonian, Eudaemon, and John of
Cappadocia. At the far end, Procopius sat scribbling away at his notes. It was
the same gallery of mirthless faces as the day previous, but today they were
even grimmer.

The Silence had been in session for fully half an hour and no one had
voiced a serious solution. One option swam beneath the conversation, the one
she read on a good many faces. The ship. As each councilor eyed the next,
she thought it a matter of little time until one dared to speak the unutterable
aloud. Who would it be? Who would dare make the proposal to flee?

Narses, well informed by a network of spies seeded in among the rebels,
including a senator who remained loyal, had just finished the update. In the
Forum of Constantine and under the sculpture of The City's first emperor,
Hypatius had been adorned with insignia from the Palace of Theodosius. From
the forum, the mob moved to the Hippodrome. A party of treasonous senators
and young racing toughs, all Greens, crowded into the kathisma with Hypatius, who dared to sit on the throne. Pompeius stood at his side as if he were
lord chamberlain. It gave Theodora no comfort to know that no emperor's
diadem existed—other than the one resting on Justinian's head. What a mis-

take it had been to release Anastasius's nephews, Theodora brooded. What a foolish mistake!

And Stephen! Narses reported that he was seen being held against his will at the back of the imperial box. He would remain loyal. She knew she had his love. She sometimes took advantage of his weakness for her, but now she realized she had placed him in an impossible situation. If he did stay true to the emperor—and to her—it could very well mean his death. Things were happening too fast. Dangerous things.

At that moment Eudaemon raised the subject no one else dared bring up. "Master, has the ship been outfitted?" he asked. He was the last person Theodora thought would possess the nerve to do so. She deemed him a timid sort of man in crisis despite his experience as urban prefect, the supposed keeper of the peace.

On second thought, Theodora decided, it was undoubtedly fear providing him with the courage to speak. He wished to save himself. She decided to make him squirm and responded first. "What did you say, Eudaemon?"

Eudaemon's gaze went to her at once, his white face going whiter. "Mistress ... I ... I asked about ... about the ship."

"Yes?" Theodora asked.

The fish wiggled on her hook. "I asked where—that is, what orders have been given, mistress."

"You mean to say," Justinian said, "there is still time to slip away."

Eudaemon swallowed hard, nodded.

"Do you have a destination in mind?" Theodora asked.

The former urban prefect looked to the others at the table, longing for rescue.

These are our closest councilors and aides, Theodora thought. Even our two renowned generals, Belisarius and Mundus, sit on their hands. These are our smartest, our bravest? The feeling of dread she had carried for days deepened now. Sensing tightness beneath her breastbone, she retreated into herself and fell silent.

John of Cappadocia broke the awkward quiet. "Hereclea would welcome you, master. They are loyal."

Others at the table nodded at mention of the city on the southern shore of the Black Sea. It was clear to her now that they had held an impromptu conference before she and Justinian entered the Hall of the Consistory. Perhaps Eudaemon had become the speaker by drawing the short straw. The conclusion that flight was the *only* option open to them hung in the air, unvoiced and deadly.

"So," Theodora said, addressing the man at the table whom she despised the most, "there are still citizens in Hereclea whom you have not cheated?"

John's face flamed red. He had no answer.

Placing his hand on Theodora's arm as if to calm her, Justinian turned his gaze to Belisarius. "General, is Heraclea safe?"

"It is, master," he answered, "for the time being."

"If things improved, master," General Mundus added, "Heraclea is close enough that you could return and retake The City. And if you recall your eastern army, you would have the might to do so."

"Ah, you mean for me to save face, Mundus." Justinian's mouth compressed into the facsimile of a smile. "Who's to say the army will remain loyal to an emperor who has fled his people? I gather you are implying we do not have the might today to make a stand, is that correct?"

Theodora studied the general, as he appeared to stare—unblinking—at something well above the royal couple.

"Master," he said at last, "is it worth it to fight if the outcome is a loss?"

The word *loss* summoned up another time in Theodora's mind. She recalled sitting—the only woman—at a conference table of men who were too willing to welcome loss. It was at the Pentapolis when it was under threat of an imminent attack from the Libyans, and as proxy for Governor Hecebolus, she had called for solutions. But the men of standing in the African province wanted no part of a solution if it was to be overseen by the young concubine of the governor. They suggested she step out of the room.

The memory brought a high heat into her face.

Justinian stared off to the side, where the painted map of the Roman world took up the entire wall, allowing a long minute to pass. Lands still part of the empire were colored in a purplish blue and properties lost to the empire since the fall of Rome a bright orange. Theodora knew his mind. He was seeing his dream of reunification come to ruin.

Finally, Justinian said, "So, both of my generals are in agreement as to the best … the best resolution. Am I correct?" Only now did he return his gaze to the table.

Neither soldier looked to the other; their dark expressions made words unnecessary.

Theodora could not help but wonder what her brother-in-law Sittas would say if he were here and not on campaign.

In the following silence, the tumult coming from the Hippodrome grew to such a volume that everyone in the room took notice.

"Most of the churches and official buildings of The City have been reduced to cinders," Justinian said. "Is there any doubt where the rabble will turn now?"

Tribonian spoke for the first time. "Surely they will not attack the palace while the generals and their armies are on hand to protect us."

"A mob can be impulsive," Justinian countered. "You have only to ask our former urban prefect. Is that not right, Eudaemon?"

"Yes, master."

Justinian turned his attention to Narses. "The ship?"

"The order went out by code, master. It should be in the Harbor of Hormisdas within the hour."

At that moment one of the double doors opened and a silentiary presented himself. The Hall of the Consistory was not nearly as large as the audience chamber, so he was not more than twenty feet away.

Color rose into Justinian's face. "What is the meaning of this?" he demanded.

"Pardon, master," the silentiary said, "I was told by the chamberlain—"

"Indeed," Narses interrupted, standing, "I gave orders that should something significant develop, I was to be informed." He hurried forward now as the young man, a Blue, stepped into the room, eyes as big as two moons at the sight of the emperor and empress at the head of the deliberation table.

The exchange between Narses and his spy did not last long. The Blue gave his whispered report and turned to go, but not without a quick last look toward Theodora and Justinian.

Narses returned to his place at the table but remained standing.

"Well?" Justinian questioned.

Narses cleared his throat and fastened his eyes on Justinian. "It seems, master, the sight of the royal ship in your harbor this morning has led to some spurious speculation."

"Speculation? Be specific, man!"

"A rumor, master."

"That is not specific," Theodora snarled.

"It was reported to the mob in the stadium that the ship bearing the emperor, empress, and their entourage had sailed." Narses paused, as struck by the news as everyone.

Theodora sat back against the chair. "So the celebration we hear coming from the Hippodrome …"

Narses nodded. "They believe that you, mistress, and you, master, have fled Constantinople."

"Holy Zeus!" Justinian cried, but he immediately caught himself. "Wait! I wonder—Can this not *somehow* be put to our advantage?"

Theodora was the first to respond. She did so, not turning to her husband but allowing her eyes to sweep the room. "What it does," she said, "is put us on a short timetable. If the ship is not already moored once again in the Harbor of Hormisdas, it soon will be. And the mongrels will get wind of it and know their information was false."

The group fell silent.

"Tell me, Narses," Justinian asked, "do they in the Hippodrome think the armies of our two generals have accompanied the emperor?"

"Surely not, master. Their warships are secured at the Harbor of Julian, southwest of the Hippodrome and in clear view, as is the strategium just above it, where the bulk of the troops have their drilling ground and tents. All in plain view."

"Then they will still hesitate to storm the palace, master," Tribonian offered.

Justinian spoke, giving vent to Theodora's very thoughts. "You are an optimist, Tribonian. If they think Belisarius and Mundus will put down their lances and lie prostrate to an Emperor Hypatius, it gives us no time." He moved his gaze from Belisarius to Mundus and back again, whose expressions struck Theodora as indecipherable.

No one responded at first. Suddenly, however, the generals seemed to ascertain that the burden of a response was on them. "Oh, master," Belisarius said in his throaty voice, "we would hold the Great Palace, you may be assured of it!"

"I agree!" Mundus seconded.

"All that is very well," Justinian said. Theodora thought him no more reassured than she. "It is a gamble. If the decision is to leave, it would be better for your armies to man your warships and follow in our wake. In that way, you could be helpful to the throne—*our* throne—at a later time."

When no one responded, Justinian said, "And so the circle of thought comes back to the ship. Are we agreed that," he paused, mouth agape as if getting the next word was hampered by a fishbone caught in his throat, "*flight* is the way forward?"

He looked from Eudaemon to Tribonian to John of Cappadocia. Each, in turn, nodded with varying degrees of hesitation. Theodora studied the surprisingly quiet Procopius at the far end of the long table, no doubt taking mental notes as to how he would write the history of Justinian and Theodora's tragic end. He looked up, face drawn down in sadness, and he nodded. Was it the face of an actor, she wondered. Perhaps he had ties to the rebels. Or—perhaps he saw a way Belisarius could emerge with a diadem.

"And now, my generals?" Justinian asked.

Belisarius and Mundus presented such faces that Theodora could imagine them standing stolidly on duty near the lighting of a bier holding one of their fallen soldiers. Each nodded now with the same crest-fallen demeanor they must have had to show on such occasions time and again. No acting here; their emotion was real.

Theodora stood to speak now, knowing that in doing so she ran the risk of changing the minds of no one in the room, her husband included.

But her time to speak had come.

The hall fell silent, and she allowed for a dramatic pause while straightening the jewel encrusted bodice of her purple dalmatic.

"My lords," she said, when she had all eyes upon her, "you have suffered through my brief comments and sometimes criticism in the past. Today, I will not be so brief. I cannot. You see, I sat at a table much like this in the Governor's Palace at the Pentapolis, thinking—in vain—that a group of men would heed the words of a woman. They did not, so I know the risk I run today when I speak to those who cringe in fear. Oh, I suspect we all cringe in fear. However, in facing the supreme loss of our government, our empire, must we not consider the wisest course? Must we not do everything in our power to save Christian civilization and realize our emperor's dream to reunite the pieces of the old empire?" In speaking, Theodora moved her gaze from man to man, holding the eyes of each in turn, recognizing, to different degrees, the fear in them.

"I do not believe flight is the appropriate response to a mob—even if it means safety. Safety at what cost? To live as a fugitive? For some, that kind of life might be tolerable. But for someone who has reigned, it is not. It is intolerable. Once, in Antioch an actress tempted me to wear the purple. I refused, for I had not the right. Today, I wear the purple as the Empress of the New Roman Empire. I am telling you, here and now, that I will not willingly part with it."

Theodora turned slightly and tilted her head toward her husband. "Emperor, you have recalled the ship that might bear us all to safety. No doubt, beyond that window, it waits in the Harbor of Hormisdas, ready to speed us away. We might sleep tonight in soft beds in some welcoming port. The royal treasure secured in the ship's hold promises an easier flight and perhaps a retirement of some comfort and refinement. But, take heed: after saving your life and losing your throne, you might find yourself wishing for death.

"Everyone put on this earth must die." Facing the eyes of Justinian, gray glistening eyes, Theodora felt her heart racing and her hand went to the dimpled area at her collarbone. In mere moments, images of their years together unfolded in her mind. Not one to suffer stage fright in her acting years, she had often bolstered the courage of fellow actors so that now she took her gaze from Justinian and peered into the faces of those around the table. Turning back to her husband, she smiled, drew herself up, as if she could attain the height she once longed for, and said, "For myself, I think the purple makes the best shroud."

When she next looked down the table, she saw Belisarius leaning over toward Mundus in whispered conversation. After no more than two minutes, both generals stood.

"Master," Belisarius said, "the words of the mistress ring in our ears like blasts from Joshua's trumpet. If it is your will, our armies are prepared to stand and fight." Mundus nodded in support.

Theodora brought her gaze back to Justinian. He was looking at her with the oddest hint of a smile, as if in wonderment.

One of Origenes' men who had been stationed outside the Hippodrome broke into the group now, huffing hard, having just rushed up the steep stairway to the imperial box. "The emperor's ship has not sailed," he announced to the small circle. "The emperor is still here!"

This new development was met with sagging shoulders and funereal faces, but no resolution was forthcoming. The discussion of what to do began again, but not before Pompeius told the others to keep the news to themselves. No one, it appeared, was to break it to Hypatius, who sat basking in the adulation of the burgeoning masses below. To do so would revive his doubts and fears.

I took this as a possible opening and drew up my own plan. As soon as the opportunity arose, I motioned Pompeius over.

"What is it?" he asked.

"How long until your brother hears that the emperor never left?" I asked.

It had the effect I expected. Eyes darting about, Pompeius paled.

"He's unlikely to see this through, Pompeius. You know that." I refrained from saying he had had his own chance at the diadem but passed on it.

"Fate goes as it must," he mumbled.

"I have a suggestion," I said.

His eyes snapped to attention. "What?"

"The letter," I whispered, nodding toward his chest where I could see the faint outline of the document.

His eyes widened, and he cast a covert look to Origenes and the others. "What of it?" His gaze now locked onto me.

I nodded toward the cabal. "They wouldn't much like it, would they?"

My threat was not lost on him. "Be wary, eunuch. I carry a knife. No one here would care about a eunuch and bootlicker to the throne."

"You haven't heard my suggestion, Pompeius. It could keep you and your brother from the executioner."

He stood still as the statue of Porphyrius the Charioteer, out on the spina.

"Give me the letter, Pompeius," I pressed. "Give it to me and tell those guarding the door to the Daphne Wing to allow me entrance."

"And?"

"And I will get it to Justinian."

"Things have gone too far," he said glancing down at his brother.

"The letter speaks for you and your brother. I can assure you I have the ear of both Justinian and the empress."

"You would speak for us?"

"I would."

Pompeius thought for what seemed a very long minute—and then shook his head with resolution. "I've enjoyed playing at knucklebones all my life, Stephen." He turned his back now, tossing off, "And more often than not, I win."

He returned to the cabal of senators. The moment was lost.

18

WITHOUT A BODYGUARD OR EVEN a handmaiden, Theodora made her way along the deserted narrow lane abutting the Daphne Wing. She passed the royal lying-in house of purple porphyry and paused. *I've obsessed over whether I would be able to use this building, and now I wonder whether my days here have all but come to an end.* She moved on, the shiver running through her earned from the thought rather than from the cold January day.

The Blue House loomed ahead. The silentiaries standing guard at the front and back doors were among the most loyal, Narses had assured her. She paused. Suddenly, sounds of the mob's uproar, as well as thoughts of an uncertain future, faded, giving way to the reality that she was meeting her daughter for the first time. Antonina had said the girl was the image of her mother. Theodora had thought so, too, on those occasions years before when she had secretly observed Hyacinth from afar as the girl helped her adoptive parents in selling chickens at the Forum of the Ox.

She felt as if her knees were about to buckle. In just moments—amidst the world's coming undone—she would finally meet her daughter.

Hyacinth knew the truth now. How had she reacted?

The two silentiaries at the front door could not hide their surprise at seeing her step onto the porch. They were confused, too, at what form of respect was expected. Theodora gave them a dismissive wave that dispensed with any show of obeisance. She nodded toward the door and one of them opened it. Her heart beat fast.

Stepping into the semi-dark entrance hall, she came face-to-face with Hestia, the woman who from the start had played the role of mother in Hyacinth's life. "Mistress," the shocked woman whispered, bowing awkwardly.

Somehow, Theodora had blocked this plain-faced, middle-aged woman from her mind. How had *she* taken the news that the baby she and her husband had adopted was the child of the empress? "You're Hestia," Theodora said.

The thin woman nodded, taking a step backward. "She is in here," she said, motioning Theodora forward and leading her into a small reception room where the pale girl stood attempting a bow, dark eyes at full mast.

Theodora approached her, realizing at once the girl was already surpassing her in height. She had been just nine the last time Theodora saw her in the forum, the day an innocent handmaiden—mistaken for the empress—was murdered in place of her. After that, Theodora dared not venture out disguised and unguarded.

Theodora longed to take her daughter into her arms, but clumsily took hold of her hands instead. Hyacinth's face was more rounded than heart-shaped like hers, but her long black hair, gathered into a ring at the back, and heavy brows that very nearly met at the middle of her forehead were much the same. "You're growing into a beautiful young woman," Theodora said, the compliment a spontaneous one. "You really are—but, why, you're trembling."

Hyacinth looked as if she would cry. She withdrew her hands.

It was no wonder Theodora had put off this meeting. She had just spoken well enough to a roomful of men, instilling in them courage where it had been short in supply, but words failed her now in addressing her own daughter.

"Do you like sweets?" Theodora asked, simultaneously berating herself for such an approach. Her daughter was hardly a child anymore.

Hyacinth nodded, as if to oblige.

"I'll send some honey-dipped dates over. Would you like that?"

"Yes." The word was scarcely a breath.

"Good! I had a sweet tooth when I was a young. However, you are quite grown now. You're fourteen now, yes?"

"In May, mistress." Hyacinth gave off a shadow of a smile and cast a quick look at Hestia before lowering her gaze. "Mistress, Mother and I would like to go home."

The girl's first words struck like a thunderclap. Theodora raised her daughter's chin with her forefinger. "I'm afraid that is not possible. The City is in revolt. It is not safe."

"But is it safe here, mistress?" Hestia asked.

Theodora took her meaning: the palace was the object of the people's ire. It was something she could imagine herself saying, but the woman's words ignited a flame of indignation just the same. She took a breath and allowed the moment to pass. Motioning to a couch just a foot or two away, she said, "Let's sit down, the three of us." She could not take her eyes from Hyacinth. My daughter, she thought. *My daughter.*

Hestia nodded and went to sit on a stool opposite the couch. Hyacinth ignored Theodora's directive to sit next to her, instead crossing over to stand next to Hestia.

Theodora forced a smile. Despite the sharp poignancy of the moment, she was finding it impossible to divorce herself from the dangers of the mob—and the decisions being made in the Hall of the Consistory.

She would remember little of the conversation that followed, only that it was awkward and filled with a multitude of silent pauses. After no more than fifteen minutes, she rose, said goodbye, and moved out into the tiny vestibule.

"Mistress," Hestia whispered, coming up from behind.

Theodora turned about.

"Mistress, if you allow us to go, we will find safety on our little farm. It's on the outskirts, just past the Golden Gates. Hyacinth will be happier there, safer."

Theodora drew in breath. "That is not possible, Hestia. That life is over for Hyacinth. Please understand that. For her, there will be no more farm, no more selling chickens in the forum."

Hestia blinked, then blinked again.

"I owe you much, Hestia, and any reward you might request I will attempt to make good—but she is *my* daughter, and she will have her place here. As for her safety, if the palace should become too dangerous, we have a fully equipped ship that will take us to a place we know to be safe."

"Mistress, I—"

Theodora put her finger to her lips, shushing the woman. "I don't have time to discuss this. Listen to me, Hestia. You are welcome to remain with Hyacinth. I owe you that. I will see to it you live safely and in comfort all of your days. Still, if you wish to return to your farm, you may do so. I'll leave orders with the lord chamberlain. However, Hyacinth *will* remain here." Theodora turned and moved toward the door.

Hestia caught up with her in the shadowy entrance hall. "But, mistress—"

Theodora pivoted toward Hestia. "Hyacinth is the daughter of an empress, Hestia. Understand that. I will see to it that she marries well." She leaned into Hestia and whispered, "Hyacinth could, one day, be the mother of an emperor."

Hestia's dark eyes went wide, and she fell back a pace, silent.

"Why, one day," Theodora added, "Hyacinth could be an empress herself."

Theodora left the Blue House now, thinking how the little scene with Hestia had played out like a short vignette on stage. But this is life, she thought, this is life. Something within her center hardened. She had to make her assurances of safety to Hestia and Hyacinth come to pass.

She picked up her pace as she passed the little house of purple porphyry. *The ship be damned!*

Plans were being finalized by the time Theodora returned to the Hall of the Consistory. Those present with Justinian were the two generals and Narses. Justinian gave Narses orders and a good deal of gold so that he and his band of eunuchs could enter and infiltrate the stands where the Blues congregated. They were not to rely on the Blue demarch's good will to distribute the gold; rather they were to spread it among all the Blues while reminding them of two things: that both Justinian and Theodora had favored them in the past and that should Hypatius take the throne, he was likely to favor the Greens, as had all the Anastasius clan. Where good sense did not prevail, gold would prove persuasive. The Blues were to be warned that returning to their homes was in their best interest. The unspoken objective was to clear as many Blues as possible from the Hippodrome before the shedding of any blood. It was a classic Roman tactic: divide and conquer.

"Listen to me, Narses," Theodora said to the lord chamberlain before he left, "Stephen is still caught up with those traitors, is that correct?"

"Yes, mistress."

"It's my fault, Narses, all mine. I don't think he would betray me. You know him well, yes? After all, you brought him here to Constantinople."

"I do know him, mistress. He was entranced by you on the ship coming from Antioch and his heart was captured. I don't think he would *ever* betray you."

Theodora sighed, embarrassed now that she had asked the question. "I know. But he is in a precarious situation, and I am to blame. Do whatever you can to see to his safety."

Narses nodded, bowed, and withdrew.

Belisarius was assigned to lead a *centuria* to the kathisma via the spiral staircase leading from the Daphne Wing. Once inside the royal box, the regiment of *bucellarii* was to take captive Hypatius and Pompeius, killing any of their supporters, if necessary, including members of the Imperial Guard who had defected.

Mundus was to order up his sizable Heruli forces that were camped nearby at the Harbor of Julian. "Make ready and wait," Justinian said. "Do you understand?"

"I do, master," Mundus said.

The generals were dismissed, and the excruciating wait began.

Justinian and Theodora returned to the audience chamber. Theodora sat on her side of the white double throne, watching Justinian pace the black marble floor.

Half an hour passed.

A silentiary knocked and entered. He bowed and delivered the news someone had passed on to him. "Master," he said, standing before Justinian, who stood near the window. Turning, he bowed toward Theodora. "Mistress."

"What is it?" Justinian demanded.

"I was told to inform you the ship has docked in the harbor and that it is at your disposal."

"Thank you," Justinian said, lifting his hand in dismissal.

When they were alone again, he turned toward Theodora, his expression saying what words could not. She read in the folds of his face the fear that they would be forced to sail and fear of what might come by choosing not to sail.

Neither spoke.

The already dark mood in the Golden Audience Chamber bled to black when a grim and breathless Belisarius returned much sooner than expected.

Theodora watched the general approach, his face foretokening a setback, and time lengthened with each step he took toward the throne.

"We failed to enter the kathisma," he announced, after a quick bow.

"What?" snapped Justinian, who had only just stopped pacing and settled onto his throne.

"Master, at the top of the spiral staircase, we found the iron door leading to the rooms adjacent to the loge barred and guarded on the other side. They would not admit us."

"They? You mean *my* guards?"

"Yes, Imperial Guards. They were not antagonistic. In fact, after an initial response, they pretended not to hear us."

"How dare they!" Justinian exclaimed.

"It's what Narses has said all along," Theodora interjected. "Most of the guard awaits fair weather. Such is their loyalty. They wish to support the winner, like at the races. We haven't won them over."

"Our fault entirely," Justinian murmured. "When we hear 'Nika! Nika! Nika!' coming to us on the wind, it is not the traditional cheer for a charioteer."

"Indeed not," Theodora said. "The chant is raised against us. Going forward, that must change!"

"If only God will give us the opportunity to implement the change, Thea."

"We cannot wait on God, Justinian. We must make our own destiny. So I ask you, what is Belisarius to do now?"

"Master," Belisarius said, sheep-faced, "the ship has returned to harbor."

"We know that," Justinian said, his eyes wide at the implicit suggestion. He turned to Theodora on his left.

Theodora wondered what expectations her husband had of her. He was looking for her reaction, she knew, but she remained still as stone. Beneath the surface, however, she held her breath, praying he knew her well enough, praying he would rise to the occasion.

Justinian stood now. "These are your orders, General Belisarius. Send word to Mundus that he is to assign half his number to close off the doors at the Hippodrome's main entrance at the north end; he should send his best lancers, and the other half is to assemble at the Dead Gate on the western side and wait to take his lead from you."

"Yes, master,"

"Now, take your men, Belisarius, *all* of them, do you hear? Take them from the palace grounds through the Chalké Gate. Do not enter into any fights with the Imperial Guard down there unless they attempt to stop you. I don't think they will. While they may not be faithful, they are not fools."

"Yes, master."

"Proceed then to the Hippodrome's entrance and follow the passage beneath the stands on the eastern side so that you enter the amphitheater directly under the kathisma."

Belisarius waited, as if to ask for something more.

"Narses," Justinian continued, "will have done his work among the Blues. Some may ignore him and remain in the amphitheater. They do so at their own peril. His next task will be to enter the kathisma through the Daphne. He will have better luck than you since he knows by name those eunuch excubitors who blocked your entrance. He trained a good many of them."

Belisarius remained stationary, unaware Justinian had finished. Any further orders, such as what to do upon entrance into the Hippodrome, were implicit.

"Dismissed," Justinian ordered.

Belisarius thrust out his arm in a Roman salute, then turned and bowed toward Theodora before backing out of the audience chamber.

I struggled to decipher the pieces of heated words among the rebel leaders a few paces away. They were still divided on the subject of whether to galvanize the multitude below into a vehicle of attack on the Great Palace or whether it was better to wait.

I shifted my attention to the crowd below in the stands of the amphitheater. The men were behaving as if victory were already theirs, joining in a chaotic variety of chants vilifying Justinian and his empress, always returning to shouts of "Nika! Nika! Nika!"

Suddenly, I noticed a glinting of white here and there on this, the Blue faction's side, a white most familiar to me. It was the white of the palace eunuchs' dalmatics. I stood spellbound by the sight. What could it mean? Eunuchs I knew by name were moving among and interacting with the Blues. Something was being passed to the Blues, something more than information. I caught glints of gold and an occasional glimpse of a purple purse. Narses himself was moving among the Blues, but in the blink of an eye, he was gone.

Near to me in the kathisma, the argument continued, the leaders ignorant of what as occurring below.

Within half an hour, the white tunics had vanished. More than that, however, the crowd of Blues had thinned considerably. In fact, a line of Blues was now moving this way, toward the portal located directly under the imperial loge. They were leaving the Hippodrome. With so many Blues gone, I realized a great many citizens remained, men wearing neither blue nor green. Just ordinary citizens.

I felt gooseflesh rise on my arms. Something was about to occur—something terrible—but what?

The minutes moved slowly, like the drip, drip, drip of a water clock.

It was already too late. From below came the unmistakable rock-crushing sound of soldiers' hobnailed boots coming down hard on stone and the frightening thumps of steel swords against wooden shields. But I knew even then—my Syrian sight?—that the Goddess of Fortune was working through Theodora. Or was it the other way around?

Most of the cabal grew silent, its members moving quickly down to the rails at the front of the loge, where they could view the amphitheater unobstructed. Two of my Green guards raced down, as well, leaving two to hold me back. Pompeius, however, stood nearby, stricken in place like a marble figure.

Hypatius used the arms of the emperor's throne to push himself up into a standing position. He appeared to teeter on the dais, his head turning as if on a swivel, fearful eyes drawn up in this direction, to his brother.

Pompeius stirred now, descending the steps of the loge. He stopped to say something to his brother, touching his shoulder as if in reassurance. Then he moved down to stand with the others at the railing.

The celebratory shouts and chants had transitioned into an eerily chilly silence in deference to the staccato pounding of studded military boots. My two remaining Green guards left me and moved down for a look.

At this moment, a clash began behind the loge, in the emperor's anterooms, where steel weapons could be heard battering at the iron door that the inconstant Imperial Guards had used—so far—to keep the emperor's men at bay. I was not about to await its outcome, for a grisly curiosity drew me to follow the Greens down the steps.

Even before I could maneuver into a space at the railing, the stillness below gave way to piercing and frightened cries, cries like I had never heard, cries of men facing their deaths. I looked down to see a snake pit of bodies pushing and shoving as men, mostly Greens, attempted to scramble away from the soldiers and toward the exits that would take them into a honeycomb of stairways and passages behind and below the tiers of benches, allowing for escape.

"It's Belisarius," Senator Leonidas wailed, "and his damn private army of pagans!" The howling below escalated to screams and shrieks as the silver flashes of swords and axes caught the dull January light, rising and falling, falling and rising. Bodies dropped like reddened sheaves of wheat into the spaces between the wooden benches; other victims were forced down atop the benches before being dispatched. With the *bucellarii* blocking the portal below us, only two exits from the amphitheater remained: the main entrance and the Dead Gate across the way. Those pushing toward the passages leading around to the main entrance found it slow going so that in their effort to elude Belisarius's killing crew, some men rushed down to the concourse, climbed over the wall, negotiated the half-filled moat, and ran the concourse around the spina—a herd going in both directions, their goal the Dead Gate, but only after crossing the moat on that side. Some Greens did have weapons and stood to fight, but their expertise was no match for mercenaries who *enjoyed* the slaughter and gave not a damn for the life of a Roman.

A wail louder than any before went up now directly across the stadium. A second phalanx of soldiers was spilling out of the portal leading to the Dead Gate. I recognized their colors as belonging to the Herulian mercenaries of General Mundus. The leather and armor bound men arrived shouting in their language, their axes and unsheathed swords already at work.

Movement all around the stadium seemed to slow, nearly stop.

The main entrance offered the only escape from the *bucellarii* and Heruli. And yet every avenue to it appeared clogged. That the thousands trying to claw their way to the exits and passages leading to the northern gate could not advance at all meant only one thing: the main entrance had been closed. I watched in horror as men crawled over one another, scaled bodies of the fallen and fought with one another in their effort to outpace the soldiers who moved from the two side entrances in every direction, encircling the stadium, bearing down on their prey like orderly, determined, paid executioners.

I looked back to see that Hypatius had fallen back against the throne, tears streaking his face. Pompeius bent over him, encouraging him to rise.

"The letter!" Hypatius shrieked, his terror-filled eyes scanning those at the rail and finally alighting on me. "The letter! Give it to him at once!" He had to shout for his words to be heard above the death cries below.

"Yes, yes," Pompeius said, simultaneously motioning me over.

By the time I moved the few steps toward the brothers, Pompeius had removed the document from his dalmatic.

Hypatius grasped the scroll and pressed it into my hand. "It's there," he mewled. "Our fate is in your hands now. See that it gets to the emperor. Please, Stephen!"

Pompeius was staring out at the monstrous violence in the Hippodrome. When he turned to look at me, I knew he would not beg as his brother was doing. He merely nodded.

At that moment the answer to the mystery of what was taking place in the emperor's anterooms above us unfolded. The eight or ten Imperial Guards that had been keeping the iron door to the Daphne Wing barred streamed out into the loge. They had chosen their side at last and opened the door. They had chosen for the emperor. Later, they would plead their case to the throne, but for now, augmented by the arrival of some fifteen palace excubitors, they marched down to the rail, arresting the rebel leaders and taking the brothers and me roughly in hand. What difference did it make that I wore the white dalmatic of a palace eunuch when they were arresting men wearing the insignia of the Senate for treason?

Things seemed to be moving too quickly. My mind's eye pictured my final moment occurring at the hands of a palace soldier. "No!" I wanted to shout. "I support the emperor!" But before the words would come, Hypatius screamed almost those very words as he was being pulled from the throne, words that made no difference to the soldiers. I will not lie. I was trembling as the three of us were forced up the stairs, swords' points at the back of our necks.

"Not that one!" came the familiar strong, but gravelly, voice. "Unhand him!"

The deadly point of the weapon at my back fell away.

I looked up. It was the first time I had seen Narses in war gear, his face dark. He motioned me forward. Upon reaching the top of the loge, I saw he held in his hand the makeshift diadem—Emperor Theodosius's golden torque—that Hypatius had been wearing atop his head. He ordered the brothers to be taken into the Daphne Wing, then turned to me. "Are you all right, Stephen?"

I nodded. "You'll want this, too."

Narses took the rumpled scroll, his eyes narrowing as he broke the red seal of the royal Anastasius clan and quickly scanned the document. His education had been limited, but his Greek was more than serviceable.

He looked at me oddly but said nothing.

The loge had nearly cleared by now but the butchery went on below. "May

I go to my rooms now?" I asked, sickened by what I witnessed and wanting no more of it.

"You may," he said, "but be there when I send for you."

After we descended the spiral stairway into the palace, Narses turned to me. "She was concerned for you, Stephen," he said. "The mistress."

19

I N MY ROOM, I WASHED up, but the stain was really within. When I closed my eyes, the violence viewed from the royal loge still seethed and roiled as if imprinted on the inside of my eyelids.

I had little time to take stock of Narses' statement about Theodora's concern for me before word came in the form of two Imperial Guards that I was to present myself in the audience chamber.

Upon entry into the chamber, I realized I had not missed much of the drama. Hypatius and Pompeius were lying prostrate before the double throne on which Justinian and Theodora perched, the royals well draped in purple and gold. They must have just taken their seats upon the purple-cushioned white marble double throne.

The rebel leaders, senators and other officials—many more than had been in the loge—were lined up against the back wall, tightly guarded by a dozen Imperial Guards. The guards who had defected to the rebels would be dealt with on the morrow. As I crossed in front of the frightened traitors to the throne, moving toward the windows and then left, toward the royal dais, I sensed the eyes of the empress on me. I came to stand off to the side of the proceedings.

"Stand!" Justinian ordered.

The brothers obeyed. Hypatius's drawn face was wet with tears; Pompeius's dry as sand.

"So, Hypatius," Justinian began, "I am told you consider your familial link to Emperor Anastasius to supersede any claim I have. Is that correct?"

Pompeius is the one, I thought.

Hypatius drew himself up, swiping at his tears. "No, master, it is not. You know me. We—we've been on campaign together. We've slept and eaten aside the same battlefields." He paused to draw breath and another thought. "You know me to be honest, master."

"Do I?"

"Yes, master." Hypatius cast a tentative glance at his brother, as if seeking approval. "You see, Pompeius and I wrote a letter meant for you that detailed our *forced* involvement."

Hypatius was trying to shield his brother by saying they *both* wrote it. I had noted at the house that only when Hypatius's wife brought it out did Pompeius learn of its existence and contents.

"This one?" Theodora asked, holding up the unrolled document, her dark eyes fixed on Hypatius.

A twitch played at the corner of Hypatius's mouth. "Yes ... yes," he admitted.

Justinian turned his gaze to Pompeius. "You appear to have your wits about you, Lord Pompeius. Tell me its contents."

Pompeius cleared his throat. "It states, master, that should the rebels take us hostage with the intention of naming one of us emperor, the time will have come for you to intercede."

"And?"

"It invited you to take advantage of your enemies while they were all contained in one closed space, whether that was a forum or the Hippodrome."

"So we could vanquish all the rebels, including the senators and palace officials standing behind you?"

Pompeius's head jerked slightly as if he was going to turn around to face those who had attempted to raise up his brother, but he changed his mind. "Yes," he said in a kind of stage whisper, his face blazing red. "Yes."

"Then, tell me, Lord Pompeius, how you were to see that this letter Empress Theodora is holding was to be delivered to us."

Pompeius visibly swallowed hard, his tongue flicking out. "I—I ..." he stammered.

Even as his brother's stone veneer was cracking, Hypatius squared his shoulders, brushed at his eyes, and found his normal voice. "We meant to, master, that is, we gave it to the eunuch Stephen."

"Which of you gave it to Stephen?" Theodora interjected.

"I did," Pompeius admitted.

"*When* did you give it to Stephen?"

Neither brother responded. Hypatius turned toward the empress, eyes blank like those of a fish on a line. He cast a side glance at his brother, clearly waiting for a rescue.

Pompeius stiffened, maintaining his hard facade, but he had no words.

"Stephen!" Justinian ordered. "Step forward!"

I obeyed, stepping over to stand a couple of paces from Hypatius.

"What do you know about this document in question?"

"I knew of its content and that it was written before we left the house of Hypatius. His wife Maria brought it out."

"Was it given to you then?"

Now I was the fish on the line. There was no saving these two. "No, master."

"Pompeius, *when* did you give the letter to Stephen?"

"I … that is, I—"

At this moment I knew the question would fall upon me. I was to be the brothers' hangman.

But I was wrong.

Hypatius spoke up. "Not long before your Imperial Guard appeared in the kathisma, master."

"And up until that time," Theodora put in, "Stephen was being held against his will. Isn't that so?"

Hypatius continued his own line of thought. "I *meant* for him to bring it to the palace before that, mistress, but—"

"Forgive us, master," Pompeius blurted, putting a stop to a possible indictment from his brother. "Have mercy. We only wish you well. Our fealty belongs only to you." Having found his tongue, Pompeius continued in this vein for several awkward and embarrassing minutes.

Finally, Hypatius turned to his brother. "Don't beg, Pompeius. Don't reduce yourself. If we are to die, we must do so without tears and lamentation."

I was touched by the implicit forgiveness he showed Pompeius, who was the one who might have freed me to take the letter to Justinian. He was the one who had made the choice that would seal the fate of the two brothers. I was also relieved my part in the sad and tragic drama was over.

"Tomorrow you will learn your sentence," Justinian said, pivoting now to his guards. "Take them away,"

Theodora caught my eye and gave me a nod of dismissal, her black eyes glistening with something more, too. If I was the judge of character she thought me, I saw in their depths concern, care, and regret; emotions that would never be voiced. I managed a tight smile and took my leave, glad to be gone before the other rebel leaders were called up before the throne.

"You won't be wearing a purple shroud, my love," Justinian said as he came into his bedchamber. He seemed tired, but he held himself erect. She sensed some of his old equilibrium and confidence had been restored.

"Not yet, anyway," Theodora countered.

It was past midnight. Justinian had allowed the senators and other officials their lives, but he was stripping them of their powers, estates, and wealth. The Imperial Treasury was filling fast with much-needed monies to begin the rebuilding.

On the wide sleeping couch, Theodora lay on her side, one arm propping up her head as she watched Justinian approach. He sat on the bed, his back to her, his tension palpable.

"And the brothers?" she asked.

"I am inclined to be merciful, Thea."

"You mean to treat them in the same way as the others?"

"Yes."

A long minute passed. Theodora held her breath and tongue, fearing her husband's new sense of composure was subsiding into—what? Weakness? She cleared her throat. "Justinian, they had the opportunity to release Stephen with that letter long before the generals took action."

"But they didn't, you're right. I know that."

"No, they did not."

"And yet, the action upon our enemies in the Hippodrome played out just as suggested in their letter."

"By *our* doing and no thanks to the letter."

"Theodora, Hypatius and I went on campaign to Persia together. It was as he said. We became friends."

"I have no doubt. Do you know that I was befriended by their mother in my time in Alexandria. She was of immense help to me in my most trying time, so you see, I have an allegiance to the family, as well." She sent up a silent prayer that he would not ask for details about their mother, Caesaria, who had helped her in the birthing of a son.

"Ah, and yet you would see me handle them harshly?"

Theodora recalled her time at the Pentapolis when her dear friend Irene warned her to take preemptive action against her nemesis Pythia. She had done nothing and lived to deeply regret it.

"Husband, to allow them their freedom even if you strip them of everything is dangerous. It projects weakness. The same band of traitors could reorganize and attempt to raise these two up again. And with all of them in their reduced positions of poverty and humiliation, they would have all the more motivation."

Justinian's back appeared to go rigid. He did not turn to look at her.

"You know," Theodora said, "my father and stepfather were bear trainers. Anyone in that occupation would tell you the same thing. You cannot allow a wounded beast to live."

Justinian gave a little shrug. "You think they are so wounded? That if allowed to live, their gratefulness would not last?"

"About as long as it would take an apple to conquer the appetite of a bear."

A minute or more ticked by.

At last, Justinian twisted about and set his gaze on Theodora. "You know, Thea, I did not see this uprising in the making. Oh, I'm at my best when analyzing old Roman law, or architecture, or the lands I intend to restore to the empire. For me, it's always some far-flung objective in the future."

"But—"

"Shush, allow me to finish. While I analyze with an eye to the future, Thea, you are contemplating the warp and woof of the present. Your mention of their mother and your own fathers also tells me that your present conclusions are governed by your past." Justinian's gray eyes held hers hostage. "Yesterday I put off the purple. Today, against all odds, you returned it." Justinian bent to kiss her. When he pulled back, he said, "We are a match, Thea. We are equals."

Monday, 19 January 532

I awoke the morning after to a grim-faced Piers informing me that at dawn Hypatius and Pompeius had been hanged, their bodies flung out into the Sea of Marmara. The cabal of shamed and newly impoverished riot leaders had been forced to watch. I walked out onto my balcony and looked out to the sea, an emptiness in my gut. I could not help but feel pity for the brothers, especially Hypatius, who had allowed a foreboding and his own good sense to be overruled by others.

There on the balcony I could hear the cries and shrieks of women searching the Hippodrome for the bodies of their loved ones. Never had the Dead Gate been put to such continuous and horrific use. Rumors as to the number of dead abounded, some placing it as high as thirty thousand.

Late in the day I asked Narses about the gossip.

His mouth curved into a tortured smile. "Thirty thousand?" he asked. "That, Stephen, is a conservative estimate."

Within the palace walls, Narses oversaw the Imperial Guard and a phalanx of slave workers as they went out into The City to extinguish the last of the fires with water drawn up from the Bosphorus. A good many nobles and eighteen senators were exiled, their vast wealth confiscated and overseen by Narses. Other nobles who had dared not revolt, but who from the start had resented the reign of Justinian and Theodora, were left to grumble in private. With false smiles, they continued in the following days to prostrate themselves before the double throne.

The actress had triumphed.

PART THREE

20

THEODORA WISHED TO BE KEPT apprised of the newly codified laws, so I sat hunched at my desk copying pages of laws Tribonian had drawn up—at Justinian's prompting—profoundly winnowed from thousands upon thousands of old Roman laws. For her benefit, I wrote in large script, but I did not translate them from the Latin because Theodora had progressed well with the language so that only occasionally did I add a few notes in Greek.

Concentration came hard because of the movements and shouts of men—the raising of scaffolding, hammering, and grinding of stone attending the construction of buildings from dawn to dark. The ruined baths had been cleared almost as fast as the thirty thousand bodies from the Hippodrome. Within just forty days some ten thousand workers had been put to the task of building another Church of the Holy Wisdom. It was my guess the architecturally inclined Justinian must have had the plans drawn up for an incredibly cavernous church even before what was already being called the Nika Riots.

When Piers admitted Tariq to my study a little after noon, I was relieved for the break in routine. His attempt at a smile was no mask to his fatigue and disgruntlement.

"Ah," I said, "that construction all about us has kept you awake. You look about to expire."

"No, it's not that. It's the damn Monophysites."

Justinian had turned the Palace of Hormisdas over to Theodora for the purpose of sheltering the Monophysitic monks and priests who had been expelled from Eastern monasteries and churches. Her attachment to Patriarchs Timothy and Severus and their followers remained strong.

"You haven't graced us with your presence, Stephen, not in some time. You would not recognize the interior."

"Well," I said with a wink, "if you take in all the scrolls and codices spilling about this room, you'll know why I seldom venture out from my study."

"The Monophysites multiply day by day. They've taken over the palace."

"The library and scriptorium?"

"Oh, Brother Leo is holding it together somehow, but his disposition has become as sour as a sewer. Every day more arrive, Stephen, sand in their sandals and stink on their tunics, from expelled bishops to filthy stylites who had been shaken off their pillars of prayer, and everyone in between. The palace echoes with their angelic hymns and canticles, and that's fine as long as you make your way about the halls holding a spring posey to your nose."

I held back a laugh. "How can they host so many?"

"Theodora is having new cells created. Some of the empress's so-called 'living saints' lie on wooden planks cramming the halls, head to foot. Some of our fellow scribes have found other, more fragrant, places to settle, but I'm staying put."

I suspected—or rather, knew—that Theodora looked to the holy men for blessings on her hopes of bearing a child, but I made no mention of it to Tariq.

Later in the day, I was called to Theodora's study in order to prepare a letter. She had already written to a number of ambassadors throughout the East, signifying her increasing confidence and power following the Nika Riots. But the letter this day had no political or religious intent. It was a letter—an order, in essence—for Probus, the cousin of Hypatius and Pompeius to present himself before her in two days. That she did not mention the emperor underscored her increasing sense of empowerment. Probus was to bring with him the eldest of his three sons. Her dictation in delivery and written word was stated directly without a hint of warmth, so I could only wonder at the prickling of cold fear that must have traveled up Probus's spine at its reception. Theodora's spies had informed her that he was residing at the country estate of his uncle, the late former Emperor Anastasius.

In leaving The City before the rioters could find him and make him the focus of their treason, Probus had no doubt thought himself removed from danger. I wondered whether he would appear. Then again, what choice did he have? The arm of the revitalized regime had grown a long reach.

Work continued on rebuilding The City. The slowly rising skeleton of the Church of the Holy Wisdom—its third incarnation, the others ravaged by fire—promised a building of spectacular size and design. Some thirty other churches were also under construction, as well as the Praetorium and a host of official buildings that had been gutted.

An underground passage stretching from the Daphne Wing to the Palace of Hormisdas was completed so that Theodora could visit and pray in secrecy with the Monophysites she sheltered. Justinian sometimes accompanied her. I suspected both he and Theodora prayed for a son on those occasions, but his presence was also a clear sign he was becoming more and more open to a truce between the Dyophysites and the Monophysites even though Justinian had supported his uncle, Emperor Justin, in the persecution of the latter.

The priorities of the two royals differed in other matters. In the busy legislative office, Justinian continued work with Tribonian on the *Codex Justinianus*. In his War Room below the Daphne Wing, he made sweeping plans for the re-conquest of lands that had once belonged to Rome but were lost now to barbaric tribes.

Likewise, Theodora was in no way reticent to wield her influence. While she supported the purchase of peace with Persia, she told me that peace between the Monophysites of the East and the Dyophysites—or Chalcedonians—of Orthodox Rome warranted greater attention. Freedom of worship became her mantra. She also believed the lot of women must be improved, demanding a new status for them, one founded on Christian principles and centered on family life. In addition, she urged reforms for provinces where governors and other officials abused their populations, while at the same time she advanced stronger support for men, money, horses, and supplies for the empire's far-flung provinces. No doubt her motivation in this regard stemmed from the lack of attention the imperial administration paid to the province of the Pentapolis during her time there as concubine to Governor Hecebolus.

With the rise of Theodora's station and power came occasional demonstrations of cruelty about which I heard second or third-hand. The empress rewarded well those who pleased her; however, she targeted with swift vengeance those who crossed her. Certain unlucky souls could find themselves subjected to whips made of ox sinews or housed in a web of dungeons beneath the Daphne Wing with a release date dependent on the whim of an empress. One object of her intense ire was Priscus, the personal secretary of her husband—and for a while my counterpart in the palace—who had openly slandered her. To my knowledge, Justinian said nothing when she had him packed off to a remote island in the Aegean Sea, where his head was shaved prior to being forced to become a deacon. He was perhaps a lucky one, for others vanished altogether.

In the Golden Audience Chamber, Theodora sat alone on the double throne when Probus was admitted. He had been on time, early even, but she kept him waiting a good hour nonetheless.

Probus moved toward her now with halting slowness, his smallish sandals kicking out from under his stone-colored dalmatic. He had been careful to dress austerely, nary a hint of his royal lineage. In his fifth decade, he was shorter than she imagined, maybe no taller than she.

Probus neatly prostrated himself, lifting his head now to kiss the toe of the red royal shoe.

An upward motion of her hand brought him clumsily upright. His perfectly round face was punctuated with dark eyes that darted in her direction, then down toward the floor. He swiped at perspiration on his brow.

"You have served the empire as a consul, yes?" Theodora asked.

His eyes came up. "I did, mistress. In 502."

"And you served well?"

"Yes, mistress."

"And yet, Probus," she said, a lightness in her tone, "in 528 you were brought before the Consistory and convicted of slandering Justinian—is that not true?"

He nodded, uncertainty washing over his reddening face.

"But the emperor forgave you. Perhaps his mercy to you then is why you recently took yourself out of The City during the rebellion? Was it your choice not to become involved in your cousins' treachery?"

Probus cleared his throat as if he were going to answer, but words eluded him.

"Never mind, Lord Probus. You need not answer." Theodora took a moment, wet her lips and said, "You've seen the scope of the rebuilding going on?"

"I have, mistress. Very impressive."

"The deaths of your cousins were unfortunate, Probus."

Probus nodded.

"I want you to know that yesterday the sea returned the body of Hypatius."

Probus's eyes went wide, and he released a nearly silent gasp.

"The body will be given over to you for a proper family burial."

Probus's forehead lifted, pushing back the sparse and graying hairline.

"Further," Theodora said, allowing no time for the words that seemed to crowd the back of Probus's throat, "your house that was burned by the rebels will be rebuilt and the property confiscated by the Treasury—or most of it—will be returned to your family and those of your cousins."

Probus's lower jaw slackened. A bolt from Zeus could not have surprised him more. He stuttered, searching for words before managing a response: "You are very generous, mistress."

"Your expression tells me you are wondering why. I will tell you, Probus. We have a mutual friend—Patriarch Severus."

Probus blinked. "Yes, I knew him before he became Patriarch of Antioch."

"You remain a Monophysite yourself?"

Probus paused, no doubt afraid of falling into a snare by admitting to what some thought a heresy. "I ... I am, mistress."

"I have reason to regret the deaths of your cousins, Probus, because I knew their mother and your aunt, Caesaria, from my time in Alexandria. We became close at a critical time in my life, and I am in her debt for the help she gave, one woman to another." Caesaria had helped her flee from a future men were planning for her, and now, for a few unsteady moments, the old emotions swept through her: first fear, then anger that men should have such power, and finally, resolve to change things.

"I see, mistress."

Theodora blinked back the memory. Now it was time for the biggest surprise. "Today you brought with you your son, Anastasius, so named for the former emperor, your uncle."

"Yes, mistress."

Theodora raised her hand to the silentiary at the far end of the chamber. The court official opened the door to admit a white-faced youth who entered with tentative steps.

Anastasius's first attempt at prostration played out awkwardly, and even though it amused her, she did not tease him by retracting her red shoe for the required kiss, as she did on occasion.

When the boy arose, she saw with some relief that he was taller and more handsome than his father. She gifted him with her most beneficent smile. "I speak to you now, Anastasius, although it could be Tyche herself smiling down on you and finding you worthy."

"Yes, mistress?" The boy shuffled from one foot to the other.

Another smile. "Yes. Today I am betrothing you to my daughter Hyacinth."

The boy's eyes became as round as brass coins and his head moved like on a swivel toward his father. The expressions of both soured, as if poisoned, to different strengths.

"She is as lovely as a butterfly," Theodora continued unfazed, "and she will give you—and the empire—children. Do you understand?"

Without waiting for the pair to arrange their faces and choke out a reply, Theodora waved again to the silentiary, signaling another prearranged entrance.

A vision dressed in a red dalmatica embossed in gold now swept into the room and prostrated herself before the empress.

"Ah, this is Lady Antonina," Theodora announced, her gaze set on Probus's son. "She will accompany you now, Anastasius, to meet your intended."

Antonina stood and motioned for the boy and his father to make their final bows and back out of the chamber. The two wore matching frowns but followed her lead.

Once Theodora deemed the two out of earshot, she called Antonina back to the foot of the throne.

"Yes, Thea?"

"You spoke to Hyacinth?"

"I did."

"She's in agreement?"

"She will come around, I'm sure."

"Handsome enough he is, I think, not to mention bearing royal lineage. Mentor my daughter as needed."

"I will, Thea." Antonina bowed and started to back out, observing the formality of the audience chamber, where, in public, she played the supplicant, rather than childhood friend.

"Oh, and Nina," Theodora said.

Antonina halted and looked up.

Theodora smiled, releasing each word like a missile: "Hands off the boy."

On a late summer's day, a quiet procession led by Justinian and Theodora made its way through the underground tunnel from the Daphne Wing to the Palace of Hormisdas, where Hyacinth was married to the youth Anastasius by a Monophysitic bishop. Tariq told me the small chapel had to be cleared of dozens of monks and their sleeping pallets before it could accommodate the guests—but the scents of beeswax candles and the woody and spicy Frankincense did not fully ameliorate the body odors left behind by these living saints and former stylites.

The couple took up temporary residence in the small Blue House on the palace grounds, where Antonina sometimes visited in Theodora's stead. Hestia, Hyacinth's stepmother, remained in attendance.

By the end of the year, confidence reigned in the palace. Justinian continued production of his *Codex Justinianus*. And with the death of Persian King Kavad I, successful negotiations with his son and successor Khosrow I were achieved, ushering in an "Eternal Peace" between the two nations. Thus, Justinian's interest turned to regaining Roman land lost to barbarian tribes. He felt secure enough on the throne to release Belisarius from safeguarding the palace, charging him with the retaking of North Africa from the Vandals, spanning the area from the western edges of the Pentapolis to Gibraltar. Justinian planned for a separate campaign to follow that would conquer the Ostrogoths and win back Sicily and Italy.

21

THEODORA BEGAN PLANS FOR A grand spring pilgrimage to Bithynia, a Roman province at the northwestern tip of Asia Minor, south of the Black Sea and adjacent to the Sea of Marmara and the Bosphorus Strait.

As I wrote out her letters of requisition that were to be delivered to John of Cappadocia, my mind faltered as to the scale and nature of her expectations. I was only too glad to send them by messenger in order to avoid the likely explosive reaction of the budget conscious praetorian prefect.

This was the Theodora I imagined within her theater life years ago, the woman who had her hand in everything: organization, writing, costuming, staging, acting, directing—except that now she was exalted high on a world stage. And the glittering production she was preparing now—well, not even the Hippodrome could contain it.

February 533

In the Hall of the Consistory, Theodora sat to the left of Justinian at the head of the deliberation table, listening to men talk of war. Aware of several absences left by traitors during the Nika Riots, she directed her gaze past Lord Chamberlain Narses and Anastasia's husband Peter Barsymes, focusing now on the faces of two men who, at the will of the people, had been driven from their public posts for their dishonest dealings, only to have been returned to the positions for which they had been denounced. She would have wished them gone, but could not always exert her influence on her husband.

Theodora knew Justinian depended on the lawyerly skills of Tribonian in creating the *Codex Justinianus*, so she said nothing when he was returned to the fold. But John of Cappadocia! Her back stiffened just to see him sitting once again at a Silence, so intense did her enmity for the once-again praetorian prefect surge. And gowned in an embroidered dalmatic worthy of a Holy Father—what gall! She looked to the small bowl of prize Syrian apples he had made a show of presenting, and she reached for one, along with the ivory handled paring knife he had included.

The plans drawn up by Justinian and Belisarius for reclaiming North Africa from the Vandals were on the table. Most of the councilors were not enthusiastic about the venture, but John was the most outspoken in his displeasure and criticism, railing against the costs—not in lives, but in gold. At no point in his speeches did he glance at her.

Theodora was torn. She did wonder whether too little time—a year—had passed since the Nika Riots that The City could ill afford to send Belisarius and his household mercenaries out on campaign against barbarians, and without a certainty of success. Nevertheless, she took her husband's part. No longer reticent to speak during the Silences, she asked, "What is it, Lord John, about the proposed defeat of heretics and the victory of Rome and the Church that irritates you?"

John gaped at her, collected himself, and attempted a smile. "*Both* are worthy goals, mistress, but the costs at this time are too high."

Theodora matched his false smile. "Why is that, Lord John?"

"Why?" he asked, flashing an expression he might use to explain something simple to a child. He released a long breath. "As you know, we are in the midst of a massive building program."

"Yes, of course. Much of the city was destroyed. Were the buildings to be left in piles of broken stone and ash?"

"No, mistress, but I am telling the emperor that with cost overruns, there is no capital for foreign ventures, such as wars and extensive tours and the like."

Tours! John's comment was a scarcely veiled reference to the requisitions she had Stephen send him for funding what was becoming her ever-enlarging pilgrimage to Bithynia. Theodora suspected he meant to bring it up once the question of war in North Africa was settled. *How much more can I despise this man?*

"My lord," Theodora said, "it was my understanding these many years that you had talents enough to turn desert stone into gold. Isn't that why the emperor returned your position to you?"

"I have no such powers, mistress."

"Really?" Theodora paused, readying her declaration of war. "Why, I know dozens of taxpayers here and all along the Levant right on into Egypt and Africa who say otherwise, so enthusiastically have they been taxed. While I say *enthusiastically*, some would say *savagely*. Of course, Lord John, surely they must be exaggerating because I know the kinds of sums they speak of have not found their way into the Imperial Treasury."

It was Justinian, who spoke as arbiter. "Lord John, we know you will not fail us. Isn't that so?"

Theodora watched John's face color. The royals' spontaneous trap could not have been better played even if planned.

John looked from Justinian to Theodora and back again. "Yes, master, of course."

Theodora's heart leaped. Her husband's war would go forward, and she was now certain John would not dare bring up the costs of her religious pilgrimage to Bithynia.

She watched the Cappadocian with some satisfaction as the Silence continued. He was afraid of her. He knew she could bring him down, as she had done to others. Her spies had informed her that he traveled now with a bodyguard and kept two nearby at night while he slept.

He could sleep for now, she thought. He was too much in her husband's favor. But the day would come when she *would* bring him down, bodyguards or not.

April 533

With no little anxiety, I held my breath in anticipation of the praetorian prefect's disapproval as Theodora's elaborate plans for the pilgrimage to Bithynia went forward, the many layers of the empress's careful, cunning goals tallying up like the many-layered and honey-drenched Athenian *plakous* cake. It was to be more than a rich display of her power, possessions, and beauty—much more.

One concern involved the empire's relationship with Persia. She invited a large Persian delegation to Bithynia so that they could witness the pomp and power of the New Rome that had come back from the brink—the Nika Riots—standing now richer and stronger than before. She felt confident that the display would discourage Persia from attempting any new challenge to the Eternal Peace.

Another concern lay in Theodora's loyalty to the Monophysitic compatriots she was sheltering. She was heartened by an edict Justinian had just issued that followed months of dialogues between Chalcedonian and Monophysitic luminaries in the Palace of Hormisdas. In the declaration, Justinian, a Chalcedonian, conceded as much ground as possible to the Monophysites without fully breaking with Rome.

One day, however, I learned of the key goal of the Bithynia excursion that was closest to Theodora's heart. It came as a stage aside to Antonina I happened to overhear. "I'll never forgive or forget him, Nina," she spat. "I prostrated myself before that befouled monk instead of expecting the same of him, and he humiliated me here, in my own palace. May he be damned!"

Theodora was referring to the saintly Dyophysitic Abbot Sabbas whom, two years before, she had begged to bless her womb, allowing her to conceive and bear Justinian a child, a son to continue the royal line. The monk had not only ignored her request, but he had told me that he would not allow the empire to fall into the clutches of Monophysites, saying, "Better it is that she is barren!"

The empress's dearest wish had not faded away. She still longed with every beat of her heart to bear Justinian's child.

As the years went by, I mistakenly began to think the subject—her desire for a child—was fading. Only now did I realize how she still grasped onto the hope that she still might bear the next Emperor of the New Roman Empire.

Theodora stood at Justinian's side in the Great Baptistery of the partially rebuilt Church of the Holy Wisdom. A close cousin of General Belisarius's household, a young man with ties to the Arian heresy, was to be baptized into the Orthodox faith prior to accompanying Belisarius on campaign against the Vandals in North Africa. By attending, Theodora was bowing to Justinian's wish to do honor to Belisarius. She smiled at Patriarch Epiphanius despite her irritation at being taken away from her pilgrimage plans, and for being kept waiting by the tardy Antonina and her husband.

At last, Belisarius and Antonina appeared side by side walking toward the baptismal crib, newly minted of Marmara white marble with its gray striping. The couple's gold-trimmed formal wear glittered in the sunshine, for the structure remained roofless. Belisarius tugged at his beard and pulled a face that begged forgiveness for their tardiness. Theodora watched from the opposite side of the font as the couple came forward and stepped apart, allowing the young cousin to advance into the breach.

Theodora drew in a silent breath at her first glimpse of the fledgling soldier. Dressed in an undyed tunic, he could have played the hero in Homer's epic. Here was the striking Odysseus whom Athena had made even more perfect. Dark curls toppled onto his wide forehead above pearl gray eyes that sparkled as they took in the royal couple and the patriarch. He bowed respectfully, no doubt confident that the setting precluded the necessity of prostrating himself. He was not particularly tall, but a single glance at his godly features forgave everything.

So then, this is Theodosius, she thought, recalling now the peculiar intonation in Antonina's voice when she had spoken of him two days earlier.

The patriarch moved toward Theodosius and Godparents Belisarius and Antonina, citing their responsibilities in a low voice and leading them in a prayer.

Directed now by the patriarch, Theodosius removed his tunic, revealing a militarily sculpted body, naked except for a white loin cloth. He climbed the three steps to the lip of the font and descended four steps into the large, oval-shaped pool. Garbed in black, the patriarch followed Theodosius into the waist-high water, prayerfully reminding his small audience of the likeness of the marble steps to those that led Jesus to his baptism in the Jordan River. Chanting in Latin, the patriarch proceeded to immerse Theodosius in the water three times.

At the conclusion of the ceremony, Theodosius was wrapped in a white robe and hurried off to the Hall of the Nineteen Couches where a formal celebration was to take place.

Theodora took Antonina aside before she could leave the Great Baptistery. "Your godson is very handsome, Nina," she whispered, her tone devoid of inflection.

"Indeed!" Antonina blurted, her sparkling blue eyes fastened on the middle distance.

Theodora reached out and covered her friend's hand with hers. "Your *god-*

son, Nina," she said, waiting for Antonina's gaze to return to her. "Remember that."

Even though I was well aware of the political and personal goals of Theodora's pilgrimage, as the days of preparation grew fewer and the plans more extravagant, I became concerned the undertaking was becoming more and more unmanageable with the number of participants, the luxuries involved, and the sheer expense. Amazingly, however, as I submitted Theodora's increasingly outrageous requisitions for men and money, the Office of the Praetorian Prefect, registered no complaint.

22

ON A BRIGHT AND BLUSTERY day, Theodora's pilgrimage began as a massive flotilla set off from four of the seven harbors in the capital. Tariq let out a low whistle as the cluster of light boats coalesced, streaming now across the Bosphorus toward the Kingdom of Bithynia. "The empress has not forgotten her theater days," he said.

"It appears so, Tariq." We stood in the prow of a boat crowded with minor officials and silentiaries. It was so true. After the dark and bloody days of the Nika Riots when The City suffered near ruination and thirty thousand deaths, Theodora's theatrical production was offering the people an event of unequaled splendor, riches, and pomp. Whether her handiwork would be well received remained a question.

The citizens of Bithynia turned out by the thousands as we docked at their harbors on the Black Sea. Tariq and I were just two of the four thousand pilgrims and attendants disembarking from the countless boats, along with four elephants and six giraffes commandeered from the animal quarters in the depths of the Hippodrome.

The three-week tour began in earnest with the slow, lumbering pace of the elephants leading the way, followed by palace officials, Monophysitic monks, eunuchs, silentiaries, slaves, and Imperial Guards. Then, like the final act of a perfect play, came Theodora's purple-cushioned litter, its gold embroidered curtains open so that she could wave to her subjects and receive their adulation.

Theodora had need of me now and then to record something for the historic nature of the event, so Tariq and I followed close. Behind us the elegant giraffes and their trainers completed the procession.

"Do you know," I said to Tariq at one of our many stops, "ten years ago Theodora and I arrived in Constantinople on the same day and on the same ship, and this is our first journey away from The City."

Tariq pointed to where Theodora sat beneath a hastily erected purple canopy, drinking a cool libation from a diamond encrusted gold goblet. "To different ends, the two of you, yes?"

I sighed. "Yes, different ends, my friend, but I do not hold her ascent against her."

He cast a glance at me that I could not decipher. "I believe you," he said.

As the procession snaked inland toward the thermal waters near Mount Olympus, we stopped at intervals when the crowds swelled, allowing Theodora to speak through her baritone herald, promising her citizens to replace the broken roads and to construct splendid new churches. She called on the people to pray for the success of the empire. The massacre at the Hippodrome was slipping into history as Empress Theodora became for the people a goddess of goodness and light. Those witnesses to the procession would take their impressions far and wide. She was well aware of that.

"She is like Demeter," Tariq marveled.

His thought caught me by surprise because I had often thought of her as Aphrodite, ever since Narses had pointed out to me a striking statue of the goddess of love and beauty. I thought about his comment awhile, then finally said, "Tariq, I'm baffled. *How* is she like the Harvest Goddess?"

"Well, Demeter chose a path unlike that of her contemporary goddesses. She would not submit to the boundaries of Mount Olympus. She went to the temples of her followers, staying close to and drawing energy from those who worshiped her. The goddess accepted their veneration and used her powerful station to give back."

"Like new churches and roads?"

Tariq shrugged. "Yes, but more than that. Demeter allowed the lowest of plebeians to celebrate and share in her good fortune. For the briefest of moments, they could share the stage with her. They could become something completely out of their reach. They could *be* her."

"I see," I said. "You know, Tariq, sometimes your observations surprise me. You're right. While she may have the beauty of Aphrodite, she has the persona of Demeter."

"Ha!" Tariq cried. "So we share in our observation."

I laughed, too. "As friends should!"

Traveling with Theodora and walking behind her litter was the humble John, the Monophysitic Bishop of Tella, a southeastern city not far from the Syrian border. John had been ousted from the See of Antioch years before by Emperor Justin's persecution of Monophysites, after which he traveled between the empire and Persia, preaching and ordaining clergy. He had served as the most effective anti-Chalcedonian debater in Justinian's dialogues at the Palace of Hormisdas, but when he witnessed no lasting results forthcoming, he continued his preaching crusade, coming finally to be given quarter by Theodora. On this pilgrimage, John spoke to the masses at each stop without use of a herald, holding them spellbound with his humble and heartfelt explanations of Christianity, thus converting thousands to Monophysitism.

Theodora's desire to capture the hearts and minds of her people while promulgating the religion of her mentors, Patriarchs Timothy and Severus, met with wondrous success.

Day by day, Theodora exulted in the sensation she was creating.

On the day before reaching the thermal baths, Bishop John approached her. "Mistress, I wish to introduce you to Lord Bishop Anthimus."

Theodora could not help but flinch at the name of a man known to be a Chalcedonian. "I know the Bishop of Trebizond." As the thin man grasped hold of the folds of his robe in order to prostrate himself, she added, "Oh, you needn't do that in this wretched and rutted road."

Anthimus smiled, nodded, and bowed instead.

When John excused himself because it was his time to preach at the front of the crowd, Anthimus asked, "Mistress, you know me?"

Theodora nodded. "While I was not invited to attend the dialogues my husband held last year between the elite members of the Chalcedonians—like yourself—and the Monophysites, I did follow them closely."

"Through your hus—the emperor, I mean to say?"

"Yes, and others. So you see, I was kept aware of the cast of players."

"As if the dialogues—as the emperor called it—were a play."

Theodora's throat tightened. *Is he alluding to my past in the theater? Is this a veiled insult?* "One without entertainment value," she countered. "My reports coming back from the Palace of Hormisdas indicated you were the strongest speaker for those of the Orthodox position."

"To your dismay, I imagine."

Theodora forced a smile and waved her hand dismissively. "What is important is that the dialogues offered a bit of hope for a future union of the two sides." She took a breath, her eyes on his reaction. "So, tell me, Lord Bishop Anthimus, how is it you have joined us here? The Trebizond Province is some distance to the East."

"Ah, but the Black Sea reduces the time it would take on the overland roads."

"Pitted, such as these, you mean?"

Anthimus offered an awkward smile.

"I'll see something is done about them. I've promised my people. Now, Lord Bishop Anthimus, you have not answered my question. Why are you joining us, if that is your intent?"

"It is, mistress. John sent word of your pilgrimage, not that he had to, for everyone in Trebizond has heard of its wonders. John suggested I come. Since the dialogues in the capital last year, John and I have struck up a fine friendship."

"Really?"

"Yes, mistress. In truth, I've had a change of heart regarding the chasm between the Orthodox and Monophysitic points of view. John is a persuasive speaker."

"This is surprising, Anthimus, if your words are sincere."

"Oh, I am sincere, mistress. You spoke of hope. Did the emperor come away from the talks with a sense of hope?"

"In time, he sees a union as possible. After the dialogues, my husband asked those Monophysites who took part how a merging might come to be. They suggested that Monophysites held only the smallest of the five sees, but if bishops friendlier to the cause—"

"Anti-Chalcedonians?"

Theodora nodded. "Or bishops open to ending the estrangement. Now, if such bishops were installed in larger episcopal sees, a union might be accomplished."

"Like Alexandria, or Constantinople, for that matter."

It was not a question, so Theodora allowed it to pass without an avowal. "In not so very many years—or months—new bishops will be needed. Come, Anthimus, let's find a cushioned chair under my canopy there, where we can talk more. Oh, my secretary is just a few paces away, you see," she said, pointing to Stephen and Tariq some yards away. "See—the handsome Syrian one—Stephen. Now, before we part ways, be certain to inform him how we can write to one another—in strictest secrecy, you understand."

Anthimus's eyebrows lifted. "I do, mistress."

We spent several days at the baths at Pythia Thermal where Theodora bathed multiple times. Twice a day, when her large and elaborate overnight tent was closed and guarded, I assumed her to be sleeping—or praying. Whether the restorative waters would bring an answer to her prayers, making her womb fruitful, remained to be seen.

Three weeks after our arrival in Bithynia, we boarded the boats to return to The City.

23

"THEA, THEA, HOW I MISSED you," Justinian said, his passion spent. He lay on his side next to her. He had come to her sleeping couch in the women's quarters.

Theodora turned toward him, giving out with a little laugh. "Why, then I shall make more such pilgrimages."

"Not any time soon, I pray. And you must never again stay away so long." Justinian pulled her closer, his sharp gray eyes capturing hers. "After all, we have our work right here. Right here."

His directness surprised her, and she felt gooseflesh rising on her arms. He seldom spoke of his—their—hopes for an heir. But there it was. She adjusted her gaze to the middle distance. She didn't answer him. Her mind slipped back to the many instances of immersing herself in the thermal pool at Bithynia and the prayers she had invoked. How she longed to feel something happening in her body, some sense of a change. However, the warmth of the water is all she felt. She chided herself now for thinking something momentous would occur at the thermal waters. Still, her hope held. If something miraculous is to ensue, she thought, it would take place *right here*, as Justinian said.

In good time Justinian rose and dressed, as she knew he would. When he bent to kiss her, she whispered, "How little you sleep." She knew well enough he was departing for the underground War Room to continue the plans to take back North Africa from the Vandals.

Alone, she lay with her hands clasped to her belly for some minutes before calling for her handmaiden Phaedra, who helped her into a purple dressing gown. It was too early for sleep. She moved into the adjacent chamber and went to the window overlooking the little house of Egyptian porphyry, dark now in the shadows of night.

Closing her eyes, she imagined herself seated in the jewel-encrusted birthing chair. *If I think it,* she reasoned, *long enough and with faith in God, it will happen. It will!*

At that moment Phaedra entered to announce Antonina, who was already rushing forward to embrace her. "Forgive me, Thea, it's late, I know. I came earlier but was told you were with Justinian and the silentiary's expression told the story. You're wicked, Theodora—no wasting time with you!" She tossed back her blond tresses and laughed.

Theodora felt a flush of heat in her face. That she could still be embarrassed about such things surprised her. Her shared past with Antonina gave freedom to their conversations. She bit her lip and turned away, glancing out the window.

Antonina sidled up to her. "Ah, the little red house," she trilled.

"More purple than red, Nina."

"Indeed. Always the purple." Before Theodora could register offense, Antonina continued, "It's thrilling, isn't it? The royal lying-in house is about to be put to use. Your prayers at Bithynia have been answered. I hear even before your boat sailed home into the Harbor of Hormisdas, the citizens were calling the thermal waters the *royal baths?*"

Theodora turned to face her friend. "What?" Was she alluding to Justinian's visit to her rooms? "Don't be stupid, Nina. There is no way to know—are you a seer now?"

"Oh my!" Antonina exclaimed. "You don't know! Of course, you don't, I can see that."

"Know what, Antonina? *What?*"

"Hyacinth is going to gift you with a grandchild."

Theodora produced a tight smile, unwilling to relay the fact they were talking at cross purposes.

I made my way down the several terraces to the Palace of Hormisdas, preferring the night air and the glittering of the moon and stars in the Sea of Marmara to the new tunnel connecting the palace to the Daphne Wing. It had been a good while since I had been here so that now I experienced the full effect of the changes Tariq had described.

Once the guards opened the doors for me, the relentlessly fetid odors struck. And then came the multitude of holy men, old and young, many ragged and reeking as if they had just come down from their columns. They were lying or sitting on pallets and planks lined up throughout the halls, passages, stair landings, and various chambers that afforded a look through open doors. One would expect them to behave like the beggars on the Mese who held out cups for coins, but these men were deep in thought or prayer; some were chanting to themselves.

Tariq answered his door.

"Holy Mithra, Tariq," I said, "Is this a palace or a marble *latrina*?"

Tariq laughed. "You get used to it. This is quite a surprise, Stephen. You've come for a game of *Shatranj*, I hope? The board is ready."

"No, sorry." I took a breath. "I'm here at the request of the empress."

"What?" Even by the flickering, weak light of his clay lamps, I saw him blanch. "It's true. She has a task for you.—Are you going to invite me to sit?"

As we settled in his small room, the *Shatranj* board on a table between us, Tariq said, "The last time I performed a task it was to tell her how her husband the emperor had been routed from the Hippodrome. I doubt she holds me in good stead."

"But she does."

Tariq poured me some wine. "All right, out with it!"

"Theodora wants you to observe two persons."

"What? Why me? She has a whole phalanx of spies. Why, weren't you supposed to have been one?"

I laughed. "That was more in jest than anything, something she and I bantered about."

"Who am I to observe?"

"A husband and wife."

"Yes?"

"Belisarius and—"

"Antonina! You're joking!"

"I am not."

"But he's about to leave for North Africa on campaign."

I nodded. "True enough. They both are."

"Both? So, this is short term, while they are here in the capital?"

"Not quite. You are to accompany them on campaign."

Tariq's mouth fell open. "And risk my life in the midst of a war with Vandals? Barbarians? You're crazy! She's—"

"Be careful, Tariq."

"Under what guise am I to pull this off?"

"The empress plans ahead. It's been worked out."

"Without my knowledge?"

I chuckled. "She is the empress."

"And the plans?"

"Procopius always brings a scribe along to act as his functionary."

"Yes, I know. A monk, Brother Albert."

"Theodora has arranged with Brother Leo for Brother Albert to be gravely ill at sailing time. He will insist Procopius settles for *you*."

Tariq's head retracted slightly. "If I may ask, why not *you*?"

"For several reasons; Theodora needs me to continue my usual secretarial tasks; also, because of my position with the empress, Belisarius and Antonina would be too cautious in front of me; most immediate, however, is the fact Procopius hates me and would rather go without a functionary than be saddled with me."

Tariq sighed in defeat. "How long will this venture take, assuming I live through it."

"Wars are uncertain things," I said, draining my cup.

June 533

On a perfect summer's day, I bade goodbye to my friend Tariq, who sailed on board the naval flagship with General Belisarius, Antonina, their godson Theodosius, Antonina's son Photius by an early marriage, and Tariq's new superior, Procopius, who evidently had not argued about the replacement. Undoubtedly, he appraised one scribe no more valuable than the next. In any event, Tariq's career as a spy was taking wing.

Patriarch Epiphanius stood a short distance away from me at the dock of the Harbor of Hormisdas blessing the assembling fleet. I silently wished Tariq well because, to hear Procopius on the subject, the forces of ten thousand infantry and five thousand cavalry committed to the re-conquest of Africa were less than needed, especially if a naval battle ensued with the substantially larger Vandalic Navy. And yet, the skin on my arms turned to gooseflesh at the sight of some ninety fast war galleys and five hundred troop transports coalescing in the shimmering Sea of Marmara, their bows pointed in the direction of the Hellespont and the Aegean Sea. In truth, I felt a bit jealous of Tariq and his new adventure.

As the flotilla began to move, I turned and glanced up at the walls of the Daphne Wing. The couple Patriarch Epiphanius had married and elevated to their thrones a few years before stood on a balcony. Justinian's hand was raised in blessing. Theodora stood beautiful and perfectly still, like the purple porphyry statue of her that had recently been erected at the entrance of the restored Baths of Zeuxippus.

January 534

On a winter's day months later, a disconcerted Piers nearly tripped over himself as he entered my study to announce in his wobbly voice: "The Mistress Theodora."

I rose to my feet.

Theodora brushed past him, purple dalmatica impeccably draped, an unrolled document clutched in her hand. "News from Tariq at last," she cried. "You must read it to me at once. His writing appears to get even smaller."

"But it wouldn't take long—"

"Oh, I don't have time for you to tamper with it. Just read it."

"Yes, Thea, of course."

She handed me the long scroll, and I sat while she took the chair in front of the desk.

Wetting my lips, I began.

We have avoided contact with the fleet of the enemy Vandals—a blessing that. After what seemed like weeks of sailing a circuitous sea lane we arrived close to Carthage, much to the surprise of its citizens and army so that we entered suffering few casualties. The king's brother fell in a skirmish. King Gelimer himself had been some distance away at his country estate, and by the time he prepared his main forces for engagement, his brother's death and burial had slowed him down, dooming his chances against General Belisarius and his ferocious mercenaries. The general says the death took an emotional toll, as well. Gelimer fled back to his country estate while the general, Lady Antonina, and the rest of us lounged in the great hall of his splendid palace, feasting on a hearty meal originally prepared for the Vandal king's expected arrival.

"Yes, yes," Theodora blurted, "the victory was impressive enough! All of that was in Procopius's report Belisarius sent today. What else?"

Tariq had been instructed to follow Antonina's movements, so I knew Theodora expected news or gossip about her. Scanning ahead, eyes peeled for her name, I found that Tariq did not disappoint.

"Thea," I said, "it appears the water supplies on the ships became tainted with algae in the barrels, causing sickness, but before sailing, the water on the flagship was well-preserved by Antonina, who insisted on bottling it and placing the receptacles in cool sand."

Theodora snickered. "A woman of many talents, she is."

"He also writes that Antonina has blamed John of Cappadocia for the food poisoning episode that occurred en route to Carthage."

"What?" Theodora sat forward, her translucent complexion waxing pink. "Procopius wrote nothing of any food poisoning! Oh, of course, John is likely to blame. He was against the whole campaign from the start. 'Too costly,' he said."

I continued with the report in my own words. "Tariq writes that it was the Cappadocian who ordered the ships' biscuits to be baked once instead of twice, and they spoiled badly, killing a good many soldiers along the route. It appears they were the only form of nourishment."

Theodora's delicate lower jaw dropped. "Some nourishment—How many?"

"Five hundred."

Theodora gasped. "If only the emperor had not reinstated the Cappadocian. The vile creature! The people were right about him. You can wager his cost cutting has somehow put gold in his own coffers!" She took a breath. "Very well, go on."

I searched again for Antonina's name. "He writes that the decisive victory against King Gelimer occurred on 15 December at Tricamarum, near Carthage. While Belisarius led the cavalry into battle, it was Lady Antonina who followed on horseback, leading the infantry into the fray."

"Ha!" Theodora cried. "I told my sisters she has the coin purse of a man!" Theodora started to laugh at her bawdy joke, but then her eyes caught mine and her lids came down in what I interpreted as embarrassment. For just a moment, I thought she would apologize, but she drew herself up and said, "Justinian will be pleased. He's reading Procopius's report now."

"Oh, Thea," I said, teasing. "You don't mean to say you read the official report before the emperor read it?"

The heavily lashed eyelids flew back, and she gave the hint of a smile I interpreted as, *What do you think?*

"I'm happy for Justinian," she said after a minute or two. "This clinches the re-conquest of North Africa and lays the groundwork for pushing on to Italy.—Any other mention of Antonina?"

My eyes scanned ahead. "Indirectly. Tariq notes that there is no love lost between Antonina's son Photius and her godson Theodosius. He is at a loss as to what the cause might be."

"Ah, she dislikes her own son. It's quite unnatural. As for Theodosius, well, is there more about him?"

"No."

Theodora's black eyes widened in surprise, as if she had been waiting patiently for some further fruit of Tariq's spying.

April 534

A single ship from Carthage arrived at the Harbor of Julian, bringing with it Procopius's report detailing the long-awaited official surrender of King Gelimer. One of Theodora's spies—acting as go-between—also saw to it that Tariq's letter was safely placed in the empress's hands. Theodora wasted no time before calling me to her private study to read it.

"Move past the details about the Vandals' surrender," she ordered. "What else does he have to say?"

I did not have to scan far down the parchment before discovering something startling, and something, I came to realize, she had suspected.

My throat went dry, so I paused, fumbling with a goblet of water. "Tariq writes," I began, rephrasing as I read, "that even before their arrival in Carthage, in the close quarters of the flagship he had begun to realize Antonina's relationship with her godson was, in Tariq's words, 'singularly uncommon'."

Theodora released a muzzled interjection of an unhappy nature, one I did not hear clearly, so I glanced up. The pinched look she gave me made it clear she was not going to repeat it.

I began again. "Tariq says he did not bring it up in his earlier missive because he could not believe a woman nearing her fourth decade could become so besotted with a youth such as Theodosius, his godlike handsomeness notwithstanding."

Theodora grunted. "Your friend has led a sheltered life."

I could do little but nod and continue. "He states here that the two—Antonina and Theodosius—are much caught up in an affair and after arriving at Carthage, they have been so bold about it that both servants and soldiers have been wagging their tongues."

"Great Hera, I did see this coming long ago."

"Your Syrian sight?" I joked.

Her gaze tightened on me as if she were to launch an arrow. She was not amused. "What exactly is the current situation?"

"He writes that as yet, Belisarius has not discovered his wife's adultery."

"I'm not surprised. He's still so much in love with her. Ha! But even a blind pig can discover an acorn now and then."

I soldiered on. "There's more, Thea. The servants have also observed both Belisarius and Antonina cataloging all the gold and riches in the sunken treasure rooms of King Gelimer's palace."

"Yes?" Her back went rigid.

"They—the servants and soldiers—are convinced a good deal of the valuables are not being tagged for the Imperial Treasury."

"Ah, thievery." Theodora clucked her tongue.

"You don't seem surprised."

"I'm not. Last week we had a secret message from some of Belisarius's officers who are questioning the general's loyalty to the throne. Oh, we are aware Belisarius has been paying his mercenaries from his own coffers, so naturally some booty would be needed to pay them, but—"

"The question is, how much?"

Theodora thought for a moment. "Well, yes, there is that, Stephen, but more importantly, there is the question of power. You know, successful generals have been known to seek their own throne."

Theodora noted the surprise on my face. "You're like my husband, I think. Too trusting. Always willing to give the benefit of the doubt or outright forgiveness. Why, if I had not stepped in, Hypatius would still be freely walking the Mese."

"And a likely rallying point for a new cabal?"

Theodora nodded. "A leader can be too good-hearted," she said, releasing a long sigh. "You see, Belisarius is being recalled, not for questioning, mind you, but for a grand public welcome to be held in the Hippodrome. Justinian isn't about to forget his past victories and loyalty, but we, or rather, *I* have a better eye on him."

Theodora gave a little nod, her signal our meeting had come to an end. When I rose and turned toward the door, she said, as if through her teeth, "As for me, I'll have some words for Lady Antonina."

24

THEODORA DESCENDED THE NARROW STONE steps into the bowels of the Daphne Wing. Avoiding the passage that ran to the right where the royal dungeons were located, she cut to the left and soon found herself in Justinian's War Room.

"I hear there was a ship from Africa," she said. "What news? What was Belisarius's response?"

"He's coming home and he's bringing Gelimer himself and cartloads of the treasures the Vandals had looted from Rome in 455."

"I see. No doubt a few cartloads have found other homes."

Justinian shrugged. "It's the way of war, Thea. His *bucellarii* and other mercenaries have to be paid."

"What about the riches he and Antonina have been holding back for themselves?"

"Reportedly so. I'll ask."

"You are too kind and trusting, husband."

"Listen, Thea, there has been no such Roman victory like this since the early days of the empire."

"I know, but—"

"And, my dear, there has been no such homecoming as the one Belisarius will experience."

"That is a mistake, Justinian. Who knows how much wealth he has been acquiring, how many apostles he has brought to himself, or how many idolizing bootlickers are ready to answer to *his* orders?"

"We tested him, did we not? We agreed to give him the choice of remaining in Africa with the enticement of being named praetorian prefect there—or returning to Constantinople with Gelimer in chains."

"So?"

"If he had his eye on the throne, he would have stayed to enjoy a seat of power that would further build his base. You've been listening to rumors at court, have you?"

"And warnings from his own lieutenants, if you recall."

"Trust me. I have a background with such military men as Belisarius."

"Do you?" Theodora asked, thinking, *But not with such women as his wife Antonina.*

"Oh, it's good we don't always agree, Thea. We complement one another."

"You're set on giving him a glittering welcome, yes?"

Justinian nodded.

"Then allow me to put my theater background to work."

"How?"

"Place me in charge of the homecoming production."

Justinian's eyes narrowed in amused suspicion. "What do you have in mind, Thea?"

"I think I know what he wants of his life."

"And that is?"

"Gold, glory, worshippers, and prominence."

"He has achieved all that, dearest."

"But I will put it on display for The City."

"Very well, I entrust you with the welcoming." Justinian waved a hand over a large table with maps spread out. "Now, I have a bit of planning to do myself."

"It's late, Justinian. What *are* you doing down here?"

"Mapping out Belisarius's next move. On to Italy."

September 534

Just as I had been involved in Theodora's preparations for the Bithynia pilgrimage, I was given responsibilities—of a letter and order writing character—having to do with the triumphant return of General Belisarius. Theodora dictated letters for the demarchs of the Green and Blue factions, city officials, Church hierarchy, as well as requests for significant funds from John of Cappadocia, who acquiesced without remonstrances although our usual courier reported dark, seething reactions.

While the Bithynia excursion proved remarkably successful, the Belisarius homecoming was to be even more magnificent, lacking only the elephants and giraffes. But it would not be without controversy.

Theodora confided in me that while Justinian wished for Belisarius to have an ostentatious show of welcome, she—fearing his ambition—meant to temper the festivities. "You see, Stephen," she said, "my husband is guileless. I do love that. But a woman's instinct is twice the worth of a man's reason."

The lead ships of the returning flotilla anchored at the Harbor of Theodosius on 06 September. Belisarius arrived at the palace the next day for a clandestine meeting with Justinian, but Theodora granted no such audience to Antonina. I was given the awkward task of turning her away, saying she was unwell, but keenly aware that she meant to save her "words" regarding Antonina's adulterous affair for later.

The homecoming spectacle was set for the next Wednesday, 13 September, the one-year anniversary of General Belisarius' march into Carthage. A long letter detailing explicit directions for the hero of the day was sent to General Belisarius's mansion, located at the far end of the Mese, near the Golden Gate at the stone double Theodosian Walls. No detail was too small. Theodora intended everything to run smooth as China silk.

From the day news of the Carthage victory had been carried back to Constantinople, Justinian, as Commander-in-Chief, took full credit for it with nary a nod to Belisarius. In fact, in his *Codex Justinianus*, the emperor gave himself the epithet "Conqueror of the Vandals and Africans." So I can only assume Theodora used her charms and velvet persuasion to allow her husband to play only a supporting role in the day's drama, for he had no part in the magnificent cavalcade. He would await the hero's arrival, along with Theodora, in the kathisma of the Hippodrome.

At eight in the morning on the given day, an escort of bishops and prelates went to collect Belisarius at his mansion. As they processed slowly, the churchmen chanted the *Ta Deum* as two acolytes swung silver censers of Frankincense. His polished bronze cuirass blinking in the sunlight, General Belisarius followed on foot, as directed by the empress, not riding in a glittering chariot, as such a hero would have done in the days of Old Rome. Behind him came Antonina, who was allowed a sedan chair manned by four soldiers. John the Cappadocian followed. Never popular with the crowds, he walked within a double line of soldiers. I wondered whether this was his reward for releasing the funds—or whether Theodora meant to humiliate him, for he was subject to some jeering.

Accompanied by the cheers and shouts of approval from citizens gathered on the battlements of the Walls of Theodosius, they moved along a private lane and into the Mese. The thoroughfare's two-mile length fairly burst with late summer flowers and billowed with colorful banners and streamers. Across the capital, church bells summoned citizens who poured out from every street, lane, and alley, swelling the masses lining both sides of the thoroughfare. "Tyche wills it!" bystanders called out. "Tyche wills it!" The Goddess of Fate was known for her fickleness. Is that what was implied—that here was the soldier responsible and hated for the killing of thirty thousand men in the Hippodrome two years previous now being exalted and wildly cheered for his victory in North Africa? Or—was the cheer meant to encourage Belisarius to greater things? Higher office?

Joining the procession from the streets near the Golden Gate—according to Theodora's precise orchestration—were a good number of the fifteen thousand Vandal prisoners, including the unchained, purple-draped King Gelimer with his clan of in-laws, cousins, and nephews in tow.

Wagon after wagon followed, brimming with riches, the treasures of nearly a century of Vandalic piracy on the Middle Sea, taxation of North African citizens, and pillage of cities, including the priceless spoils from the sack of Rome some eighty years before: silver and gold in coin and bars; golden thrones, carriages, statues, plates, cups, golden girdles and armor, all encrusted with jewels winking and twinkling in the day's perfect sunlight.

The train of men and treasure snaked along the imperial procession route, passing largely rebuilt colonnaded streets and squares, wending its way through the Forum of Arcadius to the Forum of the Ox, then passing under the triple passages of the vaulted arch in the Forum of Theodosius before entering the Forum of Constantine, where the senators and Patriarch Epiphanius greeted Belisarius and were themselves folded into the cavalcade.

Theodora once again dubbed me a fine judge of people, not only of their words and intonations, but also of their facial expressions and carriage. This notion of hers won for me a seat in the kathisma for General Belisarius's homecoming.

The stadium was crammed for the much-heralded event. Women were not allowed to attend the ordinary racing day events, considered the strict domain of men, but they were welcomed to celebrations such as this. Thus, the stands held a good many more thousands of souls than the official capacity of sixty thousand. Marble seating close to the concourse was reserved for the most elite of the attendees, much like before the Nika riots. But the majority of benches, those made of wood planking atop bricks, were gone now, replaced by one-piece benches with back supports, all carved from stone. Justinian had cleverly precluded any future instances of bench burnings or retooling the wooden planks as missiles.

Following Theodora's directives, the celebratory train entered the Hippodrome through the starting gates: the patriarch and other clerics first, then General Belisarius—to the thunderous cheering of The City's citizens. He was followed by Lady Antonina, as she had done at Carthage. Word had spread throughout The City how, on horseback, she had led the infantry into the heat of the decisive battle. She was on foot now, a jeweled tiara reining in her golden curls. The sun caught her now, and she shimmered with each step, draped in a stola that ran like fluid gold from neckline to jeweled and gilded slippers. I noticed Theodora's hands grip the arms of her throne at the sight of her but could only wonder at what her thoughts were. Was she jealous? Did she regret putting her on parade? Or, was she holding in check her anger regarding Antonina's affair with her godson? Was it, perhaps, all of these?

Some notice was given to John of Cappadocia in the way of heckling and catcalling, but for the most part and undoubtedly to his relief, the crowd's attention leapfrogged from the dazzling Antonina in front of him to the Vandal king behind him.

King Gelimer, back straight as a rod, walked amidst his noble family, wearing his purple cloak, not by choice, for Theodora had ordered it. She wanted the people to witness his daring. Cries and screams of indignation swept the stands at the shocking sight. Only Roman rulers were allowed the rarest of colors. In but minutes, however, a thousand or more Vandal prisoners, bound to each other in rows stretching the width of the raceway, brought out from the multitude gasps of awe, as well as catcalls of displeasure. The crowd began to chant, "Remember Rome! Remember Rome!" However, the mantra died away when the three dozen treasure wagons laden with gold and silver riches trundled onto the amphitheater grounds, transitioning into a stunned silence as the audience stretched in their seats to get a better sighting.

Belisarius in the lead, the massive train moved to the right, traveling the western length first, negotiating the turn at the sphendone, and moving along the eastern length to the finish line, whereupon the lead party, prize prisoner in tow, left the procession, winding their way behind the stands to the single hidden iron door that would allow access to the circular stairway leading up to the kathisma, where they were to do obeisance before the royal couple.

The rest of the train continued on, Gelimer's retinue to some stopping place and the slaves to their place of confinement. The healthiest of the slaves would be conscripted into the Imperial Army to patrol and fight the Persians—but not before Belisarius took his pick for his *bucellarii*.

It took little time for them to climb the circular stairway. Patriarch Epiphanius was the first to emerge at the top of the loge. As he was shown to his seat, Antonina stepped in, then her husband, and finally the king who was no longer a king—Gelimer.

Antonina—a vision in gold from hair to hem—descended like a goddess down the several kathisma steps, stopping in front of the thrones, and though she tried to hide her emotions, her face was as serious as Hera's when vexed by Zeus. She prostrated herself and, as prescribed, kissed the red shoes of the royals. Theodora stared impassively, her gaze passing over her friend's head.

At a motion from Justinian, Antonina stood and bowed toward the emperor and then toward Theodora, who awarded her with an icy smile and a nod toward an empty seat. As Antonina obeyed, not without visibly bristling, I noted her estranged son Photius had the seat next to her while her godson sat on the other side of him, all ice between the two. As Tariq reported, Photius had a two-fold reason to be upset: Theodosius held a higher place in the eyes of Belisarius, whom Photius idolized, and he was aware his mother was having an affair with the youthful Theodosius. This was Theodora's staging, I knew, a production meant to carry out comeuppance on several heads at once.

Belisarius and King Gelimer presented themselves to the emperor and empress now. Would they enact the script Theodora had written?

His hands clenching and releasing, Belisarius stepped forward, his bronze chest plate lifting as he drew in breath and dropped down to the floor of the loge, his arms out as if to imitate a cross. This prostration *was* his cross, I thought. He was a little closer to the emperor's red shoe where it rested on a single step above, but he had to stretch a bit to reach Theodora's. Her expression as he kissed it was no warmer than it had been for his wife.

Once bidden to rise, he announced: "My emperor, the sack of Rome has at last been avenged." He nodded toward Gelimer. "You see before you, here, and below, the fruits of your magnificent campaign."

The herald relayed his words to the audience, but his tone lacked the subtle ignominy in the general's voice, a subtlety evident only to the most observant viewers in the loge. His prostration came as no surprise to me, for I had taken down Theodora's directives. Neither would it shock senators and palace officials who could merely shrug at the sight because this was the old form of obsequiousness reinstated by the new regime. In public, it was now required of everyone, even of those belonging to the highest echelons of society. But, when the general prostrated himself, the majority of the audience, those who would never see the inside of the palace, grew silent, startled, as if the earth beneath the stands began to tremble. Then heads inclined toward one another and a hum and buzz swept the stands. How is it, the question must have traveled from citizen to citizen and bench to bench, that such a returning hero, one who could boast the greatest victory since the early days of Rome, was being made to so humble himself?

The emperor seemed well satisfied, Theodora less so. The ceremony continued as Belisarius took a step back behind the captive king, who by now had beads of perspiration forming on his forehead. Once Gelimer was in place, he undid the fibula holding his cloak and Belisarius made a show of removing the forbidden purple garment, passing it to Narses, who folded it neatly and set it aside, just as Theodora had instructed. Gelimer prostrated himself now and kissed the shoes of the rulers.

Upon the signal from Justinian, Gelimer rose, a king whose reign had ended. "I do you honor, master and mistress. My kingdom is now yours." Only Theodora, Belisarius, and I knew the words were memorized.

Justinian took his speech at face value and spoke to him as a father might have done. "You and your family will be settled and want for nothing. It has been arranged."

The crowd listened intently as the emperor's herald repeated the conversation at full volume.

A painted smile on his face, Gelimer shifted his body slightly to face both Justinian and Theodora. His chest rose and his voice boomed out almost as loud as that of the herald: "Vanity of Vanities, says the Preacher, vanity of vanities! All is vanity. What does man gain by all the toil at which he toils under the sun? A generation goes, and a generation comes, but the earth remains forever."

As the words of Ecclesiastes were repeated by the herald for the audience, I could not fully read Justinian, whose gaze was blank, distant. He seemed to be considering the meaning but had yet to figure out the intent. Theodora's expression was easier. Her brow came down, eyes narrowing. This was not part of her production. These words were not in the script she had dictated.

For myself, I knew the quotation could be taken as a self-deprecating reflection on Gelimer himself. Or—it could be construed as a caustic reminder to the two royals sitting on their thrones that all of this will pass, no matter how hard they grasp on to it. Theodora was clearly taking it in this second way.

When Gelimer launched into the lines a second time, Theodora leaned over and whispered something to her husband. He nodded and just as the herald was taking breath to repeat the lines, Justinian sent him a hand signal that immediately quashed the effort.

Later, I reported to Theodora what I observed in the loge. Even though her owl-like hearing and eyesight allowed for missing nothing, she enjoyed hearing from me how placing Photius between Antonina and Theodosius had soured all their faces. And then she went on to vent her anger at the actor whose actions and words had not played to her liking. Gelimer's unscripted speech warranted a scathing review.

The loge this day had supported quite a stew of personalities, but I was able to characterize them with fair accuracy, nonetheless. However, the crowd of thousands on the new benches below was another story. At the conclusion of the event, I turned to Narses. "I have yet to get a read on the crowd. They appear so jubilant. Have they truly forgotten Belisarius's role in the murder and havoc that unfolded in this very amphitheater two years ago?"

Narses gave an exaggerated grunt and turned to me with a bit of a smile, the first I'd seen on him all day. "Ah, Stephen, it was Demosthenes who said, 'The crowd is the most unreliable and witless thing in the world'."

25

HAVING BEEN ANNOUNCED BY A chamber servant, Antonina stood in the entryway of the women's quarters, eyes glowing blue fire. "Thea, I came to your rooms twice this past week, and I was told you were not seeing anyone."

"It was true." Theodora stayed seated on a couch near her writing desk.

"So—after all these months away doing work—and battle!—for this empire, I'm just *anyone*?"

"Oh, by the Goddess Hecate, you are not that."

Antonina tilted her head as she tried to puzzle out the answer. Clearly, still at a loss, she blinked the mystery away and straightened. "Yesterday in the kathisma and at the celebration in the Hall of the Nineteen Couches, you were so cold, as if we were strangers."

Theodora leveled her gaze at Antonina. "What is your concern, Antonina?"

"My concern is just that—your treatment of me, and more especially of my husband."

"Let's dispense with the first complaint for the moment."

Antonina blinked at Theodora's sharpness. "Am I to stand here like your handmaiden? Or am I to prostrate myself as I did yesterday?"

"That was in public." Theodora motioned her to the white damask couch cornerwise to hers.

Antonina sat, her back rigid and slightly forward. "We've been friends for so many years, Thea."

"And we shall be again."

"Again? Do you mean—"

Theodora lifted her finger in a shushing motion. "First, I wish to tell you of changes here in the empire, changes that have come about through me."

Unable to stave off a sigh, Antonina sat back against the cushion.

"You're aware of changes Justinian enacted—at my urging—before you left. How the whoremongers have been evicted and their brothels closed. Well, we've also endowed a palace dedicated to the women and girls who had been so dreadfully used so that they may now live more moral lives."

"I still see women in the streets—"

"Yes, yes—change is slow in coming. You know as well as I the fate of some actresses from our past. However, now they are allowed to leave the stage and pursue another occupation. Also, a daughter will have equal inheritance rights with her brother. A wife's dowry should be returned to her when her husband dies. And children of female slaves need not become slaves themselves. All of these things have been recorded in the *Codex Justinianus*."

"This is all very commendable, Thea, but what does it have to do—"

"With you? I am getting to that. You've seen the progress being made with the new Church of the Holy Wisdom?"

"Yes, one can't help but see it."

"As much damage as the rioters inflicted on the New Rome, Justinian is glad to have the opportunity to build something truly extraordinary: a monument to God—and a monument to his reign."

"And yours?"

Theodora ignored the question. "My husband sees himself as a spiritual vicegerent."

"Of the Holy Father?"

"No—of God Himself."

"Does it follow, then, that you are a vicegerent, as well?"

Another question ignored. "Justinian will publish an edict next year calling for universal chastity and emphasizing marriage, family, and faithfulness."

Antonina drew in a breath just short of a gasp. She caught the wind of Theodora's litany of changes and the color in her cheeks bled away. Her shoulders came forward, her body appearing to fold in on itself. "You know," she said in a whisper, her eyes round as coins.

Theodora nodded.

"Who told you?"

"Do you think someone had to tell me? I saw it at Theodosius's baptism. The way you leered at him. If you recall, I gave you fair warning."

"Warning? You're my friend."

"Exactly. That's why I saw what was coming. And then the boldness was your undoing. How careless of you, Nina."

"So others know?"

"Of course, you fool."

"Who?"

"Who doesn't? The Middle Sea doesn't stop gossip. Your servants, your slaves, your husband's lieutenants."

"But—but he doesn't know, Theodora." Antonina sat forward, face drawn. "Belisarius doesn't know!"

"I'm not surprised. Men can be blind, especially when they love deeply. You had best keep him in the dark. There's no telling how a man of war will react."

Antonina fell silent, her gaze shifting to the right of Theodora, the blue fire doused. She could summon no riposte.

"You will change, Nina?"

Antonina stood now, as if to leave, but suddenly indecisive. Long seconds elapsed as she posed immobile as marble.

"You take good time to answer me, Antonina!"

Antonina flinched, her gaze returning to meet Theodora's. "Yes," she whispered.

"I'd like to believe you. … Sit down."

Antonina obeyed. "You can believe me, Thea."

Theodora had her doubts but moved on. "Now what is it about Belisarius that bothers you? He was given the honor of a lifetime."

Antonina stiffened at the turn in the conversation, taking several moments to collect her thoughts. "Thea," she began, as if trying to rein in spite, "he was made to grovel at your feet—yours and Justinian's. For myself, I didn't mind doing it, but for him to suffer such a humiliation after the honor he's brought to the Roman Empire! The emperor had no words of praise for him. A general of his stature deserved an introduction, one of the highest praise. And a wreath or a coin minted in his honor. Why, the people were stunned to see him so treated!"

"You give the people little credit. They saw him walking the raceway. Oh, you can be certain they knew his accomplishment. However, remember, it is the emperor who is the victor, the true victor."

"But … but the wealth he's brought home to you."

"Ah, the wealth, so that should sugar over any disgruntlement, yes?"

Antonina's lower jaw dropped a bit. "What do you mean?"

"Oh, the people were transfixed by the riches, I grant you that. What I am alluding to, Nina, are the countless wagons of booty that did *not* travel here to the Imperial Treasury."

"Well … well," Antonina sputtered, "his men, those who won this victory had to be paid. They are his personal army. You know that."

"I know that he took a mountain of wealth and jewels himself. So I've been told."

"By your network of spies?"

"I'm told the general's personal wealth exceeds that of any noble in The City."

"Lies!"

"I'm told Belisarius holds back from the treasury bushels of gold and silver bars."

"Why, that's—"

"And," Theodora interrupted, "I'm told his wife holds back riches from him."

Her eyes blue as midwinter sky, Antonina drew back, deflated, as though she'd realized she could not counter the intelligence of Theodora's spies. She took in breath now, her mind at work. Suddenly she stiffened and leaned forward. "It's Procopius, who's been spying, isn't it?"

"It is not," Theodora said, amused that Antonina had come close to the mark. "But I ask myself, Nina, what aspiration would be left for a general rich as an emperor to covet? What position would remain for him to conquer?—A throne, perhaps?"

Antonina stood again and took several paces before pivoting back to Theodora. "Thea, I can assure you I have held back a few things, trinkets mostly and some lovely fabrics. There was looting of the Vandal elites among the army, but that's as expected. They see it as their privilege, you know. Why, I can tell you in all honesty that Belisarius's only ambition is to return to the East and direct the border wars with Persia."

"We have only peace with Persia, the so-named Eternal Peace. There's no need for him there. Men of skills inferior to his can maintain the borders.— So, he didn't tell you?"

"Tell me what?"

"That he will be sailing west to take back Sicily and Italy from the Ostrogoths. Justinian took him down into the War Room after the banquet yesterday and laid out the plans."

"What?" The color drained from Antonina's face. "This is true?"

"You'd better sit down again. You look as if you're about to faint."

"And … and I?"

"Oh, I heard how heroic you were at Carthage—on horseback leading the infantry to join up with Belisarius's cavalry. You're another Athena! He will certainly want you at his side again."

26

PIERS CAME INTO MY STUDY. "The Lord Chamberlain Narses to see you," he announced in an odd stage-like whisper.

"Show him in, Piers."

Piers tilted his head to one side and pursed his lips. "He has another with him, Stephen."

"Does he? Very well, Piers, show them in." I rose from my desk chair.

Narses was followed into the room by a young man perhaps as young as fifteen, a lute strung on his shoulder.

"This is Setka, Stephen," Narses said. The boy bowed nicely. "He is from Egypt. He arrived with the Belisarius victory ships from North Africa."

"I see," I said, wondering why he was accompanying Narses. Did Narses hope to train him in the Imperial Army or was he to be a scribe in Brother Leo's scriptorium, as I had begun? A second look and thought rejected both likelihoods. The boy's slimness would preclude his success in the military, and the first blush of a beard indicated he was not one of the cut ones, so I doubted Narses saw him as fit for an excubitor or a scribe.

"The mistress is aware you spent time in Egypt and know Coptic," Narses said in his gravelly voice, as if that explained everything.

"A bit." The mystery was widening, deepening.

Narses cleared his throat. "Setka is joining the Imperial Musicians."

I nodded, as did Setka, who smiled shyly. He appeared to understand Greek well enough to this point.

"The mistress requests that you host him."

So there it was.

"Host him?" I wanted to ask why. Why wasn't he to be housed in the musicians' building?

Narses saw my questions forming on my face and meant to deflect them. "The emperor requests that Setka learn a good many of Pindar's songs."

"Ah, so I am to help him with his Greek, as well."

Narses smiled indifferently, resisting validation of my theory and thus allowing the mystery to run a bit deeper.

After the lord chamberlain left, I sat and had the boy sit across the desk from me. "You're to play here in the palace," I said, attempting conversation.

He nodded and smiled. The breadth of the expression and whiteness of his teeth brought his face alive, and for the first time I realized how handsome he was. I had met numberless Egyptians in my travels, but this boy's good looks outshone them all. Many Egyptians have light skin, but his was a bit more so. His dark, deep-set eyes, almost owl-like, above a straight, narrow nose, sparkled for the first time since he arrived.

"How old are you, Setka?"

"Seventeen."

His answer took me by surprise. He was lying, I was convinced. But why? I continued my gentle interrogation. "You are Egyptian?" I asked, for he didn't quite strike me as fully Egyptian.

He shrugged, smiling as if he suddenly did not understand my Greek. One blink and the sparkle in his eyes was gone. I trespassed on his privacy, it seemed.

I called Piers into the room and he arrived in moments, making me suspect he had been standing nearby the entire time.

"Yes, my lord?" he asked, addressing me formally, as was usual in front of company.

"Setka will be staying with us. Please take him to the far west bedchamber and see he has all he needs." I turned to the boy. "Are you hungry, Setka?"

"No, my lord." The boy caught on to Piers's manner of addressing me.

"Just the same, Piers," I said, "fix him something. Setka, do you have other clothes?"

"I do not, my lord."

"Belongings?"

Setka stood, picked up his lute and strapped it to his shoulder. He shook his head. "Only this, my lord. The mistress gave little time for me to prepare."

"The mistress?"

"The general's mistress, my lord."

"I see." I turned to Piers, baffled as to how Antonina figured into this. "Have the tailor come up first thing tomorrow."

A half hour later, Piers approached me as I worked at my desk. "Stephen, if I may ask, how long do you think the young man is to—"

"You may ask, Piers," I interrupted without looking up from the codex I was copying. "But I don't know. Just see that he gets settled in, yes?"

I glanced up to see him leave the study, a bit bent. My curtness was regrettable. I was short on patience because his questions were my questions. I vowed to make amends.

In the evening Tariq stopped in for a game of *Shatranj* and I introduced him to Setka. After a bit of small talk among the three of us, Piers came in—as previously arranged—to suggest Setka retire to his bedchamber.

I could sense the questions bubbling up in Tariq as I set up the pieces for a new game.

"Where did he come from?"

"Egypt by way of Carthage, as he told you. He played for King Gelimer's court."

"I mean to say, why has he been dropped in your lap?"

"The very question I'm grappling with, Tariq. I'll have to ask Theodora. He's not a eunuch, so I'm thinking that with his looks she might think him too much of a temptation to certain musicians over in their quarters."

"He doesn't look seventeen."

"No, he doesn't. I doubt that he is. And he's as poor as the poorest palace mouse."

"But he appears to have landed well. So, Antonina brought him? Theodosius isn't young enough for her anymore?"

I laughed. "No, her interest in her godson has not cooled. Even though Theodora had what she called *words* with Antonina concerning the knowledge you supplied about her adultery, I've seen her with Theodosius since."

"So have I. Well, here's another thought. What if Antonina presented him to Theodora with some talent other than musical in mind? He's pretty enough."

"Too young for that."

Tariq shrugged. "Times and tastes change. Justinian is what, seventeen or eighteen years older than Theodora. The pendulum could swing the other way, too, you know."

I laughed again. "I know that her love for her husband is deep. Still, there's something odd about Setka. You know, when I asked him whether he was Egyptian, my tone implying, I think, *full* Egyptian, he avoided answering. He was not about to say more."

"Well, maybe he's part Vandal and won't admit it. But, then again, there's something about his features that reminds me of you."

"Me?—What?"

"Well, like me, he has the Egyptian prominent lips, large bridge of the nose, and the widest parts of his face are his cheekbones."

"You noticed all that?"

"No, what I noticed was his heart-shaped face, thick arched eyebrows, and prominent chin."

"Like me?"

"He looks … Syrian."

"I don't see it."

"Ha! You wouldn't!"

When I next met with Theodora in her rooms to go over certain laws being added to the *Codex Justinianus*, to be made public in December, she made no mention of Setka. I thought that odd. When we finished and as I was preparing to leave, I asked, "How long is the young musician to stay?"

Her dark eyes snapped to attention. "Is there a problem?"

"No, Thea, I—"

"Isn't there enough room in your suite? Do you wish larger quarters?"

"No, of course not."

"Is the boy an imposition?"

"No, Thea," I said, picking up the manuscript. I nodded and turned to leave. The subject was closed.

Overnight, I had become a part-time language tutor and full-time governor to a youthful minstrel.

27

January 535

THAT THE EXTENDED DIALOGUES BETWEEN the Monophysite and Chalcedonian believers held by Justinian had yielded nothing of substance remained a source of hurt for Theodora. Neither had anything of import on the subject changed within the Imperial Apartment. Justinian still held to his Orthodox belief, while Theodora maintained her loyalty to the Monophysitic faith she had learned at the feet of Patriarchs Timothy and Severus.

Thus, the emperor and empress were of different minds when a stylite was ushered into the Golden Audience Chamber. Zhura, a Monophysite holy man who had been tossed off his pillar in Mesopotamia by Chalcedonian believers, had been for some weeks stirring up the citizens of the capital with his preaching. People came to him with their sick and crippled in order to hear his words and receive the blessings he voiced from the top of his current column in a street off the Forum of Constantine. Rumors circulated of healings and other miracles purported to be his handiwork.

Theodora drew in a silent breath as she studied the old man in his filthy tunic and ragged sandals, wishing he were more presentable, more obeisant, less odoriferous. She had hoped for a better representative of the Monophysites she valued.

When Justinian made a motion to a silentiary indicating the stylite should be made to prostrate himself before the double throne, Theodora stayed his hand. Justinian acquiesced but nonetheless took a hard line. "You come into my capital, Zhura, and you cause a stir with your shouted beliefs. I will not have it, do you understand? The New Rome has no place for you."

The man stiffened and drew in breath as if the air gave him energy. "The City belongs to God!" he announced. "It belongs not to Chalcedonians."

"Yes, it does belong to God." Justinian's body pitched forward on his throne. "And I am the vicegerent of God!"

Zhura grinned.

"Do you doubt it?"

"I know what I know, what has been revealed. Christ had but one nature."

"You speak heresy. What brought you here?"

"I have come so that the emperor can redress the wrongs that have been done in Mesopotamia."

"Against whom?" Justinian demanded.

"Against those who follow the Monophysitic faith."

"You think I will give succor to heretics like yourself? You are mistaken."

As the argument continued, Theodora sensed the uncommon current of anger running through her husband. It was disturbing. When she placed a hand on his arm, whispering that Zhura was an old man, Justinian ignored her, pulling back.

"If your Monophysitic faith is true," Justinian said, "then send a sign! Send a sign, do you hear? Until then, an order for the death penalty will be prepared. Anyone denying the Chalcedonian faith will be put to death."

Theodora felt a tightening in her chest. Her mind raced. How was she to understand her husband? She had never seen him fly into such a rage—and in an attack on what he knew she held dear? He could not have forgotten that she was more than a sympathizer of the Monophysites—that she protected them, that she was one herself?

At a dismissive wave from the emperor, two Imperial Guards grasped him under his arms and dragged him toward the exit. At his advanced his age, Theodora would not have been surprised to hear a bone crack. "Below!' Justinian bellowed. "Below."

Theodora turned to her husband. "He's too old to survive the dungeon for long, husband."

Justinian shrugged. "Then it will be a quick end for the blasphemer."

"But the people, his followers, will—will not forget. You've promised to bridge the gap."

"I did promise and I did try. Many months were spent in the effort. To no avail, Thea, no avail." He stepped down from the throne now and moved away, leaving her.

Theodora replayed in her mind the scene between Justinian and Zhura again and again, obsessing over what seemed a full concession her husband made to Roman orthodoxy. She remained so disconcerted about Justinian's aggressiveness toward the stylite that she was relieved he did not come to her in the women's quarters that evening. She did not trust what she might say to him. Sleep was troubled so she rose much earlier than usual. At six in the morning, foregoing her customary long bath, she went directly to Justinian's rooms.

The emperor's bedchamber servant sat in the anteroom, a worried look on his face that darkened considerably upon the empress's arrival. Theodora flashed him a questioning glance.

The chamberlain jumped to attention and bowed. "Apologies, mistress," he said. "The master has yet to rise."

"What?" Theodora snapped. "He's always up by this hour. You attempted to rouse him?"

"I did, mistress. He chased me from the room."

"What did he say?"

"Nonsense. Nothing I could understand, mistress. Oh, he moaned a bit."

"He moaned?" Theodora asked, heat filling her face. "And you left him?"

"I was just now sitting there thinking what should be done."

"You're too slow of a thinker, then." Theodora deliberately modulated her tone. "If he is ill, you send for someone. The physician, if one is needed."

"Should I go—"

"Never mind that. Come with me and draw open the shutters at once."

Theodora hurried into the large dimly-lit room, the chamberlain at her heels. Justinian lay still as a block of wood beneath a pile of embroidered spreads. She went to the side of the bed, her heart pacing. It was too dark to see the rise and fall of his chest, but she could hear his shallow breathing, just barely. When she bent to take hold of his hand, he stirred, mumbling. She thought she could discern his eyelids fluttering. He retracted his hand and spoke, but his words made no sense. He moved from Greek to Latin and back again. He was delirious.

Theodora sat on the side of the bed, her hand reaching for his forehead. It was exceedingly hot, and there was something more that gave her pause and made her heart race. "Hurry with the shutters!" she spat. "Open all of them!"

When the light filtered in from the window across the way, splashing across Justinian's bed and the emperor's supine figure, she could not hold back a gasp.

At once, she stood up, turning to the approaching chamberlain, deliberately using her body to block his view of the emperor. "Go find the physician at once, do you hear?"

Theodora straightened, but even at her full height the chamberlain towered over her and when he attempted to look past her, she screamed, "At once!"

After he left, Theodora turned back to the bed and sat, daring a second look at her husband. A lumpish swelling had appeared on his head, just above his forehead. She went to touch it, but a thought intervened, and she drew her hand back at once. She had been told a rumor was circulating among the senators that a plague had visited a distant province. Her mind raced. Which province? When? Had it entered The City? Fear tightened like a wire about her heart as she waited. In little time the physician was leaning over Justinian, examining what he referred to as a protuberance. Justinian batted away his hand, muttering something in Latin.

Theodora stood at the foot of the bed. "It just appeared there overnight, " she whispered. "Ambrosius, it isn't—?"

"The plague? Oh, swellings can erupt quite suddenly, mistress. No doubt about that. But they occur in the groin, at the neck, or in the armpits. We call them *buboes*. This is not the plague but it is nonetheless a cause for concern. No, mistress, this is something else. Think back over yesterday. What did the emperor do with his time? What did he eat?"

"Nothing out of the ordinary."

"What concerns or complaints did he voice?"

"None!" Theodora lost patience and her tone turned snappish. "I didn't send for you to ask questions, Ambrosius. I'm the one with a single question: What is wrong with the emperor?"

The physician paled at Theodora's shift in mood. "Were you," he began, then shifted his approach, "that is, was someone attending him at all times?"

He meant, *during the night*. Theodora stiffened, offended by what she interpreted as a probing question about her life with her husband. "No," she answered, feeling somehow defensive because they had spent the night apart. "Why would you ask that?"

"I wondered whether he might have been alone and struck his head." The physician affected a smile. "In any case, the hope is for the swelling to come down relatively soon." He reached for his medicinal bag and withdrew a vial.

His hands trembled slightly. He was not unaware he had tried her patience. Uncorking the vial, he placed it to Justinian's lips, simultaneously massaging his throat to encourage swallowing.

"What are you giving him?" Theodora demanded.

"It's a bit of wine soaked in mandrake root. It will make him less fretful, and he should sleep. If you'll excuse me, mistress, I'll search through my codices and return presently."

"Yes, yes, if that's all you can do now."

The physician backed out of the chamber.

Theodora seated herself at the chair on the side of the sleeping couch. Mumbling Latin that Theodora could not understand, Justinian twisted in evident pain. *What if,* she thought, *what if he dies?* She could not imagine life without him. She took slow, deliberate breaths in an attempt to tamp down an upset that swirled at her core, while in her head images of what-could-be assaulted her. And then she thought, *How am I to retain power without him?*

As Justinian quieted and lay still under the spell of the mandrake, she went over in her mind every detail of Justinian's day as she knew it. At last, she struck upon an answer, one that had occurred to her early on, but she had neither voiced it to the physician nor given it credence herself because it had, at first, seemed so outlandish. Still, somehow it now seemed possible, even likely.

Minutes after the physician left, Theodora went into the anteroom where Justinian's chamberlain waited, his face screwed up in worry. He stood immediately and bowed.

"Find Lord Chamberlain Narses at once and tell him to bring the stylite here without delay."

"The stylite?"

"Don't question me! He'll know whom I mean."

The chamberlain blanched, gave a sort of nod and bow at once and backed out of the room.

Gray eyes at half-mast, Justinian lay as if in a daze, unresponsive to entreaties to speak or drink water. Theodora was applying a cool compress to his forehead when Narses entered, followed by Zhura and the chamberlain.

She ordered the chamberlain to return to his station in the anteroom and to keep Ambrosius at bay should he return. The fewer people who knew about this, the better.

Once he was gone, she turned toward the stylite, who stood staring at Justinian. "You did this!"

"No mistress, God did this."

"It's the sign?"

"The emperor requested it."

"Neither he nor I would have wished a sign that could take his life. The swelling on his head is as big as an egg! You must do something about it. Take back the curse!"

"It's a sign, mistress, not a curse."

"Take it back at once!"

"I can only pray, mistress."

Before she could respond, Zhura was stepping in front of her and moving close to Justinian, whose glazed eyes widened at the sight of the stylite.

Zhura raised his hand and made the sign of the cross in midair. His prayers were spoken in Greek and yet were spoken so quickly and so quietly modulated that Theodora could not crack the code of a single sentence. Fifteen minutes later, he turned to her, the ceremony complete.

Theodora's eyes questioned him.

"The sign is God's sign. He will recover," Zhura said, resolve in his tone. "That, too, is God's sign."

Theodora nodded to Narses. She was torn between freeing a fellow Monophysite or having him returned to the dungeon. A second nod and a flutter of her eyelids meant the latter.

When Theodora looked again to her husband, he was sleeping soundly. As she went to pull up a wicker chair to the bedside, she experienced an odd floating sensation. She reached up to Justinian's forehead. It felt cooler to her, but she would not yield as yet to hope. She took hold of his hand, kissed it, and laid her head down nearby. Within an hour, and in a less than comfortable position, she slept.

It was mid-afternoon when Justinian stirred, awakening Theodora. She picked her head up. The awkward posture had left her neck stiff, but the discomfort was forgotten when she noticed her husband staring at her, the gray eyes clear. "What are you doing here?" he asked.

For a moment her thoughts were so jumbled she couldn't formulate a response. "You … you." She had to bite her lips to hold a smile at bay. "You were so ill, Justinian, and talking nonsense."

Theodora reached up to the top of his head. "You have a … a growth right here. My God, it's gone!"

"Yes, I recall that now. You say it's gone?" He checked for himself. "It is. You're right."

"You had the physician most concerned."

"Ambrosius? What did he do?"

"Nothing, really."

"Then how …"

"It was Zhura, Justinian, who was the cause and the cure. It was the sign you asked for."

"Do you mean, Justinian, you have not been swayed in the least?" Theodora posed the question that evening after supper as they reclined on the dining couch. The servants had been dismissed.

"No. The Chalcedonian faith is my faith."

"But there can be a truce. He gave you the sign you asked for. It was a miracle! I witnessed it."

"Miracle or not, I will not bow to the likes of him."

"You don't mean to keep him in the dungeon?"

"No."

"Or to …"

"Put him to death? No."

"What are you going to do with him? You know, if he could do what we witnessed, he could do more. He could …"

"I won't have him stirring things up here in the capital again." Justinian placed a forefinger and thumb beneath his chin as if formulating a solution, but Theodora knew from experience he had already decided upon something. "Listen, Thea, talk to John. There's a property across the Golden Horn at Sycae that John has recently acquired for the treasury. Let him go there."

John of Cappadocia. How she despised him! Theodora could only imagine what crooked means he had used to capture the property and what personal gain he had scored in the bargain. Still, as disappointed as she was that Justinian could not embrace Zhura and his beliefs, this was at least something. "Is he to have a staff?"

"You would make a good lawyer, Thea. Yes—a *small* one."

28

February 535

"YOU WILL NOT PROSTRATE YOURSELF before me!" Theodora said, rising from the couch in her study and stepping forward to take the aged hands of Severus, the deposed Patriarch of Antioch, who for the past many years had lived in Alexandria under the aegis of Patriarch Timothy. Her heart hammered steadily. Here was a man who— along with Timothy— had cared for her and mentored her in the tenets of Monophysitism when she was at her lowest, an outcast from the Pentapolis where she had been mistress to Governor Hecebolus. After that, in order to secure the most vital food and shelter in a foreign land, she was coerced into a relationship with an Egyptian caravan master and was with child when Timothy took her in.

"Theodora, the years have made you even more beautiful, my child."

The years rolled back in her mind, warming her. How long since someone had said to her, "My child."

"This is such a surprise, Father Severus. No, a shock, really. When you did not come for the dialogues Justinian held, I thought never to see you in this lifetime."

"I should have come then. It was what, nearly two years ago, I think."

"I wish you would have." Theodora did not voice her thought that it might have made all the difference.

"Neither party came away with a victory, I take it."

"No. Not the union we had hoped for." Theodora attempted a smile. "It might come yet. Now—tell me, how is Father Timothy?"

Severus' face darkened. "When I left, mistress, he was near death. I wanted to stay, but winter ships are far and few between; as it was, the crossing was dangerous. Timothy insisted I go."

Theodora absently moved her hand to the dimple at her collar bone and a heaviness filled her chest. "Father Timothy …"

"You seem unsteady, mistress. You should sit down."

"Yes, yes. Come sit beside me." When they had settled themselves, Theodora turned to him and said, "You are not to call me 'mistress,' do you hear? You will call me by my name—at least when we are in private." She gave a little laugh. "Who would have thought it, yes? Hecebolus's cast-off mistress—Empress of the Roman Empire?"

"Indeed, mist—Theodora, indeed! But we—Timothy and I—always felt you carried a mighty destiny with you. It was in your aura."

"I ask one thing of you, Father. No one here knows about the son I bore. *No one must know.*"

"As you say, Theodora."

Justinian did not greet Severus with the same affection as did Theodora, but nonetheless he spent many hours in conversation with him, attempting to win him over to the Chalcedonian faith. It came as no surprise to Theodora that he was unsuccessful.

Severus stayed true to his word. No further mention was made of the child she had given birth to in Alexandria, the boy John she had abandoned. She did not confide in him the knowledge that she had signed a document before her marriage swearing she had no child other than Hyacinth. No one wanted a grown child turning up one day, especially a male who might make a claim to the throne.

On 05 June, 535, Epiphanius, Patriarch of Constantinople, died. Outwardly, Theodora mourned the Chalcedonian who had installed her as empress, but she sensed a possible closing in the chasm between the Orthodox and Monophysitic faiths. What if she could replace him with a more pliable churchman? She wrote to Anthimus, the Bishop of Trebizond, with whom she had remained in contact since her pilgrimage to the waters at Bithynia. It was there that this once-confirmed Chalcedonian told her he had found common

ground with Monophysites like John of Tella. Hope floated on the horizon. She reached for it.

For all appearances' sake, Anthimus was a stalwart proponent of Chalcedonianism. His defense of it at Justinian's dialogues proved it. Justinian, therefore, was amenable to nominating Anthimus as patriarch. When he did so, no churchman in the capitol demurred. What neither Justinian nor the churchmen knew was that Anthimus's views toward Monophysitism had shifted, softening to an understanding and acceptance.

Thus, Anthimus did succeed Epiphanius as Patriarch of Constantinople. He merely had to be carefully schooled, Theodora thought, and who better to do it than Severus?

She arranged for Severus and Anthimus to meet, and as she hoped, a pact was formed. Patriarch Anthimus wrote a document outlining his new conversion to the Monophysitic tenets. Hoping to draw the two faiths together, he sent one to Timothy's successor at Alexandria, Patriarch Theodosius, another to the Patriarch of Jerusalem who already held similar beliefs, and while a third went to Ephraem, Patriarch of Antioch, a staunch Chalcedonian, what argument could he give if Emperor Justinian himself supported the mending of the fences?

Theodora was on the verge of solving a dilemma of faith that had, in turn, simmered and boiled for centuries. The fifth and final Holy See, of course, was Rome. Unfortunately, Holy Father John II, a trusted friend of Justinian's, had died the previous May. She was certain he would have been amenable to her solution. But a very old pontiff now reigned, one about whom she knew little. Surely, he could see that hers was a way forward that would bind wounds and bring the empire, east and west, together. Much would depend on Holy Father Agapetus.

29

September 535

THEODORA MADE ME PRIVY TO secret plans going forward to take back Italy from the Ostrogoths so that crucial piece of the Roman Empire would be restored. General Belisarius, who had just been made consul, set sail with twelve thousand men, not for Carthage, as it had been put out—but for Sicily, from where the Italian campaign would begin. His forces were far fewer than he had at his command in the war with the Vandals. He was at first allotted twenty thousand troops, but Justinian peeled off eight thousand to support Mundus who was to run a diversionary tactic against the Ostrogoths in Dalmatia.

On the night before the sailing, Justinian charged Setka with singing an idyll called "The Harvest Home," written by Greek Sicilian Theocritus, who was known for his poetry celebrating the foods and drinks of the Sicilian table.

For two days previous to the supper, I worked with Setka on the idyll until his Greek pronunciation was perfect. In fact, we worked long enough for me to sing it myself—if only I had the voice for it.

Darted Golden Bees; all things smelt richly of Summer,

Richly of Autumn; pears and apples in bountiful plenty

Rolled at our feet and sides, and down on the meadow around us,

Plum trees bent their trailing boughs thick-laden with damsons.

Then from the wine-jar's mouth was a four-year seal loosened.

"The song came off well enough," Setka told me afterward, his brow furrowed. "I did start to sing one line prematurely, though."

"What did you do?"

"What most musicians do. I coughed to hide my blunder."

I laughed. "That's common, is it?"

"It is. … But really, Lord Stephen, four years! Do you suppose the Sicilians drink old wine?"

"They are known for their chefs and vintners," I said, marveling at Setka's youth. At that moment, the request for the song "Harvest Home" came to me: Justinian was celebrating in advance a different kind of harvest: that of Sicily and Italy.

Antonina accompanied her husband. In their months of respite in Constantinople, she continued to carry on her affair with her godson Theodosius, or so it appeared to everyone with fair eyesight—except for her husband. Theodora alluded to having had "words" with her, instructing her to end it, but the empress either trusted her friend overly much—or she deliberately looked the other way.

That Theodosius sailed with Belisarius and Antonina did nothing to invite the end of the affair. Further complicating the situation was the presence of Antonina's son Photius, who was still seething with jealousy about Theodosius's high place in his mother's and Belisarius's appraisals. The ambitious Procopius accompanied Belisarius, also, with Tariq in tow once again to aid him in writing the history of the forthcoming war.

As much as Tariq complained about having to go—more as Theodora's spy than Procopius's secretary—I had the impression the excitement of the

Vandals expedition had spoiled him for the sedentary life of a scribe in the Palace of Hormisdas.

I would miss my friend, but I gave thanks I was not on that warship with its incendiary brew of personalities. And I would not want to be present when someone finally tells Belisarius of his wife's adultery.

It took some months, but Setka became a part of my household. Even Piers, a manservant so set in his ways, adapted to his—our—new charge. Setka was a happy, talkative, and curious person. His curiosity, though, put me off at times because he did not observe certain boundaries of privacy. He wished to know everything about me, including how I became a eunuch and how I dealt with my "condition" as he called it. His insistence in focusing on this aspect of me, of course, dredged up dark memories of my family and how my father sold me to a Persian magus who, in turn, sold me to slavers who had me cut. His comments and questions always seemed to lead to my relationship with women. I dared not tell him I had fallen in love with Theodora upon our first meeting. I dared not tell anyone, not Tariq, not Theodora herself, though I suspected they both knew.

Despite the amount of detail Setka expected me to reveal about myself, he allowed precious little about himself come to light, other than he was taken in by monks as a child and allowed his study of music once he demurred at becoming a monk himself. Some extended relative of King Gelimer discovered him in Alexandria and introduced him at court in Carthage, where he was welcomed as an entertainer. It was there, when the city fell, that Belisarius commandeered the palace and Antonina commandeered the young singer as a gift for Theodora. His status within the palace here was little different from that of many others, servant or slave. And yet Setka walked with a subtle swagger to his thin frame, as if he were unaware his life was not his own.

Two hours were set aside each morning for Setka's lessons in Pindar's songs. In my previous position as a scribe, I had once copied a book of Pindar's hymns, but when I went to Brother Leo in my new tutor's avocation to ask for some of Pindar's works, he showed me to an alcove where a multitude of shelves were laden with Pindar paeans, hymns in honor of Dionysus, processionals, songs for maidens, songs for light dances, songs of praise, laments, and victory songs. The sheer number of works took my breath away. If he is to remain an entertainer for Justinian and Theodora and if Pindar remains the fashion, I thought, chuckling to myself, I'll be on my deathbed before we finish.

At least I was spared from helping him in the creation of the songs. I had no such musical talent and meant to keep it thus. Luckily for both of us, Setka needed no coaching in the instruments of his lovely tenor voice or lute. Setka said he was fully Egyptian, but sometimes, when he held his head just tilted so, his attention on creating harmony, I was reminded of Tariq's declaration that we looked alike.

30

WORD CAME BACK FROM JUSTINIAN'S envoy to the Ostrogothic court in Italy that Sicily fell quite easily into Belisarius's lap. The island citizens, Peter the Patrician wrote, were tired of King Theodahad's strict rule and did everything but strew flowers in the legendary general's path. I surmised that Peter, who had written a book on etiquette and court protocol well-liked by Theodora, was closer to the empress than to the emperor. He acted as Justinian's envoy to the Ostrogothic king in matters relating to the future of Italy, namely Theodahad's secretly agreeing to cede all of Italy to the empire in return for a well-rewarded exile in Constantinople. Doing double duty, Peter also acted as go-between between Theodora and Theodahad in matters of religion. When weeks passed without a response from the new Holy Father to Anthimus's document in support of Monophysitic tenets, she had me write to Peter the Patrician urging King Theodahad to put pressure on Holy Father Agapetus. The empress expected an answer, and day by day, with none forthcoming, Theodora grew more and more distracted by the issue. His seal of approval meant everything to her—and to the future of the Church.

Justinian came into Theodora's dressing area just as she was finishing preparing for supper. Pivoting on her stool away from her makeup table, she caught Justinian's expression, and her heart missed a beat. Something was terribly wrong. "What—what is it, Justinian?"

He nodded toward Phaedra, who was adjusting the jeweled diadem upon Theodora's head. Theodora dismissed her at once.

"Peter the Patrician has been arrested," he said, his face whitening.

"Arrested? But Theodahad agreed that—"

"Well, it appears he's found some courage and means to fight us."

"May Athena end his days!" She realized now that Justinian's eyes were cast down, and he was tinkering with one of his rings. "Wait, there's more. What are you holding back, husband? You look faint. Sit—sit there."

Justinian obeyed, sitting on a couch diagonal to her dressing table. He drew in a deep breath and with the exhalation came the words, "General Mundus is dead."

Comprehension came hard. How could one of the two generals responsible for saving the empire during the Nika Riots be dead? Theodora whispered, "How?"

"Killed at Dalmatia in what was little more than a skirmish, I'm told."

"It doesn't seem possible," Theodora hissed. "So your dream of uniting the eastern and western halves of the empire into one will come at a higher cost. I am sorry for that, husband."

"It is an unwelcome setback."

"It was too good to be true, I suppose. And *my* dream for the unification of faiths … now that is in peril, as well."

"Well, that remains to be seen, Thea."

"What?"

"Well, while Theodahad was acting in *good* faith, he went ahead and ordered Agapetus to come here to initiate peace negotiations between us and Italy."

Theodora swallowed hard and gave her head a shake that unsettled the diadem. "The Holy Father Agapetus is coming *here*?" Her heart raced. She could scarcely comprehend the news, much less what it might mean.

Justinian tossed off a little laugh. "The camel does not see her own hump. Don't you see, Thea? He is too late for his peace mission, but now you'll have a chance to convince him of your solution to heal the chasm between faiths." Justinian stood and motioned for her handmaiden to enter. "I'll see you at supper, dearest."

The Roman Holy Father Agapetus, old as the stone being utilized for the rebuilding of the Church of the Holy Wisdom, was coming to Constantinople. Theodora had often eschewed the notion that she had inherited the Syrian sight, but now, within her, at her very core, something stirred, like the tiny tremors presaging an earthquake.

31

March 536

WITH THE POSSIBLE BINDING OF two faiths that hitherto had been at odds concerning the nature of Christ, Theodora felt herself on the threshold of what might be her greatest accomplishment as empress. And yet, the arrival of Holy Father Agapetus in Constantinople on 07 March, one day before the predicted total eclipse of the sun, proved a vexing omen that compelled her to lose sleep and keep her eyes fastened to the water clock. Was this coinciding a bit of good luck or something to be dreaded? Tyche could be a capricious goddess.

No royal audiences were held on 08 March. As the sky darkened and day became night, so too did the dread increase within Theodora.

On 09 March, when Holy Roman Father Agapetus and a knot of five deacons in tow entered the Golden Audience Chamber, having been hosted in the Daphne Wing for two days, they were rested and well-scrubbed. While the five wore white linen tunics, Holy Father Agapetus wore over his tunic a rich bell-shaped chasuble of gold silk encrusted with ornamentation and jewels. No doubt a family heirloom, Theodora thought, for at her request, Brother Leo had looked into the Holy Father's history, discovering that he himself was the son of a priest and that he had likely familial ties to two previous Roman Holy Fathers. More disconcerting, however, was that he had recently taken a very hard line against Arian believers in Carthage once the territory was regained from the Vandals. What could she expect from Agapetus in the way of sealing the East and West divide? She trembled at the possibilities.

The five clerics were presented first, each prostrating himself and kissing a red shoe of each ruler. When it came to Agapetus, Justinian stood and stepped down from the throne's dais and as the Holy Father bowed forward—the extent of his obeisance—Justinian dropped to his knees and kissed the Bishop of Rome's ring. Theodora grudgingly followed suit. She returned to her throne while her husband managed small talk about the travel conditions. From there her eyes narrowed in assessment. She could tell that beneath a conical cap of a soft red material, and despite long, wavy white hair, his head was little more than a skull with huge eyes that jutted out, continually darting about. To an inexperienced eye, his tunic and stiff vestments might add flesh and deflect from a body thin as a stick, but in her long-ago stage days she had assisted in creating costumes, and she knew better. Something in his physiognomy—the strong posture, upturn of his chin, and assured tone—reminded her of a more worldly Abbot Sabbas, the monk who had come asking for things and who—in the most insulting manner—had refused to pray that she bear Justinian's child and heir to the throne. The comparison produced a bitter tang at the back of her throat.

Once Justinian returned to his place on the throne, the business of state finished in but minutes. Halfway along the route from Rome, Agapetus had already learned hostilities had broken out between the Ostrogoths and the Romans, Belisarius commanding.

"Your mission here on behalf of King Theodahad, Holy Father Agapetus, has been waylaid," Justinian said. "I am sorry for that. He will regret his decision."

"It is sad, indeed, master. Can we not work something out to bring the hostilities to an end?"

"I don't think so, Holy Father. By the time you return, I suspect Italy will have been returned to the Roman Empire. Your Rome will be Roman again."

Agapetus grunted. The large insect-like eyes slid sideways, casting a momentary glance toward Theodora, then shifting back to the emperor. He drew in breath. "Another matter concerns me here in Constantinople."

"Yes?" Justinian asked.

Theodora felt something like an icy hand on her heart. Her husband might be at a loss for his meaning, but she was not without a disturbing presentiment.

"It concerns the new patriarch, this, this—"

"Patriarch Anthimus," Theodora said, her posture stiffening against the marble backing of the throne.

Agapetus's head lifted slightly at Theodora's voice, but he kept his eyes locked on Justinian. "Yes, this Anthimus."

That he was unwilling to use Anthimus's title alarmed Theodora. So, too, did his air of superiority. She bit at her lower lip. It was evident that he was not about to discuss such matters with her, a woman. She persisted, nonetheless, with soft voice and facial expressions. "We have gone to much trouble, Holy Father Agapetus, to see the two beliefs find common ground." She kept a smile at the ready should he turn to her.

"I'm afraid common ground is not possible, master," Agapetus said, his gaze unswerving from Justinian. "I have seen this—this *document* Anthimus has put forward."

Justinian smiled. "Ah, then you know four of the five Holy Sees are in agreement. It is only Rome, in fact, only you, Holy Father Agapetus, upon whom we await."

"You will wait an eternity, you will. And not all are in agreement, as you say. One patriarch had forewarned me even before my copy arrived. One who is not susceptible to the heresy of Monophysitism!"

"Who?" Theodora blurted before her mind could catch up.

Agapetus turned toward her now, the round eyes intent. A little smile twitched and played at his wrinkled mouth. "The Patriarch of Antioch," he said.

Ephraem, Theodora thought. Severus had thought the Patriarch of Antioch the weak link from the start.

Justinian grunted. "He gave us no such indication, Holy Father."

"I can safely say his feelings on the matter are deep, master, even if he was timid about voicing them. Imagine how he must have felt with three patriarchs lining up against him. And—behind them the emperor himself. What could he do—but raise the alarm bell and write to me?"

"What's to be done?" Justinian asked.

"There will be no unification."

"We need not be hasty, Holy Father," Justinian said. Theodora recognized her husband's attempt to appear patient even as his patience was wearing away. "Anthimus and Severus spent tears and prayers over it."

"Severus! Of course, one deposed patriarch takes to the nest of another."

"Do you mean—"

"To depose Anthimus? Of course!"

"But so much has gone into the effort, Holy Father," Theodora said. "It is a solution to decades of disputes. So many have been persecuted over the years."

Agapetus turned on her. "Heretics, you mean? And rightly so! Heretics should die!" He gave her his full attention now. "May I ask when, mistress, did you gain your education in theology?"

Theodora sensed her husband stiffen at his charge, beneath which was a hidden barb meant to subtly draw up her early years. She detected the insult and—although Justinian could be thick sometimes in everyday matters—she saw that he had seen through it, as well. His pool of patience had always been deeper than hers, and he took a placating form now. "Holy Father Agapetus, you and the good priests have had a long and arduous trip."

"Indeed," he said, "I mean to induct a Chalcedonian patriarch and be on my way."

"This is my capital and my empire, Holy Father."

"Ah, so it comes down to power, is that it? You have the armies, too, yes? You and the mistress are thinking, what power do I have that I can depose a patriarch? You think I depend upon King Theodahad? On his army? I can assure you, I have an army in Italy, an army of Italians, true believers. For myself, I will welcome you to Italy and celebrate your victory over the Ostrogoths. However, will my citizens welcome heresy? No, they would rather keep the Ostrogoths as overlords. If you insist upon accepting heretics, your victory, master, would come much harder—and likely never come at all."

Justinian's lower lip trembled as he tried a new tact. "Holy Father Agapetus, I ask only that you afford me the opportunity for you to convene with Patriarch Anthimus so that you might hear him out. We may yet make history here."

The insect eyes stopped all movement. Certain calculations were going on inside the skull.

The Holy Father nodded.

What does he have to lose? Theodora thought. A day? She had everything to lose.

"Good!" Justinian exclaimed.

Theodora saw that her husband's tiny victory gave him hope. For herself, she had none.

"The Bishop of Rome is here, Stephen, as I'm certain you are aware. The palace buzzes like a hive." Before I could reply, Theodora said, "Sit down. I have a task for you."

I took the wicker chair to the side of her desk. I've seen her in dark moods before. This was one of the darkest. The prospect of a task was less than inviting.

"The man is despicable. Do you recall Abbot Sabbas from Palestine?"

"My nose seems to recall him, Thea."

"Ha! Oh, this one's younger and this one smells like a pot of jasmine and wears the cloth of Gods rather than rags, but he's little more than a skeleton and has the same bullheadedness, pride, and ignorance as Sabbas. Justinian is having him meet with Patriarchs Severus and Anthimus."

"I know how much you value—"

Theodora waved her hand to stop me. "Before we go into this further, I heard that a ship arrived today from Sicily. Have you received a letter from Tariq?" She left unspoken her desire to know what mischief Antonina has been into.

"I have not."

She sat back, deflated. "Very well." She sighed. "What I want you to do involves Agapetus and his five priests."

"The Holy Father—I see."

"He has asked for a tour of the library and scriptorium and who better to provide it? Your Latin is excellent, too. While he might have some interest in such things, I believe it's a ruse. He wants to see what Monophysites I have sheltered there, hoping to question them before his meeting with Severus and Anthimus. Now, I was told that when Zhura was given the property across the Golden Horn at Sycae, he took with him every soul in the Palace of Hormisdas that I had taken in. Is that correct?"

"It is. It's as if he's started up yet another monastery."

"Just to be certain, I'd like you to go down to the palace and confirm that they have vacated it. If any of them remain, drop them into a skiff and send them off yourself. The Holy Father should meet only Leo and his staff. Do make sure the place has been cleansed and the rooms fumigated."

"Is that all, Thea?" I asked, thinking it quite enough.

"No. I want you to do more than lead the tour. I have taken my measure of Agapetus, but I want *you* to interact with his five priests and take *their* measure. See just how close they are in theology and loyalty to Agapetus. Of any group of five, you can usually pinpoint one weak link, perhaps one with ambition. Take your time. Make a day of it."

I laughed.

Theodora's gaze flicked upward in annoyance. "What?"

"Once upon a time we joked about how I might become your spy."

Her lips spread slowly into a smile that seemed to say, *You are more than that, Stephen*. It was the kind of moment I treasured and locked away.

"Unless I'm no judge of such zealots," she continued, "he will want to cross the Golden Horn and see Zhura and his following himself, if only to excommunicate him in person."

"In which case you want me to accompany them."

"Yes. I don't know how we can avoid his going. I wish I did." Theodora stood. My time with her was at an end. "You do have the acumen of a spy. Remember—the weak link."

I nodded and grinned.

By the time the tour was to take place much had occurred; none of it good. Theodora sent a note detailing how Agapetus's visit had proved a calamity for her.

At Justinian's demand, he did meet with deposed Patriarch Severus and Constantinople's Patriarch Anthimus, who would not accede to the Chalcedonian Creed that Christ possessed two distinct natures. Severus proved no aid in the face of the Holy Father's questioning, and so Agapetus excommunicated both of them then and there. Severus returned to Egypt.

Subsequently, Agapetus named Menas, an avowed Chalcedonian priest, as Patriarch of Constantinople. Because Justinian remained a stout Chalcedonian and one that respected the office of the Holy Father, he gave up his support for Anthimus and the quest to bridge the two faiths. There was a third reason he unhappily broke ranks with his wife: Belisarius was waging war with the Ostrogoths for Italy and the Old Rome—a quest older than Theodora's mission to bring the Monophysites into alignment with the Chalcedonians—and he felt he could not afford to lose the theologically minded Italians.

Did Theodora understand that? I wondered.

The tour of the Palace of Hormisdas went forward.

Holy Father Agapetus was most cordial toward me when we met at the entrance to the tunnel below the Daphne Wing that would take us directly to the palace. Why shouldn't he be cordial? He had just scored a victory against Justinian and Theodora. Yes, he was thin but his chest seemed to swell with a victor's pride and his face glowed with his success.

I had spent the previous day making certain all the Monophysitic holy men had, in fact, followed Zhura across the Golden Horn. Pockets of the palace still reeked of the holy but less-than-cleanly priests and monks. Brother Leo had several scribes help me collect and destroy any remnants of their stay. Pallets and blankets had to be burned. Servants were then tasked with cleaning every inch of the palace. Oils of cypress and pine fully dispelled the stubborn musty and goaty bouquets left behind, temporarily at least.

I arranged for a silentiary to lead the procession through the tunnel, allowing me to lag behind and play spy. In his rich, red chasuble and conical cap, Agapetus and the silentiary set a sprightly pace, leaving me and the five clerics—Albertus, Vigilius, Titus, Marcus, and Pius—trailing a bit behind. Four wore white tunics, one red. As we moved through the semi-dark tunnel that ramped downward toward the palace and the Sea of Marmara, I positioned myself behind the five, listening and observing. I guessed the clerics' ages ranged from their mid-thirties to fifty. As Agapetus moved farther ahead, two clerics stayed close to him while three of the five fell a few lengths behind, whispering among themselves, heedless of my presence. In the diffused light of oil lamps spaced high along the wall, I watched the outlines of the three, one often leaning into another as some comment or secret was spoken. By the hushed nature of the exchange, I assumed that the things said would not have met the approval of the Holy Father. Of the five, these three were of a different bent. The five were not, I realized, all of a piece.

As we came to the door that led us into the subterranean level of the palace—not far from the little room where I had first lived upon my arrival in Constantinople—I heard one of the three say something peculiar to the one named Vigilius. Pius, the gossipy one, said to the one in red, "That is most certainly not how you would have handled Justinian."

The tour of the library and palace proper took up the morning. The afternoon was reserved for a ferry ride across the Golden Horn, where I gleaned Agapetus meant to excommunicate Zhura and his followers in person. At a noon meal Brother Leo had ordered, I could sense an anticipatory exuberance in Agapetus's demeanor as he chatted with Leo farther down the table. While

I could not imagine what might take place at Sycae, I knew I would not miss it for anything.

I made certain to sit next to Pius in order to draw him into conversation. I kept the amphora within range and when his cup was but half drained of good red wine, I filled it. We talked about the battle for Italy and lesser subjects. Pius had an opinion on everything, and as he became more lubricated, trying to steer the subject became more difficult. However, when he alluded to the Holy Father's reception in the audience chamber, making some comment about how the act of prostrating oneself before the throne seemed like an outdated show of obeisance, I saw my chance. As if I had been in on the tunnel conversation all along, I asked, "Why did you say Father Vigilius would have handled the situation differently?"

Pius looked up at me in surprise, then put his head down as if the dish of candied dates were the Oracle at Delphi, and he needed to know something at once. A full minute must have passed, and I thought he intended to ignore my question when suddenly his head came up and his gaze went down the table to Agapetus, who was regaling Leo with some story, his eyes bright and dancing. Pius's head swiveled back to me, eyes glazed with wine, and he said *sotto voce*: "If not for a twist of fate, Vigilius would be Holy Father Vigilius today, you can be certain."

"Really?"

"Yes, Boniface—the Holy Father before John II—had chosen Vigilius to be his successor. He held a synod and the clergy there signed a document that put it in writing."

"What stood in the way?"

"Ha! A little matter like the laws of the church, which do not allow the Holy Father to choose his successor. Boniface was forced to burn the document."

I looked over at Vigilius. His red tunic betrayed a fleshy body, and yet he possessed a narrow Roman face. I guessed him to be the youngest of the lot. Turning back to Pius, I whispered, "Did he wish to become the Bishop of Rome?"

Pius covered his mouth to hold back a laugh. Keeping his hand to his face and his voice low, he said, "Indeed! He was devastated when it went up in flames." Pius gave out with a little giggle. "Quite literally, it did. Oh, his family served high up in the Ostrogothic government for years, so he had grown used to being near the seat of power. But for real power these days, what with the Ostrogothic imperial realm in decline, you need to look to the Church, and with the wind of old Boniface at his back, Vigilius felt the shepherd's staff within his grip. Oh, he fell into such a melancholy when fate moved against him that Agapetus felt sorry for him and named him his papal legate."

"Ah, thus the reason for the red of his tunic. Did the title repair his self-importance?"

Another laugh. "Not at all."

With all that was going against Theodora since the arrival of Agapetus, I could scarcely believe what I had ferreted out. I had stumbled upon the weak link she was looking for.

None of us were prepared for the dark storm we saw in the middle distance when we left the Palace of Hormisdas and came to its dock. The ferry boat that would take us across the Golden Horn was waiting for us with another surprise. Already crowded onto the boat were some two dozen personal armed bodyguards of Agapetus's. My first thought was that the Holy Father meant to do more to the Monophysites than excommunicate them. Did he plan to put Zhura to death? What of the others? There were at least forty or more monks and priests. I had not signed on to see a bloodletting.

As we boarded the ferry, I moved close to Pius. "What do the soldiers mean?"

He shook his head. "It's not good."

I noticed the pilot speaking to the Holy Father with some animation. I believe he was warning him that on some days the crossing to Sycae could be treacherous. Agapetus vigorously shook his head, and in due time we pushed off from shore.

Ten minutes brought the pelting rain, thunder, and lightning. The seven of us were situated under a shelter, but the well-armed soldiers were forced to stand in the downpour, their soused faces set like stone.

A tempest whipped up in front of us and proceeded to blow the boat backward, toward Constantinople. It was the strangest thing. The skipper shouted over the gale forces, telling the Holy Father he was going to turn back, and they could come another day.

"I don't have another day!" Agapetus called, baring his teeth. "Continue on!"

We pushed against a horizontal wall of water that Neptune himself might have been powering.

Suddenly, a bolt of bluish lightning struck the protective reed roof above us and set it sizzling with flames.

"We're going back!" the captain said and shouted the orders.

The Holy Father stood stunned—as we all were—and offered no reply as the ferry began its wide turn.

It wasn't until we disembarked that we realized Agapetus *could not speak*.

As it turned out, the bizarre tempest was the least of the strange events. The tongue of the Holy Father Agapetus had begun to swell while he was on the ferry, and it continued to swell, preventing normal speech. He took to his bed and on the second day of the infirmity, Justinian called in a team of physicians. The tongue was lanced twice, but days went by without a remedy and gangrene set in.

On 22 April, at the age of forty-six, Holy Father Agapetus died a very painful death. His stay in Constantinople lasted less than two months. His remains were placed in a lead coffin for the return trip to Rome.

To my knowledge, no Monophysites remained in the capital, but I did hear stories of rejoicing going on in Sycae, across the Golden Horn. There, the Holy Father's death was taken as a sign from God. Others, in The City, blamed it on magic oaths made by Zhura against the man who meant to excommunicate him.

I hold neither interest nor credence in religion—pagan, Christian, or otherwise—and even though I was educated for some years by a magus, I had little faith in the oaths he engineered, so I could think of no reason for the Holy Father's death other than coincidence or bad luck. A week later, I caught a whiff of whispers that one of Theodora's spies had poisoned him. I saw no evidence of it in fact or in Theodora's reactions. No one within the Great Palace dared raise the suggestion, least of all, me.

Theodora confided little in me in the days following the death of the Holy Father. Of course, she had no reason to mourn him, but neither did she visibly celebrate. What he had done in turning out her mentor Severus, deposing her hand-chosen Patriarch Anthimus and naming a Chalcedonian in his place, as well as turning Justinian against the Monophysites' cause could not be undone. She had been at the zenith of her powers before Agapetus's arrival, and in short time he had brought her low.

It wasn't until after the death of the Holy Father that I had the opportunity to tell Theodora of Vigilius, my weak link, and how he had been promised the shepherd's staff of the Holy Father by Boniface before circumstances awarded it to Agapetus.

Theodora gasped, her eyes locking onto mine and her eyebrows lifted, questioning. "Was he disappointed?"

"Bitterly so, according to Father Pius."

Theodora swept out of my study at once, a smile breaking on the red scimitar of her mouth.

As arranged, the two silentiaries admitted the papal legate before stepping out, leaving him adrift in the massive Golden Audience Chamber. He stood there motionless in his crimson dalmatic.

"Step forward," Theodora said, her right hand lifted.

The legate approached the throne, his eyes wide but daring no more than a squint at the empress. He came to the dais and knew to prostrate himself because when the six clerics had arrived from Rome, Justinian had exempted Agapetus, but the five deacons had made the required obeisance.

"The emperor and I are saddened by the death of Holy Father Agapetus," Theodora began. "What an untimely thing and so unsettling for it to happen here. You are to accompany the coffin to Rome, I understand?"

"Yes, mistress. I will bring your condolences to Rome with me, mistress."

Theodora searched the dark blue eyes for sorrow. Finding none, she said, "I understand Holy Father Agapetus named you his legate only after you arrived here, is that correct?"

"It is."

"That's the reason for the red now? Tell me, will the title carry any weight when you return to Rome?"

"Weight?"

He understood her meaning, she was certain. "I mean, will you keep your title? Will you remain a bishop?"

"I'm—I'm not sure, mistress."

"Come, come, Vigilius, do you mean you've given it no thought?"

"I ... I—"

"Let us play above board, as we sometimes say here, though not everyone follows through. I understand not so very long ago you yourself came within a hair's breadth of wearing the fisherman's ring."

Vigilius's eyes blinked, then snapped fully wide. "Who told you? Oh!—the eunuch, yes?"

Theodora was not about to unmask Stephen as her source. He might be needed again. "Oh, I have my sources in Rome, you can be certain. Word came back to me of *Boniface's blunder*, as they called it there, but I had no face to put to the name of Vigilius who had lost the seat of St. Peter to Agapetus. Until now."

Vigilius shifted from one foot to the other as Theodora held his gaze. His face took on a deep color.

"Now, Vigilius, under the Ostrogoths your father was praetorian prefect and your brother was Urban Prefect of Rome. I suspect you sensed the days are declining for the current government and the days for the Church are in ascendance—and thus your choice of career."

Vigilius made no comment.

"Is my Greek too swift for you, Lord Bishop Vigilius? It is better than my Latin."

"No. No, *mistress*, I mean. I am following you."

"Good. The days of the Ostrogothic rule in Italy are running out quickly, like the last drops of a water clock. When our General Belisarius takes charge, things will change within the Church power structure, just as they will in the government. We *will* take Rome, you know. And then the emperor and I will have it in our power to see to your advancement."

"I seek no special advancement, mistress."

"Oh, now, Vigilius. No false modesty here, please. You and I are alone. Your sights were once set upon the highest throne. Would you sneer at having a second chance at it?"

Theodora noticed a slight flutter at the corner of his mouth, as if some spirit within were trying to answer for him.

"You don't need to answer. That it remains your fondest wish is tattooed upon your face."

The priest paled.

"Do you know what *my* dearest wish is, Vigilius? Do you?"

The legate shook his head.

"Oh, I would wager you do. You're better at this game than you let on. Do you know my wish?"

"Yes, I think so."

"Good! What is it?"

"You would have Anthimus reinstated as Patriarch of Constantinople."

"Excellent! And, my Lord Bishop Vigilius, you would see to the healing of the two faiths. In the end, this is a game that can boast two winners." Here she paused a moment, studying him, then pouncing: "What say you? Will you play?"

Vigilius cleared his throat as if to speak, but, slowly, he nodded instead.

32

July 536

I T WAS NIGHT WHEN I returned from an errand to find Piers in his usual state of bewilderment whenever Theodora visited. "Where is she? The study or reception room?"

"Neither," Piers said, eyebrows arched.

"She left? Did she wait long?"

"Oh, she's still here, Stephen." His eyes alone directed me toward the hall. "In his bedchamber."

"Setka's?" It was a mindless question. Of course, that's what he meant. My jaw dropped a bit. "How long?"

"Half of an hour."

My back stiffened. "Has he been singing or playing his lute?"

Piers shook his head, head tilted down.

Aware that his hearing was starting to fail, I said, "Maybe you just didn't hear him."

"Oh, I listened," he insisted.

I could imagine him stationed not far from Setka's doorway. We stared blankly at each other, both no doubt wondering what could go on between an empress and a seventeen-year-old musician in the said musician's bedchamber. At that moment, however, a rustle of material brought my gaze back to the hallway, where at the far end, a figure in purple and gold was gliding in our direction. Theodora was alone.

"I was about to give you up," Theodora said.

"I did not expect you, mistress," I countered, using a formal address while Piers was in the room.

"Yes, yes, I know. It's late, too, but I had some news. Disturbing news."

"Yes? I suggest we move into my reception room." I nodded for Theodora to lead the way, and a nod to Piers released him from our presence.

Theodora began even as she settled herself on a couch across from my chair. "We've had word that Rome has a new Holy Father."

Theodora had dictated a letter to Belisarius concerning Agapetus's replacement, so I was aware of her scheme to have Vigilius forcibly installed. "But Vigilius could not have reached Italy yet, or has he?"

"He has not." Theodora looked as if she had swallowed something distasteful. "The shepherd's staff has gone to a cleric named Silverius. It appears when the news of Agapetus's death arrived in Rome, this Silverius bribed the Ostrogothic king who, in turn, threatened the Roman clergy with death if they did not elect him."

We sat for a long minute in silence.

I did not dare point out the irony that the Palace of Hormisdas was named for Silverius's father, who had also been a Holy Father, one who was an ardent persecutor of anti-Chalcedonian denominations, especially the Monophysites. Neither did I waste my breath suggesting Silverius might be malleable regarding the reappointment of the deposed Patriarch Anthimus. It was no doubt quite obvious to her: Silverius held the same ironclad views as had his father. Even I deduced as much.

"So," Theodora said with a sigh, "when Vigilius does reach Rome, he will find St. Peter's chair occupied and our agreement of no value." She gave her head a little shake as if she could rearrange events more to her liking. "I'll not have my plans thwarted by simony and threats."

I could not help but think how she had meant to employ her own imperial influence to see to the naming of a Holy Father. I said nothing.

After a few moments, she announced, "When Belisarius takes Rome, there will be a realignment of game pieces."

I nodded, choosing not to inquire further.

"By the way," she asked, "we've still had no word from Tariq?"

"No, Thea."

Theodora stood to leave.

I rose, as well. "I'm sorry I wasn't here when you arrived."

Theodora shrugged and started to move toward the door. "Oh, I passed the time."

"With Setka," I said, realizing with no little alarm that I spoke it aloud.

Theodora halted and pivoted toward me, her eyes like arrows. She drew in breath and said, "Yes, he sang and played for me. He's quite talented. Justinian is much taken with him."

I stood like a statue for a minute or more after her exit. Something of a busybody, Piers had maintained Setka neither sang nor played. So—why would she lie? Knowing Antonina's fondness for young men raised my suspicion. Had she gifted Theodora with the handsome musician for more than his lute and voice? On the one hand, it seemed inconceivable. From the start, her relationship with Justinian appeared a true love match, strong as iron. But it occurred to me now that Agapetus had pitched them on opposite sides of the Christ question. Was that a wound deep enough to fracture their bond, prompting her to seek other companions? Or—and this was a truly stray thought—might Theodora be plotting—unbeknown to Justinian—to conceive an heir through this boy?

I moved down the hall with the intention of questioning Setka about his guest but stopped suddenly. *What if he is to relay my curiosity to Theodora?* I asked myself. No matter what went on in his chamber, she would not appreciate my interference. Before retreating to my own bedchamber, I found Piers preparing for bed and swore him to secrecy regarding our late-night visitant. Gossip in a palace moves like flames through tinder.

I went to my study where I had one friend in whom I could confide, one who well knew my weakness. Above the blue waters of a pond, Jati, my black-haired mosaic boy stared across at me, his dark eyes glistening in the candlelight, seeming to mirror my hurt and confusion.

Theodora meant to make good on her vow not to be foiled in the naming of a Holy Father. With supreme confidence, she initiated her scheme. Even before Belisarius began his march on Rome—she dictated a letter, or rather, an official document, to him underscoring the empire's support of the papal legate Vigilius, who was bringing the body of Holy Father Agapetus to the Holy City for burial. As if the new Holy Father Silverius were a minor official, Theodora directed Belisarius to find the excuse and means to shunt him aside, sending him to Constantinople so that in his absence an election could be held that would reward Vigilius with the position. Before the letter was sent, she managed to win her husband's signature and seal.

Several weeks later, I finally received a communication from Tariq. Because the royal couple was hosting some event in the Hall of the Nineteen Couches, Theodora would not meet with me until the next day. The temptation for me to learn the contents was too great. I read it in the comfort of my study under the watchful eyes of Jati.

Much has been happening. Procopius's version of events will likely follow on the next ship out, but know that what I write here is the truth. If someone is cast in a bad light herein, I pray that as the messenger, I'm not found blameworthy.

Someone has finally informed Belisarius of his wife's adultery, and thus began a series of wildly incredible and convoluted events.

As I have written before, numerous people attached to General Belisarius were aware of Antonina's affair with her godson Theodosius. It appears the lusty pair had the ill judgment to use the general's bed. I traced the rumors to two slave boys who were assigned to the general's bedchamber. Word spread quickly among the servants, also reaching the ears of the general's immediate subordinates, Bessas and Constantine.

It was not the only illicit affair occurring. As irony would have it, Antonina discovered her seventeen-year-old son Photius en flagrante delicto *with an exceptionally beautiful slave girl of hers, Macedonia. While Photius was lightly chastised, the girl suffered severe punishment at the orders of her mistress and consequently harbored thoughts of revenge that she acted upon. She informed Belisarius she had something to tell him, but knowing Antonina's nature, she made him swear never to reveal the source of his knowledge. When he agreed, she told him of Antonina's affair with their godson. I did not witness the scene, but his bellowing with rage made me question the girl afterward. She told me he did not believe her at first and called up the two bedchamber boys for corroboration. It was only then that he believed her. He went into a frenzy and ordered Theodosius arrested and executed.*

You might not believe what I have to say next, but Antonina's manservant Eugenius has taken me into his confidence, so my source is a primary one. He told me Belisarius called him in after having second thoughts about taking Theodosius's life. His conscience led him to change his order. Secretly, he had Eugenius put Theodosius on a ship headed for the city of Ephesus where he was to surrender himself to a monastery and take vows that include that of chastity. To do otherwise would mean his death. Eugenius said the young man accepted his fate, and he well knew the orders came from his godfather, whom he admired and feared. By now, Stephen, I suspect the boy's crown, once a black and wavy mass, has been tonsured. Antonina is despondent over his mysterious disappearance.

Subsequently, I happened to hear General Constantine consoling Belisarius on Antonina's unfaithfulness and Theodosius's apparent evasion of a penalty. It was chilling. "I would not worry so much about a youth like that," he said. "If I had been wronged by the pair, it would have been my wife *I killed. I would call it an honor killing."*

It was not advice Belisarius followed. Despite her adultery, from all appearances, he still loves his wife. And there was another reason holding him back from harming Antonina. I heard him reply to Constantine, in sotto voce, *"Oh, if I were to do that, I would be placing myself in danger with the empress. Theodora and Antonina are like confederate cousins."*

Within two days, however, there came an ad inversionem bonorumque.

I have found no witness to the turnabout, but Lady Antonina managed to extract from her husband the identities of the tattletales, as well as convince him that Macedonia and the two boys were lying out of spite for the way she treated them.

Now, in Procopius's report to Justinian the version of events he dictated to me details how Antonina and her servant Eugenius had the tongues of the three talebearers cut out prior to having their bodies minced like stew meat and thrown to sharks. How Procopius loves a good story! In actuality, the two boys were beaten, branded, and sold to the owner of a silver mine. Why shouldn't their punishment bring with it a little dividend? Macedonia suffered a different kind of branding. She was forced to enter a nunnery where she is to remain forever chaste.

Abashed by what he thought was a grievous error, the gullible Belisarius sent a ship to retrieve Theodosius. Distrustful of Belisarius's sudden change of heart, however, Antonina's lover elected to stay at Ephesus.

I will say at times I thought it would be Photius who would reveal his mother's betrayal to Belisarius, but he kept silent, and after witnessing the fates of the three who dared to do so, he must have felt a sense of relief that he had held back.

I could scarcely believe the letter's contents and could only wonder what reaction Theodora might have. Since I knew she had delivered admonishing words to Antonina in person about the affair with her godson, I fully expected to see the ire of an empress unleashed when I read the letter to her in her study. I read it straight through without looking up. She sat in the wicker chair opposite mine and remained silent throughout.

Then, when I finished and looked across at Theodora, I was surprised to find she took the flagrant disobedience of her closest friend with utter calm. She sat with her elbows on the armrests, her palms apart, fingertips together forming a steeple. "You know, Stephen," she said in a kind of drawl, "I've seen to it that such *honor killings* have been officially outlawed in the *Codex Justinianus.*"

"I do know."

The dark eyebrows that nearly joined above her perfect nose lifted, pressing up into her alabaster forehead, but she allowed no other hint of her temperament to show.

Nonetheless, she exchanged places with me so that I could sit at her desk and take down her letter to Antonina. The content was direct and emphatic—and yet coolly dispassionate. Theodora was most upset with Belisarius, who has not yet acted on the order to send Holy Father Silverius to Constantinople and have Vigilius placed on St. Peter's throne instead. Thus, she directed her childhood friend to take *any measure possible* to depose one Holy Father and elect another—and without delay. In making this demand, Theodora set aside Antonina's disregard for the recent royal edicts regarding the sanctity of marriage and any moralizing she might have expressed for Antonina's benefit.

I thought she was not even going to allude to the Theodosius affair. But I was wrong. And dumbfounded.

At the end of the letter, almost as a postscript, she told Antonina that she was writing to the Bishop of Ephesus and that Theodosius would speedily be returned to his godparents.

Now I understood. These two longtime friends who rose from a bleak and hardscrabble life shared a bond forged in steel. Theodora seemed wholly confident Antonina would follow through on her request regarding Vigilius, and in compensation, her lover would be returned to her.

My next task, then, was writing that letter to Ephesus.

33

A LETTER FROM TARIQ ARRIVED TWO days after Christmas. As Theodora sat across from my desk, I read it in its entirety.

On the tenth of the month, Holy Father Silverius violated the trust of the long-reigning Ostrogoths and ordered the gates of Rome thrown open to Belisarius, who entered riding a white-faced bay at the vanguard of a relatively small army, just five thousand strong. King Theodahad had been assassinated and the new king, Witigis, was amassing a huge force at Ravenna to take back Rome and all of Italy.

We were met by a welcoming assemblage of senators, nobles, and clergy who besought General Belisarius to ride at once to Ravenna in order to catch Witigis by surprise before his army could be properly organized. In short, no sooner had we been admitted to Rome than we were being asked to vacate. Belisarius was stunned. And stubborn. He replied by saying, "I'd much rather stay here in this lovely city and take enjoyment in your Roman hospitality."

The faces all around us soured at once. Several senators spoke up, arguing that the Ostrogoths, believed at the time to be numbering one hundred thousand, would be a tide that could not be turned back and that Rome was a particularly difficult city to defend.

"Exactly!" the general said. "I have already examined the city's defenses and I find them in deplorable condition. We'll need the time and the manpower of my army to improve them."

The next day word came that the Holy Father Silverius sought a meeting with Belisarius. Procopius told me Belisarius was too busy visiting the sites that needed to be shored up against invasion and that he arranged with Antonina to meet with him instead.

Procopius and I were present for the meeting. He had me take notes that I assume will one day work into his History of the Italian War—or whatever title he might alight upon.

We had been afforded hospitality in a splendid villa on the Pincian Hill and it was there Holy Father Silverius was ushered into a fine columned reception hall with white marble flooring. He is of average height and plain of face but for a strong Roman nose set above a full beard. His head has been tonsured but over the forehead he is bald except for a single shock of curly white that was less than becoming. When Antonina bit her lower lip and stifled what I think was a chuckle, I guessed that she found the wayward lock humorous. As the Holy Father moved toward where we stood, his eyes flicked from one of us to the next until the realization that he was not going to meet Belisarius moved like a shadow across his face. No one spoke until the three of us had knelt and kissed the ring bearing the image of a fisherman.

Lady Antonina welcomed him as Procopius and I repaired to a table off to the side where my kalamos, ink, and parchment awaited. Lady Antonina sat across from the Holy Father as if they were equals. In fact, the intense red of her stola outdid the red of his dalmatic. The Holy Father did not look pleased. He told Lady Antonina that he was hoping—or rather expecting—to speak to General Belisarius himself.

He grew less pleased when Antonina said that he would have

met with her husband if only he had found it in his schedule to accompany his clergy to welcome them upon their arrival. Silverius blinked at the barb as Antonina continued without pause, going on about how the city defenses were in disrepair and that Belisarius was doing what he could to protect the Holy City.

At this point Silverius affected a smile, mostly hidden by beard, and told Antonina that she must convince her famous husband to resign from the impossible task and leave the city. He spoke to her as if she were a child, calling her "daughter," and insisting Belisarius leave an indefensible city and confront the Ostrogothic King Witigis at Ravenna. He said that under siege Rome would face starvation.

Antonina countered by saying Belisarius would prepare the city for a siege and did not so much as flinch when the Holy Father told her they could expect one hundred thousand Ostrogoths at the gates. Silverius's next suggestion was that Belisarius return to Naples because that city made for a better defense as it was more readily shielded and paths by sea would allow access to provisions for both citizens and soldiers. He said, "Here, Lady Antonina, there is only death for you and for us Romans."

Lady Antonina had an answer at the ready. She said, "Most Holy Father Silverius, you have chosen your vocation. You are a shepherd. My husband has chosen his. He is a man of war. He knows little of your cloistered, clerical life." She paused, clearly enjoying her role. Then she said, "What can you know of his?"

Holy Father Silverius recognized an impasse, stood, and with a swishing motion of his red dalmatic, pivoted and abruptly made his exit, a scowl upon his face.

You can be certain he did not enjoy meeting with a woman on common ground, much less losing to one.

Sitting across from me, Theodora looked up when I finished, black eyes quizzing me.

"That's all," I said. "Nothing left but his signature."

"What? Nothing else?" Her chin lifted, nostrils flaring.

"No, Thea." I searched for something placating to say. After all, deposing the Holy Father of the Church had to be a forbidding kind of task. "Lady Antonina was most contentious in her dealings with him."

"Contentious?" Theodora hissed. "She was to *confront* him. She was to see to his deposition. She had him in her grasp and allowed him to slip through."

"Perhaps she wishes to pursue that end with the help of the general?"

Theodora scoffed at my suggestion. "I'm concerned that Belisarius hesitates because he feels he owes Silverius for turning traitor to the Ostrogoths and opening the city gates. You know, Stephen, military men have something of a code. And his focus right now is no doubt on the difficult siege they will have to weather. What importance would an ecclesiastical matter have in his mind? Damn him!" She sat silent, the dark eyes clouded for a few moments, then finally finding focus and rising to hold mine captive. "As for Antonina, Stephen, there's a reason why Belisarius had her lead the infantry at Carthage. She's quite capable with or without her husband."

And in that so like you, I thought.

Theodora left soon after, her expression stony with disappointment.

The next day a one-sentence letter went off to Antonina.

Be about your purpose, it read.

When a month went by without another letter from Tariq, Theodora feared her wish had been shunted aside, rather than the Holy Father Silverius. She burst into my study one day, a blur in purple. Piers, who had no time to announce her, trailed white-faced and bug-eyed behind her.

"Letters will not do," she announced; "they will not."

I stood and waved Piers away. "Will you sit, Thea?"

"I will not. I intend to send a messenger to Rome with my explicit demands for Belisarius and Antonina."

"Very well." I sat and drew out parchment, assuming I was to copy her orders.

"That won't be necessary, Stephen." Theodora reversed herself and settled into the chair across from my desk.

I looked up, noting a strangely smug smile had replaced her vexation. "The person I am sending goes with my complete trust."

"I see. Are you going to trust me with his name? Or hers?"

The black eyes locked onto me. "I am. It's you, Stephen."

34

January 537

IN THEODORA'S WORLD, MY GOING to Rome was a given, so I did not
have the opportunity to refuse. I will admit the prospect of seeing Rome
caught my imagination, but it was winter, a dangerous time for sailing,
and no ships were leaving Constantinople for Italy, neither military nor
merchant. As if reading my mind, Theodora said, offhandedly, "To wait for
April is out of the question."

On a dreary, drizzly morning, I climbed into a wagon drawn by a team
of two horses and my journey began. I was escorted by two Imperial Guards,
Cletus and Leander, who traded off the driving duties. We took the Via
Egnatia land route out of Constantinople, a seven-hundred-mile-long and
twenty-foot-wide Roman road that wound through Illyricum, Macedonia, and
Thrace. Despite repairs done by Justinian, the centuries-old road still had long
stretches where the polygonal stone slabs had crumbled from time, weather,
or the heavy trade that went on between East and West. The meandering path
took us over bridges, along lakes, jolting and jostling us through rough terrain,
mountain ranges, and more than twenty towns and countless staging stations.
The sheer traffic of travelers and traders slowed us considerably before we arrived at Dyrrachium, where we managed to book passage to take us across the
Adriatic Sea to Brindisi, on Italy's heel. We had been on the road three long
and arduous weeks, and we were about to follow the Via Appia to Orla, then
Toranto and north to Rome, a distance that was, blessedly, half the way we
had come.

Fortune was with us because the Ostrogothic forces were entrenched in
cities north of Rome while south of the capital, Belisarius's soldiers guarded

the Via Appia. My travel documents cleared the path for us, and we were favored by less traffic, so we moved at a faster rate than on the Via Egnatia. Nonetheless, with all the stops at roadhouses and staging stations, another ten or so days went by.

February 537

When Rome finally came into view, I put aside the hardships of the trip and came fully alert, all senses heightened. Nonetheless, I prayed my return to Constantinople would occur in good sailing weather so that we could avoid the overland route.

At last, our wagon clattered into Rome at its southeast side, through the Porta Appia, an appropriately grand gate in Rome's Aurelian Wall.

A guard gave us directions to a mansion on the Pincian Hill in the northeast quadrant, where General Belisarius was residing. In little time we passed unchecked through the Porta Capena, set in the old Servian Wall.

Soon the huge oval Flavian Amphitheater loomed ahead, and if I did not currently live in the shadow of Constantinople's Hippodrome, I would have been more mightily impressed. Still, the massive tiered structure rose up in the city center, an imposing site where Christians, gladiators, and animals had shed their blood.

Dusk was falling as we continued trundling up roads so that the crowds were thinning. We passed by structures and through forums that, again, did not favorably compare to The City. When we came to the base of the Pincian Hill, the road narrowed and rose toward the buildings atop it in a most circuitous way. The incline caused the wagon to slow, but my pulse quickened to think my journey of many weeks was coming to an end at last—and I would see my good friend Tariq once again.

At the top, if the well-guarded mansion did not impress, its gardens, even in winter, and its view of all of Rome certainly did hold me spellbound.

It was here I parted ways with my two guards. I could not call them friends, for as many hours and experiences we had shared, I hardly knew them. All the while, Cletus and Leander had kept their distance, talking between themselves, and including me only in regard to some aspect of the journey, such as choosing a place to stay for the night. Was it our different vocations that made the difference? That I was a eunuch? Or the fact that I was like a *pujada*, a foot soldier on the empress's *Shatranj* game board to be protected at all costs, including with their lives? It might have been all of these things, I thought, but day by day, I became certain that it was fear of Theodora that iced their personalities in my presence.

According to the request I was to hand Belisarius, he was to provide them with two good horses so that they could retrace our steps back to Justinian's service. Without a wagon and a eunuch in their charge, they would make good time. While I felt no real loss as to their companionship, I did suddenly somehow feel unanchored in this far-away city.

How will *I* return? I wondered. *When* will I return to Constantinople? To Theodora?

"It's called the Eternal City," Tariq said. "It's too dark now, but wait until you see the view tomorrow."

I had been given a room in Tariq's suite, and we stood now on his balcony looking out at the outlines of hills and buildings and flares of torches on thoroughfares and flickering of lights within windows.

"Why 'Eternal City'?" I asked.

"According to Procopius, it was given its epithet early on by a poet named Tibullus. Like early Romans, he believed that no matter what other empires rise and fall, Rome would live on forever."

"I see."

My expression must have betrayed my reaction to the mention of Procopius because Tariq said, "Oh, yes, he has the rooms next to mine. At least Domus Pinciana is big enough so that I don't have to share his suite." He wrinkled his nose. "On campaign I've had to share a tent with him."

I laughed. "He knows I'm coming?"

"That he does. He's frantic to know the reason."

"No doubt it's stirred up the old dislike. He has no clue as to *why* I'm here?"

Tariq shook his head. "I think Lady Antonina has her suspicion, but Procopius is in the dark, so you can expect to find him lurking about like the jackal he is."

"Ha! I'll be on my guard."

Tariq poured us cups of Sicilian wine, and he toasted to our friendship.

I drank, looking out at the city. "This is a lovely old mansion."

"Tomorrow, you must look to the south, there, Stephen," Tariq said, pointing. "Beyond the Flavian Amphitheater you'll see the old Imperial Palace, the Domus Flavia where it sits on Palatine Hill. Home to early emperors, it's quite an impressive structure."

"Really? I'm surprised Belisarius didn't set up his home and headquarters there."

"Oh, don't think he didn't consider it, but his wife put her pretty foot down on the notion."

"Why? She does enjoy luxury."

Tariq lowered his voice and glanced around. "According to Photius, she told Belisarius it would send the wrong message back to Constantinople."

"Ah, that his powers were ever rising, yes?"

"Yes, and that at the end of reconquering the western empire there might be a diadem glittering for the conqueror. Justinian wouldn't like it."

"Exactly," I said. "Emperors must keep their eyes on successful generals lest ambition overtake them. As for Justinian, he can be a bit thick, but he has Theodora's dark eyes on the watch for such things."

"You mean on Belisarius?"

"Yes. Now—do they know I've arrived?"

"They do. Why, Stephen, you're to have supper with them tomorrow."

"Truly?"

"Yes, now that's an honor *I've* not enjoyed."

"No?"

"Sometimes as I move about I feel like I'm wearing Hermes' cap of invisibility. It's like I fade into the wall tapestries." Tariq's voice dropped to a whisper. "I suppose that's to the good, considering I'm a spy for the empress."

"Shush, Tariq!" I hissed. "I don't want to hear some accident has befallen you."

Tariq shrugged away my worry. "Oh, you'll be treated well enough here in Rome, Stephen. In pleasing you, they will be pleasing—"

"Theodora," I said, finishing his statement.

Supper was held late to accommodate Belisarius's tardy arrival from his inspection of various fortifications. He and Antonina occupied the head dining couch, while Photius and I occupied one wing and Procopius the other, directly across, from where he glowered at me. Photius treated me more warmly but soon fell silent. Belisarius regaled us with his plans to hold off King Witigis's massive forces even while his hands picked hungrily at the bowls of diced fish and chicken. "How is the empress?" Antonina inquired. She was as beautiful as ever. With her upswept blond hair and turquoise stola, one could hardly imagine her riding at the front of an infantry division as she had done at Carthage.

"She is well," I answered, knowing this was not the time to deliver my message.

"Does she still engage you in rounds of *Shatranj*?" Procopius asked. Here was a man whose eyes, rather than his tone, sparked sarcasm.

"Less so these days," I said, affecting a smile and avoiding mention of her recent preoccupation with the politics of religion.

"You're still in her favor, though," Procopius said. He managed to sneer at me even as he stuffed a piece of chicken into his mouth. "Obviously."

It was at this moment that someone entered the dining chamber, and I was saved from replying.

"You're late," Belisarius said, bits of chicken flying out of his mouth. It was more a statement of fact than an accusation. The general nodded toward Procopius's couch. "Sit there."

Antonina waved her hand for a slave girl to come forward with a bowl and goblet for the new arrival, a tall handsome youth. She then turned to me. "Stephen, do you know our godson Theodosius?"

"Not formally, Lady Antonina," I replied, nodding and smiling at the boy. Of course, I knew who he was because I had seen her with him dozens of times as they went about The City creating no little scandal. I bit at my lower lip, realizing that at this meal there were more topics of conversation to avoid than to pursue.

Theodosius did not so much as nod at me. He tilted his head, however, his ice blue eyes questioning as if to ask, *What is this eunuch doing at our supper table?*

The meal proceeded, its awkward undercurrents of human attitudes as varied as the courses.

With the bread and bowls of fish, meat, olives, and sliced cheeses nearly depleted, Belisarius excused himself and retired. Antonina finished off a goblet of wine, her third, I think, and stood. "Stephen," she said, "it is time we talked." She left the chamber without pausing to see if I would agree. She expected me to obediently follow.

Of course, I did just that.

We settled ourselves on opposite chairs in the corner of a massive reception room.

"I think I know why Theodora sent you."

I nodded, smiling. I wondered whether I was to wait for her guess.

"Well?" she asked, prodding me to speak first.

"Lady Antonina, the empress wants to see Anthimus restored to his post as patriarch."

"She knows Holy Father Silverius is a lost cause, yes?"

"She does."

"So I am to get rid of him somehow and put this cleric Vigilius in his place."

"Yes."

"I knew this, Stephen. Now, is there some twist to her wishes?"

"Only that you follow through in good time."

"Ah—in *her* time, you mean!"

"As you say."

"She has always been impatient in her desires, ever since we were children. Ah—I suppose that is how she came to wear the diadem."

I had no answer.

"We have not forgotten her wish although my memory is better than the general's. The Holy Father Silverius opened the gates and welcomed us to Rome, but then he suggested we deal with the Goths anywhere but here—and that we pull up and leave Rome. Can you imagine? Oh, he didn't like my terse response. Why, Thea should know how angry and defeated he was by the time the audience was over."

"She knows," I said absently, for my thoughts had landed on her word choice of *audience*. Did she mean to say that she and the general had granted the Holy Father an audience—as if they *had* established themselves at Rome's Imperial Palace? As if their ambition knew no bounds?

"She knows! How? *How* could she know?"

My stomach clenched. Less than an hour after reminding myself to say little of what I knew to this cast of characters, I made my first blunder. Had I endangered my source—Tariq? "I … I don't know, Lady Antonina."

The blue eyes blazed in my direction as if she could determine whether I was telling the truth.

I stared back, feeling my face warm.

After long moments, she waved her hand dismissively, the bangles on her silver bracelet tinkling. "Oh well, never mind. I should have known we'd have one of her spies in our midst."

I forced a smile, terrified my stupid error could lead to the unmasking of Tariq.

"Well, you are in luck, eunuch. You will be able to witness in person the deposition of a Roman Holy Father."

"One day soon?" Tariq questioned. "That's what she told you? Well, that depends on whether he shows up. He's turned down their invitations twice, and he's moved from the residence of the Holy Father, the Lateran Palace on the Caelian Hill, to the more protected Church of Saint Sabina on the Aventine Hill."

"Really?"

"Oh, yes. It appears he knows he's a marked man."

"So—he's so fearful of Theodora he's almost declaring sanctuary?"

"Not *almost*, Stephen.—Now, tell me, how did they treat you at supper?"

"Procopius? With his usual scorn."

"You must have been surprised to see Theodosius. I forgot to tell you he had returned."

"I knew he was likely to be here. I sent Theodora's order to the Bishop of Ephesus that he be returned to his godparents. A proud and pompous fellow he is."

"Godparents, indeed!" Tariq said with a smirk.

"So—the affair continues?"

"It does, but she has less time for him these days. If she's not acting as Belisarius's lieutenant directing a unit of soldiers at one gate or another, then she's acting as a deputized city official overseeing who is allowed to leave Rome through those gates. She was so caught up in these activities—activities she thoroughly enjoys, by the way—that when Theodosius returned, he was no longer at the top of her agenda. She revels in her husband's growing soldierly fame, and the fact that Theodosius isn't much of a horseman and is even less proficient with a bow must find him wanting in her eyes. After all, once when a gate came under attack, I saw her take hold of a three-man catapult as manager. It is the manager who sights the target and calls 'Deliver.' Well, I saw her skewer two Ostrogoths, two for two."

As the visual played in my mind, I must have stared open-mouthed at Tariq.

"Well," he pressed, "how did *she* receive you?"

"Not with a catapult," I said. We both laughed. "But she treated me like the messenger I am, I suppose. You would never know I was the one to rescue her from her life at Madame Flavia's brothel."

"Don't expect any kind of recognition or respect from her ilk."

"Because then I was merely an imperial messenger?"

"Well, yes, but more so is the fact that you are a—"

"Eunuch," I said, once again finishing his sentence.

35

S EVERAL WEEKS WENT BY AND I began to think Antonina's assurance she would act on Theodora's order was all bluster.

For me, they were not weeks spent idle or bored. Tariq took me on daily tours of the Eternal City. I had noticed little on the evening of my arrival so caught up I was with locating the Domus Pinciana and how the delivery of my message to Antonina would be received. Add to that my extreme exhaustion after grueling weeks of travel.

Now, day by day, I grasped a true sense of the city. What I noticed was shocking. One certainly could feel the grandeur and magnificence of Rome's best days of the early empire, but the decades spent under the control of the Ostrogoths had rendered this center of civilization a stagnant, forlorn, and fractured place. Rome was a city in decline.

Each day we walked through one of the various neighborhoods. In each, I observed temples, libraries, and palaces that had been closed or abandoned, their costly decorations of marble, gold, and bronze stolen or stripped to adorn new buildings, often done with corrupt city officials' license. Statues were defaced, mutilated, or missing entirely from their pedestals. Baths and fountains, once flowing with fresh and sparkling waters, had been stilled because the ingenious aqueduct system fell into neglect and decay, resulting in deposits of dank and fetid swampland in various parts of the city that was believed to cause outbreaks of serious illnesses.

The tenor of the population matched that of the miasmal and dissolute surroundings. A few of the upper class families that managed to survive the onslaught of the Goths did so in a condition of poverty whereby they currently resided in just a few rooms of their once-luxurious mansions, or had been reduced to living in tenements. Those who were able to leave Rome repaired to Ravenna or Constantinople. At its height, Rome had boasted one million citizens. Now, the population numbered no more than forty thousand.

"Eternal City, indeed," I said to Tariq. "That poet you spoke of—what would he think of it today?"

Tariq did his best to counter my melancholy at what I was seeing. "You have to remember, Stephen, Rome has been sacked four times. Besides the plundering, it's suffered fire and earthquake."

"Does that excuse the neglect?" As we were passing one of the swampy areas, I took the cloth of my sleeve's cuff away from my nose. "So—this is the city of gold Justinian is determined to win back? Why, I wonder what he would say should he see it. Tariq, he used to take me on long walks along the aqueducts of Constantinople, all the while praising the Roman masterminds who had conceived and built them. I pray he does not ask me about my observations here."

"What if Theodora should ask you?"

I shrugged. "Oh, she will, but I'm not sure it will matter much to her. She is more concerned with uniting the two faiths."

"You know, Stephen, the odd thing is that in his reports to Justinian, Procopius paints everything here as silvery bright and full of promise. Why would he do that?"

"I don't know, but I do know he has no alliance with the truth."

"It may have to do with the patina he wants to lay on Belisarius and his accomplishments. I can tell you in his *Histories* he downplays the general's foibles and defeats."

As the days fell away, I began to realize that as the old glory of a Rome renowned for its legal minds and military might receded, a new city was rising, an episcopal city of newly built churches, cathedrals, convents, and hospitals. All of this, as well as the entire Christian community across the world, was led by the Bishop of Rome who had, since the days of St. Peter, resided in the Domus Faustae, the episcopal palace close by to the Basilica of St. John Lateran. However, Silverius, the current and unconditionally Orthodox Bishop of Rome, had abandoned the Domus Faustae for the safety of sanctuary in the Church of Saint Sabina, aware he was the target of Theodora and her longtime lieutenant, Antonina.

And I was here to document the deposing of the Holy Father. I placed no faith in Christianity or in any faith, and yet the enormity of what Theodora had ordered made me shudder.

21 March 537

"He's coming," Tariq said, shaking me awake. "He's coming!"

"Truly?" I asked, pulling myself up to the side of the sleeping couch. "Today?"

"Tomorrow—after he says his Sunday Mass."

"Why—after so many refusals?"

"Antonina used her gatekeeping position to have him charged with treachery. Evidently a warrant signed by General Belisarius was enough to goad him into agreeing to appear."

"Treachery? What treachery? Does she mean treason?"

"I don't know, Stephen. It could be a trick. The tale will unfold tomorrow. Her attendant Eugenius says she will face him alone."

"What of the general?"

"Eugenius said the two had quite a spirited debate over deposing Silverius. Remember, Belisarius is an Orthodox Christian, and I suspect he'd rather face a thousand Ostrogoths alone than bring an accusation against the Holy Father of the Christian Church."

"Whereas Antonina is Christian in name but has pagan roots."

"Exactly!—I expect Antonina will say that her husband is 'busy elsewhere'."

22 March 537

Lady Antonina made sure I had a good seat in the court hearing featuring her as judge and Holy Father Silverius the accused. She must have known Theodora would be waiting for a moment-by-moment account of the event. Tariq had been correct: Belisarius wanted nothing to do with the proceedings and busied himself elsewhere.

So that the Holy Father would not disappoint Antonina again, Belisarius had ordered Photius—flanked by a bodyguard of ten—to escort him from the Church of Saint Sabina to the Domus Pinciana, where he arrived promptly at noon, the prescribed hour. The six attending clerics were made to wait in the atrium as Photius and his bodyguard led him into the reception room. I suspect the presence of the stone-faced military men took him by surprise—and perhaps suspicion and fear. In any case, he gave no argument.

In glittering vestments of gold and red, Silverius entered the reception room serving this day as a courtroom. Beneath a gold diadem, his face was pallid as the white pallium draped about his neck, his body stiff as the gold shepherd's staff he carried. His darting eyes betrayed his anxiety.

Antonina sat in an oversized chair that had been painted silver, her long, polished nails tapping the armrests, looking every bit the part of a judge—or empress. Her golden curls had been gathered high on her head and held within a band of gold. She might well have imagined it a diadem. I sat at a table off to the side with my writing materials, Tariq seated beside me. The ten soldiers posted themselves at the side walls of the large room. Silverius approached Antonina, his red shoes kicking out in measured steps. She gave a dismissive wave of her hand to Photius, indicating his task was finished, and he was to leave. He answered his mother with a scowl but obeyed.

Antonina did not stand, kneel, or kiss the Holy Father's ring. Silverius offered a bow, stood erect, drew in breath, and in strong voice asked, "On what grounds have I been called? What charges have been made against me?"

Antonina offered a vague smile and nodded to a chair that had been placed next to where he stood. "You may take a seat, Lord Silverius."

I took the raising of his bushy white eyebrows as surprise at Antonina's familiarity of address. I expected him to correct her for not addressing him as *Holy Father Silverius*, but I was wrong.

"I'll stand," he said.

"As you wish."

"Where is General Belisarius?" Silverius demanded.

"He is securing the city. I have been deputized."

Silverius's head jerked back slightly. "You?"

In answer, Antonina merely smiled.

"What is it, then, I am accused of?"

"You are accused of treason."

"That's preposterous."

"You are accused of signing a letter offering to open the city to King Witigis."

Silverius's jaw dropped a bit. "As I did for the general? Never!"

"Why would you expect me to believe that a person willing to betray once would not do so a second time?"

His eyes widened. He paused for a moment before taking a different tack. "Because, Lady Antonina, it is the heir to Saint Peter that assures you I am innocent of such a thing."

"Oh? And is that the same heir who, when he heard of Holy Father Agapetus's death in Constantinople, rushed to the Gothic king with satchels of gold as a bribe? The same whose interest King Theodahad—a heretic, I might add—took up, threatening the Roman clergy with death should they not elect him? Or rather—you, *Lord* Silverius."

"Lies!" Silverius cried. It was more than the misappropriation of his title that brought about a quick empurpling of his face. "Call in my fellow clerics from the atrium. They will tell you so."

"Are they the same ones who were cowed into voting for you? Or was bribery all it took?"

"You have no proof of these accusations! I see no witnesses sitting here who will dare speak against me."

"Here is my proof, Silverius." Antonina held up a scroll. "It is the offer you made the new Ostrogothic king, Witigis, to open up the Asinarian Gate at midnight on the day of his choice."

Even with his full beard, gray as stone, I could see Silverius swallow hard.

"It has your signature, Lord Silverius, and it has your seal. Do you not wish to see it?" Antonina held it open on the table.

Stepping forward, Silverius bent over the document and scanned it in a cursory manner. No more than a minute passed before he straightened himself. "A forgery is this. A forgery! I ask you again to call in my clergy."

"They are your clergy no longer. You are hereby removed from your ill-gotten position."

"What? You have no right—"

Antonina gave a nod to a soldier nearby. "Just what right did an Arian Goth have to install you as head of the Roman Church?"

Before Silverius could draw breath to answer, a crush of soldiers surrounded him. Beneath his finery, his body was thin, so that when two soldiers grasped him under his arms, they had an easy time of it lifting him off the floor and carrying him to an adjacent chamber. The door closed and all went silent in the reception room. Her blue eyes flicking in our direction, Antonina smiled slightly and slumped back in her chair.

Some six soldiers remained in the room, as did a palpable tension. Tariq and I did not dare to share a word or even a glance between us. I'm certain he was wondering the same thing as I. *What is going on behind that closed door?*

Fifteen minutes later, the door opened and Silverius was escorted back to Antonina's table. He had been relieved of his diadem, vestments, red shoes, and staff. He stood before her in a monk's brown robe, cord tied at the middle.

A eunuch who had been in that side chamber to oversee the disrobing appeared now and placed a small item on the table in front of Antonina.

"That's Eugenius," Tariq whispered, "her trusted secretary."

I had guessed as much. "What did he give her?"

"It's the signet ring of the Holy Father's office. It bears the imprint of a fisherman."

Shamed and embarrassed, Silverius collected himself, his chest rising as he prepared to speak.

Antonina spoke first. "You must realize what the penalty is for treason, Lord Silverius, do you not?"

Whatever impromptu speech Silverius had prepared deserted him. His shoulders tightened, neck moving forward, tendons protruding. He understood—probably for the first time—the true depth of the danger facing him.

Antonina kept her silence for a full two minutes, watching her fish twist and turn on the line, his face blanching, a tic quivering on his cheek. Finally, she spoke: "You will spend the night in the palace guard house. If we were to execute the law prescribed for traitors, your death in the morning would come only after the most gruesome torture."

For a moment, I thought he was going to fall on his knees and implore her for his life. But he would not allow Antonina the satisfaction of seeing him beg for mercy. He stood erect, silent.

"The court is inclined to be merciful, however," Antonina went on, "so we have chosen banishment rather than execution. At dawn, you will be placed on a ship and sent to Patara in Lycia, where you will live out your days as a monk."

"And—and my attendants?"

"They will remain in Rome. They've been told of your sentence and have given statements. Some, I suspect, will have a vote in the choice of your successor."

29 March 537

I was glad I had waited to write to Theodora about Silverius's deposition because the epilogue to the story followed hard upon.

In but the space of one week, Rome welcomed—or rather, accepted—a new Holy Father. While not partaking overtly in the deposition of Silverius, General Belisarius was shaken into action by his wife. He made it clear as Alexandrian glass to the Roman clergy that they had one choice only: Vigilius. Thus, as ordered by the empress, Vigilius was consecrated Holy Father, Bishop of Rome, in an understated ceremony at the Basilica of Saint John Lateran.

After the formalities, Tariq and I wandered about the basilica, a marvel of architecture from Constantine's day. Tombs of the previous Holy Fathers were in the nave, several chapels, and the atrium, where I found myself suddenly facing the tomb of Holy Father Agapetus, his exceedingly brief reign chiseled into white marble: 535-536. A cold shiver ran up from my lower spine to the back of my head.

As I turned away, Tariq caught up with me. Glancing at the tomb, he asked, "Strange to find someone you know?"

I shook off a chill and pivoted away. "Let's go."

Vigilius wasted no time in taking up residence in the Domus Faustae, the traditional palace of the Bishops of Rome.

02 April 537

"What are your plans now?" Tariq asked, his face drawn as he came into my room. "You've sent your letter to the Augusta?"

"I have," I said, looking up from my small desk and turning over his first question in my mind and answering the second. "Fully detailed. My hand is cramped."

"The contents should make her happy."

"Indeed."

"Will she expect you to return promptly?"

"I expect so."

"Stephen, please put her off. I have so enjoyed having you here. You've been an oasis in a desert."

"But I thought you had come to enjoy your status of secret spy."

"Status?" Tariq scoffed. "When no one knows I'm here acting as the empress's personal ferret, I have no status. I'm very much ignored. And if someone were to find out—or ..."

"Like Antonina?"

Tariq nodded. "Or Procopius. Well, that would be the end of me. Seriously."

"Should I ask Theodora to recall you?"

"Yes, though I don't know what good it would do if she hopes to have more information. Please stay in Rome awhile."

"I'll put off my return until sailing weather is perfect. I don't want to do overland again. I'll tell her June."

"We haven't covered all the sites yet. As June approaches, you can delay it till summer's end; I know you can."

"Tariq, we're both forgetting something. Rome with its weak defenses and few soldiers is under siege by the massive Ostrogoth forces. We could both be dead by then."

"Well, there is that."

We both laughed.

36

537 Late Summer

I DID REMAIN IN ROME THROUGH the summer, but it proved no idyll. The Ostrogoths continued to amass outside the several gates to the city, a city already stalked by fear and famine. Whether Antonina's charge against Silverius was true or invented, Belisarius worried over those Roman senators who might resent the hardships of the siege, preferring their past Gothic rulers; consequently, he took precautions against nighttime treason. Sentinels were doubled and locks to the gates were changed weekly.

My walks with Tariq about the city were anything but pleasant. The citizenry was starving, existing on meager rations of corn and what greens they could scrounge: cabbage, herbs, dandelions and such. People resorted to eating cats, dogs, pigeons, rats—most anything. Children in rags ran up to me, begging. I gave what I could, a coin or a bit of bread and always a piece of my heart. Meats, like horse or mule flesh, were costly and only occasionally graced the table at the Pincian Hill mansion of Belisarius and Antonina. Tariq and I, the uninvited, ate in his suite. Wine at least was in abundance because Belisarius's men had raided the cellars of every palace and mansion in the city.

During this time Belisarius sent urgent messages to Constantinople demanding reinforcements. A few replies raised hope but no additional soldiers. As a result, he would not chance a pitched battle, instead sending out forces from alternating gates and at irregular times to storm the camped enemies in frequent surprise sorties. It was a masterful plan and execution, and yet the number of Ostrogoths grew.

Garbed in purple and white, Holy Father Vigilius received me in the large reception room of the Domus Faustae, one of the few buildings in Rome that had been splendidly maintained. The acorn-shaped bearded face was the same, but his middle had filled out a bit since the day I had first seen him in Constantinople. It appeared the famine had passed over a good many of the clergy in the city.

"Well? What is it, eunuch? I've been expecting you."

"You have, Holy Father?"

"The empress wrote. Again."

"Then you know—"

"What answers she wishes me to give. What deed she wants to be done … yes!"

"And?" He kept me standing, but I didn't care. The shorter this task, the better.

"You're going back to Constantinople, I take it." He crossed his arms. "You're here to interview me and bring to her my answers."

"It's not to be much of an interview, Holy Father, just two questions."

"Fair warning, eunuch. She will not like the answer to what I know is the first one. Ask me now—I have a busy schedule today."

"The empress wishes to know when you will reinstate Bishop Anthimus as Patriarch of Constantinople."

Vigilius let out a sigh strong enough to send the stink of garlic in my direction. "She thinks I am procrastinating."

"The empress's exact words were, 'In an honorable enterprise there must be no delay'."

"Ha! Not her words, eunuch. They're from an old Platonic philosopher—Nigrinus." Another sigh. "But I wouldn't expect a Syrian to know that." My heart dropped a bit when he rose from his chair and nodded toward two carved chairs with red upholstery; I knew this was likely to take more time than I wished.

I settled into the plush cushioning, glad he was sitting at a right angle so that I could look away if his gaze—or breath—made me uncomfortable.

"Tell me, eunuch," Vigilius asked, his expression masked behind his pointed beard, "are you a religious man?"

I did not expect to look away so soon. "I am not. My father was Pagan. I have no religion."

"Good! Then perhaps you can see from a neutral standpoint."

My gaze went back to him and I nodded.

"You see, when I spoke with the Augusta, I was in the Eastern realm, where the dialogue between the Chalcedonians and Monophysites was taking place. The empress believes the two sides can meld together, that both sides believe in the Christ, no matter whether he had a single divine nature or a nature both divine and human. She thinks both beliefs can exist in one unified Church. I have to say, at the time I was swayed to her thinking."

"I see," I said, thinking the offer of St. Peter's throne no doubt played a part in his receptiveness to her thinking. "And now, Holy Father?"

"Here, Stephen, the story is different. The Diaphysites here in the Western realm give no consideration to the notion of a single nature. None!"

That he called me by my given name took me by surprise. It was a sign that he hoped to take me into his confidence, to win me over. To what end, I wondered. How much influence did he think I had with Theodora?

"So," I ventured, "the powers here would not accept your reinstating a Monophysite as Patriarch of Constantinople."

"That is the sum of it." His dark eyes held mine. "I am told you have the ear of the empress. What is the history between you two?"

I gave him the abridged version of meeting Theodora on board ship and facilitating her meeting with Justinian. He nodded occasionally, seemingly impressed.

At last, he came to the point. "How do you think she will respond to my hesitancy?"

It was more than hesitancy, I realized. He had no intention of following her instructions. "The empress is accustomed to having her way."

Vigilius stood and took several paces toward a window. Facing away from me, he said, "So I have gathered, Stephen. So I have gathered."

When I stood to take my leave, he turned around, a shaken man. I was surprised he allowed me to catch him without his veneer of confidence. The empress frightened him—but not enough to bring him to heel. "Perhaps … perhaps you can explain to her my conundrum."

Having no answer, I smiled weakly and made a quick exit.

Holy Father Vigilius was not the only one chilled by the thought of Theodora's disappointment. After all, *I* was the one tasked with delivering the news. The empress had been a woman of the stage in her younger days, and I think she still viewed her position and power in terms of stagecraft. On stage, tangled conflicts arose, came to a dramatic conflict, and ended with an untangling and a neat, gratifying end. How different life was, however. One could not count on the number of players, much less their motivation, the pacing, and actions. And the final act—as now with the Anthimus question—was liable to ignite the volatile anger of an autocratic director.

I resolved to stay in Rome a few more weeks before boarding a pack ship for Constantinople so that my letter would reach Theodora long before I did. I had no wish to be scorched black like Apollo's white raven that brought him the news his lover had been unfaithful.

37

September 537

"MY LORD STEPHEN," A BREATHLESS Piers cried when I entered my suite for the first time in many months. "Oh! It is good to see you."

"And you, Piers," I said, grasping his forearms.

"You came by boat, yes? You'll want a meal, I expect."

"A small one," I said, releasing him. "Some fruits and vegetables, if you please. I've had my share of twice-baked biscuits on board ship, if you take my meaning."

It took Piers just a few seconds to do so, whereupon he gave me a second glance, and we laughed.

"And after, a long sleep, Piers. Tomorrow I'll meet with the empress."

"I think not."

"What?—What do you mean? Is she in ill health? Is she—"

"She's healthier than you or me."

"Well, then, what do you mean?"

"She's not here."

"Not here?"

"She's at Hieron."

"The summer palace Justinian is building?"

"Oh, it's built, Stephen. She's been there most of the summer. Justinian says it's to be hers exclusively. In the summers there are to be two palaces, two courts."

"Really? I thought it wouldn't be ready until next year. What about my letters—I've been sending my letters here."

"Not to worry—I put them on the morning boat to Hieron no more than a day after their arrival. There's at least one sailing each day, supplies going and people coming and going all the time, you know. I assumed you must have known about the move and you were still sending them here to me as a security measure."

"I … I didn't know. Her letters to me were brief and focused on a particular wish of hers."

"Has the wish worked out?"

"No."

"Ah! Then a little more time before you see her is a good thing." Piers chuckled. When he saw that I was resistant to his humor, he cut a quick exit, saying, "I'll get your fruits and vegetables, Stephen."

Entering my study, I nodded and smiled—stupidly, I suppose—at Jati, suddenly comforted to feel his enigmatic expression again—even if he was made of tesserae. Dropping down onto the desk chair, I stared absently at my container of pens, ink well, and blank scrolls. Piers saw to it that the desk was newly polished—and neater than it would be on the morrow.

I toured Hieron the year before in the fall as the palace was being built. Situated in an extension of Constantinople across the Sea of Marmara on the Asian side, the new summer palace shared the site with an old temple of Hera. Positioned on a peninsula known for its wide variety of greenery and flowers, Hieron was very much an opulent citadel, boasting colonnades, exquisite buildings, and baths created out of marble and rare metals. Countless containers of cement had been sunk to create a private harbor for the royal ships. The expense of the project continued to gall John of Cappadocia, who—her spies reported—railed against her at every opportunity, thus deepening the divide between him and Theodora. I imagined things getting no better in my absence.

I wondered if Piers was correct in saying Hieron was to be exclusively Theodora's. If true, what did that portend? A chasm coming between the imperial couple?

In little time, Piers came in and placed on my desk a plate of carrots, radishes, olives, pomegranates, apples, and dates. "You're lucky we have dates now with Setka gone. He has a sweet tooth that—"

"Gone?—I assumed he was in his room."

Piers neared the door on his way out. "No," he said, turning around, his eyes locking onto mine, "oh no, Setka has also been at Hieron all summer." His words were free of inference, but his eyes told a different story.

I nodded and picked up a radish, hoping my expression was free of concern. Piers pivoted and left the study.

I dropped the radish onto the plate. My heart beat fast. So, Justinian remained in the Great Palace, and the new palace was to be Theodora's alone, a body of water between them. And Setka, the handsome young Egyptian, now plied his music at Hieron. Oh, Tariq still maintained that Setka's features resembled mine, but I didn't see it. I pushed the plate away. Why did I consider this a personal affront? Why did I feel the jealousy that Justinian should be feeling? Did he trust her more than I could?

That a year had passed since I entertained a particular suspicion I deemed too wild did not mean it had faded away. Theodora was thirty-seven now, and I knew she still harbored hope she would bear a child, an heir to the empire. I also knew—because I had done the research for Theodora—that Justinian's bout with orchitis some years before might very well have left him sterile, prompting me to wonder if she meant to conceive a child with Setka, a child meant for the throne. And most likely done without Justinian's knowledge.

I looked across the room to my mosaic boy seated on the side of the fountain. "Is it possible, Jati?" I asked aloud. "Is it so outrageous of a thought?"

The flame on the standing lamp next to the mosaic sputtered as the oil ran dry so that only an eerie, flickering play of light and shadow moved across the boy's handsome face. Was that his answer?

I went to bed a shaken man. Sleep was long in coming.

An indelicate flood of sunlight awoke me in the morning. "I brought some mountain tea and fruit," Piers said as he finished adjusting my shutters. "They're on your bedside table."

"Do I have time before the boat sails?" I pulled myself up to the side of the sleeping couch.

"That you do, my lord. No sailing today." Piers brought my tunic to the bed and stood before me. "She's coming home this afternoon. I heard it from Narses. He's most eager to see you and hear the news."

"Not as eager as Theodora, I'll wager," I muttered.

"I've read your letter, Stephen," Theodora said. "Three times. Now, tell me *exactly* what Vigilius said, Leave nothing out."

We sat in Theodora's study. She called for me less than an hour after her arrival. Her greeting after so many months was short and rather formal. Seated across from her, I recited for her my conversation with the Holy Father nearly word for word because in anticipation of this moment, I took notes immediately after the meeting. When I finished, she stood quickly and walked to the window, keeping her back to me. "So the priest has had *his* wish granted, thanks to me, and now he thinks he can put off payment. He procrastinates. The question is, how long will he delay?" She drew in a deep breath and pivoted to face me.

I knew Theodora well enough to know what the next question would be. It was why she sent me to Rome.

"And you, Stephen, with your nose for people and their character—how did you judge him? Will he make me wait long?—How long?"

"I ... I am not certain, mistress." The formality of this meeting precluded my calling her *Thea*.

Theodora blinked, her heart-shaped face swiveling slightly, the black eyes capturing mine. "Ah," she said, "you don't think he will keep his part of the bargain at all! Isn't that so?"

I could do nothing more than nod my head. She knew *me* well.

"By the bones of all the Caesars!" she cried. "I've taken down a consecrated Holy Father only to be set adrift by a creature such as Vigilius!" She returned to her chair and sat, her face aflame. "This news, plus that of John of Cappadocia. Will nothing go right?"

I hesitated to inquire as to her meaning, but curiosity overcame caution. "The Cappadocian?"

"Yes, Stephen. My husband has placed his name in contention for one of the two consuls ordinaries for next year. Just watch his head get even bigger, his nerve bolder. One day ... one day—"

"One day?"

Theodora looked, her brow wrinkling, as if suddenly remembering I was in the room. "Oh, never mind, Stephen. You may leave me," she said through gritted teeth. "But don't think I was pleased with your procrastination about returning home."

Ah, thus the reason for the cool homecoming.

"Your friend Tariq will be my eyes and ears in Italy until Vigilius finally makes his move."

Or doesn't, I thought. I stood, gave a slight bow, and walked to the door. As I made my exit, I heard her mutter, "Thank you, Stephen."

The *thank you* stayed with me as I made my way downstairs to my suite. I was at once appreciative of it, yet I despised myself for accepting so little for my months of travel and time away. I felt a bit guilty, too, because it was clear the task she had given me regarding the Holy Father now fell on my good friend Tariq.

And throughout my interview with Theodora, I kept wondering about her relationship with Setka. I hoped for some little clue that my suspicion they were lovers was foolish on my part.

As I entered my suite, Piers whispered, "He's in his room." So, Theodora was not the only one to know me well.

And, yes—I did so wish to question Setka about his relationship with Theodora, but I held off out of fear he would alert her to my interest. And then, too—some part of me wished to stay in the dark.

In the following days, Setka continued to play and sing at the imperial suppers. He absented himself from my suite most afternoons, always with some excuse I thought could be proved false, had I the inclination to do so.

Theodora had such strong faith in my nose for people and their character, and yet I had no such faith in my judgment of the Augusta herself.

38

27 December 537

As Piers and I made our way across the Augustaion on the day of the dedication of the Church of the Holy Wisdom, I regretted Tariq's continued absence from The City. He had stood with me in the former church as witnesses to both the marriage and coronation ceremonies of Justinian and Theodora. I vowed to write to him, supplying every detail possible.

This was the third building on the site, the last one having been burned to the ground in the Nika Riots. Justinian had told his architects Anthemius and Isidore he wanted the building to be majestic, that it should reflect heaven itself. Mosaics and other decorative works were not yet finished, but the bulk of the building was complete, less than six years after the former cathedral's destruction. No amount of money was spared. My thoughts went back to the Rome I had left and how that kind of money could have revived the city and supported its citizens for five years or more. The cathedral, with an exterior clad in gray-streaked white Proconnesian marble, was imposing enough, but it merely hinted at the majesty within. As we entered, passing through the outer and inner Narthexes and coming into the nave, the sight made me realize I could never begrudge the imperial couple's extravagant spending. The interior far surpassed the considerable lavishness of the original church.

Even for a man of no religion, I felt as if I had arrived, wide-eyed, in another world. Windows glassed in reds, blues, and greens and arranged in both flat and curved walls let drop shafts of diffused light at various angles into the massive nave, enlivening the white marble slabs of flooring set in patterns meant to resemble the waves of the sea.

My eyes moved higher to the titanic dome and its circular bank of some forty windows glassed in purple, the rays from which propelled my gaze down and to the east, toward arches of descending sizes and, finally, to the apse of the sanctuary and to the floor. We stood there in the nave, bathed in streams of coruscating colors that streamed down—and seemingly through—our bodies, its effect at once unearthly, mystical, rapturous.

A multitude of lamps were hung from brackets extending from the galleries' cornices. Most striking, however, were a dozen tall silver sculptures of trees standing in large silver bowls in the sanctuary, each with more than two dozen lamps set among five branches.

I drew in breath. It was only now that I took in what stood between the sea-like flooring and the heavenly light. Enormous marble columns of dark green mottled with white, as well as those of red porphyry, took my eyes up, gliding over walls inlaid with upright slabs of the red porphyry and green marble, banded above and below by beautiful onyx. The second floor consisted of columned galleries looking down at the nave from the north, west, and south. The West Gallery had a separate section for the empress and her ladies.

For some moments, I felt alone and unmoored, unaware of the increasing crowd. I looked to Piers, whose wrinkled, yet radiant, face was no doubt a mirror to the wonder overwhelming me. He caught my eye and gave a little shrug that told all.

We went to find our places for the ceremony.

On a past occasion, I had heard Procopius tell Brother Leo that Justinian knew nothing about architecture. If that were the case, then I would have to believe in Divine Inspiration. My lack of faith, however, made for another conclusion: Procopius was a fool, or as Tariq would say, an ass.

At the front of the cathedral, Theodora and Justinian stepped down from a golden coach and passed through the wide gilded door meant only for the emperor, empress, and their entourage. She felt his hand tighten on hers, and she turned toward him, noticing how when he tucked in his chin, his shoulders drew up and added to his height.

How proud he is, she thought. This was his moment. For years now, he had given of heart and body to this miraculous cathedral. He was a man who needed little sleep. In the small hours of the night he would be toiling away at a new codex of Roman law, or his plans to win back Roman provinces lost to barbarians, or his architectural projects, chief among them the Church of the Holy Wisdom. His objective was for it to be a place where the imperial powers unite with the divine. How many nights in the past few years had he left her bed to go to the construction site? Often, he went without a single guard and that worried her. Well, now, it was finished, or nearly so.

As they processed the length of the nave, she sensed the silent awe of the worshippers who stood shoulder to shoulder on either side, and she reveled in her husband's success. Why, she thought he actually relished the destruction of the previous church because it gave him the opportunity to create a magnificent and perfect structure that would allow his name to live on for centuries. "And your name, as well," he had told her.

Taking three steps up into the sanctuary, the royal couple genuflected before the altar. It was at that moment she saw how Justinian had made good on his promise. Beneath the ciborium—silver with gold embellishments—the altar consisted of a single block of porphyry, its face inscribed in gold: *We, Your subjects, Theodora and Justinian, offer to You, Oh Christ, what is Yours from what is Yours.*

Theodora's heart leapt.

Justinian took her hand now, and they moved to the right, toward their thrones. Once they were seated on the gilded chairs, the pinch-faced Patriarch Menas climbed the steps of the ambo to begin his sermon regaling the miracle of the cathedral and the vision of Justinian.

Even as he spoke—and Justinian after him—Theodora's concentration was drawn away. That their words echoed back to the sanctuary after some ten seconds added to her disconnect in thought.

The news had come that morning. Earlier in the month, Silverius had died on the island of Palmeria, off Naples. Starvation, she was told. Was the place so poor in food—or had he meant to starve himself? Was it even possible he was murdered?

The irony was not lost upon her. Here she sat in the greatest gift to God any emperor had ever created, her name upon the altar—and blame in her heart. She had Holy Father Silverius deposed so that Bishop Anthimus would be restored to the office of Patriarch of Constantinople, a restoration that would pave the way for the acceptance of Monophysites by Orthodox believers. To those ends, she had forced the election of Vigilius. And what had come of her game plan? Holy Father Vigilius knew her wish, agreed to it—and yet, he still procrastinated. Stephen intimated that he might never bend to her will. In that case, Silverius's death would have been for nothing.

Theodora placed her hands on the golden arms of the throne, grasped tightly and held, her gaze moving to the rear of the apse where Patriarch Menas now sat in the bishop's throne in the synthronon, priests on either side. If only Bishop Anthimus had not been deposed, she thought, longing to approach Menas and pull him down from the patriarchal silver throne.

39

April 538

TARIQ SOMEHOW MANAGED TO ALWAYS have his own letters arrive before the reports of Procopius. One of them detailed the end of the siege of Rome. After a full year and some days, Witigis, King of the Ostrogoths, gave up the siege and began a retreat toward Ravenna, the Ostrogothic capital. Belisarius waited until half of the enemy had crossed the Milvian Bridge on the River Tiber and then led out his forces to spring a surprise attack on those who had yet to cross. The Ostrogoths resisted at first but, in the end, untold numbers were slain or lost to the river.

A few days later, Theodora said the report was much the same as the one Justinian received from Procopius although Procopius put a much brighter shine on Belisarius's strategy and victory over the Witigis. She added that Procopius's report had ended with a plea from Belisarius for reinforcements. Ravenna and other cities and outposts had yet to be taken. The Ostrogothic war went forward.

I had hoped Theodora might allow Tariq to come home, but knew not to ask because his task regarding Vigilius had not yet yielded anything, and the fact he made no mention of the Holy Father in his letter was a source of displeasure to her. Adding to her distress was the recent news two of her favorites had died, one day apart. Severus, one of her mentors during her time in North Africa, died on 08 February in his beloved Alexandria. And John of Tella, the bishop who won over legions to the Monophysitic faith during Theodora's now fabled Bithynia pilgrimage, died for his beliefs on 09 February in an Antioch prison. The two deaths seemed to make her desire to bring the Monophysites into the Chalcedonian fold even stronger.

June 538

A T LAST A LETTER ARRIVED with some mention, if not real news, of Vigilius. Tariq wrote that Holy Father Vigilius continued to obfuscate regarding reinstating Anthimus as Patriarch of Constantinople. In the meantime, I learned that Anthimus—who vanished after being deposed—has been hiding in plain sight all the while under Theodora's auspices in the recesses beneath the Daphne Palace.

General Belisarius had continued his requests for reinforcements all these months since my return. Justinian at last sent a force of seven thousand men led by Lord Chamberlain Narses, of late a general who had failed in his first assignment—to support a Monophysite, Theodosius, as Patriarch of Alexandria. The mission had come from Theodora, but it ended badly with Theodosius's deposition. He appealed to Theodora when he fled Alexandria, and she made space for him at the Palace of Hormisdas.

When Narses told me of his new assignment, my face must have flashed surprise, not because of his failure in Egypt, or his status as a eunuch, for it was outweighed by his renown for decision making—but because of his advancing age of sixty-two.

"I've kept my ambition to myself," he told me, "but the military has always drawn me in. I find it a fascinating challenge, Stephen. It appears my abilities during the Nika Riots made more of an impression on Justinian than my feeble performance at Alexandria. Or perhaps Theodora put in a word for me."

I thought the latter. And even then, I must say, I thought the move on Theodora's part was another way to keep an eye on Belisarius.

In the late afternoon, the *carpentum* drew to a stop in front of the mansion clad in white marble. An excubitor stood outside the coach, waiting to hand Theodora down from the purple-draped interior.

She drew in breath, her stomach tightening. She peered out at the building she had given to her sister Comito on the occasion of her marriage to General Sittas. It was a magnificent edifice expropriated from a wealthy eunuch. Even though Comito had been to the Great Palace any number of times these past years, this was only the third time Theodora had visited their home. Her two sisters were her only family, and the bond with her older sister Comito was strong, their love impermeable. She should have visited often, but it seemed she was always caught up in some event or occasion. And to come here now— with such news. She thought she would be ill. Urging herself to move, she reached out a manicured hand to the excubitor and realized she was trembling.

A crowd was gathering as she walked up the stairs where a eunuch was stationed, his eyes wide at the surprise visit. "Tell your mistress I am here," she said, stepping into the grand vestibule. "I'll find my way to the atrium."

In less than a minute, Comito came running. "Thea! You should have warned me! We're hardly ready to entertain you. Oh! Something's wrong! You never could mask bad news. What is it?"

Theodora conjured up a tight smile. "Let's sit, shall we?"

"Come into Sittas's office. It's private. Will you have something to drink?"

"No, nothing." Theodora sat on a couch next to her sister and took her hand.

As if sensing the gravity of the visit, Comito spoke first. "The last time we sat here, years ago now, you brought good news. Sittas had excelled in battle and you were very pleased."

"I remember."

"And now?"

Theodora squeezed Comito's hand. "Now it is not good news, Comissa."

"Tell me, Thea, please." Comito's eyes suddenly glistened with tears. "It's Sittas, isn't it?"

Theodora nodded, whispering, "Yes, dearest."

"He's dead." Comito's tears spilled now.

Another nod.

"How, Theodora—how?"

"He got caught up in a skirmish while putting down the Persian rebellion in Armenia."

"Generals don't die in skirmishes. He was Master of the Soldiers."

"A title he deserved. He had earned it."

"But, I mean to say, how does the general in charge die in a skirmish? Where were his bodyguards?"

Theodora sighed. Hoping to spare Comito the details, she had planned to lie. She intended to insist it was a skirmish and that his death was sudden and nearly painless, but to do so now would only delay the truth. And it had to come from her. *Now.* "It was an Armenian, Comissa, acting as a mercenary for the King of Persia. It was more than a skirmish. Sittas was taken by surprise. It was an assassination."

Comito pulled back her hand from Theodora's grasp. "How?"

"A spear to his back."

Comito declined against the cushioned back of the couch, face flushing red. "A wretched way for a courageous soldier to die," she cried.

Theodora looked away, staring absently at Sittas's desk, one scarcely used because of his foreign duties. "I blame myself," she offered. "When the command position in the East opened up, I convinced Justinian that Sittas was the right soldier."

"That he was. He was so proud to take it up.—Thea, do they know the identity of his assassin?"

Theodora dreaded the question. She had prayed Comito would not ask it. Yet, somehow Procopius had found out the Armenian's identity. "His name is Artabanes, Comito."

"Has he been captured? Is he dead?"

Theodora shook her head.

"He goes free?"

Theodora wanted to tell her he would be caught and punished, but it would be an empty promise. She had no control of things that happened in the East. "He's returned to the Persian court, Comissa."

The slightest shuffling noise came from the doorway. Theodora glanced up to spy a young girl in a pretty yellow tunic standing there. Unable to turn her gaze away, she drew in a deep breath. "We have company, Comito."

Comito looked up, eyes widening, tears streaming down her cheeks.

"Mother," the girl cried, "what's wrong?"

"Come here, dearest."

The girl seemed uncertain.

Comito wiped at her eyes. "Sophia, come to Mother."

The girl slowly came forward, her dark hair and delicate features eerily more a match to Theodora's visage than to Comito's. The wide, black eyes kept stealing the quickest of glances at Theodora. When Comito took her into an embrace, the girl drew her head back and wiped at her mother's tears. "Why are you so sad?"

"We'll talk later, Sophia." Comito blinked back her tears. "Your Aunt

Theodora has come to see us. You should make a little bow for the empress, like you practiced."

Sophia obeyed, executing the bow perfectly.

"That was lovely, Sophia," Theodora said. "How old are you now?"

"Seven," she said, all hesitancy gone. She then brought her eyes up to meet Theodora's. "You've brought Mother sad news, empress, have you not?"

At a loss for how to react, Theodora forced a smile. *How quick she is*, she thought, chastising herself for not seeing the child since her baptism. But to see her now was a kind of revelation, one she would have to ponder.

"Now, now, Sophia," Comito said, "go find your teacher. It's time for your Latin lesson. But before you go, give your aunt another bow and address her as *mistress* this time."

Sophia looked from her mother to Theodora, her expression in a pout. She knew very well she was being stage-managed, but she obeyed and left the room.

"I—I didn't know what to say," Theodora said.

"I'll tell her about her father a little later, but I suspect she already has an idea."

"Comissa, I want you to bring her to the palace sometime next week. Will you do that? Justinian should get to know her."

Comito pressed her lips together in what seemed an attempt to smile. Taking hold of Theodora's hand now, she said, "Yes, of course, Thea."

Seated in the *carpentum* for the return drive, Theodora again reproved herself for having avoided interaction with her niece. Alone now, she had to admit it was intentional, perhaps not overtly so, but at least at some level deep within she had no wish to involve herself in the child's life.

Now she had to confront the truth. While her sister had borne Sittas's child early in their marriage, she herself remained childless. No amount of prayers or magic or noting the most generative phases of the moon had brought forth an heir for her and Justinian.

Theodora had passed her thirty-eighth birthday. Despite continued efforts, the likelihood of bearing a child diminished day by day. Whether the fault was hers or the disease, orchitis, that had struck Justinian, what did it matter? The result was the same: They were childless. They were without an heir.

Sophia came back into her thoughts. She was just seven now, but thought must be given to her future—and to the future of the family and the empire. She would arrange a marriage for the girl, thinking at once of Justin, the son of Justinian's sister Vigilantia and her husband Dulcidio. Justin was a decade older than Sophia, but that did nothing to preclude the match.

She had left on a mission to relay news of a death, but by the time the coach clattered onto the paving stones of the palace, the plan for a marriage that would further unite the two families was falling into place.

An old proverb came back to her now: *A society grows great when the old men plant trees whose shade they know they shall never sit in.* She was neither old nor a man, but the truth rang in her head like a bell made of crystal.

40

As I sat on my balcony on a cold but ordinary Thursday evening, I noticed a peculiar fire in the sky. At first, it didn't appear to be moving, but it was. The alien object was a comet, but a singular one for its large size, elongated shape, and pointed anterior. It moved so slowly its fire appeared to flame and coruscate in place, a sight both wondrous and frightening.

It was there the next night, and the next. People came out of their houses each evening. At its first appearance, the soft roar of oohs and high-pitched yelps moved in waves across the rooftops. People lost sleep by viewing it—and by worrying over it. The year ended, a new one began, and still it came. Theories about it arose as various as the streets of Constantinople. It was a sign of wonder and Christ's coming. It was a sign of destruction for The City. It was a forerunner of the End of Times. It meant Monophysitism would triumph—or Orthodoxy. Clergy, stylites, fortune-tellers, and soothsayers made a holiday of it.

From Italy, Procopius wrote about the strange phenomenon. He called it the "Swordfish Comet" because its body was quite long and it led with a sharp, sword-like point. He pronounced that the fact it was moving from west to east signified that the empire was being reunited once again, from Rome to Constantinople and beyond. To me, it made as much sense as the other suppositions. None.

The comet gave the illusion of just hanging in the air. I took seeing it each night for granted and thus missed its final appearance—on 30 January 540.

March 540

Dressed in his gold-embroidered purple dalmatic, Justinian entered Theodora's study, his neck sloping forward, arms clutched at his chest. He moved with the slow gait of a mourner. "I am sorry to interrupt, dearest, but there is news."

"Yes?" Theodora looked up from her desk, smiled, eyes questioning—for his benefit.

"Holy Father Vigilius has written." Theodora nodded and he continued. "He has at last taken a stand and it is not to our liking."

"No?"

"No, Thea. It's about Anthimus."

"He's decided against us, yes? He's taken up the same position as Silverius had, damning the Monophysites and refusing to reinstall Anthimus."

"Yes.—You're not surprised, even a little?

Theodora gave a little shrug, her eyes shifting momentarily to a scroll on the right side of her desk. It was a copy of the letter written large by Stephen, one she had already read, one of many arranged to come to her desk first. "How could we be surprised, Justinian? He's put us off too many months."

"That is true, my love. I'm sorry for you. I know how the matter is close to your heart."

"He's played us for fools, Justinian. One day, we must make him regret doing so."

"You taught him to swim, Thea, and now he seeks to drown you."

April to May 540

I gave no credence to any of the theories regarding the Swordfish Comet. However, if Procopius's hypothesis about the phenomenon were correct, the reunion of the Roman Empire's two halves was taking longer than hoped for. The continuing battle for Italy became protracted and complicated. Justinian had sent Narses to support Belisarius, but the two generals mixed no better than oil and water. Before his departure, Theodora had cautioned Narses to beware of Belisarius's ambition. That he took it to heart turned out to be a direction Theodora came to regret.

Tariq wrote frequently of the chaos involved in the attempt to prevail in Italy. Theodora noted that often Procopius's reports were not so dark, but the two accounts were alike in that both stressed Narses' repeated questioning of Belisarius's decisions. Their inability to act in unison lost the city of Milan, resulting in the slaughter of many thousands. For once, Procopius did not varnish the facts, placing the number at three hundred thousand; in so doing, he motivated Justinian to recall Narses, a boon to Belisarius's leadership. The move followed Theodora's needless error of encouraging Narses to obstruct Belisarius.

Italy was subjected to widespread hunger and sickness when crops failed. Cannibalism was not unheard-of. Tariq wrote of a guest house owned by two women who, over a year's time, killed and ate close to twenty guests—until one intended victim woke up in time to take his revenge.

As the Italian campaign went on, Procopius's reports became fewer and less revealing, while Tariq's letters divulged secret dealings between the Ostrogothic forces and Belisarius, dealings that increasingly put Theodora on edge when I read them to her.

The negotiations culminated finally when the Ostrogoths offered to surrender Ravenna—but only if Belisarius would agree to remain in Italy and create, in effect, a separate Ostrogothic and Roman Empire in the West, one in which he would reign as emperor.

"It can't be! It's not true!" Theodora raged even before I finished the reading of the offer. "Oh, Belisarius is ambitious, but he would not dare go so far! Antonina would surely have warned me if her husband intends this—this treason!" Her face nearly as purple as her dalmatic, she stormed off, muttering, "She will write. She must."

For the next few weeks, Theodora was fraught with worry, checking two or three times a day to ask if Tariq had written. He hadn't; neither did Antonina write. While we both worried that perhaps Tariq had been found out by Antonina or Procopius, I reminded her that trustworthy couriers were not always at the ready.

Theodora paused before the door leading into the Hall of the Consistory. She was making a late entrance because she had rushed down to Stephen's rooms in the hope that some new word had come from Tariq. The errand had been in vain.

She drew in several deep breaths. Justinian had called a Silence to discuss General Belisarius's fate. Her husband had many more spies than she had, and the news about the Ostrogoths' offer came back hard upon Tariq's writing. In private, Theodora had tried to soften Justinian's suspicion and soothe his anger, but he seemed willing to believe the spies who wrote that Belisarius did, in fact, plan to accept the diadem of the West.

Theodora entered now and proceeded to her place next to Justinian at the head of the table. She was startled to see only two councilors present. Half-way down the table and situated across from each other, Narses and John the Cappadocian stood and bowed to her, their faces serious as physicians at a deathbed.

"Are we waiting for the others?" she asked, even as the councilors' demeanor augured the answer.

"No," Justinian answered. "The three people I trust most are in this room." He nodded to the silentiaries at the near and far door, and they left the chamber.

Theodora's calculation was immediate. Telling Narses he was to be a check on Belisarius had been a grievous move on her part. He came home an enemy to the general. And John—well, she had learned to expect nothing good from him.

Justinian laid out the covert messages that had come, most from Italy, but one came from the Persian court, as well.

"News must travel at breakneck speed among spies," Theodora said, "for it to have gone to the Eastern front first. How can it be trusted?"

"They are well-paid for their accuracy," Justinian said. "They take oaths upon their honor."

"And what about the honor of your generals who have served you well time and again, as has Belisarius?"

"Begging your pardon, mistress," John said, settling back in his chair, his dark hair and beard combed to perfection. He wore a deep blue dalmatic embroidered in gold. "I believe Belisarius has been planning his move for years."

"He's told you as much?" Theodora asked.

"No, we have not been friends, but I'm sure you recall the events following his taking of Carthage. His own officers sent word of their suspicion that he would raise himself as emperor of North Africa. Can we doubt his ambition?"

Justinian turned to his left. "Theodora, you will recall his men did write with considerable concern at the time."

"I do recall. But it came to nothing," Theodora replied, returning his gaze. "Here, we will see the same." She sucked in breath. This was a twist she had not counted upon. She herself had worked to seed the distrust of Belisarius in Justinian's mind, and now she had to speak on his behalf, all the while praying her belief in Belisarius and her oldest friend, Antonina, would be validated.

John was quick to answer. "It came to nothing because taking North Africa from the Vandals meant a small reward when compared to taking the bigger pearls of Sicily and Italy from the Ostrogoths."

"But, John," Justinian said, "he didn't know that's where I would send him next."

"It was a good wager, master. Who else would you have sent?"

"I had options ..."

The Cappadocian shrugged.

"Narses," Justinian said, "you're quiet. You were with him not long ago. What are your thoughts?"

Theodora tensed. *Here's where my plan ricochets. I should have spoken to Narses before this.*

Narses stood to answer. Over the white dalmatic, his general's highly buffed bronze cuirass gleamed. "I was wrong to obstruct the general's plans in some instances, master. I see that now." His eyes went to Theodora, then flicked away. "But, at the time, I might have questioned his loyalty."

"And now?" Justinian demanded.

"Now, master? ... I don't know."

The Cappadocian stood. "We gave him too much when he came back from defeating the Vandals. Too much attention. Too much adulation. Too much gold, much of which he and Antonina merely took."

"So many loyal officials take," Theodora said.

The Cappadocian flinched. The comment's intent was not lost on him. That he was voicing the very things she had said at the time of Belisarius's triumphant return from Carthage was not lost on her.

John recovered quickly. "If I may, master, I suggest my proposal is the best alternative."

Theodora sat forward, her back at once rigid. "Proposal? What proposal? What have I missed?"

"Before you came in, mistress," the Cappadocian said, "I posited that a solution to the problem at hand would be to offer Witigis a better bargain than what is on the table in Ravenna, a deal richer than anything the general can provide the Ostrogoths. Should Witigis take it, Belisarius's dream of a diadem would vanish."

Theodora felt a rush of blood to her face and a thrumming at her temples. "What are the details of this—this proposal?" she demanded, her eyes locked onto the Cappadocian.

John offered a slow, tight smile. "First, mistress, let me point out that the empire is hard-pressed in several areas of the world. New rebellions are rising in Armenia and Persia, all while the Italian campaign crumbles. My proposal is we cut our losses in Italy and sue for peace with Witigis, putting forth a treaty that would divide the isthmus into two parts, ceding the land north of the River Po to the Goths. How much better for Witigis it would be to claim a smaller kingdom than prostrate himself before Belisarius. As for the general, you see, mistress, his dreams of a diadem would wither at once."

"And is Belisarius the one to negotiate this?" Theodora asked.

"If ordered," Justinian put in, "he had better do so."

"If ordered," Theodora repeated, turning toward her husband. "Do you mean to do so?"

"It is a plan," Justinian said, averting his eyes. "Narses, I would have your opinion."

The eunuch cleared his throat, his gaze flicking from Justinian to Theodora and back again. "It would, in fact, check him, master."

"At what expense?" Theodora snapped, her tone starkly informal. "We're to lose half of Italy on the mere supposition that Belisarius has been disloyal? What becomes of your dream, husband? Your dream to recreate the empire? You could not do so with just half of the Italian boot!"

Justinian smiled sadly. Rather than turn to her, he covered her hand with his, and she knew she had lost.

The Cappadocian had won.

Theodora left the Hall of the Consistory seething with anger. She knew it would be of no use to try to change Justinian's mind. Once he formally approved something in a Silence, he did not rescind the decision. Foreseeing a danger that a vain and ambitious Belisarius might balk at Justinian's order, she went directly to dictate a letter to Antonina describing Justinian's decision. She warned her friend to make certain her husband ignores the offer from the Ostrogoths and maintains loyalty to his sovereign by agreeing to put forward whatever plan comes from Justinian's desk. She could not reconcile herself to the plan settling for half of Italy, but the prospect of Belisarius's yielding to the temptation of a throne was worse, much worse. No one could tell where that might lead, where a true taste of power might take him. It could take him to the East.

She paid handsomely for the letter to be sent by ship that very day.

June 540

The news was long in coming, but a letter came at last. Theodora sat biting at her lower lip as I read Tariq's letter aloud in my study.

The first sentences raised the hairs at the nape of my neck, and I could only imagine what angst they conjured in Theodora. Tariq wrote that Belisarius *had accepted* the Ostrogoths' plan—but that he would put off his installation as emperor until he was well within the walls of Ravenna and in the presence of King Witigis and his nobles. The details of the evolving plan and responses made by Belisarius were many, and Theodora grew impatient, admonishing me to hurry to the outcome, her hand held to her throat.

I came to the key information. Belisarius's desire to take the Goth capital of Ravenna and all of Italy was stronger than his wish to obey his emperor. He did not put forward the plan contrived by John the Cappadocian. Instead, he allowed the Ostrogoths to believe he agreed to their plan and that he would accept the diadem once inside the capital. They took him at his word. As had occurred with Rome, Belisarius and his army entered Ravenna without the loss of a single soldier. However, Belisarius shocked the enemy when he did not accept the diadem. In fact, he arrested the nobles who had devised the offer and proceeded to lock down the significant treasury of the Ostrogothic kings. King Witigis was placed under guard and plans were made to bring him to Constantinople. General Belisarius would be called to account for his disobedience, but who would fault him for the results? No personal ambition was at play. His loyalty to Justinian held fast, as did Justinian and Theodora's claim in the West.

Theodora slumped back in the chair, her exhalation audible. She smiled now for the first time in weeks.

Belisarius's return to Constantinople from Italy resembled that of his home-coming from North Africa in that he brought a conquered king in chains, his nobles and family members, and the wealth of a treasury of gold and riches, but that is where the similarities ended. He had been recalled from Italy almost at once. The spies' speculation and gossip had done their work, causing cracks in Justinian's faith in him. While Belisarius still had the hearts of the masses, his welcome at the Great Palace ran cold. No public celebration was held, and the treasures he brought were not put on public display.

In the matter of a subdued reception, Theodora agreed with John the Cappadocian for once, albeit for different reasons. John had his accountant's eye on the cost of a public welcome, while Theodora, always leery of a general's rising power and popularity, did not wish to add to what could become insufferable vainglory. Justinian and, to a lesser degree, Theodora considered the general's decision to ignore the emperor's treaty offer to the Ostrogoths and proceed with his plan to deceive them—its success notwithstanding—an act of insubordination. It was not to be richly rewarded.

I personally celebrated the return because it was Tariq's homecoming, as well, and I looked forward to countless games of *Shatranj* and stories of Italy to accompany them.

I embraced Tariq warmly when he arrived at my suite the day after their arrival. "It is so good to see you, Tariq."

"And you. It's such a luxury to be home. I pray my spying days are over."

"Won't you miss the drama and excitement?"

"Excitement? Ha! Do you know Ravenna is built on pilings driven into a lagoon? Why, its main populace consists of frogs and mosquitoes! Although they are more preferable companions than is Procopius."

I laughed.

"I can laugh now, too, but I'm serious. So, Stephen, shall we have a game tonight?"

"Insubordination?—Belisarius?" Antonina cried, leaning forward in her chair. "Theodora, how could you think that?"

"Because that is what his actions amounted to. Spies and others at Justinian's ear have warned him that Belisarius meant to take the diadem."

"He put the empire first—as he has *always* done."

"He chose to ignore the treaty offered by the emperor and did as he pleased."

"And in so doing, if that's how you see it, he brought *all* of Italy back into the empire. Be reasonable, Thea. Wasn't that Justinian's longtime dream?

Why, we even thought that the treaty offer might be a forgery. We could not understand why Justinian would settle for less than all of Italy."

"It was the Cappadocian's plan. I didn't agree to it, but Justinian was desperate, Antonina. We have problems everywhere we turn. Most especially with Persia. King Khosrow has not kept his word so that the Eternal Peace is no longer eternal. We have too few soldiers to defend the eastern border. Worse—Persia has sacked Antioch. "

"Antioch! That is terrible news."

"Indeed."

Antonina set aside the news of war, saying, "Theodora, did you not speak up to your husband and the naysayers about Belisarius's loyalty? *Our* loyalty. You know if my husband were guilty of treason, I would have confided as much in you. Our ties are stronger than those of any husband. ... Theodora?"

"What?—Yes," Theodora said, giving her head a gentle shake. "I believe that, Nina. For a short while I doubted both of you. I'm sorry for having done so. Forgive me. And I think Justinian has thought again about Belisarius. They're in conference now. He's planning a spring offensive against Persia."

Antonina grew pale. "With Belisarius?"

"Yes."

"Oh! Let Athena strike me down here. I don't think I could weather another campaign. I really don't. Listen—"

"I'll see to it that you don't go this time, Nina. At least not right away."

"Yes?"

"Yes, I'm going to need your help here."

Antonina drew back against her chair, blue eyes questioning.

"I need to rid myself of someone."

"The Cappadocian?

Theodora smiled.

"Now, there's someone with ambition," Antonina said.

"Indeed. And ambition is a beast that must be fed—or starved!"

Late one morning, Piers announced Tariq's arrival.

"Have you heard, Stephen? Witigis has been granted patrician status and been given an estate in Galatia."

"I know. Much in the same gentle way Justinian treated King Gelimer. I can't say as I understand it, but Witigis had to renounce his Arian faith first, as well as give up his bodyguard detail, so they could be trained as Imperial Guards and sent to the Danube frontier."

"It's strange, too, the cold shoulder the general has received from the Palace while the people worship him, following him up and down the Mese shouting their hurrahs."

"There you have it, Tariq, the reason for it in the same sentence."

"What?" Tariq paused a moment, then his eyes widened. "Ah, I see. The people."

Just then a noise came from the hallway, and we both turned our heads to see a figure pass.

"Was that—" Tariq began.

"Setka? Yes."

"He's *still* living here? Why, I have heard—"

"Heard what?"

"Gossip."

"You shouldn't listen to gossip," I snapped. I took a breath, quashing my sudden anger. "Actually, Tariq, I've grown—accustomed to his presence. What with you gone and Theodora often preoccupied with affairs of state, I've had no one with whom to share a game of *Shatranj*. Piers did try to play but in the evening he'll fall asleep in the middle of a move."

We laughed at the servant's expense.

"Setka is a good young man," I offered, "and an excellent musician."

"What you mean to say is you've become *attached* to the youth, rather than *accustomed* to him. So, Stephen, my friendship has been replaced." The corners of his mouth twitched, as if fending off a smile.

"Nonsense! We'll have a game whenever you wish. And it will be good to sit on that bench again watching the ebb and flow of the Marmara as we discuss the mysteries of life. I've missed that."

"But what about the mystery of Setka and his relationship to the empress?"

"We've come back to that, have we? I—I don't think about it."

The moment froze in awkwardness.

Tariq seemed unconvinced but turned the conversation, nonetheless. "I took a tour of the new cathedral yesterday. Stephen, it is an architectural wonder!"

"It is quite the wonder," I said, relieved for the diversion. I proceeded to bring him up to date on details regarding the architects, workers, materials, and costs, as well as the clashes between Justinian and the cost-cutting Cappadocian.

Later, as I sat alone in my study, my reaction to Tariq's comment about Setka replayed in my head. Why I had become so irked, even angry? Just thinking about it now brought heat and blood into my face. I knew some people gossiped about the special attention Setka received from Theodora. I had no wish to be told about it. Besides, I had warmed to the vulnerability and seeming innocence of the youth. Now, what was it that bothered me? Was it that people thought and spoke disrespectfully of the empress? Was it that I cared too much for Theodora, always had? Was it jealousy of the young man who took up so much of her time? Was it anger that the gossip about an affair might be more than gossip? Was it *all* of this?

41

April 541

TWO WEEKS AFTER GENERAL BELISARIUS left for his assignment in Persia, Theodora sent for me. "I have a task for you, Stephen," she announced even before I sat. "It's rather a delicate one."

"Delicate?" I asked. "Is that a code word for dangerous?"

Theodora let loose her tinkling laugh. "Do you suppose I would put you in the middle of a riot—again?"

I laughed, too, but as I watched her rise, come from around her desk, and perch on the couch across from me, I could not be certain of anything.

"I need your listening and writing skills, Stephen. You're to observe an interview and record it exactly as it occurs, word for word."

Something in her tone gave me pause. "It sounds like a trap to me. Am I to be present at the interview?"

"Ha! You are shrewd. I like that! No, you are to be seated nearby—unobserved. So, there, you see? I told you some years ago you could be my spy. But I chose you for secretary."

"And now I can be both?"

"You are in good humor today, I see. Yes, you shall be both secretary and spy! So, will you play?"

"Have I ever said no to you? But how is the trap to be set? It would be advantageous for me to know the rules of the game."

"That's only fair." Theodora called for a silentiary and ordered wine and an afternoon meal.

"What is it? You look so serious." Tariq said, his high voice cadenced with suspicion.

For the first time in many months, we sat on our familiar stone bench situated on one of the cascading terraces built into the escarpment above the Sea of Marmara. On this breezy Spring day, the salty scent of the water wafted upward, laced with the intoxicatingly sweet fragrance of the jasmine vines growing near the shore. I stared out, knowing I had to break the spell.

"Well?" Tariq persisted.

"I've been asked to help bring someone down."

"Well, I needn't inquire who asked you to do it. So tell me who her victim is this time."

"John the Cappadocian."

Tariq whistled. "Now, that could go wrong, Stephen. Spectacularly wrong."

"Indeed."

"The man is evil, vindictive, and dangerous. But you agreed?"

I shrugged.

"Details, man, details!"

"Lady Antonina is going to entrap him in a plot to stage a government overthrow."

"You're joking."

"I am not."

"The last such power play ended with thirty thousand dead. How is this little scenario to play out?"

"It appears the Cappadocian has a daughter of an impressionable age— Euphemia. Antonina has been priming her with an abundance of attention in order to gain her confidence. It was not so hard. She's just seventeen, her mother is dead, and her father is busy at all hours of the day, no doubt devising ways to relieve people of their fat purses. Well, Antonina first won her confidence. Then she began complaining to her about how badly the emperor has treated Belisarius, despite his having retaken lands lost, brought back kings in captivity, and infused the treasury with untold wealth—all to little acclaim and reward."

"To an extent, the case is true, you have to say, Stephen."

"Perhaps, but now for the part that is not so true. Antonina told the girl the evil ones on the throne should be cast off. The Cappadocian's hatred of Theodora, as well as his fear, has been passed down to Euphemia, so the gullible girl was quite enthusiastic about taking part in an overthrow of the *cruel and unjust* regime. Antonina convinced her that Belisarius had no wish to wear the diadem because he was a soldier first and foremost."

"Let me guess … but maybe Euphemia's father would be persuaded to take on the role of August?"

"You're quick, you are Tariq."

"Don't mock me, Stephen," Tariq said with a laugh. "So, what did she say?"

"The little fool sashayed right into Antonina's snare. In fact, Euphemia confided in her that some soothsayer had told her father some years before that one day he would sit on the throne, that one day he would be August."

"Ah! Then this would be the realization of that prediction. How perfect."

I nodded. "Euphemia promptly told the Cappadocian, and he agreed at once to meet with Antonina."

"When and where?"

"All in good time, Tariq. First, Theodora has asked me to enlist your help."

Tariq's lower jaw dropped. "Me? In an overthrow?"

"An overthrow of John the Cappadocian. Not the government, Tariq."

Tariq ignored the quip and looked toward the sea. He took good time to deliberate. "I don't know," he said at last. "I've only just started to sleep soundly again." He swallowed hard, his Egyptian looks darkening. "Have I got this right? We have John the rightly feared praetorian prefect on the one side and the headstrong Empress of the Roman Empire on the other. Why, it's like standing between Zeus and his greatest enemy, the monster Typhon, as the sky explodes in storm. Are two lowly eunuchs going to escape injury?"

Our eyes locked. I managed a smile. "Do you see Theodora as Zeus or Typhon?"

"Does it matter?"

"Ah, I see your point, Tariq," I said, allowing myself a low laugh. "One is as dangerous as the other."

"Shouldn't *that* give us pause?" Tariq continued in a rush. "That's my point. Does it not give *you* pause?"

I broke eye contact. "Zeus and Typhon? Ha! I didn't know you could speak so poetically," I said, holding tight to my mask of comedy.

In my study later, I admitted to Jati, my muse, that Tariq's caution had caught me unawares. He had good reason to hesitate. Until then, I don't think

I fully realized that if either Procopius or Antonina discovered that he was playing them both false by spying for Theodora, his life would be in peril.

I hesitated, too, considering how quickly I had signed onto the scheme. If my decision turned out to be a reckless one, I would accept the consequences. I regretted, however, having placed my friend back into the lion's mouth.

Tariq and I stood on the bow of a commandeered dromon, the navy's new warship, its fifty oars slicing through the waves of the Bosphorus, heading for the Asian shore. The contrived meeting between Antonina and John the Cappadocian was to take place at a villa Belisarius had purchased called Rufinianae. Antonina would be there waiting for us. For her, it was a stopover on her way to join her husband on his eastern campaign. Also on board were Narses and his successor as Commander of the Imperial Guard, Marcellus, both of whom had been conscripted by Theodora for the plot. They were the enforcers and were supported by ten or twelve troops.

"Nervous?" I asked, my gaze set forward.

"Nervous? What, me?" Tariq teased. He turned his gaze toward me. "I must say, I am grateful that the empress had Brother Leo invent an illness for me so that I could skip this latest Persian campaign shackled to Procopius. Now, tell me, Stephen, is Justinian aware of this little intrigue?"

"She did tell him just today about her scheme." I looked him in the eye. "But what she didn't tell him is that once treason has been confirmed—by us—her order to Marcellus is to kill the Cappadocian on the spot."

Tariq blinked back his surprise. "So, he will not be the only one on the spot, as you say. You and I are to witness a political murder."

"Does that bewilder you? Why, he was ousted once on the eve of the Nika Riots and managed to regain his power afterward. Theodora calls him a Lazarus and is taking no chances this time."

"Ah, she knows her husband's soft heart. Why, he was even ready to forgive Pompeius and Hypatius."

We arrived at the sumptuous Roman villa, and Antonina received us coolly, as if nothing were out of the ordinary. Like Theodora, she was sliding gracefully into her fourth decade, her frame still quite voluptuous, hair a yellow-gold mane, eyes vivid blue as a spring sky.

Tariq and I were placed on a balcony above the atrium where Antonina would lay out the temptation to the Cappadocian. Our seats and a small writing table were set back far enough, but at opportune moments we could lean forward and observe the goings-on below. Narses, Marcellus, and the palace excubitors were placed in two rooms off the atrium. Once John revealed his hand in very specific words, words that could only be defined in the language of treason, I was to send Tariq down to alert Narses and Marcellus.

We did not have long to wait.

John the Cappadocian arrived at the appointed hour, seven in the evening. While we expected him to have a bodyguard or two—for he had enemies numbering beyond Theodora—he came with as many as twelve. This unexpected force did not appear to put Antonina on edge; of course, like Theodora, she had trod the stage in her youth. She proceeded to place them in two rooms on the opposite side of the atrium from Narses and Marcellus.

"Why, it's almost like a scene from one of the old Aristophanes comedies," Tariq said, his hand over his mouth. Considering his initial hesitancy to join the subterfuge, I was surprised he could eke out a bit of humor. I found none.

Breathless, I leaned over the railing to observe Antonina—all smiles—direct John to a couch. "No one is to be privy to our discussion," she told him.

"Perhaps, then, you should have someone open the pipe to the fountain."

I looked down at the fountain with its three stone maidens, each holding a horn of plenty, and imagined the difficulty I would have hearing the conversation against the gurgling and splashing.

"It is a beautiful fountain, John, but, alas, the pipe is broken." Her lie dripped honey, and without missing a beat, Antonina launched into her planned tirade on the administration of Justinian and Theodora, bringing up wrongs done not only to her and Belisarius, but to the population of Constantinople and beyond. John offered no argument, for some truth resided in each tale. Soon enough, he began to inject his own experiences. Eventually, Antonina came to her very specific plan for the overthrow of the evil pair, assuring him Belisarius was on board and that he had no wish himself to become emperor. Someone within the palace government was needed. Someone like the praetorian prefect.

Next, Antonina complimented John on his daughter, what a lovely girl she was. And how magnificently he has raised her, all without a mother. John basked in the praise so that when Antonina mentioned the soothsayer, I didn't have to see his face because his voice gushed enthusiasm.

"Oh, yes, I was told years ago the throne would one day be mine. I just had to wait."

"Well then, Lord John," Antonina said, striking her most logical and lilting tone, "it's time for us to take an oath together, so we can remove this scourge from the empire."

I shot Tariq a knowing look. His part in this drama was about to be played. He stood now with his back near the stairway that led down, his eyes on me.

Antonina pretended to make up the oath that would seal the scheme as she spoke, but to my ear, it was well-prepared ahead of time. He listened and then walked blindly into her netting, swearing on his own life and that of his daughter he would not rest until Justinian and Theodora had been pulled down from their white double throne.

I signaled to Tariq. He turned and took the stairs. I leaned over the railing, and in less than a minute observed Tariq knocking at the one door, then the other.

Narses and Marcellus responded at once.

I made the mistake of taking up my writing and carefully placing it into my dalmatic before moving toward the stairs. I say *mistake* because I missed seeing John's reaction when Narses and Marcellus made their appearance, the Imperial Guard behind them. As I hurried down the stairway, I heard the Cappadocian's angry voice shouting orders to his bodyguards.

By the time I came into the atrium, the two forces had clashed, and I was nearly run over by the praetorian prefect's men in their retreat.

John the Cappadocian vanished in the midst of them. Marcellus lay near the fountain, bleeding at the shoulder. At Narses' order, Marcellus's men stayed with him, rather than give chase. Narses told me later, out of Marcellus's earshot, that the Imperial Guard was more show than substance and no match for the Goths the Cappadocian had hired for protection.

Antonina stood shaking, seriously rattled, her stage face evaporated. Undoubtedly, she was fearful of telling Theodora that the prescribed outcome—the Cappadocian's death—had gone awry. She looked from the supine Marcellus to Narses, and then to me. She drew herself up, set her jaw, and took an unladylike stride toward me.

"Well, eunuch, did you get it? Did you write everything down?"

Late the same night—as Theodora had insisted—I gave her my written report of Antonina's meeting with the Cappadocian, after first providing her with a halting verbal account of the brief clash that followed it.

"What?" she demanded, black eyes ablaze. "The Cappadocian escaped? With Narses and Marcellus present? Should I have sent cavalry, Stephen?"

I did my best to explain the situation.

That Marcellus had been wounded made little difference. "What good is the Imperial Guard?" Theodora snapped. "*Where* did he go? The man has more lives than a cat."

"Narses said he would likely come back to The City."

"Listen to me, Stephen, you are to tell Narses to have the entrances to the palace patrolled. If the Cappadocian shows, he is to be apprehended and brought directly to me. If we allow him to plead his case to Justinian, he could invent something that would place him in a good light. Even if what's in your report is incontrovertible treason, he could say he was trying to set a trap for Belisarius and Antonina."

That Theodora's thoughts ran a step ahead came as no surprise. "Would Justinian believe him?" I asked.

Theodora shrugged. "He might."

As it happened, John the Cappadocian was not smart enough to create an excuse for himself of the sort Theodora feared. Panic must have set in, for he took up sanctuary in a church and was found two days later. Reading my report convinced Justinian of the Cappadocian's disloyalty, so he allowed Theodora to have him physically removed from the church. She did so, but only after enjoying the irony of forcing him to be ordained a monk and given the name "Brother August." Thus, in an ironic twist, the soothsayer's prediction that he would one day reign as August was fulfilled. Mention of it never failed to bring out Theodora's charming, tinkling laughter. Much of his wealth was confiscated, but common knowledge had it that he had squirreled away a treasure room of gold for his daughter's future. If he had been smart, he would have moved far from the capital to live out his life, but he stayed. Maybe he thought he would one day be reinstated as praetorian prefect; after all, it had happened once before. He had no friends left, no one with whom he had dealt with honestly. And he should have known Theodora would not forget, that she would be watching, waiting for another chance to complete the task of bringing him down.

42

Fall 541

I FOUND MYSELF PRIVY TO AN exchange of letters between Antonina and Theodora concerning Theodosius.

Even as Antonina traveled east to reunite with Belisarius while he was on his Persian campaign, Photius, fed up with his mother's coldness and no doubt jealous of the place Theodosius had taken in her life, revealed her adultery to the general. This time Belisarius believed the tale, and rather than follow through on a run of victories against the Persians, he lost the military momentum and pulled back to lie in wait for her arrival.

Belisarius confronted Antonina when she appeared and placed her under guard. Theodora assumed he avoided doing her harm, or even arranging an honor killing, not merely because it was against Roman law, but because he still loved her. While I agreed that his love held, the most practical reason for sparing his wife was her status as Theodora's closest friend and, masterful general or not, he feared the power and whims of the Augusta, as so many did. Indeed, when Antonina managed to bribe someone to get a letter to the empress detailing her predicament, Theodora dictated a royal order recalling Belisarius and his wife to Constantinople and convinced Justinian to sign it. I suspected it was against his better military judgment.

The general left his troops to winter in the East while he and Antonina returned to Constantinople, where Theodora forced an awkward reconciliation between husband and wife.

Photius, meanwhile, took it upon himself to apprehend Theodosius, confiscate the wealth that war had yielded him, and hold him captive. In striking at his mother through her lover, he did not take the caution Belisarius had taken when he avoided angering Theodora.

In little time, Theodora had Photius arrested and placed in the dungeon beneath the Daphne Wing. He refused to reveal Theodosius's whereabouts even under a series of lashes from a whip made of ox sinews. In the end, however, Theodora's spies found the abducted lover.

"Lady Antonina has arrived, mistress," Phaedra announced.

Theodora sat, watching Antonina enter her reception room in the women's quarters, hesitancy in her step, brow lifted in a questioning expression. She still cut a striking figure; no one could deny her beauty. Once, she had felt a jealousy toward Antonina for her blond hair and blue eyes, likely inheritances from her charioteer father's Gothic bloodline. The years, however, and their friendship had mitigated the feeling. Still, she wondered whether her own beauty had worn as well.

"I came as soon as I received your note."

"I see that. Come, sit across from me." Theodora nodded to her hand-maiden, a signal to leave the room.

Antonina sat on the couch, eyes cast down, hand running back and forth, smoothing out non-existent wrinkles in her pink stola. "Are you still angry, Theodora?"

"Angry? What makes you say that?"

Antonina brought her eyes up to meet Theodora's. "You seemed so the other day when Belisarius was here."

"Ah! That was more for his benefit. How has he treated you?"

"A bit cold. But I think things between us will improve."

"He still loves you, you know. He can't hide that."

"Thank you for bringing us together, Thea. I—I thought you would still be disappointed with me for allowing the Cappadocian to escape."

"An unlucky thing, that was. Still, you managed to bring about his down-fall. He's gone from the palace and from Justinian's ear. I owe that blessing to you, Nina. He'll not stage a return. He's already played that trick." Theodora stood. "I searched for just the right jewel with which to reward you. Stand up, dearest, and come along."

"Jewel?"

"A pearl, to be exact." Theodora took her friend's hand and led her to the curtained doorway leading to her study. "The pearl is in here, Nina." She pulled back the curtain.

There, not five feet away, stood the handsome Theodosius, black curls tumbling from the crown of his head and a toothy smile wide as a river.

Antonina blinked, her perfect jaw dropping. She gasped. "Oh, Theodora," she cried, her eyes locked on her lover, "what have you done?"

In answer, Theodora pushed her into the room.

"Why would she do that?" Tariq asked.

"You mean since she has been behind the Sanctity of Marriage laws Justinian has put forward?"

"Yes."

"It's a reward for Antonina's part in destroying the Cappadocian."

"You're right. There is that. And might there be something else? While Antonina is able to cavort with Theodosius, so too—"

I put my hand up to hush him.

"What—oh! Is Setka here?"

"Shh! Not so loud."

Tariq dropped his voice to a whisper. "Is he here?"

"In his room. Let's talk about something else."

"Come, come, Stephen!" Tariq challenged. "Tyche has painted them with the same brush. Why, half the palace is talking about Theodora and Setka.— You don't mean to say you still give her the benefit of the doubt."

"Yes," I said, attempting to sound firm.

After Tariq returned to the Palace of Hormisdas, I sat lost in thought— and a kind of sadness—.

Tariq had forced me to face what appeared to be the truth regarding Theodora and Setka. But how was it possible? The laws she had fostered regarding the sanctity of marriage and women in various situations demanded a stricter code of behavior. She had successfully lobbied Tribonian and Justinian for myriad laws now included in the *Codex Justinianus*. Simple incompatibility was no longer a reason for divorce, as it had been in the old Roman law. And whereas a man previously had always been able to seek divorce based on variable reasons, the woman had little recourse by comparison. Now, however, the laws provided the woman more latitude. The instances of a man living with a mistress in the same house as the wife or keeping a mistress elsewhere in town were seen as sufficient cause to grant the woman a divorce. A man convicted of rape now suffered the death penalty. Procopius scoffed at the changes that made women more equal in the eyes of the law, but women celebrated them—and celebrated Theodora.

Theodora was an enigma. Since the day the ship left Antioch, she has been my puzzle. Despite the part she played in the Sanctity of Marriage laws, she engineered the reunion of Antonina and her young lover. Antonina had been instrumental in deposing one Holy Father in Rome and electing another, as well as negotiating the downfall of John the Cappadocian, tasks earning complete loyalty from her childhood friend. I understood why Theodora not only looked away at Antonina's adultery, but also why she facilitated it.

I had stood in the old Church of the Holy Wisdom and watched Theodora marry Justinian. Despite being happy for her at the time, a piece of my heart had been torn out. Notwithstanding my love for her, I adapted to her marriage, happy only to be of service to her. She was a goddess, and so I looked past her many divine imperfections.

But now, to think her behavior with Setka ran parallel with Antonina's affair with Theodosius made me feel strangely unclean. I could not accept it. Complicating my thought was the fact that the young musician's friendliness and zest for life had won me to his side.

While I clung to my faith in Theodora, the truth that she facilitated Antonina in her adultery was incontrovertible. In fact, the empress housed Theodosius somewhere in the Daphne Wing because I would on occasion see Antonina stealthily moving along the stairways and halls to or from an assignation with her young lover.

"You should be elated," Tariq told me the next day, "that the empress didn't order him to board here with you."

"What?" I rejoined, laughing. "Where? In the room next to Setka's?"

"Why not? They are two sides of the same coin. Think what comradeship would develop."

Suddenly, the humor dissipated. "Stop, Tariq!" I demanded, angry that he had broached the subject of Theodora's rumored adultery again. Not accepting what he and others thought left me with a whisper of hope.

I came to wonder about Belisarius. He must have known about the renewal of the affair between Antonina and Theodosius. Did he ignore it, or was he slavishly knuckling under to Theodora? I would not find out which was the case because the liaison ended in a heartbeat—Theodosius's.

He lived well for the time-being, enjoying the attention and favors of Antonina. He basked, too, in a palace suite and in an empress's promise to see that he realizes his dream to become a highly placed army field commander.

43

December 541

ANTONINA BURST INTO THEODORA'S STUDY, Phaedra on her heels and too late to announce her.

"Theodora!" Antonina cried. "There are guards on Theodosius's door!"

Theodora stood, waved the handmaiden away, and moved around from her desk. "Come in ... and lower your voice." The handmaiden bowed and left.

Theodora took hold of Antonina's forearms. "Nina, you didn't attempt to enter?"

"I know better than to fan the flames of gossip."

"*Do* you?" Theodora blurted before realizing the sarcasm was inappropriate to the moment. She released her friend.

"Well, to be honest, the two guards would not allow me entrance."

"Come, sit with me here."

Antonina settled herself on the couch beside Theodora.

"He's ill, Antonina—very ill."

"It's the dysentery, I'll wager—tainted water, no doubt. He'll recover. He survived it once before—in Rome."

"Our water is good, Antonina. This appears to be different, more serious."

"What is it, then? I want to see him."

"The room is guarded for a reason, Nina, and no one enters, other than the physician and his assistants. They—we, that is—are being very cautious."

"Of what? ... Theodora, tell me!"

"Well, something of an epidemic has been recorded in Egypt."

"In Egypt? That is half the world away. Why should we worry here?"

"Because, Nina, reports have come that there have been isolated cases in port cities along the Levant, like Gaza and Jaffa."

"You're talking about the plague, aren't you?"

"Yes, Nina," Theodora whispered. "It is fierce and it is deadly. The reports are bone-chilling." She drew in a long breath. "They say it could come here."

"Here?" Antonina's lower jaw fell slack. "Here?—And ... and they think that Theodosius—"

"Now, now, don't jump to conclusions. Alexander of Tralles is the physician in charge. He's the brother of our architect Anthemius and just as renowned in *his* field of expertise. He is highly revered, Nina."

"Yes, yes, I met him in Rome. Belisarius called him in to attend Theodosius. They call him 'Alexander the Physician'."

As if on cue, Phaedra returned to announce the physician. Theodora nodded her assent.

Dressed in a gold embroidered green dalmatic, Alexander the Physician swept into the room. The white hair and well-trimmed beard betrayed the fact that he was into his sixth decade, but his stride was quick, his posture perfect. He bowed to Theodora. "Mistress." Only then did his dark brown eyes shift to Antonina, widening in recognition. He afforded her a nod. "Lady Antonina," he murmured. Theodora assumed some interaction of a negative sort had transpired between them in Rome. She suspected he was aware of her interest in Theodosius.

"What are your findings, Alexander?" Theodora chose not to stand because she would be dwarfed by his height.

"The man is quite ill, mistress."

"Is it ... is it—"

"No, it is not the plague, mistress."

"Then he will recover?" Antonina pleaded.

The physician turned to her. "Only God can say. Your godson is deathly ill."

Although Antonina seemed of one mind, Theodora recognized the knife's jagged edge on the word *godson*. The physician was reminding Antonina of her true relationship to the young soldier.

"No!" Antonina cried, paling. "But you helped him through this once before. You did!"

"This is not mere dysentery, Lady Antonina. Quite the opposite. Rest assured I've given him the appropriate amulet and ordered a diet of dates and cereals, among other things, but—"

"That hardly sounds so serious," Antonina interrupted.

"In his case, it is." The physician's face went dark. "It's called gastroparesis. He is experiencing severe abdominal pain, nausea, and vomiting. His limbs are weak as a newborn's, and he has night sweats at all hours. I'll spare you the other details."

Gasping, Antonina pushed herself up from the couch. "I want to see him!"

The physician looked from Theodora to Antonina and back again. "I advise against that. You would be at risk."

"I don't care!" Tears were coming fast now. "I must see Theo!"

Theodora reached up and took Antonina's hand before she could barge past the physician. She drew her back onto the couch. "The physician has determined a risk, Nina. You cannot see him."

"But, Theodora, I—"

"You heard me," Theodora snapped as she turned to her friend, her gaze locking onto the stormy blue eyes. "I won't have it!"

Theodora held the physician back after Antonina left the chamber. They sat facing one another. "Doctor, I have questions of a nature other than a plague."

"Yes, mistress?"

"Justinian and I have been praying for an heir."

"I see." Alexander tried to conceal a smile. "It takes more than prayers, mistress."

Theodora could not help but give a little laugh. "We have been doing more than praying, you can be sure."

"Ah! I see," he said, hesitating before venturing to ask, "How old are you, mistress?"

Theodora responded without hesitation: "Forty-one this past June."

Alexander nodded. "And—and do, that is, do—"

"Yes, yes, my courses still run."

"Well, then, I think—"

"Wait, before you deliver a message of hope, I want to mention my husband."

"Yes, mistress?"

"Will you swear to secrecy?"

"Certainly. Subjects of import between me and my patients are always in confidence."

"Should word get out, I would know the source."

The physician's head drew back. "I understand, mistress."

"Some years ago, before we were married, Justinian was diagnosed with a disease called orchitis."

The physician's eyes widened, his forehead wrinkling.

"Oh, you needn't be embarrassed. I'm well aware that it's a matter dealing with the testes." When he gave a hesitant nod, face reddening, eyes cast down, she continued. "The royal physician at the time was Philoxenos. He was hesitant to speak to me of it, much like you are now, but a little research revealed the disease could result in Justinian's becoming sterile. Is that true, Alexander?"

"Well, mistress, in some cases, yes, I've found it so."

"I see, but not in all? So I might still be able to bear a child?"

"Pardon, me, mistress, but you've already borne a daughter. Have you ever lost a child in childbirth?

"No."

"I see, but—have—have there been other children?"

The question caught Theodora by surprise and quickened her pulse. She had but a moment to decide whether to tell him of the boy John she had delivered in Alexandria, where the Patriarchs Timothy and Severus had taken her in. Her first thought was that perhaps it could have some bearing on the physician's counsel regarding her fertility. However, the next thought sent a chill of fear up her spine. She recalled the document she had signed upon her marriage, swearing that she had birthed no other children than the girl, Hyacinth. She took in a deep breath and steeled herself. No one must know about the boy. No one.

"No," Theodora said, her gaze set on the physician. Eyes were windows that projected truth, and avoiding eye contact would surely give her away. She had learned in the theater how to stare at an actor or an audience without seeing them. It was a trick she employed now so that he would not see through to her lie. After some moments, she allowed him to come back into focus. To her surprise, it was he who avoided eye contact; he had adjusted his gaze off to her side, as if the wall were more interesting. Her pulse slowed.

She noticed now that his face had reddened. "Mistress," he said, "it's often the case with preeminent men of government, or even of the church, that they form liaisons, attachments that … well, that yield …"

Great Hera! Theodora suddenly realized he meant to ask whether Justinian had fathered children with someone else. "Alexander," she said, biting back spontaneous anger, "I can assure you that line of questioning will get us nowhere. I want to know what of *these* circumstances?"

The physician cleared his throat. "I'm not of much help, mistress. You and the emperor should continue to have hope and to—"

"But, after all these years, it is likely that Justinian is sterile, is it not?"

Theodora held his gaze now as a lawyer might interrogate a witness so that he dared not look away. She would know if he lied. She saw him swallow hard as he took some seconds to fashion his response.

"Yes, mistress," he rasped, "it is likely."

Theodora felt the world falling away, as if she were dropping into a void. These were words she thought she had prepared herself to hear, and yet they cut into her with the precision of a surgeon's scalpel.

"Are you … are you well, mistress?"

"What? … Theodora looked up to see him standing in front of his chair.

"Thank you, Alexander," she said at once, hoping to deflect him from coming toward her. "Please take your seat. We kept that possible consequence of the disease from Justinian all those years ago. I took the blame for our childless marriage, as I do now. He is not to know, do you understand?"

A nearly invisible tremor occurred at the corner of the physician's mouth. He nodded.

Theodora would never make good on her promise to see that Theodosius become a general. She was saved from having to do so. He died a week later on 26 December, Saint Stephen's Day. Theodora told me both Belisarius and Antonina were inconsolable. However, I knew it weighed more heavily on the one godparent.

A rumor was whispered in corners of the palace that Theodosius was poisoned. This, I thought unlikely, for his one serious enemy was Antonina's son Photius, who remained Theodora's prisoner in the dungeon below the Daphne Wing. When he did find his way to freedom, he would keep his distance from Theodora all of her remaining days.

44

January to April 542

WHILE ALEXANDER THE PHYSICIAN DETERMINED Theodosius's cause of death was not the plague, news of disease nonetheless became a topic of gossip when word came from North Africa that a high number of people were falling ill, many dying. The news inspired little worry at first because it was well-known that a certain confined pocket on the eastern edge of the Nile Delta—with the city of Pelusium at its center—hosted this deadly disease, had done so for as long as anyone could remember, centuries, in fact. However, for some reason no one understood, this year the disease broke out of its historical environs.

Slowly, gossip evolved into concern when later reports had contagion traveling from Pelusium west to Alexandria and east to the cities of the Levant. Death tolls rose as the pestilence moved north into Palestine, devastating Gaza and Jerusalem. Now called a plague, the disease struck Syria, depleting the population of the Persian-held city of Antioch by half.

Here, in the New Rome, Spring brought the opening of the sea lanes, and half of the population went dauntlessly on with daily life, somehow confident that the plague had no means of travel. Occasionally, a fearless jester would excavate an old quote from Socrates: "There's always something new from Africa."

But fear stalked the other half. And they had good reason to fear.

May 542

Somehow, I lived through The City's most terrible calamity.

Silently, invisibly, the Angel of Death entered Constantinople from the waters, at the harbors—not the small royal one used by the royals, the Harbor of Hormisdas, but three large commercial ones: the Harbor of Theodosius, just south of the Forum of Theodosius; the Prosphorian Harbor, at the entrance to the Golden Horn; and the Neorion Harbor, west of the Prosphorian. Sailors, travelers, dock workers, and the legions of those working in the many nearby storehouses were stricken first. Like its namesake, the New Rome possesses seven hills, and it was at the base of those hills where the pestilence began its inexorable climb to the churches and homes of every stratum of society. Fears mounted as the plague spread, infecting a few hundred a day at first—and then, thousands.

In the first few days, numerous government officials, nobles, and senators moved with their families away from The City. Wealth translated to security at summer homes. As the plague closed in, Alexander the Physician recommended isolation to citizens who remained in The City. Justinian ordered the bronze gates of the Chalké barred. No one was to be admitted to the palace grounds; those who left could not return. I thought perhaps he and Theodora would sail across the Marmara and seek refuge at Hieron, but the two remained in the Daphne Wing. A decade had passed since she had convinced her husband and his male councilors not to run from the Nika Riots, and I could not help but think she exerted a like influence on her husband during this plague time.

Within the Great Palace environs, court physicians had little to do at first; still, they were forbidden to leave. Those remaining behind the walls waited with fear-imprinted faces, listening to the lamentations echoing from every quarter. Outside, doctors paid by the government and sworn to tend the public, rich or poor, quickly became overworked, many falling victims themselves to the *demon*, as the plague was sometimes called.

Inevitably, the pestilence stole its way into the Great Palace, afflicting soldiers, servants, and slaves first, but in no time striking two senators and several government officials who had not fled The City. Word had it that within the Palace of Hormisdas three scribes had fallen ill, as well as at least the same number of Monophysites whom Theodora sheltered there. With isolation in place, I had no way to check on Tariq, whose well-being was foremost in my mind.

For me and those who shared my suite—Piers and Setka—a new confined and circumspect manner of existence became the normal. My meetings with Theodora came to an end. Setka was denied her company, as well, and he brooded about it incessantly. When she had translations or works to be transcribed in larger script, we would hear a brief but insistent knock. By the time we opened the door, the assignment sat there on the hallway floor, along with the date by which I was to have it finished.

June 542

One day, I heard a commotion in my little vestibule and went to investigate. The door stood wide open. Piers lay on the red tile, mouth agape and eyes closed, a spilled container of flour nearby.

Calling for Setka, I rushed to his side and went to my knees, fearing his age had brought on a paroxysm of the heart. The boy was there in a minute. "Close the door!" I ordered, because in just those few moments my thoughts went to another likely diagnosis, and I didn't want some passing person witnessing the scene and spreading yet another bit of panic-inspired gossip about the plague.

Setka closed the door, came over and dropped to my side. "Is he breathing?"

"Yes, but it's troubled." I laid my hand on the furrowed forehead. "He's a bit feverish."

Setka put the back of his hand to Piers's forehead, and when he took it away, he shot a clouded look at me. "I'll take his upper body," he said, "if you'll take hold of his legs. Let's get him to his sleeping couch."

I had no time to argue. Once I would have bristled at this youth who was directing me in my own residence, but we had come to friendly terms.

We had no sooner laid Piers upon his bed than his eyes opened as wide as I had ever seen them. It was the first time I realized they were not black, but a dark gray. He looked from Setka, who was kneeling at his side, up to me, where I stood.

"What happened?" Piers asked in a voice more raspy than usual.

I told him.

"Oh! The flour!" Piers cried. "The royal kitchens have little left, and they wouldn't part with even a dusting. There was but one bakery I found open on Baker's Row, and the price I had to pay was ridiculous." His voice dropped to a whisper. "Not to mention the bribe I paid at the gate to be let back in." He started to push himself up from the narrow couch, but Setka gently held him back. "I must—"

"You must rest, Piers," Setka said in a tone allowing no argument.

"You are warm to the touch," I put in, "nothing to worry about. Still, Setka is correct. You're to rest all day today. I'll salvage the flour. The threshold goddess must know you keep the vestibule floor clean enough. Still, you should not have gone down into the streets."

Piers looked from me to Setka and back again. "Oh no! I know what you're both thinking—that the plague's got me." He struggled anew against Setka's hold. "I'll show you."

"No you won't, Piers," I said. "And we don't think that's the case at all, not with the tepid fever you have. However, I do insist you stay in bed until tomorrow. If you get up, we'll only put you back in bed, like a child. Do you understand?"

Piers fell back against the cushion. "Then you don't think—"

"No, I don't," I interrupted. "But you're not as young as you think, either. You've exhausted yourself. The two of us can manage the household though you might not think so. I insist you rest."

Piers's head rolled away from us. "Very well," he said, "the flour bin is—"

"I know perfectly well where it is," I said.

His gaze toward the wall, Piers took a few deep breaths and stopped resisting. We left him once he promised us he would rest—and sleep.

Outside the bedchamber, I turned to Setka. "You didn't assure him it's not the pestilence," I said, opting for a word other than plague.

"I couldn't," he said.

"What? His fever is so mild. Other than that—"

"That's the way it often starts, Lord Stephen."

"How do you know?"

"Because this is how it started for my father."

"What?" I was caught unawares. This was the first mention he had made of his parentage.

He nodded. "It came on much like this. We lived very near Pelusium, on the Delta, where it struck every year ever since I can remember. Some say it originated in the south and traveled up by way of the Red Sea, but no one really knows."

I took in a long breath. "Did he survive it?"

"No," he said, a sharpness in his tone. "A madness overcame him and before long his body betrayed him."

"I'm sorry, Setka." Sometimes, I realized, information comes unbidden and roundabout. "And your mother?" I knew I was pressing my luck.

"She lives."

"You'll go back to her one day?"

Shrugging, he gave me an indecipherable glance, and said, "I'll get some bedding and stay with Piers tonight."

"You'll do no such thing. We've already been exposed."

"I was in Carthage when my father took ill. Had I been there to comfort him and see that he ate and kept himself clean, he might have survived. Instead, he died, crazed and alone."

"You should *not* put yourself at risk," I pressed.

"If I can be of comfort to Piers, I might be easier on myself for not being with my father when he died. Then again, maybe I can save him." The youth turned and made for his room.

I went to sweep up the flour.

After dark, I took soup and cheese for two to Piers's chamber. Setka came to the door, took the tray from me, nodding—but he meant to block my entry. I motioned toward a pile of clothes on the floor behind him. "Is that his dirty clothing? Let me have it, Setka."

"No, no—never mind. I'll see to it. When he went down to Baker's Row, he came back infected with some little flour mites or bugs. I'll burn the clothes." With that, he closed the door.

In the morning, when I heard nothing coming from Piers's room, I knocked, fully planning to enter, but Setka appeared in a flash, again blocking me. I looked over his shoulder to see Piers struggling to throw off his covers. He was naked.

"How is he?" I asked.

"Delirious for much of the night, Stephen. The truth is he's exhausted from battling me, as well as some demons in his mind."

"What's to be done?"

"This morning he has the buboes."

My throat closed and I suddenly felt unsteady. I knew what those swellings meant. "Where?"

"In his groin and under his arms."

"I see," I said. "And now?"

"We can only wait and hope the buboes break open and the poison drains out."

"Otherwise?"

Setka shook his head, gently backed me off the threshold, and closed the door.

Later, when I went out onto the balcony at sunset, as was my custom, I noticed a small pile of ashes. Bending over to take a closer look, I spotted a tiny patch of material, the tiniest scorched piece of what had once been Piers's tunic.

I was able to put thoughts of the buboes from my mind for the rest of the morning and into the afternoon but, somehow, the sight of those scraps of material that symbolized an old man's humble existence on earth brought home to me the realization that life as I had known it was no more. Tears came in a rush. The way forward was dark and dangerous.

In the afternoon of the next day, a knock came at my door. I answered it and stood speechless at the visitor.

"What?—No servant to answer the door today? The times we live in!" Without invitation Procopius crossed the threshold and pivoted toward me. "Oh, don't look so surprised, Stephen. The empress asked me to stop by."

I closed the door. "We can talk in my study." He wore his usual immaculate brown dalmatic, and as he turned, I noticed a small tag hanging on a string around his neck. I put down the urge to ask him about it. We were not friends.

"Your study, yes," Procopius said, already in motion. Several paces down the hall, he called back, "I know the way."

His words dripped with equal parts sarcasm, irony, and bitterness. Oh, he did know the way. No doubt he considered me an interloper. He had little liking for me before Theodora commandeered his apartment—and less afterward. He was now relegated to rooms beneath the ground floor. Only later would I learn the true depth of his resentment and to what lengths he would go to regain the suite and its proximity to the Imperial Apartment.

By the time I caught up to him, I chose to annoy him, so I sat at my desk chair and had him sit in front of the desk, as if he had come to beg some favor.

Once seated, he turned in the chair, craning his neck to view the wall behind him and the chief difference in the study since it had been his: my treasured mosaic boy sitting on the parapet around a pond with its blue water and golden fish. He grunted and turned back toward me, a sneer forming.

I spoke before he could deliver his critique. "Actually," I said, "Piers fell ill a couple of days ago." I was curious to see how he would react to mention of the servant who for years had served him in these rooms.

Procopius leaned forward, at once intent. "What?"

I immediately knew I had blundered by saying that much. "Yes," I said, searching for a way to extricate myself, "he collapsed after coming back from an errand. He works himself too hard. Surely you remember that."

"Well, then he's a changed man from the days in my employ, but perhaps he's more motivated to work for you. ... Exactly *when* did this occur?"

"The day before yesterday."

"Three days? And he's *still* bedridden?"

I nodded.

"Did he come down with a fever?"

"Only a slight one," I replied, becoming nauseous at the questioning. I had given him just enough of an opening for his lawyerly skills to take over.

"And now?"

"It persists."

"What else?"

"He's ... uncomfortable."

"Damn, Stephen! Does he have the buboes?"

My face flushed with heat. I could prevaricate no further. He had backed me into a corner. "He does."

Procopius sat back and drew in air. "You—you act as if you don't know the seriousness of this. It's the plague, eunuch! The plague!"

"I didn't want him taken elsewhere, Procopius. If he's to die, he should die here with what little comfort we can provide."

Procopius's eyes went to full mast. "We—*we*? Where's Setka? Where, Stephen?"

I swallowed hard. "Setka is in with him now."

"What?" The word came like an explosion.

"He's been his nurse. His father died of the pestilence. He knows the risks."

"But do you know the risks to allow this to go on? Do you have any idea what it's like out there in The City? *Do you?*"

My spine went rigid against the chair's back "I know food is scarce, the bakeries have closed, and the fishermen have fallen ill or gone to their homes."

"Goddess Hygieia protect us from your ignorance, eunuch! If only that was all! The poor *and* the rich are dying at an alarming rate. Strangely, a good many of those stricken imagine demons have come to collect them. Some have returned to the old gods, foolishly thinking they can save them."

"Like Hygieia?" I asked, unable to resist the taunt.

"Oh, you can mock the idea of religion, Stephen. I forgot you hold no belief. But the bodies are piling up and the tombs have been filled. Justinian has ordered pits dug to the north of the city, but even those are filling fast with thousands. Those charged with the burials have to walk across the bodies in order to press them down and allow for another layer."

"I … I didn't realize—"

"Nor did anyone ever think it would come to this. However, the warnings were in the sky if only we'd had someone to divine them. There was the comet."

"The one you called the Swordfish Comet? Didn't you tell Justinian that was a kind of salute to the reunification of the empire?"

"Yes, yes, I did. But I am no diviner of such things."

No, I thought, but you are a flatterer of emperors.

"There was another sign, too," Procopius said.

"Yes?"

"Yes. Just a few years ago a veil of dust blotted out the sun."

"I remember. It lasted a year, a very cold year."

"No—eighteen months it went on. Crops failed and thousands upon thousands of people died. Some believe a volcano many times more powerful than Vesuvius was the cause." Procopius sighed. "But—again, there was no one to read the sign."

"And," I put in, "nothing to be done even if there had been."

Procopius stood. "Theodora sent me here to look in on you and Setka. What can I tell her?"

"That we are fine."

"Fine? I dare not tell her about Setka and his recklessness. I can't fathom why she holds dear that skin-and-bones singer, but she does, doesn't she?" Here was Procopius, ever the lawyer, alluding to the gossip concerning Setka and the empress and plumbing for information.

"Does she?" I asked. "I don't know, Procopius."

Contrary to Procopius's description, at twenty-two now, Setka had filled out and was more handsome than ever.

When Procopius finally made ready to leave, I again noticed the tag hanging on a string. Curiosity got the best of me. "Lord Procopius, if you don't mind my asking, what is that you're wearing?

"Haven't you seen people with them?"

"I haven't been out."

"I *must* to go out. I have duties. Everyone is supposed to wear them." He turned it over so that I could see writing. "It's my name you see there. People have dropped down delirious or even dead on the street with the plague. This bit of identity was the urban prefect's idea so that the victim—or the body— could be returned to his home."

"So, it's the duty of the urban watch to collect the bodies?"

"No!" he bleated. "Not a chance. Too many victims for the police. Besides, they've lost a good many of their own. No, believe it or not, the Greens and Blues are working together, collecting and burying the dead. No seer could have predicted that!" Procopius gave out with an irreverent snort.

I could not resist a final taunt. "Won't you look in on Piers?"

"No," he snapped. "I have business to attend. I'll see if I can scare up a physician. Be certain to tell Setka to keep his distance from the sickroom. Get him out of there, do you hear?"

"He has a mind of his own, Procopius. Perhaps you can talk to him?"

"Me? I think not." He moved out into the hall, and as we passed his former servant's room, he brought up the wide sleeve of his dalmatic to cover his nose and mouth. "I don't intend to tell Theodora about Setka's foolhardiness. She's known for blaming the messenger, they say, and with good reason. "But I warn you, you had better amend the situation by igniting some fear in Theodora's musical prodigy."

At the door, I took hold of his other sleeve. "How is she?" I asked.

"Theodora?" Procopius shrugged. "It will take more than a plague to knock her down. While Justinian feels compelled to continue to meet with his councilors or citizens who have somehow breached the gates to come begging a moment of his time, Theodora has not stepped out of her confinement. And word has it she luxuriates for an hour or more in her scented bath before breakfast every day, without fail. I can't help but think the habit has served her well." He leveled his gaze at me. "What is it, Stephen, are you missing her attention?" He pulled away now and stepped out into the hall, tossing off a final quip: "Or is it the image of Theodora at her bath?"

I sat at my desk, feeling tightness across my chest. How I resented Procopius! It was more than the fact he had gotten in an insult about my closeness to the empress. It was the fact that it had hit its target.

The truth was, I did miss her. And she? Procopius said she had sent him to see how we were—Setka and I. Was her concern more for the musician? I seldom allowed the rumors of their relationship to enter my thoughts. I had built a wall to hold them back, but now, they came scaling over the top. Was she no better, no nobler, than Lady Antonina, who was no lady? Had she fallen in love with this youth?

And Setka! Against all odds and strong initial emotions, I had come to like the boy and enjoy his company.

That night, in order to fall asleep, I talked myself into believing Theodora was concerned for the welfare of *both* Setka and me.

45

No one really knew how this plague was being passed one to the next, but in the days following, I tried to convince Setka to spend less time tending to Piers. However, the youth remained moored to the servant's room.

Procopius advised Theodora of Piers's illness, and she sent Alexander the Physician to make a call.

Setka and I watched from a corner of the bedchamber as the physician drew back the sheet Setka had just changed and examined the patient, who lay inert but awake. He prodded the lime-sized buboes with a blunt-edged instrument. Next, he held his palms hovering over each site, chanting: "Through the grace of God, I abjure thee, foul contagion, to take thyself away from this good man. Begone!"

His chant reminded me of the incantations my first owner, the magus Gaspar, would chant for his customers. Whether they were prayers or curses, we never stayed in any one town long enough to determine whether they had any effect. For once, I thought, I will find out if they do.

When the physician had finished, he drew me out into the hall. I deliberately did not introduce him to Setka out of fear he would relay the youth's continued risk-taking to Theodora.

"You're the empress's secretary, yes?" Alexander inquired.

"I am."

"What kind of ink do you use?"

"Iron gall ink," Doctor."

"Good. Take a small but thick piece of parchment and with iron gall ink, write upon it, 'Evil, stay your distance'. Cut the parchment into the size of a medallion, make a small hole in it, and draw a gold chain through it. When the amulet is ready, place it around your patient's neck."

The physician turned to leave and took long strides toward the door, where I caught up to him. "How is he, Doctor Alexander? Will he—"

"The abscesses appear as if they are ready to suppurate. That will allow the poison to drain."

"I'm told that's good."

"It's no miracle but it means he *might* recover. I've seen it happen. Had he developed internal hemorrhages, as some do, he would have no hope. Or, if it entered the lungs, for that matter. Death comes quickly for those struck in those ways. But maybe they are the lucky ones."

"And the amulet?"

"Make it as I directed." The doctor sighed. "For a patient struck down by the plague, it is the physician's duty to diagnose it, to see he has good care and is kept clean, and to merely stand by, sometimes offering hope. In such cases as this, the amulet may have no more power than that—hope. His family can see it. The patient can hold it. ... I must go now, Stephen."

I touched his elbow, detaining him. "What if, what if the buboes do not—discharge their poison?"

The physician's lips flattened into a contrived sort of smile. "Then he is fated for the burial pits. He will be in crowded company. Goodbye, Stephen."

The next day, Setka stood at the doorway, again barring my entrance to Piers's bedchamber. "It's for your own good, Stephen," he said. He took the amulet from me that I had prepared during the late hours, and I watched from the doorway as he secured it around Piers's neck.

That night and into the next day, the swellings in the groin and armpits erupted, draining the yellow, fetid pus. Setka tended his patient fastidiously, keeping him clean, even entertaining him with his playing and singing the songs of Pindar. Having resigned myself to Setka's self-chosen position as care-taker, I felt foolishly helpless.

With each new day, Piers improved. My father would have said, "Mithra be praised!"

July 542

One night, I was shaken awake.

"What is it, Setka?" I turned to my side and opened my eyes.

My intruder stood there, holding a clay lamp, orange light flickering on his face. It was not Setka.

"Piers?" I blinked. My first thought was his delirium had come back, and he was wandering about. Such was not the case. He appeared to have recovered. "What is it?" I repeated, "Piers?"

"Yes. It's Setka, Lord Stephen. He's fallen ill—very ill."

I sat up, pivoting and bringing my legs to the side of the bed. I wiped at my eyes. "Where is he?"

"I managed to get him to his room. Stephen—he has the swellings."

A vise took hold of my heart. Within a minute or two, I was up and stumbling along a dark passage.

Unless Setka had been hiding symptoms, his illness had struck with virulence and the suddenness doctors were witnessing across The City. Citizens were dropping dead in the streets.

Weak as a newborn, Setka cycled through fever, chills, and fever again in the following days. He had the buboes in the usual places, as well as a smaller swelling on his forearm, the tiniest of pinpricks at its center, as if he had been bitten.

Piers insisted on staying at his bedside. "He nursed me back to health," the servant said. "Now I must do the same for him."

Two weeks passed. The buboes grew to the size of apples, and we began to lose faith they would break open. From time to time, Piers and I exchanged despairing expressions. Alexander the Physician had told me in cases such as these death wins out.

I knew I should alert Theodora, but I held back.

Two more days passed. From the doorway, I studied Setka, watching him struggle to breathe and wishing him well, but I had little hope. He was dying.

Procopius called unexpectedly. He seemed more stunned by the reversal of fortune for Setka than by that of Piers's recovery. Saying little, he made an excuse and abruptly left, never having crossed my threshold.

I felt an odd ache in the back of my throat. It did not take the sight credited to my Syrian blood for me to know only too well where he was going. How he would love bringing bad news to her. He hid it well in front of Justinian, but he hated Theodora; he always had.

I drew back the bolt, unlocking the door to my suite, and waited for the visitant.

Within the hour, Theodora pushed her way in, the dark eyes wild and yet intent. "Where is he?" she demanded.

"Theodora, I don't think you should go in. We don't know how it's passed from one to another. Setka became ill taking care of Piers."

"Never mind that, Stephen. Which room?"

Forgetting myself, I put my hand on her arm to detain her. "But—Thea, you're the empress."

Her ebony eyes dropped to where I held her, then flared up at me as if she could slay me.

I dropped my hand and nodded toward the room where Setka lay dying.

Theodora was well-used to scented oils and expensive perfumes so that the fetid and stifling room struck her like a thunderclap. But it was a sudden coldness that ran upward the length of Theodora's spine when she saw Setka, tangled in a mass of covers on the narrow sleeping couch, his skin white as powdered lime.

He appeared more unconscious than asleep as she settled into a chair Piers had kept placed next to the bed. His lower jaw hung open a bit, and he emitted a wet, crackling noise as he struggled to breathe.

However, his eyes opened when she took up his hand. This is not happening, she told herself. It can't happen like this. Not to Setka. *Not now.*

But she had seen people die and knew Death stood in the wings.

"You have come," Setka said, each word a struggle. "I'm glad." He closed his mouth, its corners seeming to twitch a bit in an attempt to smile. "I waited, you know. I waited for you."

"You'll be well again," Theodora managed to say despite a painful tightness at her throat.

Setka's head moved haltingly, side to side.

"You will, Setka. You'll play and sing once again for the emperor. Must I command you?" She attempted to summon her best stage smile. His expression told her it was not good enough.

Setka's eyes closed and he appeared to sleep. Theodora held to his motionless hand. An hour—or two—passed. Theodora remained silent, daring not to speak, not to offer false hope. Little by little, the rattle in his throat increased.

Theodora herself drifted into a space between sleep and wakefulness, dread and hope, when suddenly she realized Setka's fingers were curling to take hold of her hand. Her heart caught. She blinked away the fogginess, focusing now on his visage. The film over his eyes seemed to lift. He returned her gaze.

"Don't mourn me." Now able to move only his eyes side to side, Setka said, as if the movement intimated the whole of the Great Palace and its life, "This—this has been *all*." He paused for breath, struggling unsuccessfully to lift his head from the cushion. "You," he said, a single, solemn tear breaking from one eye, "have been everything—Mother."

Setka labored at life for several more minutes before the death rattle stopped.

Theodora took good time for her tears to dry and her regrets to retreat. As she lifted and kissed the hand of the child she had left behind so many years before, she saw that his fingers were blackening. Her stomach clenched, and yet she reverently placed his hand upon the comforter, fending off disgust. She recalled someone saying that nearing the end, the victim's extremities blacken. She stood, turning to see Stephen in the doorway. Her heart thumped.

How long had he been standing there? *Had he heard?*

I sat at my desk, drinking wine. I lost count of how many cups I had drunk, only that the amphora was empty—and yet the liquor had done nothing to obscure the heaviness of my thoughts.

I looked across the room at Jati, my mosaic muse, and silently shook my head as I thought how Tariq had been so accurate in saying that Setka's features were similar to mine—Syrian. Those features had come directly from Theodora and her Syrian mother.

Setka had put his life at stake in order to nurse Piers. He had done it even knowing from his experience in North Africa how dangerous it was to do so.

I regretted that it had taken a good while for me to warm up to him; nonetheless, I was glad that in recent months we had become close. In time, I did give him the benefit of the doubt, rejecting the idea he had become Theodora's lover. More than a few palace dwellers believed as much, and I confess at times my own doubts were stirred.

Now those doubts were quashed. That Setka was her son changed everything. I now grieved for Setka—and, more, for Theodora's loss.

From the two Blues who collected the body came word of outside the walls of the Great Palace. In its fourth month now, the urban prefect claimed the disease was claiming as many as four or five thousand a day. It was not an uncommon event for a city household to be completely emptied of servants, slaves, and masters. The man holding the Office of Referendarius, the official usually in charge of presenting citizen petitions to the emperor, was now charged with the thankless task of organizing the burial of countless bodies.

"We have dug pits for the dead at every open bit of land within the city walls." The husky young Blue spoke not in answer to a question, but rather as a way to vent a complaint. As he and his partner shifted Setka's body from the sleeping couch to a stretcher, he continued, "The pits have been filled and still the bodies pile up in streets and alleys." In neither face nor voice, did either Blue betray emotion, merely exhaustion.

"That's why an occasional wind will bring a stink with it," I suggested.

"No, my lord, what you smell comes from the towers."

"What? From the Theodosian Walls?"

The Blue nodded.

Justinian and I had walked to the far city walls years before, investigating the square and octagonal fortification towers spaced out the whole length of the double line of walls.

As they carried the remains of Setka from the room and down the hallway, the Blue continued: "It was the idea of the Referendarius, it was. And a bad one, at that, if I do say so. They removed the roofs of those towers and piled the dead one atop the other. Just dropped them in from the top with no order, mind you, haphazard, like partridges into a pot. The towers filled up fast, they did."

"*That's* the stench we smell?"

"If the wind is from the west, it is. Oh, they put the roofs back on the towers but it did no good."

When we reached the door, I put my hand on the speaker's sleeve to detain him. I nodded toward Setka's body. "What of this man?" I pressed, fearful he would be so badly disrespected.

"He's a lucky one, he is," the Blue said. He gave a twisted smile, seeming to appreciate the irony of his statement once it was out. "Must be somebody, yes? He's to be buried here on the palace grounds. The grave is dug already." He nodded to his partner, and they moved out into the hall.

"Where?" I asked, relieved.

"Secret," he called back.

If guards had not been stationed at the Daphne exits to keep people from leaving, I would have followed him.

46

September 542

ACH NIGHT, WITH NO ONE to share her grief, she shed a river of tears over the son she had just come to know. If only she had told Justinian about Setka … if only …

Dawn was breaking when Theodora awoke. She lifted her head and saw that her husband—contrary to habit—had remained in her bed rather than descend to his subterranean War Room, where he had most recently waged war on the pestilence crippling The City.

Justinian lay on his side, facing away. Theodora propped herself up on her elbow and pulled at his shoulder so that he moved onto his back. He muttered something incomprehensible but did not awake. His face glistened with wetness. She placed the back of her hand to his forehead. He had a slight fever.

Theodora's stomach went rock hard. Her thoughts ran together, blurred. It had come, as she feared, as she knew it would. She froze in place, allowing minutes to pass. If the plague could claim her son, it could take her husband—everyone. What to do? *What to do?*

Theodora reached over and gave Justinian a gentle shaking. Too gentle. She tried again—and again.

Al last, he stirred. "What? What is it, Thea?"

"You were saying something in your sleep."

"Nonsense!" Justinian lifted his head and looked at her, blinking away the sleep.

"You were. And you have a … a fever."

"I think not," he said, his gaze going past her, toward the shaded windows. "It's fully light out!" he gasped. "I've overslept. But how? I never oversleep."

"But you did. It's the fever, Justinian. I'm frightened—"

"No. No reason to be! I must get up. I have an appointment with Procopius." He sat up and swung his legs over the side, but instead of propelling himself up, he sat there.

Theodora heard his quick and shallow breathing. "Procopius can come another time. You're not going anywhere." She shot out of bed, heedless of her nakedness, and went to stand before her husband, who was trying to push himself up. "You're to stay in bed, Justinian."

"I am a bit dizzy. You're thinking—"

"Let's not think anything. Let's just put you back in bed. Now lie down. Do as I say." Theodora bent over and lifted his feet onto the down comforter as he pivoted his upper portion.

"Perhaps another hour of sleep," Justinian said, his words slurring as he settled into the softness.

"Yes," Theodora said, reaching over to his forehead again.

"Is it …"

"Hush," she whispered as she drew back, "hush." She stood, turned, pulled on a robe, and hurried into her study, where she scratched out a note. She was about to ring for Phaedra when the handmaiden appeared in the doorway.

Theodora went to her and thrust the note into her hand. "Take this down to my secretary at once."

Phaedra paled. "Mistress, just yesterday, you said we weren't to leave the apartment under any—"

"Yes, yes, I know, but this is different, and he's but one flight down. It's important, Phaedra. If you're afraid of the plague, knock hard upon the door, push the note under, and come back."

"But—"

"What, Phaedra? What?"

"It's Lord Procopius. He's out in the hallway."

"Oh. Well, as you leave, tell him the emperor has canceled his meeting. Say no more and be certain not to admit him into the women's quarters."

"Yes, mistress."

"Hurry, now!"

She stood immobile, heart racing, body trembling. For weeks, whether awake or asleep, the Angel of Death had been haunting her. Daytime imagination and nighttime dreams admitted into the palace the grisly, ghostly horror whose sword would cleave soul from the body.

And now it had come.

"May God have mercy," she said aloud.

Theodora stood to greet me as I entered her study. She was always clever at disguising her disappointments, anger, trepidation and the like, but on this morning, pain and fear were carved into the lines of her face. "Stephen!" she cried, her chin trembling. "Something terrible has happened, terrible."

"What? What is it, Thea?"

"Justinian," she said. "He's ill! Oh, Stephen, what if he … what if he has—"

"What are the symptoms?" I attempted a businesslike tone, hoping to lessen her anxiety.

"He was talking in his sleep and awoke with a fever. He didn't have even the energy to leave the bed. And you know he's not one to sleep late. Then he sank into a deep sleep. He won't awaken."

"You've sent for the physician?"

"No, Stephen, I sent for you."

"Me?"

"What is it you think I can—"

"You've had two patients in your rooms, as well as a visit from Alexander the Physician. I don't want to set off an alarm, you understand. I have no doubt you have some knowledge of the—the illness. You tell me what you know and that way I'll have some idea of what to do. Now, follow me."

I obeyed. I understood her wish to keep the emperor's condition quiet, especially if it was what she could not name, and yet I wondered how it would be possible to keep it quiet.

Justinian was stirring and twisting in discomfort when we entered Theodora's bedchamber. He had thrown off the covers. I'm not certain what I expected, but the light, knee-length tunic he wore was much like any other man might wear, one doubling as an undergarment and sleeping attire. His, however, was made of fine silk. He was unaware of my presence as I approached.

"I'll have to examine him," I said, biting at my lower lip and feeling oddly trapped by the awkwardness of my situation.

"Yes, yes, go on."

I took hold of the tunic's hem and turned to Theodora, wishing she would leave.

"Go on, Stephen!" she snapped. "It's nothing I haven't seen before."

My stomach churned with anxiety as I lifted the emperor's tunic. It took no second look to recognize a bubo swollen to half the size of my hand in the emperor's groin. Theodora's gasp indicated she could see it even from where she stood at the foot of the sleeping couch. Neither of us spoke.

Further investigation revealed buboes in the emperor's armpits and small ones behind the ears.

I straightened the tunic, stood, and turned to Theodora. Her expression precluded any need for me to put the diagnosis into words.

"Now Stephen, tell me what you know."

I looked down at Justinian, assuring myself he was unconscious before I spoke. "I'm told it strikes differently Thea, but it will often begin with a fever, even a mild one. For some, it attacks the lungs and others have small pustules spring up all over their bodies. The fate of such victims is—is death. It often comes swiftly."

"And for my husband? The buboes?"

"According to Alexander, if the buboes get to the stage where they suppurate—that is, break open and release their poison—the chances are good the patient will survive."

"But—not always?"

"No."

"What if the buboes never break open?"

I merely shook my head.

She understood. Her dark eyes pooled. She adjusted her gaze from me to her husband. Whole minutes must have passed.

Still facing away from me, she said, "This is to be kept quiet, Stephen. It must be."

I stood, rooted to the spot, dumbfounded. How could the emperor's illness be kept from the people? "Listen to me, Theodora. The emperor should have a doctor. People will find out."

"I will tend to him. Phaedra will help. I trust her implicitly. No one else must know."

"As you say, Thea." The disappearance of the emperor from court would cause concern and suspicion. It was a flawed strategy, but I knew not to argue. Not now, anyway.

"You do understand, Stephen?"

"Yes," I said, with less resolve than she no doubt wished. I wondered if she wasn't considering her own situation should her husband die. *Could she retain the throne without him? How?*

I found myself drawing back a couple of steps, wishing I could leave—but sensing something else was on her mind.

Her gaze still locked onto Justinian, Theodora asked, "And Setka?

"Setka?"

"His buboes?"

"They did not suppurate, Thea. ... I'm sorry." Those words—*I'm sorry*—were no sooner out of my mouth than I realized I had intoned them with a spontaneous intimacy that might have revealed too much, namely, that I knew about her true relationship with Setka.

The sound of glass breaking came from the adjoining study. I turned my head in that direction, glad for the diversion.

"Never mind that; it's only Phaedra. Listen, Stephen. I have things I must do now, but we'll talk soon. Come back tomorrow evening. I'll have had time to think. And—not a word, you understand?"

"No, of course not."

"Good! Leave me now with my husband."

I was only too glad to go. As I passed through the curtains into Theodora's study, my foot kicked a shard of glass. I looked down and saw the remains of a vase that had been knocked from a pedestal, its pieces cast about. I glanced up at once, expecting to see Phaedra, but instead I caught a fleeting vision of a cloaked person scurrying on silent feet down the length of the hall and disappearing. The person was wearing a heavy cloak, and the hood was raised so that identification was impossible.

47

"**B**UT NO ONE IS TO leave their suites," Piers told me the next day, his face a mask of worry. "You did so yesterday and now again?"

I affected a little laugh as I moved toward the door. "At the request of the empress, Piers," I said, pivoting back toward my hand-wringing servant, who stood in the hall just outside my study door. "Do you think I should decline?"

"Well … no, I guess not." He drew a deep breath. "Surely it's not to resume the board game you play?"

I shot what must have seemed a supercilious smile at him but said nothing.

"What is it, Stephen?" he pressed. "Is something amiss?"

It was a difficult thing to pretend annoyance with this man who, having survived the plague dared to risk it again in caring for another, but I inclined my head and glowered at him.

Piers flinched and went silent.

I turned and left the suite, a bit guiltily.

Upon my arrival, Phaedra announced me in Theodora's small reception room. I sat in a chair opposite Theodora, a table with the Shatranj board between us. She was in as unnerved a state as I'd ever seen her.

"How is the emperor?" I asked.

"No better." The intensity of Theodora's dark eyes held me transfixed.

"There's something I have to know, Stephen. And I'm not going to pace about a bowl of hot milk, like a wary cat."

I held my breath, knowing, fearing what she was about to say. "What—what is it?"

"You *know*, don't you?"

"Know?" I asked stupidly. I swallowed back saliva that suddenly collected in my mouth.

"Oh, you heard Setka's last words, Stephen, his last breaths." She leaned forward, shortening the distance between us, her eyes holding me. "You heard him call me *Mother!*"

"I—I did, Thea."

"Setka was my son." Tearfully, almost as if she had forgotten she once told me about giving birth to a boy across the Middle Sea, Theodora related to me how she had been forced to flee one relationship in the Pentapolis to find herself—poor and alone—in Alexandria and a victim of an Egyptian caravan master, Haji. Carrying Haji's child, she sought shelter in the tender care of Patriarch Timothy, who mentored her in the tenets of Monophysitism. Theodora planned to give the child up to a good family; however, when the time came to give birth, Timothy insisted she stay in Alexandria and marry the father. Unwilling to submit her life to a man who had exploited her, Theodora fled immediately after the birth and began a long trek that would take her back through the deserts and towns of the Levant to Constantinople.

"I named him *John*, Stephen. I came to terribly regret my abandonment of him. But he learned his history and Fortune managed to intervene at Carthage. It was there Tyche brought him and Antonina together. Or, perhaps, merely chance." Theodora forced a little ironic smile. "Setka was Nina's gift to me, but not in the way some gossips here think."

Theodora went on to say how much getting to know her son had meant to her—and how much hurt came with losing him to the plague. That she could not share the hurt with her husband magnified the pain. At the time of her marriage to Justinian, she had signed a document declaring she had but the one child, Hyacinth.

"After he came into my life, I was biding my time before telling Justinian." Tears began to stream down her face. "I wanted the two to bond first. Now—now I dare not tell him the truth, ever."

My heart broke for her. Theodora bent over and covered her face, sobbing, body trembling. I had never seen her like this. How I wanted to go to her, kneel by her, take up her hand and console her. But she was no longer the woman who once cleaned my sandals and washed my feet of human waste after I had tried to aid an ungrateful stylite. Theodora was an empress now. She had quickly grown into the diadem and flourished. I dared not touch her, dared not approach her. I sat there like a sorry fool, waiting for her storm of sorrow to abate so that I could present her with a new problem. She must be told that someone had most likely heard our conversation about the emperor's illness.

At that moment Phaedra bolted into the room, her pretty face disfigured by worry and panic.

"Mistress!" Phaedra cried, still running toward us. "Mistress!" The hand-maiden advanced too fast and came too close to the empress. She halted mid-stride, nearly stumbling over the game table. She gasped in humiliation at her blunder and silently stepped back from us, head hanging.

Her face still wet, Theodora stood at once, her hand flying to the dimpled area at the base of her throat.

I stood.

Phaedra had gone dumb, as if the message had evaporated.

"Phaedra!" Theodora cried. "What is it?"

I could almost see Theodora gulping back fear and dread as she took on once again the veneer of an empress.

"It's the … the—" Phaedra's gaze flicked to me, as if my presence gave her pause.

Theodora read her hesitation correctly. "Just tell me, Phaedra. Tell me!"

"Yes, mistress, yes." Phaedra took in a long breath and blurted out the message. "It's the physician, mistress. He is with the emperor and sent me to bring you without delay. He told me to make haste. I'm so sorry, mistress."

"Never mind that," Theodora blurted, her vocal pitch rising. "I'll come with you at once." She looked across at me now. "You should leave now, Stephen."

I thought of telling her that I would wait, but if the emperor had taken a turn for the worse, if death was at hand, my presence would be awkward. I returned to my suite.

It was the most fateful decision of my life.

In late morning, Theodora was sitting at her husband's bedside when Phaedra hurried in.

"You've come to relieve me for a bit, have you?"

"No—well, yes, mistress, but—"

"But what, Phaedra?"

"I must tell you something."

"What?" You might be faster than Hermes, but you are a dark-faced harbinger of bad news. Why, yesterday, I thought my husband was dying."

"I'm sorry for that, mistress, but Alexander the Physician was very abrupt with me. I thought that might be the situation. I'm so glad it wasn't—"

"Alexander should have been more specific with his message. Justinian came to his senses but for the briefest time. Today he merely sleeps. Now, Phaedra, what is it today?"

The handmaiden's eyes widened, forcing her brow to wrinkle. "It's … it's, well, word has gotten out—about the emperor."

"What?"

"It's true. Several people have approached me, asking if it's true. Is he sick, they ask. I said nothing, but some immediately declared that it must be the plague."

"But how?" Theodora felt as if an abyss opened up beneath her, and she was falling through space. A sense of powerlessness overcame her.

One minute passed. Two.

"Mistress …" Phaedra gasped. "What's to be done?"

Theodora blinked, forcing herself to react. The girl was right to ask. Something had to be done, plans made, protections taken. "Send for Alexander the Physician, Phaedra." After the girl left, Theodora stood and hurried to her desk in the study where she prepared a note that would go to her lead palace spy, Rufus.

48

I WAS OUT ON MY BALCONY watching the sunrise when Theodora's secret police burst into my suite and hustled me down to the dungeons beneath the Daphne Wing.

Five years would pass.

49

"HE WON'T AWAKEN THIS MORNING," Theodora said. "He just sleeps."

"The emperor is in a *koma*, mistress," Alexander the Physician replied, "a very deep sleep."

"What are we to do?" Theodora implored. "You must know of something that can be done!"

"There is nothing for now, mistress. We must wait."

"Is this how it strikes—the plague?"

"Sometimes, mistress. I'll prepare an amulet and return later with it. In the meantime, allow me to say some prayers."

As Alexander chanted his prayers in a soft voice, Theodora knelt at the foot of the sleeping couch and tried to follow along with her own prayers, but her mind took her elsewhere.

What if he is to die? What, then? It would be my duty to command, she thought. But it was the next thought that touched something at her core and strengthened her resolve. *It is my duty to command now. Now!*

She and Justinian had been a pair since taking the white marble double throne, each with different skills, interests, and opinions, but always a couple. Until Justinian's illness, no matter their disagreements on political or religious matters, they had been as one. And now came the unexpected and unwelcome thought that she could be left alone. It was inconceivable.

Theodora was crying freely when she heard Alexander finish his prayers. She sensed his eyes upon her as she used the bed to push herself up onto unsteady legs. The physician blinked in surprise at her appearance. Almost immediately, she felt a thickness at the back of her throat and a kind of nausea at her center. Her hands moved up to tardily push away the wetness. Even before taking the throne, she had always been so careful to show only strength. Putting aside regret over her tears, Theodora brought her back into perfect alignment, recalling her mother's coaching: *Walk proud as a peacock.* Assuming a façade of practicality, she asked, "When will he awaken, Alexander?"

"In my experience, mistress, it's impossible to say."

"But the Monday Silence is tomorrow. There is much to be discussed, much to be done. What am I to tell his councilors?"

"The Silence will go on without you, mistress."

"No, it mustn't. I should be there."

"Your place is here, at his side. If he awakens, you should be here. It is your duty."

"Affairs of state are to be decided. No, Alexander, my duty is to attend, most especially because the emperor is unable to be present and make decisions."

"Let his councilors do their jobs, mistress."

Unwilling to argue with the physician about the nature of her duty, Theodora changed the thread of conversation. "So there is hope," she pressed, "hope that he will awaken from this—this *koma*?"

"Yes," Alexander said.

Theodora, so used to defining people by way of their eyes, could see no hope in his glassy dark brown eyes.

"What are the likely discussions to be put forth at the Silence?" Theodora asked Narses, who had responded at once to her summons. They stood in the large reception room. She hoped she could trust him, just as Justinian had for many years. Narses had disliked her at the first, but over the years a fondness blossomed between them; at least, she felt that it had. In this crisis she prayed he would prove as impartial and trustworthy as he was knowledgeable in every facet of the government.

"Public health will be at the top of the list, in light of the plague, mistress, as well as a few legislative considerations, and a host of military decisions. As to the latter, we have active war fronts. In Italy, since General Belisarius was withdrawn we've lost a good part of what had been won there. In his new deployment in Persia, the general and his *bucellarii* have made inroads due in part to some masterful strategy, but also because King Khosrow is said to be afraid of what he calls 'Justinian's Plague'."

This was the first she heard of the disparaging epithet. Theodora swallowed hard. Her anger flared. "Justinian's plague?" She could scarcely get the words out.

Narses' eyes softened. "Yes, mistress." He paled slightly. "I'm sorry. I should not have told you."

"No, no, you did the right thing. You *must* tell me anything of importance. Are there other matters?"

"Yes, mistress. Besides the difficulties in Persia and Italy, the empire is under attack in the Balkans, and revolts continue in North Africa."

Theodora's breath came with difficulty. "May Athena guide us! Is your litany finished?"

"Those are the key points, mistress."

"You make my head spin with these crises, Narses." Theodora paused. "Now, I must come to *my* point. Let's sit down."

The two settled in an alcove where two chairs were placed cornerwise.

Theodora smiled tentatively. "You know, as I'm certain everyone does by now, that the emperor is ill."

Narses nodded.

"Well—I plan to attend the Silence as I often do—but in the role Justinian is unable to fill. I will not be a spectator. I will make decisions."

"I see, mistress."

"Ah, you don't seem surprised."

Narses' ironical smile spoke for him.

Theodora took a moment to collect her thoughts. Even though the lord chancellor was slight of build, he was long waisted so that, when seated, Theodora had to look up at him. "I am hoping to receive good advice and help from you, Narses."

"You shall have it."

"Good! Before the Silence I will consult with the physicians and find my way through the public health labyrinth. Now, while I have kept to my interests in religious matters and equality for women, my husband has handled all of these military matters. In them I am at a loss."

"You and the emperor have held the reins of power close to the throne. Now, you should know, mistress, with the emperor seriously ill, the councilors will make a play for power."

"Ah, I am not surprised. Well, I will not surrender power. Neither will I make any decision Justinian would frown upon."

"I have an idea, mistress. When an issue out of your sphere arises, I will stand and sum up the two or three arguments before you. You'll know from my eyes and perhaps a hint of a smile as to which one Justinian would likely favor."

"Excellent!"

After plans for the Silence were further fleshed out, Narses stood to leave. "Mistress, if I may ask—what has become of Stephen?"

"He has disappointed me. That is all you need to know."

"I'm told he is kept—below." Narses' gaze dropped to the floor.

"I forbid you to see him or contact him in any way. Do you understand?"

"Yes, mistress."

Theodora watched his dark brown Armenian eyes as he answered, as she had done all through the interview. She believed a person's eyes were the conduit to the heart, and she determined now that she could trust him.

Alone at the head of the deliberation table in the Hall of the Consistory, Theodora felt the weight of Justinian's absence. She sipped from a goblet of water to remedy her parched lips and throat, all the while forcing herself to maintain eye contact with the councilors, most of whom averted their gaze. Their prattle had ceased the moment she entered the hall. Clearly, they did not expect her to attend. Now, as she watched the dozen men— senators and officials—squirm in their seats, resistant to the power of a woman, she prayed Narses' plan would work. Bringing him into her confidence could prove risky, but she had to take the gamble that he would remain true to the throne. In another time, she would have asked Stephen about Narses' character, but that time had passed.

Her thirst quenched, Theodora set down the goblet and sat back against the hard backing of the carved chair. She would make it work. The recollection of another time in that chamber washed over her, a time when she encouraged the men at the table to collect their courage and stand strong against a city-wide rebellion, the Nika Riots. She had meant to hold onto the purple then, and she meant to do so now.

Narses had told her that Tribonian, who had been restored to his position of Quaestor of the Great Palace after the riots, would be in charge of the agenda for the Silence. Tribonian was so loved and respected by Justinian for his work as commissioner on the compilations that made up the *Codex Justinianus* that she allowed him his role at the Silence.

When Tribonian announced the public health crisis as the first subject on the agenda, Theodora stood and politely but firmly announced that she wished to question Theodoros, the referendarius who had instructed bodies to be thrown—one haphazardly upon the next—into the fortification towers that ran all along the double Theodosian Walls. As the plain-faced and white-bearded official stood, an exchange of expressions traveled across the table while whispers and muffled comments were traded, one to the next, on both sides.

Just as her appearance had been a surprise, so too was her boldness in asserting herself. She worked to hold back a smile at the reaction. And so began her power play.

"Lord Theodoros, please describe for us the manner in which bodies were placed at the Theodosian Walls. Now, I can't say buried, can I? They were not buried, in truth, were they?"

"No mistress."

"Then tell us how they were disposed of?"

Theodoros was easily into his fifth decade, and Theodora guessed from the unlikely combination of fear and wonder that washed across his face that he, like most at the table, had never been called into question by a woman. She was well aware that she was simultaneously placing the others on notice. Theodoros explained now that every bit of available land within The City's walls had been utilized for burials, and the towers spaced along the Theodosian Walls were seen as receptacles for the continuing number of victims.

"I'm told that bodies were carried up to the battlements and thrown down into the towers. Is this true?"

The man's face bled to the color of milk. "It is, mistress."

"I see. Now answer this very carefully, Theodoros. *Why* would you do this?"

"Why, mistress?" he asked dumbly.

"That was my question. Theodoros, you have a good nose. I see that you do, a bit larger than most perhaps, but no doubt as efficient as any in this room. So I ask you, has your nose not taken in the stink that has inundated The City? For days, the foul stench of death and decay has been flowing down toward the Sea of Marmara, pervading the palace walls, even into this very chamber. Can you not smell it?"

The man stood at his place, his upper body leaning forward as if it would collapse on itself. "It … it seemed a good idea, mistress. And the emperor did—"

"I don't want to hear about the emperor," Theodora interrupted with a quiet but cutthroat tone. "I want to hear that it is to be *undone*—at once."

"Yes, mistress," the referendarius said, nodding and taking his seat.

"Perhaps you misunderstood, Theodoros. Stand up."

The referendarius obeyed.

"I said *at once*."

The bureaucrat understood. With no little embarrassment, he bowed and backed out of the chamber, an action made all the more awkward because his chair was far removed from the exit.

Narses' plan to send her signals regarding needed decisions worked perfectly. Her handling of Theodoros set the tone so that for the resolution of each issue on the rest of the agenda the councilors looked to the empress for the final decision. The throne lost none of its luster despite the absence of the emperor.

At the end of the Silence, Theodora accepted well wishes for Justinian and stood, thanking the councilors and assuring them with all the fervor she could muster that his recovery would be soon and it would be complete. She prayed that her eyes did not give her away.

In leaving, she smiled to herself, knowing that the attendees would not be able to hold to the rule for which the meeting of the consistory was named a Silence. The palace would soon be astir, even with its inhabitants confined to quarters. To her mind, the drama of the Silence finished as a thorough success. If it were not for Justinian's tenuous condition and unknowable prognosis, she would have left the Hall of the Consistory in a state of bliss.

50

D AYS WENT BY ... ONE WEEK and another. Justinian remained in a *koma*. The physician stayed close by, at regular intervals employing a reed-like device in Justinian's throat to force down water and liquid nourishment.

Within the Great Palace confines, Theodora prayed with the Monophysites she safeguarded in the Palace of Hormisdas, as well as with Anthimus, whom she had hidden in a nicely appointed chamber beneath the Daphne Wing.

Against the counsel of Narses, Theodora left the palace each day, crossing the Augustaion to the Church of the Holy Wisdom, where the colored window glass of reds, greens, blues, and purples coalesced for an ethereal rainbow that brought the presence of God to mind and infused her with hope. Then she took to visiting churches, monasteries, and hospitals. Declining use of a carriage or sedan chair, she walked instead, wearing the jewel-encrusted diadem, gold-trimmed purple cloak, and red shoes. Some ten or twelve excubitors accompanied her as protection from citizens, angry or adoring. As her habit of leaving the palace each day became known, more and more citizens—despite their own losses and fear of the plague—stood on the sides of the Mese, as if she were on parade. Some followed her.

In this way, Theodora experienced the true nature of The City. Most of the shops were shuttered; the bakeries also, so that increasing numbers of beggars sat or lay along the colonnaded thoroughfare and in the forums. With regularity, carts laden with stacked bodies of the fallen rattled lazily toward the far reaches of The City, beyond the Theodosian Walls, where she had ordered new burials to take place. The stench of death still permeated the streets. More than once she had to be directed around the prone form of a plague victim who had died in mid-step.

"The people are hailing your bravery, mistress," Narses told her one day upon her return.

"Ah, but you think it's stupidity, yes? The risk? Don't answer. I often think so myself. But I need their prayers. I need *them*."

Wherever she stopped, she addressed the people, assuring them that she was praying for them and begging that they pray for the emperor. Response was tepid at first, but soon the whispered naysayings and mutterings fell away and the chant that had always welcomed a royal took precedence: "Glory of the purple, joy of the world!"

Narses attended her on her little pilgrimage on one occasion, his ever vigilant eyes missing nothing. "You say you need them, the people, mistress," he told her afterwards. "I say the people need you. I watched them, listened to their words and tone. You've brought life back to The City. Just as the cathedral's interior inspires you, you inspire the people."

It was a thought that stayed with her, one that helped her navigate the days going forward.

One day, Theodora stopped to pray at the chapel in the Saint Panteleimon Hospital, a huge edifice now covering the grounds where her little rental house from those early years once sat, the house where the daughter of a bear tamer met the nephew of the emperor. The memory of meeting Prince Justinian came back to her, as did the sharp fear that their years were coming to a close, the chilling fear of losing him.

As she was leaving the hospital, a woman called out, "Mistress, God bless you! May Emperor Justinian rest in peace!"

Theodora stopped at once, pivoting toward a small group of citizens. The words were daggers that stabbed at her heart. "Wha—what?" she stammered. Then louder, "What did you say?"

"The emperor is dead," came another voice, a man's.

"He is not dead," Theodora managed to say, reining in a shriek. "He is *not dead*, do you hear?" She did not wait for a further response, turning instead and hurrying along toward the Mese and then turning in the direction of the Augustaion, her excubitors in tow. By the time she entered the Chalké—heart racing—terror suffused her, terror that her people were right, terror that Justinian had died while she had been away. And guilt, heart-rending guilt.

By the time Theodora climbed the stairs to the Imperial Apartment, she was gulping for breath. She entered the anteroom to Justinian's bedchamber where she found Narses, as if standing guard.

"Is he—is he—?"

"No, he's not," Narses told her, reading her expression at once. "Alexander was at his bedside just a little while ago. He gave him some nourishment through that device of his. The emperor's condition is unchanged."

"Thank the Christ!" Theodora cried.

"Phaedra is with him now. Take a seat, mistress." Narses poured out a cup of red wine. "Drink this," he said.

Theodora sat on the edge of a chair. Somehow, she found consolation in his directions. She sipped at the wine. Her heart slowed.

"However," Narses said, a catch in his voice, "it is a serious rumor, and it's spreading like a fire in the filthy back alleys." He sat across from her.

"People are so gullible," Theodora said. "What about here—behind the palace walls?"

Narses swallowed hard and nodded.

"And talk of succession?"

Narses gave a little shrug.

Theodora drew in a long breath. "If succession is up for discussion here," she posited, "the senators and officials are venturing to suggest names of a successor, I would wager. They would have me set aside. Am I correct? Don't sugar over it, Narses."

"You are."

His words struck like poisoned darts. She took a moment, then asked, "What names have come up?"

Narses, ever the model of self-control, flinched. After some seconds, he said, "Germanus."

"Not while I have breath! I loathe the man. Why Germanus?"

"I speak for others who say his bloodline as cousin to the emperor is reason enough, mistress. Others cite the reputation he's made with the military."

"But not to such an extent as has Belisarius! I'll wager the talk about him is the more serious."

"It is, mistress."

"He is the real threat, isn't he?"

"Well, mistress, since the Italian campaign, there is no love lost between the general and me, but I will say he did turn down the diadem of the West offered to him by the Ostrogoths. He stayed true to your throne."

"Yes, there is that. And yet, the diadem of the *entire* Roman world might sparkle with more allure—yes?"

Narses answered with the tightest of smiles.

"Just listen to us, Narses," Theodora scoffed. "Why, it's almost as if the rumor were true. The emperor is *not* dead! We must counter the talk."

"How, mistress? The emperor sleeps as if he *is* dead. We have nothing to convince those within the palace or without that he is still among the living."

"You need to assure the senators and other officials. I shall continue my daily walks. I shall speak the truth to the people. We will put down this gossip."

Narses shrugged. "I have no better suggestion, mistress."

"Oh, and Narses, should my husband die, I have no intention of giving up my throne."

"For that, mistress, I am glad."

51

TWO WEEKS LATER, A LETTER from Tariq arrived. Without Stephen to transcribe it into script large enough for her eyes, Theodora called upon Narses to read it to her.

"You will always surprise me, mistress," Narses said when he learned of the task she had in mind.

"Have I turned out differently from that fallen woman on the ship from Antioch all those years ago, the one you told Stephen to disavow at once? I'm certain you had colorful words for me."

"You embarrass me, mistress. I was referring to my surprise at your placement of Tariq as spy into the nest of vipers surrounding Lady Antonina. Has it been thus since the Italy campaign?"

"I'll not tell," Theodora joked. "Now, read the letter."

The letter offered nothing to the good. Word about Justinian's illness and unfounded prognosis of "imminent death" had arrived at the Persian front, prompting Belisarius's staff to spit out long pent-up grievances against both royals who sat upon the throne.

Bouzes, one of Belisarius's generals, Tariq wrote, railed against the regime, saying how Belisarius is unlike Justinian in that he is respected by his men and, most especially, loved by the people. While Belisarius didn't respond at once, the conversation among the officers moved to whether the army's allegiance extended to both the emperor and empress.

Tariq quoted Belisarius as saying, "I swore allegiance in the old way—to Justinian alone. The empress is an administrator of some talent, but, as much as I admire her, the law does not allow for a woman to rule alone. Can you imagine the Goths, Armenians, or any other people under our aegis accepting the rule of a woman? One rebellion would follow another."

"And so," Bouzes replied, "it will be to the dustbin with Theodora."

Late into the night, Theodora was sitting at her husband's bedside when Phaedra entered the bedchamber.

"I'll sit with him through the night, mistress."

"No, you go rest now, Come back when it gets light."

Phaedra obeyed. She knew not to protest.

Theodora held Justinian's hand, keenly aware of his weak pulse. "You must come back to me, Justinian," she whispered. "You must." She spoke her thoughts to him each night, praying her words would somehow pierce his consciousness and awaken him. "The empire needs you, dearest. Without you, it will all fall apart."

Justinian lay on his back, his mouth slightly open, breaths scarcely noticeable. The only times he showed movement occurred when he struggled against the nourishment and healing medicines the physician administered or when she and Phaedra made certain he was kept clean and in a fresh tunic. No one else was allowed to enter the bedchamber. Excubitors stood outside the door to the suite. Several times a night, Theodora—heart pounding in fear—felt compelled to lean over her husband in order to ascertain from breath or heartbeat whether he was still alive.

The letter from Tariq still rankled. She had not waited even a day before sending the imperial summons to Belisarius, Bouzes, and several other witnesses to the talk of treason. This was the third time the general had to be summoned back from his campaigns. This time there would be a trial. She would see to it. It would likely muddy her relationship with Antonina, but so be it.

Theodora was sitting at her husband's sleeping couch two nights later when the oil in the clay lamp ran dry, bathing the bedchamber in inky shadows.

Watching her husband labor for breath, Theodora felt for his pulse and allowed her hand to rest there. She waited, her stomach in flux, her mind racing with dark scenarios. She prayed for Justinian to recover, shutting out any other possibility. Her prayers and the people's prayers would recall him to life. They would. *They must!*

She waited for the arrival of Generals Belisarius, Bouzes, as well as Antonina. The summons had made it quite clear that Justinian was indeed alive. They were taking their good time, however. What if they were already plotting a coup? Should he awaken, what would Justinian say about the summons with his forged signature? He had always been lenient, had always turned a blind eye to Belisarius's hubris. What if Justinian does not come back to life before they arrive? Or worse, what if … no, she would not think the worst. She couldn't. Her hand still clasped Justinian's wrist, as if she could hurry the pulse.

Yet she had to think about it. Should she be left to rule alone, her power would be in immediate peril. Without Justinian, if the generals or senators did not make a play for power, the Chalcedonians might very well feel emboldened to revert to religious persecution against the Monophysites she kept sheltered—and against her. She would fall with them, along with the deposed Patriarch Anthimus. John the Cappadocian would have been the first to take the reins of government had not Antonina served her well in orchestrating his downfall. While Theodora could thank her friend for that, it was Antonina's husband, Belisarius, who loomed as the most likely—and most deadly—threat to her holding the throne. The people loved him. Everyone loves a military hero. No matter how she considered it, she would have to act at the very hour he and Bouzes reenter the capital. No delays. No mercy.

The words of General Bouzes haunted her: "And so to the dustbin with Theodora." Her hand tightened on Justinian's wrist. "Come back," she whispered. "Come back."

Belisarius had been in the Hall of the Consistory a decade before when she declared that *purple makes the best shroud.* "Dustbin?" she said aloud. The memory of the Nika Riots came back to her now in full. She had said: *I wear the purple as the Empress of the Roman Empire. I am telling you now that I will not willingly part with it.*

Theodora continued her daily walks. Hope was as hard a commodity to find as bread in a Constantinople without bakers. Doubts and distrust followed her as she made her way along the Mese. The crowds that waited for her became sparser, day by day, a stark reminder of the sheer number of dead. Narses reckoned half of the city was gone, some to more rural areas, many more to mass graves. He dared to lecture her once, in his gentle, fatherly way, about her risk-taking. She replied by saying, "If Tyche has brought me this far only for me to meet my end in such a way, then the laugh will be on me."

This day, with just five excubitors, she traveled a good distance along the northwest branch of the Mese to pray in the Church of the Holy Apostles. After its destruction during the Nika Riots, she had taken an active interest in its rebuilding, which was ongoing. She spoke to those few worshippers who were well enough to listen, beseeching their prayers and promising her own for them.

Upon leaving, she turned to see two excubitors hurrying up the thoroughfare, their hobnailed boots click-clacking on the paved slabs, faces intent.

Presenting themselves before her, they began to follow protocol, but a wave of her hand released them from prostrating themselves.

"What is it?" she asked, stiffening with cold fear.

"The Lord Chamberlain Narses sent us, mistress," one said. "He wishes you return to the palace."

Theodora's mouth went dry. She straightened, collecting herself. "He said nothing further?"

"No, mistress."

"Has General Belisarius arrived in The City? Is that it?"

The faces of the two excubitors went blank. The silent one shrugged.

Theodora absently moved her hand to the cleft at the base of her throat. If that was not the reason for the message, there was but one other.

Theodora swallowed back a gasp, pivoted, and started downhill, walking quickly, her excubitors—seven now—trailing.

For once, she wished she had taken a carriage.

The distance seemed to spread out before her, the palace and the Sea of Marmara a great distance away. Her jeweled red slippers were not meant for quick travel. She stopped, bent low, removed them, and stood. Reaching up, she removed her diadem. Holding the slippers and diadem in her left hand, she grasped the folds of her stola and tunic with her right hand and hastened on.

When she was a child, she had often gone barefoot as she followed her older sister Comito about The City. Her feet became callused and inured to the hard polygonal stone slabs of the Mese and the crushed gravel of the lanes and alleys. But that was a lifetime ago. Years of good shoes and long baths had made the soles of her feet soft as baby skin. She began to run now, mindless to the shocks that came with each hard footfall, every cutting stone.

The eyes of the guards at the Chalké widened to see the perspiring empress hurry through, barefoot, hair undone.

She dashed into the Daphne Wing, and climbed the staircase, feet slapping against the cold marble.

Narses was waiting for her. The beads of perspiration that populated her forehead dripped onto her eyelids, blurring her vision so that his face was a blur. She could not read his expression. She was out of breath and could not get words out, could not ask the worst. Behind Narses, through the doorway, she saw Phaedra and Alexander the Physician standing at the foot of Justinian's sleeping couch.

"Mistress," Narses started to say, "the emperor—"

But Theodora brushed past him, trembling at the sight she conjured in her mind, and rushed into the bedchamber, diadem and red slippers still in her grasp.

She stopped suddenly, pivoting to the left, blinking away the moisture in her eyes.

Disbelief.

Justinian, garbed in a purple tunic, was sitting against the cushions at the head of the bed. He looked up, forehead furrowing enough to push back his diadem a fraction. Clearly startled by *her* appearance, he nonetheless smiled.

PART FOUR

52

A SINGLE WHITE HORSE DREW THE cart bearing the carved ivory coffin containing Theodora's body, a purple shroud enveloping her, as was her longtime wish. Some fifty white-robed eunuchs led the funeral procession, their angelic voices chanting the "Christos Anesti."

Christ is risen from the dead,
Death trampling down death
And upon those in the tombs
Bestowing life!

Citizens lined the Mese in such a crush one would think The City's former population had shaken off the plague and come back from the dead to see their Augusta laid to rest. Some three hundred thousand had died within Constantinople and millions more to the east and west. I wondered if—strangely enough—Theodora had perhaps saved me from succumbing to the plague by locking me away. Was Tyche enjoying the ironic twist? I blinked away the odd thought and studied the crowd. In all of them, I saw myself. Some faces were prayerful and tear-stained, others passive, and still others stony with contempt, perhaps for some transgression attributed to the empress. And yet, all had turned out to bear witness to the final goodbye to one of their own, a woman who had risen from their midst to become what she had felt destiny called her to be: a great lady. Oh, Tyche had called her to be so much more.

Wrapped in his purple dalmatic with its gold trim but bent with grief, white-faced Justinian appeared older than his sixty-six years. His diadem slightly askew, the emperor followed the gold-painted cart on foot, attended by his family that included his sister Vigilantia and her son Justin; Theodora's sisters Anastasia with husband Peter Barsymes; the widowed Comito with her daughter Sophia; finally, Theodora's daughter Hyacinth with her husband Anastasius and their three sons.

Narses, who had organized every detail of the funeral, had me walk side-by-side with him. Behind us came a phalanx of monks and priests, followed by senators, nobles, generals, and palace officials.

We passed the Hippodrome, where Theodora's determination had steadied the nerves of men and saved an empire. Slowly, slowly, we went, passing through the forum of The City's founder, Constantine, then through the Forum of Theodosius, after which we veered onto the northwest branch of the Mese, climbing to the brow of the fourth hill, and at last arriving at the Church of the Holy Apostles.

As the coffin was being carried up the many stone steps by excubitors, a great wailing went up from the crush of mourners standing many deep all around, those souls who would not be allowed to enter the already-packed church. The earsplitting intensity of the keening raised the hairs on my arms as I took the steps, my eyes on the coffin's intricate ivory carving. The cry went up and resounded: "Glory of the purple, joy of the world!"

And I cried.

Theodora had held a special place in her heart for this church, the original of which had been destroyed during the 532 riots. While Justinian had overseen every detail of the rebuilding of the Church of the Holy Wisdom, she had worked with his architects, Anthemius and Isidore, in the imaginative recreation of this church, fashioning it nearly equal in beauty and second in size only to that of Justinian's project. It had yet to be finished, so she was to be laid to temporary rest beneath the altar. She had told me that upon the church's completion and consecration, a two-domed mausoleum large enough to accommodate sarcophagi of her and of Justinian, as well as vaults for their family, was to be built next to the church, abutting the northern arm.

Despite the pomp and glory of the funeral procession, Theodora would not have been pleased, for the service was strictly Orthodox, presided over by Patriarch Menas, who, along with a dozen attendants, led the procession down the center aisle. The deposed Monophysitic Patriarch Anthimus remained in hiding beneath the Daphne Wing. On her deathbed, Justinian had promised to continue working to bring the Monophysites and Diaphysites together, but her funeral gave no evidence of the effort.

I practice no religion, but I respectfully watched the communion service take place, my mind wandering. My eyes turned to the northern transept of the church, and I tried to visualize the imposing mausoleum that was to be built just outside of it. Theodora had so wanted to give Justinian a child, a son to continue their newly royal bloodline. Failing that, she looked to the future, engineering not one, but two relationships. She arranged for Belisarius and Antonina's daughter Joannina to fall in love with her grandson Anastasius, younger by two years. Playing them like two pieces on her *Shatranj* board, she saw that they were married while Joannina's parents were still on campaign in Italy. The other bond linked Justinian's sister's son, Justin, with Sophia, the daughter of sister Comito. If the diadems were to go to Anastasius and Joannina, Theodora's blood would continue in the royal line—but not Justinian's blood. However, a marriage between Justin and Sophia would unite both her bloodline and that of Justinian.

Standing there, taking in the mix of sharp incense and sweet aroma of beeswax candles, I recalled standing with Tariq as witnesses to Theodora's wedding to Justinian, the Easter Sunday coronation of the two, and the drama at the Hippodrome when they stood in the royal loge, taking in the adulation of a city. How I missed Tariq, who was currently attached to Procopius in Italy, where Belisarius—still favored by Justinian—once again fought the Ostrogoths. Guilt was a heavy burden for me because I felt responsible for his being chosen as Procopius's secretary in order to play spy for the empress. Neither of us had any idea the task would take him away for years at a time. We had begun an exchange of letters after my release the year before, and he relayed no regrets about his fate, but that did not lessen mine. For my biography of Theodora, he supplied information relating to what went on during the five years of my incarceration, gaps left by the death of the empress. However, the events he enumerated concerned the wars at the Persian and Roman fronts, as well as the continuing antagonism between the Chalcedonians and the Monophysites, all conflicts active when I was arrested—and when I was freed. It was as if five days had passed, not five years.

Suddenly, I came into the present as the chanting of the eunuch choir echoed in the unfinished church:

Christ is risen from the dead,
Death trampling down death
And upon those in the tombs
Bestowing life!

Patriarch Menas was coming toward us. The recessional had begun.

Neither Narses nor I spoke on the return to the Great Palace. I think he was brooding. In that, we were confederates.

53

July 548

WITH THE INTENTION OF PLEADING for substantial reinforcements for Belisarius's efforts against the Ostrogoths in Italy, Antonina arrived in Constantinople to find her childhood friend dead and buried. She seemed shocked and sorrowful, but not so heartbroken that she didn't become incensed upon learning that before her death, Theodora had already engineered the meeting, engagement, and marriage of Antonina's daughter Joannina to Theodora's grandson Anastasius, all without the consent of parents Antonina and Belisarius. Narses said Antonina arrived upset that Theodora and Justinian had offered her and Belisarius little support in the Italian campaign, but Theodora's machinations with Joannina enraged her to such an extent that she had been heard vowing she would see the marriage dissolved, this, despite the reality that Joannina and Anastasius had fallen in love. Should Antonina prove successful in breaking up the marriage, she would reduce by half the possibility Theodora's lineage would continue as part of the royal bloodline. Here's the hazard for Antonina, however, and possibly a good laugh for Tyche: Justinian's new divorce laws, inspired by Theodora, could thwart Antonina's intention because they did not include as cause for divorce an irate mother-in-law.

July 549

I had not been privy to Antonina's parleys with Justinian in 548, but she evidently had begged him to recall her husband to Constantinople. Her request was granted a year later, and so on a hot summer's day, Belisarius arrived, Procopius and Tariq in tow. Perhaps at Antonina's urging, Justinian named Belisarius Commander of the Imperial Guard, an advancement Theodora would have strongly vetoed, for she was fearful of any general amassing too much power.

My stomach roiled with anxiety as I sat in my study, waiting for the arrival of Tariq, whom I had not seen in some seven years. While he was in Rome, I had been hounding him with requests he turn his spying skills to searching out the book Procopius was writing about Theodora and Justinian. A day did not go by without my thinking about my pledge to Thea that I would ensure it never comes to light. In the last letter he wrote before leaving the Italian front for Constantinople, he confirmed that with the death of Theodora, Procopius had indeed finished his history on the corruption of Justinian's reign and, more especially, Theodora. "Yes," Tariq wrote, "I've seen it, and it is more scurrilous than you could ever imagine."

The message took my breath away. The question now remained: how was I to confiscate the codex and see it destroyed?

My servant Basil appeared now to announce Tariq's arrival. I stood, came out from behind my desk, and was halfway across the room when he entered. We embraced at once and then I held him at arm's length. "My God, it's good to see you!"

Tariq pulled a comical face, mouth gaping and eyes widening. "'My God'? Have I been away so long you've found religion, my friend?"

"Ha! Not that long! Why, look at you! You're brown as a berry, Tariq, but you appear no older." He had gained around the middle, as eunuchs who were cut before puberty were prone to do, but I made no mention of it.

"It's the Italian sunshine. Oh, Stephen, she kept you well-hidden for those years. I began to think you dead. Oh—how I missed you. But *you* don't look any worse for the years, either."

"Ha! You should have seen me when I emerged from—from below. Thin as a broomstick and wan as a mushroom!"

We embraced again, both laughing.

"Come, let's sit," I said.

We sat across from one another, chatting about his voyage home, the war effort in Italy, Belisarius's recall, all the while my cheer at the reunion diminishing as my chest tightened more and more with unease.

At last, I could contain myself no longer. "Tariq—the book, my friend—what about the book?

"It's finished. *The Secret History* is finished."

"That's what he has called it?" I drew in breath. "Were you able to—"

"Steal it? No."

"Damn. Then he has it in his possession. Perhaps—"

Tariq put his hand up to silence me. "Stephen, did the empress tell you why she took five years of your life?"

Tariq had a way of touching the heart of the matter with a needle. But why raise this hurt when I was more interested in the codex Procopius had written? "Well, she intimated she had lost trust in me."

"Did she say why?"

"She was not one to admit fault," I said, prevaricating. "Why are you asking this now? What I want to know is—"

"Because, my friend, when I wasn't reading Procopius's *Secret History*, I was foraging through his personal journal. The man writes night and day, and he has the vanity to think that how many times he pisses in a day will someday be interesting to someone." Tariq let out a good laugh.

My mind was in ferment. I did not join in his laughter. "And?"

"And *he* was the cause of her losing trust in you."

"What?"

"It seems he had overheard you and Theodora discussing in specific details the fact that Justinian had contracted the plague, and inside of a day the news got around the entire palace. Rufus and his league of spies traced it to Procopius. She confronted him and he put it off on you. Suddenly, you—"

"Disappeared. Tariq, there *was* a robed person who was in the adjoining room when Theodora and I had that conversation. I'm certain now that it was Procopius. The possibility had crossed my mind at the time, but I couldn't imagine what business he would have in the women's rooms of the Imperial Apartment. But … but wait, Theodora would not believe him without even questioning me. She wouldn't!"

Tariq's eyes softened as he held my gaze. "Well, Procopius was quite convincing."

"How do you know that?"

"I told you he wrote down everything. He recreated the scene with Theodora as if he were Sophocles or one of the old playwrights." Tariq laughed again. "Everything played out in his account but the required choruses."

I waited.

"Well, he went before the throne well-prepared. He told the Augusta that he heard the details of Justinian's symptoms not from you, but from Piers."

"Piers?"

Tariq nodded. "He convinced her that he remained close to his old servant and that Piers was still faithful to him."

"And that I had told Piers about the emperor's illness? A lie!"

"Of course. However, it worked. Oh, he's quite proud of how he survived her wrath and sent you into Limbo with one stroke. You know, what puzzles me is why she silenced you if the secret was already out?" Tariq's Egyptian eyes narrowed in suspicion. "What would make her do that? Stephen, do you have any idea?"

Of course, I did. Shortly before she died, she told me herself. I stood now and walked to the window, keeping my back to Tariq. Other than a physician, Alexander of Tralles, I was most likely the only other person who knew that the royal couple's inability to produce an heir had been the likely after-effect of orchitis, a disease that Justinian fell victim to, one that was known to cause sterility. She meant it to be kept secret because she would rather have people believe she was barren than think the emperor was sterile.

The other secret was probably even more important to Theodora. I was quite certain that only I knew that Setka was her son.

For me, the missing piece of the puzzle had been the catalyst that sent me to the dungeon. It came to me now: Theodora no doubt weighed the thought that if I had revealed the secret that Justinian was bedridden with the plague in such a careless way as Procopius claimed, why would I keep the other two to myself? At last, I had a complete answer to the question I asked myself every day of my term in that dark, dank, rat-infested dungeon.

In fact, if she did believe Procopius, she had every reason to have me killed. And yet, she hadn't …

"Well, do you?" Tariq asked, jarring me from my thoughts.

"Do I … what?"

""Do you have any idea why she locked you away?"

I merely smiled.

He tilted his head slightly to the side in an attempt to read me. Then he shrugged. Sometimes a good friend just knows when not to push further.

"What about Piers?" I asked, changing the subject. "I was told he died soon after I disappeared."

"Not true, according to Procopius's journal."

"She ... she didn't—"

"Have him killed? No, but she thought him possibly dangerous for some reason I can't fathom and had him packed off to a monastery in Alexandria for his final days. According to Procopius's notes, he lived another two years."

I sat in silence for a minute or two, numbed by Tariq's report. Theodora must have considered the possibility that Piers had become my confidant and knew something of Setka's true identity—or Justinian's sterility. He did not.

Tariq broke into my thoughts. "Stephen, will you avenge yourself on Procopius? Tell me that, at least."

I took a minute or two before answering. "I have good reason, yes? Not just for me, but for Piers. However, if I can destroy his *Secret History*, that would be my revenge, mine and Piers's. And Theodora's."

Tariq smiled. It was a smile only the best of friends could decipher.

"Wait one moment! You know more about it," I said. "It's written on your face. *What* do you know, Tariq? Where does he keep it? Tell me!"

"He does not have it. He left it at Saint John Lateran's Scriptorium to be copied, along with several of his history codices."

"But, why?"

"He dared not have anyone in our scriptorium see it."

"Someone like me, no doubt."

"Or anyone who might inform the emperor of its existence. I can tell you it is full of half-truths and outright lies and slander."

"You've read it, all of it?"

"Yes, I spent several late nights doing so by the light of a single candle, with Procopius lying snoring in his room, drunk as a Goth."

"What are his plans for it? On the one hand, Theodora's death might embolden him to publish it, and yet his reward from Justinian might be the gallows."

"Exactly. It will also take the deaths of Belisarius and Antonina before he makes it public. They are all caught up in a morass of intrigue, corruption, and sin, all tied together with a tissue of truth."

"He hopes to outlive them all?" I sat back against the cushions, silent.

"Procopius sets precious store on his position as Palace Historian," Tariq continued. "It's my belief this *Secret History* is a companion work to his various codices on the Persian war, the Vandalic war, and the Ostrogothic war. It contains incendiary information and lies that he dares not include in those works while its subjects live, at least not without reprisals. I think he plans to blend the one into the others when he feels safe."

"I have to lay hold of it, Tariq. The question is, how? Will you go to Rome with me?"

Tariq's lips flattened into a strange sort of smile.

"What?" I demanded. "I know that smirk! You know something else, yes? You're holding back. Now, spill it! Please!"

"Fine. I've led you on long enough."

"What? What do you mean?"

"I accompanied Procopius to Saint John Lateran's Scriptorium two days before we set sail. That's when he turned some ten codices over to the cleric in charge, Bishop Alberto. The two had formed quite a friendship during the years of our occupation. I returned the next day, alone. I wore an exceedingly large tunic so that I might rescue the codex in question for you."

"You devil!" I cried. "You did get it, after all."

Tariq held his hand up. "Unfortunately, I did not, Stephen."

My stomach clenched. "What, then?"

"I waved a paper at Bishop Alberto and said I had been sent to place it in one of the codices. He showed me to the shelf where they had been consigned and disappeared around the corner where I heard him talking to one of his monks. I knew I had but moments. I quickly drew down *The Secret History* and went about the business of trying to secure it under a belt I wore beneath my tunic for just that purpose."

"And?"

"Well, as I struggled with the book, I heard him conclude the conversation with the monk. His footfalls were returning to the alcove where I stood. I had no time to conceal the clumsy thing, so—"

"You put it back." My heart dropped.

"The shelf was on eye level, you understand. I was about to replace it when I saw a horizontal gap in the wall at the base of the shelf. Setting the codex on its side, I pushed it into the gap. I heard it fall to the ground behind the bookcase which happens to be *built into the stone wall*."

I felt suddenly light-headed. My mind struggled to put together the pieces of what he was telling me. *Could it be true?* "So—it's gone." I held my breath.

"It is, Stephen. And *The Secret History* is not likely to be found in our lifetimes."

My heart pounded. "Holy Mithra!" I blurted. "Tariq, I can't believe it! I've never known you to be impulsive before."

"As many games of *Shatranj* we have played over the years, Stephen, you know I seldom miss an opportunistic move."

In another conversation, I would have countered him on that contention, but instead, I jumped up, bent down, and kissed him on the cheek. I stood at once, rigid and embarrassed by my own impulsiveness.

Tariq looked up at me, eyes squinting. "With all her blemishes," he said with a bit of a drawl, "with all her faults, and with all her crimes, you loved her, didn't you?"

I longed to turn away, but his gaze held me transfixed. I bit at my lower lip, searching fruitlessly for words.

I smiled.

HISTORICAL NOTE

Procopius died some twenty years after the conclusion of events in *Too Soon the Night* without having published *The Secret History*.

In 1623, more than ten centuries later, Nicolò Alemmanni, a Vatican Archivist, came across Procopius's long-lost codex and published it as *Historia Arcana, The Secret History*.

When Justinian died in 565, his nephew Justin acceded to the throne, a throne he shared with Theodora's niece, Comito's daughter Sophia. As with Justinian and Theodora's reign, the new emperor and empress shared power. Thus, some seventeen years after Theodora's death, her plan to see her blood and that of Justinian continue the royal line met with success.

JUSTINIAN deeply mourned his beloved Theodora. Most likely in her memory, he moved away from Chalcedonianism and toward an extreme branch of Monophysitism. He continued to follow his dream of restoring the Roman Empire, to some success. He died on 14 November 565, at the age of eighty-three. The Eastern Orthodox Church canonized both Justinian and Theodora as saints. Justinian was honored for his spiritual and legal reforms; Theodora for her support in those reforms, as well as for her influence in the matter of women's rights. Both are commemorated on Justinian's death date, 14 November.

PROCOPIUS continued in the good graces of Justinian, who provided him with high honors and exalted positions. Despite being so favored, Procopius wrote scathingly of the Justinian-Theodora rule in his *The Secret History*.

NARSES achieved great success as a general in the continuing struggle to win back Italy. Surviving Theodora, Justinian, and Belisarius, he died in old age sometime in the 570s.

BELISARIUS continued his military career as a general and is highly regarded by historians for his tactics and strategy. He was placed on trial for treason in 562, found guilty, and incarcerated. Justinian forgave him and returned him to favor. He died in the same year as Justinian, 565.

ANTONINA appears to have been unable to scuttle the marriage of her daughter Joannina to Anastasius. Procopius credits Antonina with restoring Belisarius to Justinian's favor. After Belisarius's death, she reportedly went to live with Justinian's sister Vigilantia, the mother of Justinian's successor, Emperor Justin II.

GLOSSARY

ANASTASIUS (Emperor 491-518): Was a Monophysite, placing him in conflict with the Orthodox Church.

ATRIUM: center of a Roman house, the open roof sheds light on the rooms nearby; contains an impluvium, or pool, directly under the opening to catch rain water for use within the house.

AUGUST/AUGUSTA Terms of honor from the Latin (great, magnificent) used for Roman and Byzantine emperors and empresses.

AUGUSTAION: The public square at the east end of the Mese, south of the Church of the Holy Wisdom, and north of the Great Palace.

BATHS OF ZEUXIPPOS: Luxurious public baths named after a Thracian deity and located on the northeast side of the HIPPODROME.

BLUES: Supporters of the charioteers of the Blue faction.

BUCELLARII: Personal troops often acquired from defeated armies and employed by high ranking military leaders, like Belisarius and Sittas.

CENTURIA: The Roman tactical unit of one hundred men.

CHALKE: "The Bronze Gate" serving as the ceremonial entrance or vestibule to the Great Palace.

CHALCEDONIAN CREED, The: Adopted at the Council of Chalcedon in 451 CE, the view of the ORTHODOX Church that Christ be acknowledged from two natures, man and God, rather than in two natures. The view is not accepted by the Eastern Orthodox Church. Followers of this view were called CHALCEDONIANS or DIOPHYSITES.

CHURCH OF THE HOLY WISDOM: (also called the Hagia Sophia) Significant edifice on the Augustaion. The first burned down in 404, the second during Justinian's reign in 532. The third was built by order of Justinian and it still stands.

CISTERNS: An ingenious system of aqueducts and cisterns—open, covered, or underground—was built to effectively supply fresh water to the city population, even in times of siege.

CODEX (Plural: CODICES): A book constructed of pages made of papyrus or the more durable parchment and enclosed with hard covers.

CURSE TABLETS: Scrolls of thin lead, engraved with curses thought to be harmful to those cited in them.

DALMATIC(A): A wide-sleeved and heavier garment worn over the lighter tunic by both sexes, but mostly by men. A robe.

DAPHNE PALACE or DAPHNE WING: One of the many buildings comprising the complex of the GREAT PALACE, it is located on the western perimeter and houses the Imperial Apartments.

DROMON: A galley warship; the type used by Belisarius in the Vandalic wars, were likely single-banked galleys employing fifty oars, twenty-five on each side, and featuring LATEEN sails, which were early fore-and-aft triangular sails, meaning they could harness the wind before and after, rather than square sails that allowed for only sailing before the wind.

EUNUCHS: Men who have been castrated and who often performed important parts in the church, army, and civil or palace administrations.

EUPHEMIA: Empress and wife of Justin I; desired that the diadem be passed to Justinian, but much opposed to his marriage to Theodora.

EXCUBITORS: The Imperial Guard.

FACTIONS: Supporters of the BLUES and GREENS, chariot teams named for their colors. The REDS and WHITES had fallen out of favor and been assimilated into the other factions.

FOLLIS (Plural, FOLLES): Largest of the copper coins, it was valued at 40 NUMMI or 1/288 of a NOMISMA.

GREAT PALACE: A complex of many imperial buildings created at the southeastern end of Constantinople amidst pavilions and gardens at the edge of the Sea of Marmara.

GREENS: Supporters of the charioteers of the Green faction.

HALL OF THE CONSISTORY: The meeting chamber in which the emperor met with his councilors; meetings were called SILENCES because the business discussed there was not to be revealed elsewhere.

HALL OF THE NINETEEN COUCHES: One of the Great Palace buildings used for imperial ceremonies and banquets.

HECATE: Greek Goddess of magic, witchcraft, the moon, and ghosts.

HERUL (Plural: HERULI): An early Germanic person/people, possibly from Scandinavia.

HESPERIDES: Nymphs of the sunset in Greek Mythology, usually depicted as three in number and as caretakers of Goddess Hera's garden near the Atlas Mountains in Africa. In the Garden of the Hesperides there grew a grove of apple trees that bore golden apples capable of dispensing immortality when eaten.

HIPPODROME: Capable of accommodating perhaps 60,000 citizens, the U-shaped race track next to the Great Palace was used for chariot racing, public entertainment, imperial ceremonies, as well as military and political demonstrations.

JUSTIN I (450-527; reign 518-527): Sought his fortune as an excubitor in the reign of ANASTASIUS I, became commander and then emperor upon Anastasius' death; adopted his nephew Justinian who was named co-emperor with him, and who became emperor in his own right four months after Anastasius' death.

JUSTINIAN I (483-565; reign 527-565): Succeeded his uncle, Justin I as emperor; ordered the codification of Roman law and sought to regain parts of the empire lost to barbarians, including Rome, North Africa, and Spain. Went against most of society by marrying actress Theodora.

KATHISMA: The Imperial loge at the Hippodrome attached to and accessed from the Great Palace.

KNUCKLEBONES: An ancient gambling game like dice adopted by Romans and Greeks and utilizing the bones from the ankles of sheep.

LEVANT: An approximate geographical term referring to the eastern Mediterranean; a broad definition roughly refers to the territory from Greece to Egypt.

LORD (or GRAND) CHAMBERLAIN: Highest ranking attendant (usually a eunuch) to the Byzantine emperor, with whom he held great sway.

MAGUS: A member of a priestly caste of ancient Persia; a sorcerer; wizard; conjurer; charlatan; trickster.

MESE: Main thoroughfare traversing Constantinople from the MILION west to the outer city walls. One branch split off to the northeast.

MILION: Marble obelisk near the Church of the Holy Wisdom and just outside the AUGUSTAION, it served as the point from which distances in the empire were measured.

MITHRA: Pagan Sun god. Also known as MITHRAS.

MONOPHYSITISM: The doctrine that Christ had a single divine nature, whereas the Orthodox Church held that Christ had both a divine and human nature and considered MONOPHYSITES heretics.

MOUNTAIN TEA: an herbal tea made from the leaves and flowers of a plant called sideritis (ironwort). It is plentiful in mountainous areas of northern Greece.

NARSES: A eunuch serving Justinian first as a chamberlain and then as a general and commander of the forces that reconquered Italy.

NOMISMA (Plural: NOMISMATA): Gold coin.

NUMMUS (Plural: NUMMI): Smallest copper coin.

PALACE OF HORMISDAS: A palace within the Great Palace complex located at the water's edge of the Sea of Marmara and used by Justinian before coming to power.

PATRIARCH: Head or bishop of a diocese. The five dioceses in Theodora's time were Rome, Constantinople, Alexandria, Antioch and Jerusalem.

QUADRIGA: A chariot drawn by four horses harnessed abreast.

SASSANID EMPIRE: the name used for the Iranian Empire from 224-651 CE.

SHADE: the spirit of a dead person.

SHATRANJ: Indian board game and forerunner of chess.

SILENTIARY: An official of the court acting much like an usher, staying silent while standing guard over imperial personages.

STOLA: A long, pleated dress for women worn over the tunic, usually woolen or linen, but sometimes silk for the rich citizens. Often worn with a belt placed just below the bustline.

STRATEGIUM: Site of an army's drill ground and tent barracks.

STYLITES: Holy men or "pillar saints" who lived atop tall columns.

SYNTHRONON: a structure in the apse of an Eastern Orthodox church placed behind the altar and against the east wall, combining the bishop's throne with seats or stalls for other clergy.

TANTALUS: A evil king in Greek Mythology whose punishment by Zeus was to stand forever thirsty and hungry in a pool of water that would recede when he bent to drink and beneath branches heavy with fruit but out of reach.

TARTARUS: In Greek Mythology, the abyss used as a dungeon for the wicked.

TESSERA (Plural: TESSERAE): Small pieces of stone or glass used in the creation of mosaics.

THEODORA: Actress who became Empress of the Eastern Roman Empire through her marriage to Justinian I.

THREE FATES, The: In Greek Mythology, the three goddesses who determined a person's fate. They were Clotho the Spinner, who spun the thread of life; Lachesis the allotter, who determined the length of life; and Atropos the inflexible, who cut the thread of life, ending it.

THUCYDIDES: (460-400 BC) A well-respected Greek historian.

TORQUE: In jewelry, a metal collar or neck ring.

TUNIC(A): Replaced the toga, over which upper class males often wore a DALMATIC and females wore other garments, like the STOLA or a mantle. *Tunica intima*: A woman's under tunic.

ACKNOWLEDGMENTS

An abundance of sincere thanks goes out to those who have travelled with Theodora and me along this journey: Kitty Killackey Mitchell, John Rdzak, Scott Hagensee, Mary Rita Perkins Mitchell, Pam Sourelis, Elizabyth Harrington, Natalie Dale and members of Portland's 9-Bridges Downtown Saturday Meetups.

ABOUT THE AUTHOR

A native of Chicago and longtime teacher of English and Creative Writing, James Conroyd Martin holds degrees from St. Ambrose and DePaul universities. He has received IPPI Gold Medals for his novel ***The Boy Who Wanted Wings***, as well as for the works in **The Poland Trilogy** (*Push Not the River*, *Against the Crimson Sky*, and *The Warsaw Conspiracy*), novels inspired by the diary of a countess in 1790s Poland. In the Chanticleer International Book Awards, the first book of The Theodora Duology, ***Fortune's Child***, won the 2019 Best Book Grand Prize.

READING GROUP GUIDE

1. In what ways might people belonging to different echelons of society (slaves, peasants, patricians, government officials, clergy) reflect different attitudes toward the rising of Theodora to power?

2. Theodora seemed confident that Stephen would write an accurate account of her life. What might have inspired that confidence?

3. Why would Theodora keep from her husband the knowledge that he was likely sterile? What might this say about her?

4. The *Encyclopedia Britannica* cites Theodora as "probably the most powerful woman in Byzantine history." She is also remembered as an early feminist and one of the first rulers to foster the rights of women. Cite examples from the novel that support or undermine these characterizations.

5. Theodora could be viewed as failing in her first two experiences as a mother. Do you think she would have found success as a "good mother" had she been able to give birth a third time? Why or why not?

6. Given the importance of the two remaining secrets Stephen held (Justinian's likely sterility and Theodora's relationship to Setka), why didn't Theodora have him executed?

7. Theodora no doubt is capable of cruelty, but to what extent might she exhibit empathy?

8. At a critical moment in the novel, Theodora stood before Justinian and his councilors, all men, and changed the course of history:

"Turning back to her husband, she smiled, drew herself up, as if she could attain the height she once longed for, and said, 'For myself, I think the purple makes the best shroud.'" What aspects or moments of her life experience brought her to this critical occasion?

9. In a poignant scene, Justinian tells Theodora: "While I analyze with an eye to the future, Thea, you are contemplating the warp and woof of the present. Your mention of their [Hypatius and Pompeius's] mother and your own fathers also tells me that your present conclusions are governed by your past." Comments invited.

10. The Plague of Justinian, or the "Justinianic Plague," as it came to be called, was the first (Old) World pandemic. In light of our more recent world pandemic, what parallels could be drawn? Are we able to identify/empathize in a pandemic from the sixth century?

AFTERWORD

Truly~I never planned on two books for Theodora. While she may have been diminutive in height, she was, as I'm sure you can bear witness, bigger than life. And once Stephen entered the story, one book was not enough.

This author would so appreciate it if you would write a little review on Amazon, B&N, KOBO, Google Books, Smashwords, Apple Books, or Goodreads.

And stay connected in order to learn where my writing journey might take me next. I do have an idea.

PLEASE subscribe to my rather infrequent freebies, bonuses, booksignings, contests, recommendations and news: **http://jamescmartin.com/announcements/**

LIKE me on **Facebook**: https://www.facebook.com/AuthorMan/

Follow me on **Twitter** @JConMartin

Follow/add me on **Goodreads**:
https://www.goodreads.com/author/show/92822.James_Conroyd_Martin

JConMartin on **Instagram**

DANGER: TEASER AHEAD!
NEXT STOP: 1791 POLAND!

Some years ago, I came across the translation of a diary written by a Polish countess. I thought it then a *Gone with the Wind* kind of epic. Sure enough, that's the tag critics latched onto when St. Martin's Press brought out **Push Not the River**.

With this sample chapter from the novel, you will now time travel from Byzantine time to the eighteenth century and meet some characters you'll love, and a few—well, not so much.

Not to worry~each book in The Poland Trilogy stands alone.

Go ahead, take a chance on Chapter One …

PART ONE

There are three things that are
difficult to keep hidden:
a fire, a cold, and love.

—POLISH PROVERB

1

HALICZ 1791

S HE STOOD MOTIONLESS NOW, IN a painter's tableau of flowers and grasses, a long distance from home, alone. It was only recent events—not the intervening years—that made Anna question her childhood attachment to the mythical. Today, in fact, the young girl who stood poised on the threshold of womanhood questioned the very world around her.

The afternoon was idyllic, the meadow at mid-day a canvas of color and warmth. A breeze stirred the wheat and barley fields nearby, coercing the spikes into graceful, rippling waves. Next year the meadow in which she stood would be made to produce also, but for now it was thickly green with overgrown grasses and rampant with late summer wildflowers, birds, and butterflies.

To all of this Anna was coolly indifferent. She stood there, her black dress billowing in the breeze, vaguely aware of a bee that buzzed nearby. In time, though, her eyes found focus as she observed a few fallen leaves hurl themselves at the trunk of the solitary oak, whirl away, and come back again. In them—their detachment and their restless movement—she somehow felt a comradeship. She was as mindlessly driven as they. And from somewhere deep at her core, a keening rose up, piercing her, like that of a mournful siren from some unseen island.

How had it come to this? Only months before, upon the passing of the Constitution in May, Anna's universe had been complete and happy. The reform seemed to place her father in a good disposition. The Third of May Constitution did not threaten him, as it did some of the nobility. Count Samuel

Berezowski was of the minor nobility, the *szlachta,* his great-great grandfather having been conferred the title of count when in 1683 he aided the legendary King Jan Sobieski and much of Christian Europe in keeping Vienna—and therefore Eastern Europe—from the Turks. The count managed his single estate himself and he already allowed his village of twelve peasant families liberal freedoms of thought and action. As was the custom, the peasants addressed him as Lord Berezowski.

It was a happy time for Anna's mother, too, because she was eight months with child. As a young girl, Countess Teresa Berezowska had gone against her parents' wishes, foregoing marriage into a magnate family for the dictates of the heart. This did not preclude, however, her own ambition to bring into the world children who would go on to make matches that would distinguish the family. Though her heart had been set on a first-born boy, she rejoiced with Samuel in the birth of their healthy, green-eyed girl, Anna Maria. She was confident that many childbearing years were left to her and that there would be a troop of boys to fill up the house. Instead, a succession of miscarriages ensued and her health grew frail, her beauty fragile. Still, the countess persisted against doctors' advice, until at last—seventeen years after the birth of Anna—it seemed certain that she was to bring another child full term.

Anna's relationship with her mother improved after the incident with the crystal dove, but a certain distance between mother and daughter remained. Anna came to realize that while she was loved by both parents, her mother was much concerned with bringing boys into the world. While Anna's father gave his love freely, her mother inculcated in her—through the spoken and the unspoken—a sense of inadequacy that sent her into herself, into her own realm of imagination.

Alone in her books of fable and fairy tales and the myriad places they took her, Anna longed for a brother or sister to anchor her to the real world.

But it was not to be.

Feliks Paduch, one of Count Berezowski's peasants, had always been trouble. Since adolescence he had been involved in numerous thefts and brawls. At thirty, he was lazy, alcoholic, and spiteful, a man who questioned and resented his lot in life. Some peasants whispered, too, that he had been involved in the murder of a traveling Frenchman, but no one dared accuse him.

Countess Berezowska had encouraged her husband to evict Paduch, and he had nearly done so twice, but each time relented. A few days after the passing of the Third of May Constitution, Count Berezowski set out for the Paduch cottage in response to a local noble's complaint that Feliks had stolen several bags of grain. The *starosta* should settle the matter, the countess insisted, but the count, claiming he was ultimately responsible for his peasants, would not leave the matter to a magistrate.

It was on that day that life changed forever for the happy family. Anna was sitting in the window seat of her second-floor bedroom reading a French translation of *A Midsummer Night's Dream* when she heard the commotion below. She looked down to see eight or ten peasants accompanying a tumbril in which her father's body lay on a matting of straw.

Because of the sincere mutual respect between the count and his peasants, this time they seemed unafraid to name Feliks Paduch the murderer. It was Anna who had to tell her mother, and who—in her own bereavement—had to listen to the countess mourn her husband while in the same breath rail against him for playing estate manager and attending to most ignoble business well beneath his station, business like Feliks Paduch.

Countess Berezowska was devastated. Anna believed that it was the traumatic effects of her father's murder that precipitated the premature birth of the baby. The boy lived only two days. The countess never recovered from her husband's murder and the difficult birth—thirteen hours it had taken. After the baby's death, the countess stopped taking nourishment. A week later, in a delirium of grief, anger, and despair she died.

And so it was that within a matter of days, Anna had lost everyone. The fabric of her peaceful life at Sochaczew had come undone, never to be made whole. She stood alone in her garden that day, the day of her mother's death, somehow unable to cry. How her mother had loved the flowers grown there. In fact, Anna had taken to gardening, initially, to please the countess, who so loved to have flowers in the house. Her father had helped her start the garden that year, the year the five-year-old precocious child had brought home the crystal dove. She had been allowed to keep it and wanted so to please her mother by producing bushels and bushels of flowers.

The garden venture took no time at all to instill in Anna a passion for growing things. Her father gave her an array of bulbs, imports from Holland. She dutifully planted them in the fall, wondering to herself how such funny looking things could ever produce something delicate and pretty. But in the spring the green feelers peeked out of the brown earth, and amidst fine rains, reached brave, thickening arms upward. Anna had arranged them in neat rows, like soldiers, so that when the heads burst open with hues of reds, purples, oranges, and yellows she could scarcely contain her delight. It seemed a miracle. That first bouquet to her astonished mother was her proudest moment. In time she came to see in the flowers an almost symbolic difference between her parents: while her father loved the living, growing flowers still rooted to the earth and warmed by the sun, her mother preferred them cut, placed in cool water, and set out in shaded rooms to be admired.

Anna's lesson with the crystal dove so many years before had provided a defining moment for her relationship with her mother. Anna persisted in her love for her mother, but its foundation seemed to be one of fractures and fissures which, while they never fully broke away, seemed always to hold the threat of doing so. The difficult truth was that she questioned her mother's love for her. The countess' love was a cool kind of love, taking the form of a nod or a light pat on the head, a love given out sparingly, like formal candies in tiny wrappings, and on occasions few enough for Anna to store away in a half-filled memory box. Anna, in turn, grew up confident only in her father's unconditional love, a love that radiated like sunshine. She came to fully place herself in his guardianship, so much so that at his death she found that her reservoir of trust had been emptied. Even he, in dying, had failed her. If what he had done was place himself in the way of destiny, no good had come of it.

The Countess Berezowska's older sister, Countess Stella Gronska, arrived with her husband and daughter Zofia for one funeral and stayed for three. When they left Sochaczew to return home to Halicz in southern Poland, they insisted on taking Anna with them. The count and countess would provide guardianship for her until she reached eighteen.

At first, Anna was grateful. Her world shattered, she was happy to have someone deciding and doing for her. And her aunt and uncle were warm and loving people. Zofia, too, was welcoming. Anna found her cousin very different from herself, so outgoing and worldly-wise.

The Gronskis tried their best to be a family to her. But as the days at Halicz wore on, Anna came to miss her home and its familiar surroundings more and more. Sleep brought with it dark dreams of abandonment, of isolation. At night she sometimes awoke to her own voice calling out for her father. Her aunt and uncle responded to her melancholy with genuine concern, but she would only pretend to be comforted. What she longed for was the cocoon of her father's library, where she had spent countless hours of her childhood transported to other times and places by the stories on the darkly varnished shelves. And, most of all, she missed the opportunity to mourn at her family's graves, to touch the earth that held them, when she could not.

Anna often wondered why it was that *she* survived. Had she *done* something to lose her whole world? Sometimes she found herself wishing she could join her family in the earth on that little hill where they and three other generations rested amidst daisies, cornflowers, and poppies. What did living have to offer now?

Her life had taken on a tragic dimension, one that reminded her of the many tales and legends she knew. So often they, too, ended tragically. Why? In growing up, she would often read a tale only to the point when things went wrong. Then she would stop in order to provide her own, happier, ending. Her favorite story was of Jurata, Queen of the Baltic. If Anna could not quite identify with the mythical beauty of Jurata, she did acknowledge that they had in common their green eyes. What she admired most about the goddess was her passion. Oh, Anna wished for such passion in her own life.

Jurata lived in a palace of amber under the sea. One day a young fisherman broke one of her laws, but the kind Jurata forgave him. Falling in love with the fisherman, the goddess courageously defied custom and law, swimming to shore to meet him every evening. Anna thought the myth very romantic. It was at this point that she chose to amend the story. She had no taste for the unhappy ending that went on to depict the god of lightning and thunder, Percun—who loved Jurata—flying into a rage because Jurata, too, broke a law: that magical beings marry only among themselves. Percun destroyed the palace with his thunderbolts and Jurata was never seen again. The pieces of the broken palace, then, accounted for the bits of amber found in the Baltic area.

In Anna's ending, Jurata chipped away at her amber palace, breaking it down bit by bit, a mythical feat in itself. She then cleverly created among the gods and goddesses a great desire for the yellow stones. At last, she was able to assuage Percun's anger by presenting him with the largest cache of amber in the world, thus making him more respected and powerful. Jurata's passion was so great that she assumed a human form, giving up her immortality for the love of her fisherman.

Now, transfixed in the meadow, Anna was aware of the sights and sounds about her only in a peculiar and distant way, as though she stood—an intruder—in some French bucolic painting. She wondered if this panorama were even real. Perhaps her very life was no more than a dream. Might she be *dreaming* her life? Strange as it was, the notion caught hold in her imagination.

Was such a thing possible? Somehow, at that moment, it made sense. *If only recent events were illusions,* she thought.... *If only*—

Suddenly a voice shattered the trance: "You must be the Countess Anna!"

The deep voice jarred her into consciousness, and an instinctive, fearful cry escaped her lips before her mind could work. She wheeled about, shielding her face against the western sun, her eyes raised to take in the mounted rider.

Her skin felt the full heat of the afternoon sun. His visage was at first little more than a silhouette cut against the sunlight, like a black-on-yellow paper cutting. Still, she knew he was not from the Gronski estate.

"It is a fine day, is it not?" He was smiling at her. A smile she could not interpret.

"Who are you?" She hardly recognized the voice as her own. It sounded distant and tiny. Her heart beat rapidly against her chest, and for a moment she thought of running.

"I'm sorry if I startled you." The smile was fading. "I assumed you would have heard my horse."

"You did—and I had not." Anna swallowed hard. She fought for composure. She would not run. "You might have called out from a distance."

"Truly, I am sorry. Really, Countess Anna—it *is* Countess Anna?"

She mustered decorum now. "*Lady* Anna Maria. My parents didn't use their titles."

"Forgive me." He was maneuvering his horse around her now. "Around here you'll find that many of the *szlachta* do."

"Do you often go about sneaking up on people?" She lifted her head to him, feigning boldness. She found herself turning, too, in a half circle until it was no longer necessary for her to shade her eyes against the sun. She was certain that he had initiated that little dance for just that end.

He was laughing. "It's a habit I thought I had broken, Lady Anna Maria."

His cavalier attitude was disconcerting. Anna chose not to answer.

"And what," he pressed, "is it that brings you out here, milady?"

Anna conjured up one of her mother's smiles that wasn't a smile. "I might ask you the same question."

"Fair enough." It was he who was shading his eyes now, but he took his hand away long enough to point. "Your uncle's land ends there to the west with that wheat field. This meadow is mine."

"Oh." Anna felt her confidence go cold and drop within her, draining away like a mountain stream. How neatly he had put her in her place. "I am nothing more than an interloper then, is that it? I'll go back immediately."

He smiled. "You need do nothing of the kind, Lady Anna. There's no key to the woods and fields."

It was a saying she had heard her father use, one she had thought was his alone. Her gaze was held by the stranger. She answered: "It's just that I found the meadow so very peaceful, so conducive to thinking."

"Ah, so pretty—and thoughtful into the bargain!"

"Are they qualities so incompatible with each other?" The man was impossible, she decided, her spine stiffening.

"No, of course not. It was a stupid comment." The cobalt eyes flashed as he stared down at her.

She smiled now, her head lifting to meet his gaze. "At last we agree on something."

He laughed.

Anna sensed her little victory a hollow one. Was he laughing *at* her? She turned away. "It's well past time for me to return to the house, so if you'll excuse me—"

In one quick movement the stranger swung down from the black stallion.

Anna felt fear rise again. She took a cautious step backward.

"Oh, but we haven't met yet," he was saying. "Allow me to detain you but a moment longer. I am Jan Stelnicki." He bowed, stood erect, gazed down at Anna. The dark gray trousers tucked into high black boots, white silk shirt, and red sash around the waist made for an impeccable appearance. His costume was a mix of western and Polish influence, but that he wore no hat was neither western nor Polish.

Anna nodded, lifting her eyes to take in his considerable height. "Well, since you seem to already know my identity, there's little else to say." She persisted in her petulant tone even while her mind was seeking its own course. Despite the missing hat and familiar manner, his nobility was evident in his speech and bearing. Once he stood in the shade of the great oak, she took in the aristocratic and masculine features chiseled under a mane of wavy yellow-gold, the laughing smile above a dimpled chin, and those dark blue eyes. Some current at her core stirred: something profound and alien. *No man should be so beautiful.*

"Lady Anna," he was saying in a voice almost intimate, "may I offer my sincerest condolences? I was saddened to hear of your parents' deaths."

"Thank you, Lord Stelnicki."

The mourning which for months had consumed her life took on a strangely distant quality now. Her impatience with the stranger was giving way involuntarily to a dichotomous mix of caution and attraction. She watched the motion of his mouth, the porcelain flash of teeth. He wore no moustache. This, too, ran against the Polish mode of the day. There was a mesmerizing presence about him and a strength, not merely physical strength—though he possessed that, too—but a force that came from deep within and resonated in his gaze, in his voice.

"Will you be staying with the Gronski family long?" he asked.

Her immediate response was to tell him that it was of no concern to him, but she took just a moment too long to formulate the reply and her annoyance dissipated. She heard herself telling him that she would be staying with the Gronskis for some time and that, yes, they were treating her very well. While he turned to tether his horse to a wiry branch jutting from the thick tree trunk, he continued his questioning, asking why they had not previously met. Studying him at his task, Anna replied that she had been to visit her aunt and uncle twice several years before. He took studies at the University then, it seemed. When he turned to face her, Anna averted her eyes, politely asking where. In Kraków, he responded, then two years in Paris.

Anna feigned nonchalance. She had never been to Kraków, but she had been to Warsaw—not often, even though her home was so near Poland's capital. Paris, however, seemed worlds away. Paris was the City of Light: the quintessence of European culture. She longed to see it. Now, of course, the unrest there made it quite unsafe.... How old is he? she wondered. Twenty-two? Twenty-three?

"I am glad that you will be staying," he was saying. "I trust that I will be allowed to show you the sights here at Halicz. Our Harvest Home will be concluding with much celebration…"

Her mind a blur, Anna watched as the young man went on speaking of the local autumn customs. What emboldened him to speak to her as though he had known her all his life? She absently fingered the dark lace at her throat. The voice was so warm, so musical, the eyes inviting as a lake in August. Still, she wondered at his sincerity. Did sincerity and boldness coexist? "Lord Stelnicki," she managed when he took a breath, "I am afraid that such festivities are out of the question for me for some little while yet."

"Of course. Forgive me." He bowed from the waist. "But once you are out of mourning there will be many winter gatherings to which we shall look forward—parties, sleigh rides, and—"

Anna interrupted, smiling indulgently. "Oh, I'm afraid that in a few weeks my aunt and uncle will shut up the house. We are to winter in Warsaw."

"Of course. For the moment I forgot the Gronski custom. Why, were you staying, I would personally organize a *kulig*. Our joyrides are well-known around here and no Halicz manor home turns away a sleigh party!"

"At least," Anna laughed, "until the master's vodka reserve has been drained!"

"I expect so." Lord Stelnicki laughed, too. Then he let out a great sigh and his face fell with an exaggerated disappointment. "Ah, winter will not be such a happy prospect for me."

He was so glibly forward that Anna could only stare. *This* comment, certainly, was insincere.

But the mocking attitude vanished suddenly and he brightened. The blue eyes held Anna's. "Time is the world's landlord and he may be friend or foe. May he be our *friend*, Lady Anna Maria."

Anna had never heard this saying before, but she knew his meaning and she felt her face burn. His forwardness unnerved her. No man, and certainly no stranger, had ever behaved toward her with such familiarity. Her throat, already dry, tightened as she sought a diversionary tactic. "Do you not winter in the city, Lord Stelnicki?"

"You must call me Jan. Please."

She longed to extinguish that expectant smile. Did this man ever meet with resistance? Even as she thought this, she found herself nodding in acquiescence. Silently, she promised herself to ignore the request.

He was satisfied, nonetheless, and told her that in years past he had spent December and January in Kraków—where his father lived now—but that he enjoyed the country far more. Yes, he assured her, even in winter, admitting himself to be an odd sort. His mother, it seemed, had died some years before and he assured Anna from experience that Time would help to heal the hurt.

Despite his forwardness and her own awkwardness, Anna was surprised by some interior part of her which sought to prolong the conversation, but having been reminded of her mourning, Duty, not Time, prompted her to insist that she return to the house.

"Very well, then," he said, "I'll lead my horse to the Gronski home, if you would care to ride?"

"Oh, no!"

"You do ride?"

"Of course, but I did come out for the walk, you see. Otherwise, I would have ridden out myself. I look forward to walking back." The words had spilled out in a rush, but he seemed satisfied with her excuse.

"Well, Lady Anna Maria," he said, bowing, "I welcome you to Halicz and look forward to our next meeting. I hope that one day soon we will ride together. The countryside is breathtaking. When do you put off your mourning?"

"In three weeks' time." His deep voice was no longer alien and startling. It was somehow a lyrical voice she had not known but had held always within her, like some ancestral song, primal yet soothing. Is his interest as keen as it seems, she wondered, or am I too vulnerable in my grief? Or merely too easily snared by my own imagination? What stupid and easily-caught bird was it that Polonius had compared Ophelia to? A woodcock, that was it. Is that what I am? Her heart was quickening nonetheless. He wanted to see her again. The thought was at once exciting and unnerving.

"Forgive me for disturbing you today," Lord Stelnicki was saying. "It was just that from the distance I took you for Zofia and so I rode over. I will make a point of calling on the Gronski family in exactly three weeks. What is it? Why, Lady Anna, I do believe that you're blushing!"

Anna inwardly cursed him for pointing out her embarrassment. She forced out a little laugh. "It is funny, I should think. I have never been mistaken for my beautiful cousin, I can assure you. I could only wish for such beauty."

"Why, Anna—it's only fair now that I address you so—you have little reason for such wishing." He mounted his black steed. The leather creaked as he settled into the saddle with the grace and ease of one who has ridden all of his life.

Once again Anna found herself staring up at him.

"Look!" he said, gesturing in a sweeping motion. "See the two meadow flowers, the yellow and the violet? One is as different from the other as day from night. Yet who will say that one is more beautiful? Oh, a fool might. But only a fool." The saddle groaned again as he leaned over, motioning her nearer, as if to impart some great secret. "But do you know what may determine the desirability of one over the other?" He spoke with a great earnestness.

The intense eyes held Anna's, and she could only shake her head in mute response.

"The fragrance!"

The playful, widening smile, set against a complexion colored by the sun, revealed the even white teeth. Suddenly, he drew up on the reins, and as the animal reared, he waved and turned the horse into the wind. Anna stood close enough that she felt the earth tremble when the horse's forelegs came down. She took a stumbling step backward, feeling a quick breeze made by the swish of the animal's tail.

As the horse thundered off, Jan Stelnicki called out his goodbye.

Her lips apart as if to speak, she stood and stared until the figure crested the hill and fell from sight.

Anna's legs quaked. She felt as one abandoned by the enemy on a battle-field. The man was incorrigible: insufferably confident, proud, strutting. He caused defenses within her to rise like drawbridges. And he was toying with her to the last. *Yellow and violet flowers, indeed. You are a scoundrel and a rogue, Jan Stelnicki!*

And yet she was drawn to him. For a short while, her life had been filled with something other than death and darkness and mourning. Anna sank now to the ground, the stiff satin skirt billowing up around her like a great black cushion.

The world went on as it had before he arrived. The leaves were continuing their circuitous movement. A butterfly fluttered among the meadow flowers. A tiny sparrow sat appraisingly upon a nearby branch.

The meeting with Jan Stelnicki played out again in her mind. She tried to make sense of her feelings. Of course, he is strikingly handsome, she conceded. There was something else about him, too, a special manly grace or energy that accounted for an immediate and deep attraction. A simple meeting, and yet Anna felt that somehow her life had changed. Was this to be the kind of mythical romance of which she read, dreamt, invented?

Doubt ran close behind and she scoffed at the notion: I will not be some easily-snared woodcock. I am too old for such a wishful and girlish infatuation.

But her mind grasped and held to one thought, one memory. Anna's mother often had told her that she herself had known she would marry Anna's father from the very first meeting. And she *had*, despite the concerns of her parents and offers from other wealthier and higher-placed nobles.

She had known! It is possible. Anna's heart surged at the thought. *Might it be so with me?*

Her mind was not through playing devil's advocate, however, conjuring up myriad reservations and fears. Maybe Jan Stelnicki is less than sincere, she thought. Maybe he is merely taking advantage of his looks and charm. To what end? Perhaps he has long been skilled in the arts of seduction. Perhaps it is only his ego....

But there was something deeper—some mysterious link—which attracted Anna and gave profound meaning to what seemed a happenstance encounter, a link that the blacksmith of the gods, Hephaestos himself, might have forged.

Anna sat, her eyes alert now, suddenly aware that the meadow about her teemed with color and movement and warmth and life. This experience of intense attraction she savored for the first time in her life. She drank it in like a fine French wine and it lifted both her body and mind to a strangely ethereal plane.

Rainless clouds came and went. The sun slowly moved over her. Anna stood at last, and the movement stirred the little sparrow from its perch. With purposeful steps she set out in the direction of the Gronski home.

Perhaps she was to have a future, after all. If the endings of myths might be changed, why not the ending to *her* story?

A gusty wind began to blow, catching the folds of her black skirt as it might a sail, pushing her along.

Anna laughed to herself as she broke into a run. She was thinking about his expression that Time was the world's landlord. She would conscript Time as friend rather than foe. "After all," she said aloud, "it will take time to learn how to ride a horse!"

Made in the USA
Monee, IL
12 August 2023

40821308R10246